A Magnificent
Book Two (

Contact Patrol

Pat Cunningham DFM

Pecsaeton Publishing

Published by
Pecsaeton Publishing

Flat 13, Clare House,
7 Lime Avenue,
Derby, DE1 1TU, England
patrick@pecsaeton.co.uk
www.pecsaeton.co.uk

ISBN 978-0-9556325-3-2
© Pat Cunningham 2008

First published July 2008
The rights of Pat Cunningham as author of this work have been asserted by him in accordance with the Copyrights, Design and Patents Act, 1993
All rights reserved. No part of this publication may be reproduced, stored in a retrieval system or transmitted in any form or by any means, electronic, mechanical, photocopying, recording or otherwise without the prior permission of Pat Cunningham.
British Library Cataloguing in Publication Data: a catalogue record for this book is available from the British Library.

Printed by Book Printing UK,
Remus House, Peterborough

Maps
The Western Front, British Sector, mid-1916 .... page 4
The Somme Front, 1st July 1916 .... page 24
Vélu Area, 1916 .... page 166

Illustration
Monosoupape Gnome rotary engine ... page 303

Front cover: author's draft enhanced by Book Printing Design
A de Havilland DH2 Scout, seen through a 1916-pattern Aldis gunsight

'If the air war was a diversion, it was a magnificent diversion.'
Preface to, *The Great Delusion,* Neon (Marion W. Acworth), 1927. Ernest Benn: London

'Did they have aeroplanes in the First World War?' Wies White

Books by the author:

Non-fiction
Peakland Air Crashes series: Landmark Publications
Peakland Air Crashes: The North
Peakland Air Crashes: The Central Area
Peakland Air Crashes: The South

Blind Faith: Joan Waste, Derby's Martyr   Pecsaeton Publishing

'Now We Are Ninety'
'The Elephant Box'
'By Fell and Dale, Volumes 1 # 3'
'Frozen Tears' (a Polish family's odyssey)
'Brat to Well Beloved' (autobiographical series)
'Apprentice to a Pilot'
'The Kind Commander'
'The Simple Captain'

Fiction
In Kinder's Mists   Pecsaeton Publishing

A Magnificent Diversion: series (1914-18 Aviation)   Pecsaeton Publishing
Book One   *The Infinite Reaches*
Book Two   *Contact Patrol*
Book Three *Sold A Pup*
Book Four   *The Great Disservice*

'Though the Treason Pleases' (Irish Troubles)
'Flotsam' (short pieces)
'Jetsam'

In preparation:
'East Midlands Operational Aircrew' series
'The Ignorant Walker's Companion'

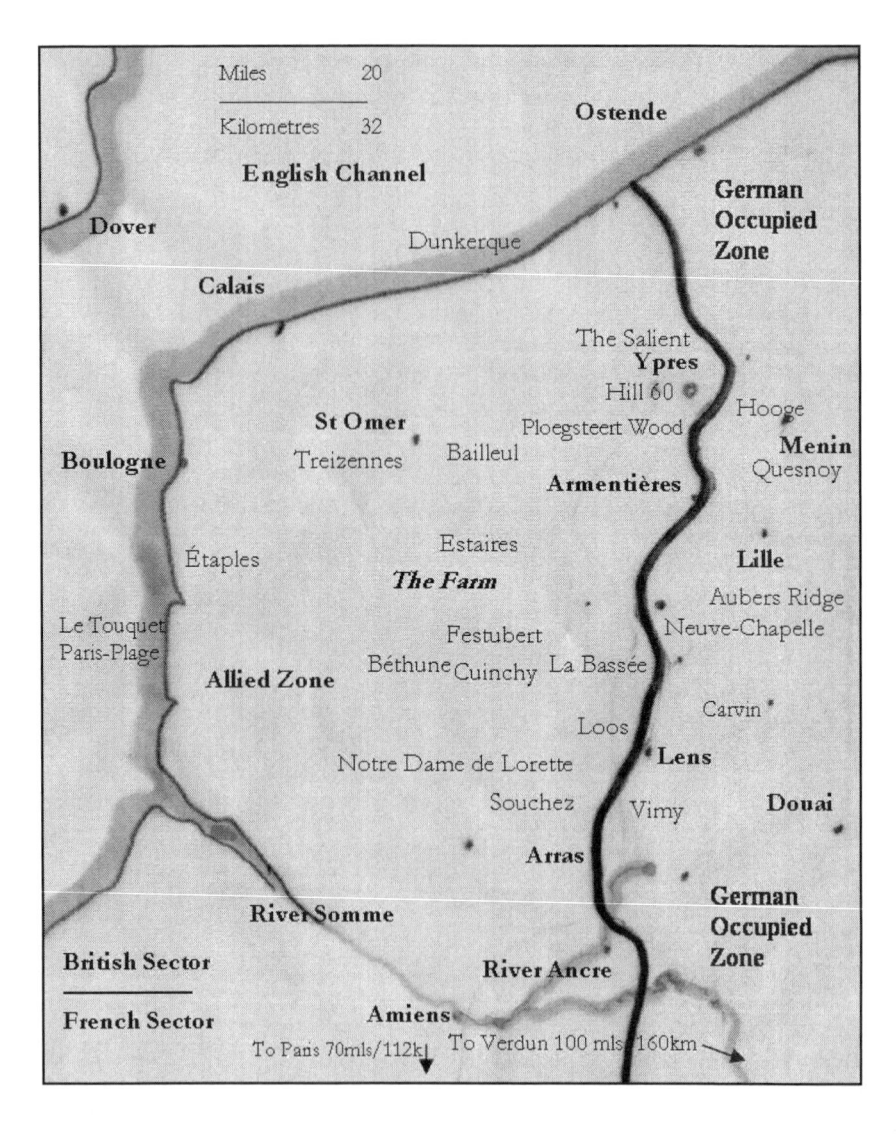

British Sector, Western Front, 1916

Contact Patrol

Chapter One

Lieutenant Paul Cowley swung down to the platform, wincing slightly as his right knee made itself felt. The city's morning rush was still an hour away yet St Pancras was already jammed with khaki-clad figures from the Midlands. It struck him that he might have been struggling through a cattle market – one without the discipline of pens. And the apathetic acceptance reflected on the faces around him made the comparison chillingly apt.

Paul saved himself a journey to Royal Flying Corps Headquarters at the Embankment by begging the phone from the Railway Transport Officer's harassed sergeant.

'Pity we can't get together.' Major Frank Taylor's voice was reedy down the phone. 'But I'm tied up until this afternoon. I report to Handley-Page's tomorrow although I'm keeping my office here.'

Paul had to shout to hear himself above the hubbub.

'What's that?' Frank had evidently raised his own voice. 'Laura and Baby Christopher send their love. So does Diane. In fact, General Cousins phoned from Derby just minutes ago to say the Voluntary Aid Detachment people have promoted her to nurse's aid, so she'll be joining you in France any day now. But –' Paul heard the raillery enter his friend's voice, 'she was telling us that this lady friend of yours from Darlington, Catherine Tomlinson, is a widow-lady. So what about it?'

Paul seized upon the transport sergeant's desperation to get his phone back to cry off answering Frank's question, pressing instead to be transferred to postings, and promising to write.

The transferred connection was no clearer.

'Yes, report to Airco. At Hendon,' bawled postings. 'They know all about you. Phone us from there.'

The sergeant, either psychic or blessed with especially keen hearing, reached for a book of travel dockets. 'Hendon, sir?' He looked towards the RTO but seeing that his officer was tied up with two young subalterns whose drafts had been allocated the same block of carriages, initialled the docket himself. 'That'll do for the taxi.' Then, as he lifted the phone to his ear, 'And the best of luck over there, sir.'

The taxi-driver nosed his way out of the station and into the traffic, plunging almost at once into a labyrinth of streets. Paul registered signs pointing off towards Camden, Hampstead, and Golders Green but for the most part he sat fighting off that depression that always came to him with anything more than passing exposure to the immensity of London. As a counter he turned his mind to Hendon.

Hendon, and the London to Manchester flight of 1910, unbelievable as it seemed, now six years behind him. Initially an open 'first-man-to-complete' endurance challenge which had developed into a contest and then into a nail-biting race. How well Paul remembered playing his motorcycle headlamp alongside those of the cars gathered in the Northamptonshire field where Englishman Grahame-White had put down at nightfall! Together they had floodlit his last-ditch 2.50 a.m. take-off aimed at snatching back the lead from Paulham, the Frenchman; the night take-off being the first in Britain, and not that common even now. After that, Paul had continued to thread his bike through the lanes, initially leading, and then, when overtaken again by those shadowy 42 mph wings, following the exhaust flare. Consequently he had been on the spot when the fifty horsepower Gnome rotary engine had failed at Polesworth, near Tamworth.

He remembered, as a side note, crowding around the downed machine with the other helpers, declaring, in his youthful enthusiasm, that it was the loss of English prestige that hurt, not the loss of the Daily Mail's £10,000 prize money. And he remembered the look one of Grahame-White's mechanics had given him. The same sort of look, he imagined, that businesslike Catherine Tomlinson would give him today in similar circumstances. And with the thought of her all traces of depression fell from him and even the drab streets outside the taxicab seemed brighter.

A *widow-lady!* He shook his head. Major Frank Taylor was, at times, he reflected, regrettably lacking in sensitivity ...

Soon after the Manchester race, Paul remembered, Channel-flyer Monsieur Blériot, had opened Hendon as an official aerodrome, staging not only full displays of night-flying with illuminated aircraft, but 'military' demonstrations during which Grahame-White had dropped sandbag 'bombs' and the celebrated Gustav Hamel – so recently lost in mid-Channel – had carried dispatches between Hendon and Aldershot, outstripping telegrams by up to half an hour. Paul remembered too, how, despite the unfavourable weather, carefully-concealed army units had been spotted from the air. In how many ways events at Hendon had proved a forerunner of the present day!

Paul recalled too, Lieutenant Parke of the Royal Navy – the second pilot to have survived the dreaded spinning nose-dive, but the first to realise *how* he had done it – setting off for Oxford in a Handley-Page monoplane in bad weather and stalling to his death near Wembley. But above all he remembered the *spirit* of Hendon, the striving to popularise and to make a success of all that the fledgling endeavour of aviation stood for.

The taxi having dropped Paul off at Airco – Holt Thomas's Aircraft Manufacturing Company's works –, he turned to see a man advancing from a hutted office with outstretched hand and a beaming smile.

'Lieutenant Cowley? I'm Charles Walker, I work on design. I thought you'd be arriving about now, so I was hovering. I've been dabbling with the DH2 for the last eighteen months so you're just the chap to tell me how my dabbling's working out.'

Briskly taking Paul in tow Walker found them places in the works canteen. 'So – our "Spinning Incinerator", how do you like her?' There was a speculative glint in his eye.

Paul grinned. 'The De Hav Two scare stories? What would you like to hear about first? Its lethal spin characteristics, how fragile the airframe is, how the rotary engine breaks up in flight, or how perishing cold it is to fly?'

Charles Walker inclined his head. 'Quite,' he acknowledged, smiling. 'But really, we're always delighted to hear first-hand experiences.' He paused. 'It was a great worry when we began hearing of problems, because from the start the DH2 was designed to be straightforward. As you're probably aware, many of our component parts are so simple that we sub-contract them out to other firms.' He pointed to a large van manoeuvring alongside an unloading platform. 'Ribs and spars – we're ordering them by the hundred now.'

Paul nodded, watching the unloading with more than normal interest. Only days before Mr Abercrombie, the merchant-banker who was helping finance 'widow-lady' Catherine's business ventures, had quizzed him about the feasibility of mass-production methods in aircraft manufacture, and here it was, already happening!

'As you'll understand,' he said now, 'it was those early accidents that gave the machine its bad name in the Corps. It seems that pilots were saying it was too light an airframe, too powerful an engine, that sort of thing.' He pushed aside his empty coffee cup. 'Strangely enough, I was asked to have an unofficial look at the morale problem when I re-trained recently – I'd been off flying after a motor-bike accident.'

Walker looked up, eyebrows raised. 'Ah! those reports started with you, did they? Jolly good, very useful!' He paused, frowning. 'And wasn't there something else, more recently?'

'Seat harnesses, possibly? Shoulder straps as well as lapstraps.'

The other's face cleared. 'That's it. In fact, we'd already got it in hand. But we're really waiting for the harness Oliver Sutton's producing; that's very exciting. I'm afraid, though, the machine you're taking out's only got the lapstrap.'

Paul nodded understandingly. 'I did rig up a full harness on my squadron bus but Wing weren't keen on approving it for wider use. Besides, there's always the argument that the more straps, the more chance of getting trapped in a smash.'

'Quite, everything in this game involves some sort of compromise, doesn't it? But how can one cope with pilot superstition, and what you called the scare stories?'

As both of them were well aware, although the RFC was growing by leaps and bounds bad tales had no difficulty in keeping pace.

Walker shook his head dolefully. 'And so the DH2 retains the reputation of being a pilot killer.' He pursed his lips, 'I have a theory that fliers thrive on rumour – the boss is just as bad as the rest of you.'

Paul was well aware that 'the boss' referred to was not Holt Thomas, Airco's businessman director, but Geoffrey de Havilland. For de Havilland, now an RFC captain, had built and flown his own aeroplanes long before becoming chief designer and test pilot at Airco. Indeed only a year ago, in the grimly uncertain months following his motor-bike accident, Paul had tentatively approached de Havilland about a job: had he not been able to pass his medical board, and had the RFC not kept him on, he might well have followed up his application, for not only was the DH2 fighting-scout de Havilland's brainchild but it was generally held that there were other equally exciting things to come from the same source.

'Of course,' Paul smiled, continuing with his invited critique, 'having the tail stuck back there on those four spindly-looking tailbooms doesn't help the new lads – it takes some accepting that it's one of the strongest of configurations. That aside, it's so dependable. And such a delight to fly.'

Walker fairly beamed with satisfaction. 'Well, what a splendid young man you are! But then you're an engineer yourself, of course: M.I.C.E., with an aerodynamics speciality.' He laughed at Paul's evident surprise. 'You applied to us for a job, remember? I looked out your letter when they phoned to say who was coming today.' He got to his feet. 'Care for a short tour?'

The tour of the factory was swift but comprehensive. Having shown Paul around the main operation Walker drew his visitor into a corner.

'Do you recognise this?'

Paul sensed that the question was in the nature of a personal assessment. 'A Dennison compression tester, isn't it?'

Walker nodded, pleased. 'Compression and bending. Are you familiar with the method?'

Paul shook his head. 'Not really. Or, I should say, only the theory of it. I had virtually no practical workshop experience after I qualified. But I did a little stress testing in the course of a summer job.'

Walker led the way towards another machine. Paul looked at the work piece prepared for test.

'A control cable?'

'It was on the DH2 that we began testing cables and turnbuckles. Now we test all spliced cables. I have a theory that aerodynamic stressing is going to be big in the future, especially the way speeds and loads are set to increase.'

'I hadn't realised testing was that advanced.'

'Well,' Walker conceded, 'to a large extent it's still a matter of guesswork – if increasingly educated guesswork. As you know yourself, a while ago it would have been unthinkable to put machines through the strains you chaps put them through every day out there. Yet there's still no complete structural testing, so most things are worked at a safety factor of four, four and a quarter, something of that order.'

'What particularly impresses us,' Paul told him with feeling, 'is the way the DH2 sustains damage and still keeps flying.' He thought of the thirty-seven bullet holes – and the cavalryman's lance slash! – found after his abortive attempt to pick up young Andrew Barton. Heavens! Was that only ten days ago? How Major Hallam had flayed him for endangering himself and his machine! Ten days ago – that made it unbelievable aeons since. Back in BC indeed! – or Before Catherine.

'But can't you beef up the performance a bit?' he asked. And instantly feared he might have sounded ungrateful, although it was clear that this was the very the place to raise problems, when he could get answers straight from the horse's mouth, as it were. Just the same, it was certainly not worth mentioning that he had toyed with diverting engine exhaust-air to provide some foot-level heating in the scout: with so little power in hand in the first place that had really been a non-starter: but during his spare time in France it had been a sanity-preserving alternative to staring at the ceiling and dwelling on one's thoughts.

'The limited speed range,' he explained, 'gets a bit critical at times. Especially as we hear the Hun has something very hot on the stocks.'

'The new Albatros, I fancy,' said Walker evenly, taking no umbrage at the criticism. 'For our part we're looking at the Le Rhone 110 horsepower and possibly the Clerget: their 110. I must admit the 100 Monosoupape-Gnome hasn't been nearly as successful as we'd hoped.'

They finished the tour by looking at a temporary armoury housing spares and ammunition for the single Lewis machine gun which was as much as the DH2 could usefully carry.

'You don't normally arm up here, do you?' asked Paul.

Walker shook his head. 'No, but the pressure's on, as you well know. So for the last couple of weeks they've supplied RFC fitters to do the final Service touches here. Saves time – and the ferry flight to Farnborough or Hounslow.'

'No union objections?' asked Paul. Union disputes had been a major factor behind the shortfall in artillery-shell manufacture that had come close to bringing the country to its knees the previous year.

'Not so far, touch wood.' Walker tapped a spar. 'But the way the pace is quickening ... However, as things stand, we're all working well together. So – they'll want you to go straight to St Omer. You'll gather they're desperate for all the machines they can get.'

Paul nodded. That he had managed his full ten days' allotment of leave was still a source of wonder to him. Many had been less lucky, among them erstwhile ambulance-driver and ward-orderly, now VAD nurse's aid, Diane Cousins. She had seen her Rifle-Corps fiancé recalled to France three days back. And the newspapers were making no secret of the way things were hotting up: on the train down from Derby that morning he had made a point of catching up with them.

Heavy shelling, they reported, was creating 'havoc and desolation' along the ninety-miles of the British Front. And they noted that French reports – in view of this 'general quickening of activity' – actually seemed more interested in the British Fronts than in their own! Even German sources spoke of 'the great violence' of the artillery fighting.

But below the headlines the papers were speaking too of the 'very unfavourable weather conditions', with heavy rain that had flooded the trenches and left the ground 'almost everywhere' covered by deep mud. Paul knew what General Cousins – Diane's grandfather – must be thinking of that: retired though he was he would undoubtedly be on the telephone, arguing even harder that the new 'tanks'– *his* tanks as Diane insisted, despite the modest old boy's disclaimers – should not be committed until they were mechanically sound, and then only in vast numbers and over carefully chosen terrain. Unfortunately, as Paul now knew, the barely-proven Mark 1s were already in France; and piteously few of them. And were to be pressed into use!

But whatever the weather, and the vulnerability of the new weapons hovering in the wings, it was certain that the much talked about 'Big Push' was imminent, if not indeed, already under way, and that the Flying Corps would be eager for every machine they could get their hands on. Particularly fighting scouts.

'Clement is up putting yours through its final paces at the moment,' Walker told him. 'So we hope to get you away soon.'

'I'd best get phoning, then,' said Paul. 'But before I do, have you nothing in the cupboard at all, to match the new Albatros?'

'Walker shook his head regretfully. 'Not a thing here. But Tom Sopwith's got another beauty in hand – not the Pup, another one, and that's besides his Triplane. And Bristol's have a good one in the slips as well.' He paused. 'I have a theory that development breeds development, so we shouldn't be that far behind.'

Paul grinned. Walker seemed to have a theory about virtually everything. 'So is Airco building nothing new then?' he chivvied.

The blurting of a Gnome drew their attention as a DH2 came spiralling down from directly overhead, its wings almost transparent against the sky with only the ribs to give them form.

'Ah!' exclaimed Walker. 'Here's Clement, with your machine.'

He began to lead the way back to the office, walking at a near trot, but looked back after a few paces and at once slowed his pace. 'Bad knee?' he asked.

'The motor-bike smash I mentioned,' Paul explained. 'My own silly fault. Took me out for almost two years, very nearly stopped me flying altogether. Which's when I contacted Airco.'

'I'm surprised the docs still let you fly, with that limp.'

'Oh! it's no real trouble,' Paul told him hurriedly. 'It's just got a bit stiff with travelling.'

The machine landed, its propeller shivering to a halt even as the handlers swung it into line outside its shed. Moments later a fur-clad figure clambered down and after a brief word with the handling party, came angling across, stripping off gauntlets and helmet as he came.

'Clement,' Walker smiled. 'This is Paul Cowley who's come for the machine. Paul, Clement Gresswell.'

The two pilots shook hands, Gresswell frowning slightly as if to place Paul's face.

'I once helped you start,' Paul supplied, grinning, *'for Ashford.'*

'For Ashford?' Gresswell frowned. And then, recollecting, he groaned. 'I might have known I couldn't live down my murky past.' Chuckling, he half-turned towards Charles Walker. 'There was a return race to Brooklands. Of course, Hamel – poor old Gustav! – returned a magnificent round-trip time, fog or no fog. But I got a trifle lost and began to panic about my fuel so I put down where I could: as it turned out, just a stone's throw away, at Ashford, Middlesex.'

He held out a hand to Paul. 'So what were you doing, helping around?' As was to be expected, although the handshake was warm, the proffered hand was still icy cold.

'That's right,' said Paul. 'On the lookout for a flight. Any flight, in any old thing. I used to motor-bike down at weekends.'

Gresswell directed a grin at the wings on Paul's chest. 'And now look where it's got you!' With a turn of his head he indicated the de Havilland. 'She's a good 'un. I think you'll like her. She was a little tail heavy this morning, but she's OK now. Come and see.'

Walker held out his hand, smiling. 'I'll get on now then, Paul, but nice to meet you. And do let us hear from you.'

The fitters had just about completed replenishing and checking the machine over by the time the two had walked the few paces to the apron. The senior hand, a grey-haired man in overalls which might well have been white once, gave a final rub down to the tailplane, glistening, as always, with the castor-oil the Gnome had shed; another mechanic extricated himself from between the tailbooms where he had been checking the rear-mounted engine and propeller assembly.

'Everything's fine, by the look of it. So she's all ready for you, sir. Just the paperwork to sort out.'

'I don't think there's much new,' Gresswell said, shadowing Paul as he began his walk-around. 'We've settled to a standard production model now. Gun rigidly clamped fore and aft – and the windscreen's the standard.' Beckoning upwards he directed Paul's attention to the centre section of the upper wing. 'Hucks brought the gravity fuel tank in from the port wing.'

'Hucks? He's testing here too, is he?'

Paul's thoughts carried him back to Darlington, rarely out of mind nowadays, being so intimately associated with Catherine. But Hucks' name took him back to 1914 and the town's Annual Show where the pioneer flier had been billed as the first British airman to 'loop the loop'. So Paul had motor-biked from tramping in the Lakes just to see him do it – and until recently that was all Darlington had ever meant to him. Later it had meant Corporal Bill Timkins, bleeding to death in his arms in a shell crater in the Ypres Salient. And as a direct result of that, it now meant Catherine. Catherine Tomlinson. Catherine, with her grey-blue eyes and the warm, tender, north-eastern lilt to her voice ...

He forced his mind back to Hucks.

'It's only a couple of years since I rode halfway across the country to see him loop.'

'It all seems such a long time ago now, doesn't it?' said Gresswell. 'But he's still very much in harness. As for the testing, the boss used to do it all himself, but once they went firm on the DH2 instead of the FE8 he needed help. For they're talking of three or four hundred all told. But Old Hucks can't wait to get to grips with the bomber.'

Paul pricked up his ears. This was where his interest really lay: long-range bombing, using purpose-built machines. Frank Taylor, lucky devil, was to oversee Handley-Page's bomber at Cricklewood. But this was something new.

'A de Havilland bomber?'

'The DH4,' Gresswell told him. 'It's going to be big – it's going to dwarf the DH2, as you'd expect – and it's going to be a good'n.'

So a de Havilland bomber! And that was why Airco were letting Sopwith and Bristol build the next generation of scouts! Paul turned, intending to pump Gresswell for all he was worth, pilot to pilot: he seemed likely to prove a little more forthcoming on under-wraps subjects than Charles Walker had been. However, a hail from the office forestalled his evil intent.

'Lieutenant Cowley? – phone.'

'Oh, heavens!' Paul groaned. 'I forgot to phone HQ.'

'I'll button things up for you here,' Gresswell laughed after him.

Orders did not take long, and half an hour later, with all the paperwork completed, Paul was ready to go.

'Fancy a tea first?' Gresswell asked.

'Best not,' said Paul. 'I've just been, and I'm doing St Omer direct, overflying Dover, so I don't want to get caught out.'

Paul settled into the cockpit, feeling at home at once. Even the smells – of burnt castor-oil, petrol, leather, and doped fabric – were English and familiar, unlike the 'sauerkraut and sausage' flavour he would now always associate with the captured Fokker *Eindecker* monoplane he had ferried over to Catterick from France at the start of his leave. He checked the red safety tag which indicated that the machine was armed, then reached over the lacing of the nacelle, each side in turn, to jam the spare Lewis magazines, two by two, yet more securely into their external stowages. These were the standard-Lewis 47-round drums, although Charles Walker had shown him the new stowage for the 97-round drums soon to be issued. If this machine eventually finished up on the strength of his own squadron – Major Hallam's – or on that of No.24 Squadron, the drums would be moved inside the cockpit. He exercised stick and rudder, and finally craned back over his shoulder towards the engine and propeller to grin towards the mechanic, presently hemmed into what amounted to a cage between the tailbooms, standing ready to swing and start him. Satisfied, he faced the front and signalled his readiness to the senior hand beyond the nose.

'Switches off?' the man called. It was both question and order.

Moments later, the starting drill completed, the 100 horsepower Gnome behind him roared lustily into life. Almost as second nature Paul adjusted the fine-setting then thumbed the button switch, momentarily cutting the power until the workmen could pull away the chocks and run clear. He awaited the signal that the propeller-swinger too was out of harm's way, and letting the engine have its head, gave a cheery wave to Gresswell. Then the grass was streaming by as the eight, so well-remembered, original hangars fell beneath his wings. And what fond memories the now-faded signs brought back as he swept past! 'The Blériot School' across the front of two sheds, and 'Grahame-White', necessarily squeezed tight to fit all the letters on a single roof. He banked gently, turning away from the newer sheds, crossing the main road, and climbing out over the seemingly unending housing beyond.

It was nearly midday on the thirtieth of June 1916, and His Majesty, King George the Fifth, now owned another DH2 fighting scout. And by this time, if things had gone as planned up north in Middlesbrough, Catherine Tomlinson, hairdresser, milliner, youthful war widow – and soon to be couturière –, now owned her third hairdressing salon!

Paul spared one fleeting glance below him for the past – Hendon –, and one to the distant north-east for what he so much hoped would be the future – Catherine. Accordingly it was with a poignant sense of melancholy – half-regret, half-anticipation – that he set heading for the coast, for Dover, for the Channel – and for France.

Chapter Two

If St Omer had been crowded ten days before, now it was packed to capacity. A sergeant checked-off Paul's machine against a list on a clipboard and directed him to a lieutenant sitting behind a table outside the dispatching office. The officer smiled briefly.

'Welcome to Chaos.' He ruffled through a sheaf of papers, selecting and scanning one of them. 'Glad to see you, but we'd like you out of here the moment you can leave.' He pointed at the DH2. 'You've just picked that up in Hendon? If it's all right, then you're keeping it.'

'It's fine,' Paul told him, handing over his travel orders. 'Just top me up and tell me which way to point and I'll get out of your way.'

'You know your squadron's moved south?'

A clerk looked up from a pile of papers and muttered a reminder.

'Ah! yes.' The recording officer searched through his own papers again. 'Found it – thanks.' He scanned the paper. 'Yes, Seventy Squadron's been caught short. They should've received eight Sopwith One and a Half Strutters already but it looks as they're going to be left four shy for a few days. You're to join up with two others from your squadron and operate as detachment commander under Seventy's admin until we get 'em sorted out. It might be as long as a week. They're at Fienvillers.' He looked up. 'Do you know where that is?'

Paul shook his head, pulling a map from his pocket and unfolding it. 'Where's it near?'

'It's where "Boom" has his advanced headquarters.'

Paul shook his head again. Last time he had heard Major General Trenchard, the Officer Commanding the RFC in France – the British army blandly treated Belgium, France, and French Flanders as one –, had established his headquarters at St André aux Bois. For just a moment the officer seemed somewhat peeved at Paul's ignorance, but then he grinned. 'Sorry, old boy, he probably didn't think to tell you he'd upped sticks, did he? It's down towards Amiens.'

'South-west of Doullens, sir,' said the clerk, writing on without looking up.

Paul traced his finger down the map, finding Doullens, and then Fienvillers. 'Got it – thanks.'

'A Very's light for those three,' ordered the recording officer.

The nearby crack and flutter of a signal cartridge signalled take-off permission to three Morane Parasol scouts; four other machines in a row were just starting up. A corporal clutching a batch of newly-arrived signals stood hovering at the lieutenant's shoulder.

'I'm off then,' said Paul, grinning.

'Any other time, old boy,' promised the recording officer, reaching for the signals. 'But as you see ...'

Paul followed the road south, losing it as it passed through Doullens but picking it up again on the far side, staying with it then as far as Beauval, when he turned due west. He was now in Fourth-Army country with the Beauval Aircraft Park falling behind him and Candas coming up on his left, and positively stacked with machines. He raised his eyes, and there was Fienvillers, a hub of minor roads, with a windsock and a clutch of canvas hangars just beyond the trees. The field was not overgenerous even for France, and there were men and aeroplanes everywhere; RE7s, BE2s of various marks, and what seemed to be a score of Martinsyde Scouts. As he crossed the hedge, blipping his switch, he caught sight of two DH2s parked before a double row of bell tents. Alongside the DH2s were four elegant and purposeful-looking Sopwith One and a Half Strutters: a double triumph then, he had found both Fienvillers and No.70 Squadron!

Two nimble air mechanics darted from a shed and helped to swing Paul into line beside the two de Havillands. He cut the switch and heard the engine die, his ears dulled from the din. He pulled off a glove with fingers made awkward by the cold, and looked at his watch. It was just gone four. He wriggled his icy toes inside his fleece-lined boots and took off his helmet. It seemed ages since he had said goodbye to Catherine yet only minutes since he had waved farewell to France. He jumped down from the cockpit, stiff limbed and staggering slightly as his legs gave way beneath him, glad of the momentary assistance of a supporting arm. An arm donated, he found, looking up, to a grinning Peter Mainwaring.

'Good leave, Paul?'

'Feels like I haven't been away.'

He had to shout as a flight of RE7s bumped past across the field: No.21 Squadron, he recorded mentally. Gauntleted hands waved at them and they waved back, watching the grass brush down in a white, feathered wash of slipstream as the veteran two-seaters gathered speed.

There was another face he knew, Dick Fisher's.

'Mike sent us to look after you,' the youngster grinned, 'said we were to show you the ropes.'

'How did he enjoy Paris, and its firing range?'

They both laughed. 'Le Touquet Paris Plage, not Paris itself,' Peter remembered appreciatively. 'At the end of the day he was the only one who hadn't tumbled to it. He was fit to burst when he realised.'

'How is he?' asked Paul.

'In the pink,' said Peter. 'Ah yes, and he said to tell you Andrew Barton's been hospitalised over there.'

'Great news,' said Paul, ashamed to admit, even to himself, that he had all but put the sad figure of Barton from his mind.

It might never be known whether the boy had suffered some intermittent power loss and decided to land under control rather than crash at a time not of his own choosing; or whether he really had been wounded; even lapsed into some form of shock. Or whether he had consciously made the decision that he simply could not face the strain of war flying any more. If the last was the case, Paul reflected, then Barton was as much a casualty as any of the others from this insane carnage: at least now he would get whatever treatment he required.

'A Hun dropped the message over the lines: or rather in 'em,' Peter went on. 'And there was one for you: Roly has it.' They were both grinning widely. 'The Uhlan Hussars and the German Air Service join to invite the other pilot to stay longer next time.'

'Did it really say that?' asked Paul, disbelievingly.

'Cross me heart,' said Peter.

Paul laughed. 'I can't believe it,' he said. 'Although it's a nice thought.' Then he sobered. 'But what must the major have thought? The Huns rubbing it in like that. He was mad enough as it was.'

'He's even madder now,' said Dick. 'Spitting mad. Because they've given you a "Mention". Came through yesterday.'

'But – ?' Paul was overcome. And quite at a loss to understand it. A 'Mention in Dispatches' would have had to originate with the squadron, surely? And Major Hallam had made his feelings perfectly clear.

'He's mad because he put you up for an MC,' Peter told him, grinning. Beside him Dick laughed outright at Paul's evident surprise.

'Bosh,' Paul said firmly. 'Couldn't have done.'

And yet there was a glow of satisfaction deep within him. So the major had put in for a Military Cross! He found himself grinning.

But would Catherine have been impressed? Convinced as she was that Big Business had started the war in the first place and was deliberating prolonging the conflict for its own ends, a conviction that caused her to hate the carnage all the more because of that.

He sobered again. 'Any news of Harry?'

Peter wrinkled his brow interrogatively.

'Saunders,' Paul elaborated. 'He went missing after a balloon attack.'

Mainwaring shook his head. 'Sorry. That must have been before we arrived. We've lost Trent and Padden off the squadron since you've been away. But then you wouldn't have known either of them. Padden was a flamer ...'

Paul mulled this over. There was little enough to say. He looked around the field. 'What's the form here?'

'Major Lawrence is CO of Seventy,' said Dick, 'But he's at a meeting "Boom" called, over at the crossroads.'

'There's a buzz that tomorrow's the big day,' explained Peter. 'Major Lawrence apologised for not being around to meet you but if you're not too tired, and if your bus is OK, he wants us to fly a line recce to get the lie of the land. I've got a sector map marked up for you.'

A flight sergeant appeared from around the tail.

'Good afternoon, sir,' he said, saluting, 'Welcome to Seventy. I'm Flight Sergeant Morgan and I've been detailed to look after your flight while it's with us. If you'd like to rest up a bit before you go up again – have a cuppa and so on – I'll get the machine ready.'

'Thank you, Flight Sergeant.' Paul looked at his watch. 'Perhaps you'd give me a shout when it's all ready?'

'Ours is that Armstrong hut, second in line,' Peter told him.

'I need *that* hut first,' Paul told him, pointing to an adjacent construction. 'After that, we'll get under way.'

Just as Paul remembered, Peter Mainwaring flew confidently and well, keeping station about fifty feet behind and to Paul's right. Dick Fisher was as keen as ever but still diffident, although his over-concentration showed only now and again in certain jerky movements that on occasion caught Paul's eye. Paul grinned. Fisher would be all right.

Climbing gently from Fienvillers he led them in a wide orbit, signalling them to pull in somewhat closer as Fisher's handling became steadier. He reversed the direction of the turn, dipping his wings to the right towards Peter Mainwaring and nodding approvingly as the other pilot sank down and dropped back slightly. On Paul's left Dick Fisher had to work harder to make up the extra distance and Paul watched the way he slid closer to cut the corner. Paul gave them a few moments before reversing the turn again, this time against Fisher, noting the momentary wing twitch as the boy tensed up as Paul's machine loomed towards him. Despite that he coped, and Paul waved approvingly. Satisfied that both were capable, he levelled off at 2,000 feet, heading due east towards the lines some twenty miles away.

The area they were flying over was scattered with woodlands, an agricultural region well served with small roads, most of them running south-east towards the lines. From two thousand feet any contours were flattened but looking ahead towards the horizon the ground rose somewhat to culminate in a series of low ridges, turf-covered where there were no woods, and with chalk showing through wherever the surface was broken by cuttings or quarries. It was a landscape of small, prosperous-looking farms and villages, a vista of green untroubled downs and woodlands, neat and quite unspoiled by war. And yet even before the section crossed the main road running south from Doullens to Amiens there were signs of the storm to come.

Every road had become a river of movement with mile after mile of vehicles threading their way past columns of marching troops. There were equally long columns of horse transport with wagons and limbers taking up supplies and guns, and now and again a staff car darting in and out of the main stream like a self-important minnow. Here and there at road junctions the flow came to a halt, only to resume after a stretch of uneasy confluence; undoubtedly the military police would have their work cut out to keep the traffic flowing free.

Nor was the traffic just one way, for an equal number of vehicles was moving west, empty vehicles presumably, on their return journeys, squeezing their way with difficulty against the unending opposing flow with men spilling off into the countryside where necessary in order to allow them room to pass. In places whole bodies of troops could be seen resting on the march, sprawled out in the fields, or half-concealed beneath the shelter of the trees, their faces pale as they turned them to the sky: a bad practice they would have to be swiftly schooled out of!

The nearer the flight came to the lines the more the constituent parts of the flow turned aside, pooling into vast camps, into horse lines, into dumps of stores and parks of transport, into rows and rows of ordnance laid out ready for use; and all with only the sketchiest attempt at concealment from the air. There were acres of round tents and temporary huts, mostly in ordered cantonments but often set down in haphazard fashion as the terrain permitted. Paul's attention was drawn to a new light-railway line along which men still laboured at the rails. Behind them, dogging their heels, waited two fully-laden trains, one still pushing up a lively plume of steam.

Peering down at the mass of men and materiel thronging the narrow ways Paul was once again forced to pay grudging tribute to the Allied Offensive Policy, for the Flying Corps alone had bought this battle-eager Army freedom of movement. And paid the blood-price for it. Even now, if the enemy's heavy artillery were permitted eyes to see, then these crowded roads and indeed the whole green *Département de la Somme* could become a bloody slaughterground. He lifted his gaze to the horizon, to where a long-strung line of kite-balloons kept watch – British alone, and yet another mark of the Policy's effectiveness.

He steered towards the red-tiled roofs of Gommecourt, the German-held village at the extreme north of the Somme sector. And now the crenellated pattern of the trenches began to appear, running left to right across their front in a tumble of chalk and clay. On the enemy side the Germans had spent up to two years consolidating their defences. The British had been given far less time to develop what they had taken over from their French counterparts. Even so the network of Allied trenches was impressive.

Stretching away to the south where the detachment's beat would run were thread after thread of chalk burrowings, rising with the hills, bisecting woods, dipping through valleys and even through villages, disappearing at times into folds in the ground, but always re-emerging to run on into the distance. There were stretches where one could easily grasp the basic layout of the lines: the rearward assembly trenches fronted by varying numbers of support trenches, and finally the front line trenches themselves behind their mazes of barbed-wire. There were other places where the scheme of things was complicated by the terrain, where the lines of trenches changed direction inexplicably, or were oddly-spaced, the front and rear schemes wide apart, or conversely, crowded one against the other in a narrow cord of chalky spoil.

Always less easy to follow were the communication trenches linking the main systems, narrow ditches for the most part, often dwindling to little more than tracks in places where the ground was deemed dead to enemy observation. Further forwards, out beyond the front-line trenches themselves and projecting into no-man's-land, would be the saps and listening posts. There was also talk of tunnels where large mines had been laid to blow gaps through the enemy defences. How busy the sappers and the infantry must have been!

Paul circled well short of Gommecourt, signalling the section to open out and test their guns. He checked to right and left, getting thumbs-up signals from both his followers, then headed south for neighbouring Hébuterne, itself in British hands. He ran a gloved finger down the Somme front as marked out on his map, assimilating the basic details. In practical terms, ten miles running due south from Gommecourt, to a village named – Fricourt? He peered closer, bracing his shoulder against the bumps that were unsteadying him. – Yes, Fricourt, when the line turned south-eastish for five or so miles to reach the wooded village of Maricourt: a total length of fifteen miles. Fricourt, he saw, backtracking with his finger, lay just a couple of miles east of the key town of Albert.

For the first ten miles, running beneath the rising ground to the east, the front was dotted with a whole string of villages whose names were as unfamiliar to him as the area itself. He picked them out: Gommecourt and Hébuterne, and then, almost equally-spaced, Beaumont-Hamel, Hamel, Authuille, La Boisselle, Fricourt – and then around the corner – Mametz, and finally Maricourt; some in British hands, some in German.

Five miles down from Gommecourt the sleepy, partly-canalised River Ancre passed from the high ground to the east to cross the British lines and follow them for a while, threading south through woodlands before bearing away to battered Albert, clearly visible on the horizon, the largest town in the area and the focal point of the British defences.

Paul led his vic south, climbing to 4,000 feet and heading directly for Albert, keeping at a respectable distance from the lines: long-armed

Archie would be watching and the present job was merely to look and learn, not to be shot at. He eyed the road that ran north-east out of Albert and directly into Hunland for a dozen die-straight miles to reach Bapaume. La Boisselle, over the German line, was the first village along that road, with Ovillers just a little beyond.

With Albert slipping beneath them, and keeping a discreet distance from Fricourt, Paul wheeled the section south-east towards Maricourt, visible five miles distant and framed by trees. Even so he must have misjudged the run of the lines and strayed too close, for all at once a black puff appeared ahead and slightly above him. Then another, and another. He saw flashes from the outskirts of Fricourt's neighbour, Mametz, and he shied away, accepting that the German anti-aircraft gunners, at least, knew for certain where the front ran.

Peter waved reassuringly from his right, while Dick sidled in close, tapping his Lewis and pointing interrogatively down towards the villages. Paul shook his head firmly. 'Not-on-your-life,' he mouthed. Was he surrounded by bloody heroes? Or would-be suicides?

Gradually he edged to the right, heading for Maricourt and turning just short of its wood. Here, at the end of their beat, the lines turned sharply again to run due south towards the village of Suzanne where the French Front began amid the pools and marshes of the River Somme.

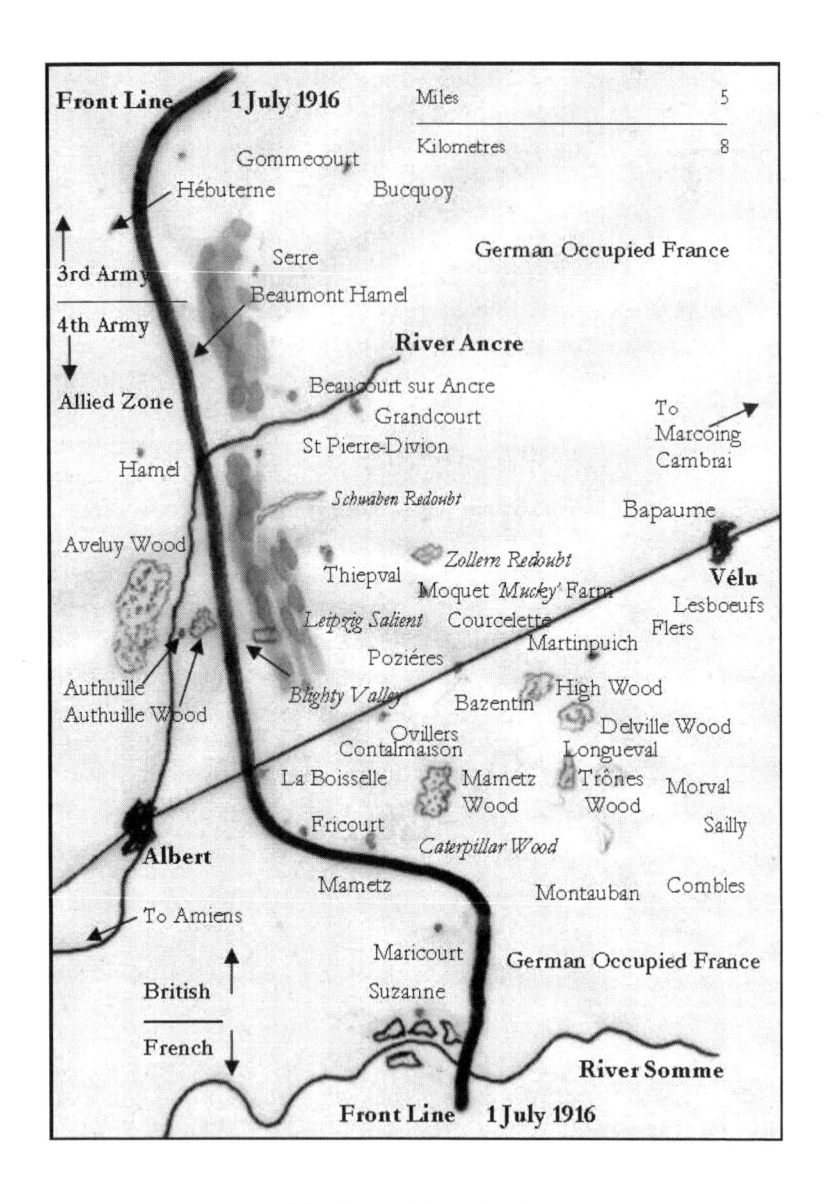

The Somme Front, 1st July 1916

Chapter Three

Paul held a lazy turn that brought them down over the edge of Suzanne, looking for signs of French aerial activity south of the river but seeing none; although there was a fair amount of movement on the roads: here too the build up was progressing towards some imminent conclusion. And if the response from Fricourt and Mametz was anything to go by the Germans were not in the least bit unaware.

From Suzanne he led them back to circle Albert, picking out the celebrated basilica. They were too high to make out the golden, shellfire-tilted figure of the Virgin and Child that surmounted it still and he decided against losing height to sightsee now.

The shots fired at them had drawn specific interest from the British guns for, following a series of flashes from the good side of Albert, Paul saw eruptions of smoke as shells burst beyond Fricourt village. Moments later another salvo burst just short of Mametz. But he was lucky to have picked out this solitary exchange from all the other activity, for nowhere along the line had the British artillery been still.

Checking the height he suddenly realised that he must be flying well within the trajectory of many of the shells! At which juncture, as if to give point to the realisation, Fisher's whole machine lifted suddenly and then careened onto one wing, to hang there nose high.

'Don't spin,' Paul gritted.

He watched, mesmerised, dreading to see the beginning of the flick that would leave the boy whirling out of control towards the gloating ground. But the nose came down and the machine fell away into a spiral dive. Paul relaxed as Fisher rolled wings-level and eased out within a matter of feet, climbing up into position again, grinning and waving to show that no harm had been done. Paul tapped his helmet in acknowledgement. It must have been a big shell. But going up, or coming down: theirs, or ours; and just how close had it come? Who could tell? And did it really matter?

Four miles along their northerly run from Albert, coming up to Hamel, where a localised firefight appeared to be taking place, they passed abeam an area on the German heights which seemed to be taking a particular pounding. Paul thumbed the map. – Thiepval, and just north of it, down the spur towards Hamel, St Pierre-Divion. Indeed British shells were bursting everywhere along the crests and he realised soberly that all the ground of any height was German-held, the enemy overlooking the British positions at every point along the battlefront. Battlefront being the word, for it was clear that the offensive could not be far off now. The bombardment had been unceasing for days, the lads had told him, and when he flicked off the switch, allowing the Gnome to run down momentarily, the noise became a tangible presence. He recalled his few hours in the shell-crater: on what the South Staffordshires had called a quiet afternoon! What must it be like under the hell being created over there, he wondered? What opposition could be left?

He sank lower, bringing what contours there were into sharper definition. The crest itself, he saw now, rose from the undulating plain which held the River Ancre to form an identical plain only eighty to a hundred feet higher; indeed from any reasonable altitude he might well have missed the fact that there was a rise at all! Now he studied the Ancre, running towards him from the higher ground, locating Grandcourt, on its southern bank, and Beaucourt-sur-Ancre, closer by a mile, on its northern. He marked how the river swung south, washing hostile St Pierre-Divion on its left and friendly Hamel on its right, the heights of its re-entrant valley, insignificant as they were, dominating the British lines. It was, therefore, with a feeling of trepidation that it came home to Paul that, though deprived of balloons and aerial observation by the RFC's Offensive Policy, the Germans nevertheless maintained surveillance over the whole of the northern sector, simply by virtue of holding the highest ground.

And more than just surveillance, for as he brought the section around to skirt Beaumont-Hamel so German batteries opened up in a fierce counter-barrage, bursts falling in a wood across the river and filling the air with smoke and dirt along hundreds of feet of front. Paul signalled to the others and clawed for altitude, circling away from the lines and climbing to 2,000 feet where he had a better chance of tracing the source of the counter-fire. Eyeing the bursts of shortfall-shells he followed the trajectory back to where a minor road climbed from Beaumont-Hamel towards a tiny cluster of houses, seeing flashes by the score. He drew an imaginary line north-eastwards over the map, and grunted – Serre. No more than a hamlet, but on the ridge, and evidently massed with artillery well-ranged upon the British front.

He marked the location on his map, taking additional comfort from the fact that at least two balloons had the area under observation. There would be little then the staff did not know about the Serre concentration. So undoubtedly they had something in mind for it before the troops were committed.

From 2,000 feet Paul could see little of the men manning the lines but in places the trenches themselves seemed to have suffered badly both from the shells and from the recent rains. Viewed aslant from his moving machine the whole area seemed a mass of glinting ponds, the very mud glittering in a myriad points of light as the perspective changed, while a support trench, running for some way along their line of flight, shimmered like a small canal. Paul thought back to the bogged-down tractor he and General Cousins had seen in the fields the week before, outside Lincoln. At least the general's fears regarding the tanks should be allayed on one head: determined as they might be to press the new tanks into action at the earliest possible moment, the staff would never contemplate deploying them in ground as waterlogged as this.

Paul kept the patrol up for an hour until he felt confident that he could find his way around the sector without reference to the map, reeling off to himself the names of the main features of the sector and registering the inter-relationship of each. After that, having less need to concentrate so particularly on the ground features, he began to look for aerial activity across the lines. From time to time he had seen scout formations at high altitude, two-seaters for the most part, but once it had been a section of de Havillands, well over, and heading even further east.

Just then Peter Mainwaring pulled ahead to warn of a German two-seater approaching the lines amid a cloud of shell bursts. It was the only German machine they had seen and Paul searched the skies, wondering if it was, indeed, on its own. He turned and began to climb for height, but forestalling him, two Morane Scouts, obviously awaiting just such an attempted incursion, streaked from on high, gunsmoke drifting back from the leader's machine as its pilot fired a frustrated burst towards the now-fleeing two-seater. At once the German anti-aircraft fire became punishing and the Moranes turned away in a snakelike climb to pass two or three thousand feet above the DH2s before heading back across the lines to see what else they could flush out.

On the final leg to Fienvillers Paul contented himself with identifying the bolt-hole landing fields marked for him by Peter, some regular aerodromes, others makeshift. He had not been able to see Baisieux, that had been too far off their track, but he had no trouble identifying Warloy, Léalvillers, and Beauquesne, and as they turned in south of Beauval to return to Fienvillers, Vert Galant on the Doullens road.

They landed back at Fienvillers after one and a quarter hours in the air finding the place strangely bereft of men and just one handler each to see them in. Paul jumped down, wincing with pain, yet patting the fuselage nacelle fondly just the same. His knee was throbbing with overuse, but the new machine had done him proud.

It had been a full day already but it seemed that it was not over yet. Flight Sergeant Thomas appeared with a summons. Major General Trenchard had left some time before but the detailed briefing was still going on. Would the officers join the rest the moment they returned?

The meeting was being held behind one of the hangars, so that as Paul and his two companions rounded the corner it was to discover a whole crowd of men, some on chairs, but for the most part sitting, squatting on the ground, or leaning against the hangar sides. Ranged behind two blanket-covered trestle tables were several senior officers. A lieutenant colonel was speaking but he stopped, acknowledging their salutes and waving them to find a place.

'Quite a crowd,' Paul whispered.

'There are three squadrons here,' Peter told him, shielding his mouth, schoolboy-fashion. 'Seventy – what there are of them yet – and Twenty-One and Twenty-Seven.' He nodded towards the table. 'Major Lawrence – that's our man: OC Seventy Squadron – on the end there? On his right, that's Major Waldron, he's got Sixty, at Vert Galant.'

The lieutenant colonel waited until the wave of unrest caused by the late-joiners had died down.

'So there you have it, gentlemen, an ambitious plan on an immense scale which, with your help, will produce the breakthrough expected of it. It only remains for me to wish you all, Godspeed! and to hand you over to your own squadron leaders for your individual instructions.'

The attending staff officers, serious-faced, followed as he left the table. The gathering, officers and men alike, waited at attention for just a moment before breaking into an excited babble of discussion.

'But the guns have done sweet bugger all!' said a captain flatly. 'And they know it as well as we do. It's going to be bloody murder.'

Major Lawrence came towards them through the crowd.

'Cowley?' he smiled, holding out his hand. 'I'm Lawrence. Sorry to have rushed you off back into the air like that but things are about to break. "Boom" gave us the larger picture – and even *he* had to shout at times to be heard over the guns. Our OC, Lieutenant Colonel Dowding – OC Ninth (Headquarters) Wing, that is –, was just setting the scene for individual squadrons.' He led the way around the corner and found a relatively quiet spot where mechanics were already servicing the three newly-landed de Havillands. Beyond them the four Strutters seemed ready for whatever the future might bring.

'It's Paul, isn't it?' The major gave the others an acknowledging smile. 'Peter and Dick I've already met, of course.' He turned back to Paul. 'Sorry to be the cause of dragging you from your own squadron at a time like this but I've still only two flights in France – and only one here – and the thought is that you can do most good by liaising with our effort. Headquarters Wing, as you probably know, is basically a special-duties wing, so we can be tasked for most things.' He pointed to the map in Paul's knee pocket. 'May I borrow that?'

Paul having unfolded the sheet, they formed a huddle.

'You missed the preamble so I'll just paint in the picture. – You've just come off leave?'

'That's right, sir. So the area's new to me. Or was until an hour ago.'

'The recce was useful then?'

'Very much so, for my part.' And Paul saw Peter and Dick nod in corroboration.

'Good,' said the major. 'Then here's the scheme as it was just put to the rest of us. Bits of Third Army are to attack in the north of our sector, that is, from Hébuterne, running north. Fourth Army – our concern – is to launch an offensive from just south of Hébuterne, down past Fricourt, to Maricourt.' He looked at the three of them and waited until they nodded assimilation.

'South of Maricourt, and in conjunction with the British, the French will be attacking on both sides of the River Somme.'

He ran his finger down the route they had just been patrolling.

'So the whole attack will be launched upon about twenty miles of our front, and eight of theirs. It should have started on the twenty-eighth of June but was put off because of the weather.' He looked at Paul. 'Out here it's been nothing but rain and more rain.' He paused. 'So it's tomorrow at 7.30 ack emma.'

He waited again as they looked at each other, knowing that each would need a moment of reflection. Resuming, he again addressed himself to Paul, 'The guns have been going for almost a week now.' He paused. Then announced, 'The final bombardment will start soon and will only lift when the troops leave the trenches at 7.30. Your job will be to fly contact patrol and later to liaise with our Strutters.'

Once more, he looked at Paul. 'Have you done any contact patrolling?'

Paul shook his head.

'And Dick and I,' Peter said, 'only started at it when we heard about the detachment.'

'Not to worry. We'll have a look at that in a moment. After tomorrow, of course, you'll be the specialists and can tell the rest of us all about it. We're all learning.'

He spanned a section of the map between thumb and forefinger. 'Your area for the kick-off will be the five miles from Hébuterne down to just south of Beaumont-Hamel, north of the river.'

'The Ancre,' Paul murmured.

'That's right. Now, the job of Number Eight Army Corps is to capture and hold the ridge back here.' They leaned forwards, Paul pursing his lips as he saw where the major was pointing.

'Uphill all the way,' said Dick Fisher.

The major nodded gravely. 'That's right. But as you see the ridge runs from Serre to parallel the lines right down to the river. So once they've taken it they can provide a secure defensive flank for all the troops further south.'

'Once they've taken it.' Paul barely caught Peter's mutter, but knew a moment of unease.

'Right, now!' the major changed tack. 'Contact patrol!' He turned to Dick Fisher. 'Let's hear what it's about, Dick.'

The boy actually blushed, and looked about him nervously. A pilot and an observer who had been tinkering with something on one of the

Stutters sauntered over to join the group, saluting as they approached. Fisher looked more embarrassed than ever.

'Come on, Dick,' Peter urged him. 'We won't laugh.' But they all did, the major among them.

'Contact patrols,' announced Dick firmly, as if about to recite. He half-turned and addressed himself to Paul, evidently finding it easier to talk to one person than to a crowd. 'Well, the guns are going to be firing a "creeping barrage". It's failed before but this time they reckon they've got it right. And hopefully they have, for they've been practising it for weeks, apparently. The troops will march forwards at –', he hesitated, evidently searching for a remembered phrase, 'at a measured pace: that's all been calculated out too. And as they begin to move so the guns lift and drop their shells further on in front of them. And so on. That way the troops move up under a constant protective barrage.'

Paul nodded. The troops would be shielded from enemy fire by the barrage while the barrage itself would not only finally cut any barbed-wire entanglements inadvertently left uncut but would keep the Germans' heads down until it was too late and the British stormers were among them.

'And it works?' he asked.

'Like clockwork across the practice trenches,' said the No.70 Squadron pilot dryly. Paul recognised him as the captain who had been so scathing about the results achieved by the guns. By the looks of him he seemed to be a level-headed sort of man and Paul felt another flicker of discomfort.

'On contact patrol,' Dick went on doggedly, 'it's our job to fly right down on the carpet keeping in touch with the storming troops and carrying back reports so that HQ always know where they are.'

Again Paul nodded. It made sense. With all this bombarding going on telephone lines were sure to get broken and runners would be equally vulnerable. An aeroplane, on the other hand, would be able to see what was going on and to report with the minimum loss of time. It seemed a useful concept. Provided that the airmen could see where the troops were in all the chaos. What intensity of fire the low-flying machines would draw upon themselves remained to be seen, although it might well turn out that the Germans would be too busy with the ground action to spend much time on aircraft – at least at the start. It sounded like an exciting undertaking all round, and Paul found himself totally unenamoured of the prospect. Contact patrol, he could see, like shooting down observation balloons, was definitely not likely to prove a pensionable occupation.

'The stormers will display coloured signal panels so that we can see where they've reached,' Dick went on determinedly. 'And they'll be carrying mirror things on their backs, and flares too, so we'll always know where the forward troops are. Oh! and our machines are to be fitted with klaxon horns to tell them to signal us. We sound, AAA. Then, when we've got their positions, we turn back and drop a message bag at forward headquarters.' He had been gaining confidence throughout, Paul noted with approval. Now he looked towards Major Lawrence. 'I think that's about it, sir.'

'Yes, well done, Dick, I think you covered everything,' said the major. 'The Strutters' – he acknowledged the captain and his observer –, 'will have their wirelesses, of course. And that then,' he told Paul, 'is contact patrol.'

He paused. 'As you'll appreciate, our task here is directed by the local army corps, and our responsibility is to the troops, therefore you Army-Wing fellows'll become Corps-Wing chaps for the duration of your detachment. So while you've got your heads down, looking at the ground, your chums back in the Army-Wing squadrons will be keeping the Hun off your necks.'

'Or at least ...' grinned the captain irreverently.

Or at least, Paul finished off silently, that is the plan ...

As soon as he could Paul led his own party away towards the squadron office to report himself to the adjutant – the recording officer, out here in France. The Sopwith captain waved a sardonic farewell before turning to receive his own instructions from the major. At his shoulder his observer gave a cheery grin.

'Tell me,' said Paul, having given his details to the recording officer. 'One of your pilots said something about the guns having done nothing. What did he mean?'

The other officer grimaced. 'Wing have been sending back our reports about it to Army for days. Wire cut at night is mended by next day and we believe that most of the shells, even the heavies, aren't even touching the dugouts they've built. Yet the whole theory is that the guns will obliterate the wire and keep Fritz's head down so that the troops can simply stroll across no-man's-land.'

'At a measured pace,' acknowledged Paul dryly. 'And what does Army say?'

'They say, "Thanks for the reports, maties," and do bugger all about it.' The tone was bland.

'What about "Boom", though?' pressed Paul. If his reputation was anything to go by it was hardly likely that Major General Trenchard would let RFC reports be disregarded.

The recording officer sighed. 'Someone asked him that at the briefing earlier on.'

'And what did he say?'

'He said, "Take a note, Baring," to his aide.'

They laughed together. 'Boom' Trenchard was well known for having notes taken, but he was even better known for getting things done as a result of those notes.

'I fear, however,' said the recording officer, 'that on this occasion High Command have made up their minds that the barrage will do the trick and a little bit of proof from the RFC isn't going to sway their judgement, even when it comes from "Boom" himself. Besides, even if they did decide to take notice, an offensive this big has a momentum of its own. It would take the Day of Judgement to stop it now.'

They left it at that. Paul spread out his map and pointed to the mark he had made, at Serre.

'There's a large concentration of guns running right back north-east from here. There were two of our balloons covering the area, so the concentration'll be known about, but the ridge there really does command our whole front. It's the one Major Lawrence told us Eight Corps has to take as its starting objective.'

'Serre, still.' Thoughtfully the recording officer shoved forwards his bottom lip. 'Right ... I'll pass that on straightaway – again. True, they may have thought they'd neutralised them. Although I doubt it.' He traced north-east from Serre to a village marked as Bucquoy. 'They say the Hun has up to a hundred batteries around there.'

'A hundred batteries?' Paul echoed. 'But from what I've just seen the Serre to Bucquoy heights control the whole way south! And they haven't knocked them out before this! It's unbelievable.'

The other smiled sadly. 'Believe it,' he said.

Chapter Four

'Did you have a good leave, sir?' Robinson asked.

Paul shot up in bed. 'Robinson! What on earth – ?'

The batman grinned. 'Thought that'd surprise you, sir. Major Hallam sent me over last night. It was late, so I didn't disturb you.'

Paul grinned, rubbing at his chin. 'Home from home,' he said accepting a mug of tea. 'It's good to see you, but what's the time?'

'Five ack emma, sir. Misty but it'll soon clear.'

'Five o'clock?' Peter Mainwaring groaned from a bed across the hut. 'God, what a lousy war! I swear I didn't get a wink.'

'With a hideous row like that,' grumbled Dick Fisher, 'they don't mean anyone to sleep.'

Paul concurred. The barrage, though dulled by distance, had been incessant all night, swelling as new batteries took up the roll, a drumming to no particular rhythm, diminishing as various elements paused to reload or re-range, and then intensifying once more.

'If the troops aren't going over until 7.30 what are we getting up this early for?' Peter grunted.

'*Je ne sais* bloody *pas*,' answered an even more disgruntled voice from a bed near the door, 'So put a sock in it you early birds.'

Stars were still visible in the pre-dawn greyness, nevertheless some RE7s from No.21 Squadron were taking-off. And No.70's Sopwiths, it seemed, had been long gone. Major Lawrence walked the DH2 pilots to their machines to wish them well.

'You couldn't be better off,' he told them, 'the bombing machines will disrupt everything far back, your own Army-Wing chums will keep the Hun from even approaching the lines, and defensive patrols will take care of any that still manage to get close. So you won't even need to watch your tails.' They grinned at him, and he had the grace to grin back. 'Your buses have had klaxons fitted,' he went on, 'so we'll just have to see how it'll work out.'

There was time to spare but the pilots used it to best advantage in making their own careful inspections of their machines.

'Your chaps have done a great job for us, Flight Sergeant Morgan,' Paul said sincerely, and saw the technician grin with pleasure.

'Ay, they're not bad lads, sir,' he replied gruffly.

Leaving the machines the three of them made their way the few yards to the armourers' tent. The de Havillands' guns had all been cleaned and serviced during the night but Paul took the opportunity of giving his own a further close inspection, the other two following suit. No.70 Squadron's armourer officer, a lieutenant seconded from the Middlesex Regiment, grinned. 'Guaranteed not to jam,' he told them cheerfully.

Paul pulled back the cocking lever and checked the action, then opened it again, eyeing what he could make out of the seer.

The armourer nodded approvingly. 'Yes, the seers've been a bit of a thorn.'

'But this should be all right, it's straight from the factory,' Paul told him. 'I just picked it up.'

The other smiled. 'So was the oil they sent out recently. But it froze at altitude. Wrong bloody oil, it turned out.'

Two of the armourer's airmen were scooping rounds from a cartridge-box, scrutinising each round for deformity or damage before loading it into the drums. Peter lifted one of the circular, fluted drums, rubbing his finger round it a little dubiously: if just one of the forty-seven rounds jammed at the wrong time!

An aircraftman looked up grinning. 'This lot isn't bad, sir, we've slung all the American stuff.'

'Notwithstanding which –' The armament officer pointed to a heap of a dozen or so rounds on the table before him, apparently identical to all the others but found wanting, nevertheless.

Paul grinned appreciatively at all three. 'We're clearly in good hands.'

They got airborne at 7.10 a.m., circling towards 3,000 feet and climbing above the mist-shrouded fields into a clean, clear sky. Below them trees stood proud through a fog layer so thin that it was evident that the sun would indeed soon burn it off.

Almost at once they could see activity around them. First a ragged flight of Morane Scouts descending off to the south, returning to Vert Galant from some pre-dawn take-off job. Minutes later two flights of BE2cs took off from Bellevue and climbed away towards the north-east, closely followed by a third flight: No.8 Squadron, then, heading for the Gommecourt sector at the very north of the line and their left-hand neighbours today. Paul peered over to see if he could make out anything of No.3 Squadron whose Moranes would be operating on their immediate right, but drew a blank. On the other hand there was plenty of activity on the ground at Marieux where the BE2cs of No.15 Squadron were getting ready to work alongside those of No.9 Squadron further south. In all, it looked as if the sky would be pretty crowded.

Paul checked his watch. Since first opening his eyes to Robinson's awakening summons the throbbing of the barrage had never been out of his ears. Now they were passing over the bigger artillery pieces. He thumbed off the switch, and at once the bombardment filled the air with such a cacophony that it was a relief to switch on again and let the Gnome drown out the sound once more. He pulled at his lapstrap and lifted in his seat to ease some wind, then moistened his lips behind his face-mask. Four dots appeared slightly above, and he tensed, but then relaxed as they took shape and he recognised the four Sopwiths of No.70 Squadron whose pilots and observers, back from their long reconnaissance, waved and cushioned heads on arms at the stay-abed de Havillands as they dived past: they must have been off at some utterly ungodly hour. Paul grinned, and waved back airily.

They could see the ridges ahead of them now, the softly rounded contours bisected by shallow valleys each with its ribbon of mist, and here and there villages, red-roofed and white-faced, no longer undamaged, but preserving still at least a vestige of their form. They slipped beneath the balloons, rocking their wings as they passed, seeing the observers in their baskets take their binoculars from their eyes and wave back. 7.18 a.m. And not a German balloon to be seen!

The mist blotted out much of the terrain but Paul could just make out the roofs and copses around the village of Beaumont-Hamel, forlorn already and almost certainly destined to become even more so in the next few hours. Keep five miles clear, the orders said, until 7.20 a.m. Paul checked his map and edged a little further to the left. He positively identified brigade headquarters where they would drop their signal bags, noting, as he momentarily flicked his switch, that the guns were, if anything, noisier than before: little wonder that people were already speaking of this as the greatest bombardment the world had ever known. And 'great' was the word they were actually using!

Passing over the signal area he switched off once more, and on sounding the klaxon could just hear it, a raucous croak, torn thin and ragged in the airflow. Obviously it carried well enough, however, for immediately the signal panel winked a black and white acknowledgement. Powering up again Paul began a circle back to face Beaumont-Hamel, glancing at his watch, and waving Dick and Peter further out as a precaution. Batteries were flashing continuously from a thousand points, some from concealment in their net-draped pits, others from the shelter of woods. Lighter pieces were everywhere, some even firing from open fields, risking aerial discovery should any Hun penetrate the defences. Yet again, Paul re-checked his watch. It could only be a matter of seconds now.

The explosion came when they were halfway around the turn. There was a rumble that overrode all other sounds followed an instant later by a torrent of disturbed air that tossed Paul's de Havilland nose-high into the air and onto its side, leaving him confused and the machine near-stalled. He turned his head frantically, centralising stick and rudder and locking hands and feet, waiting for gravity and the aircraft between them to sort the situation out. Instinct insisted that his engine had blown up but reason told him differently, and there was no mistaking the fan of smoke and dirt rising to a height at least twice that of his own for anything but what it was. 7.20 a.m., and the mine at the Hawthorn Redoubt, Beaumont-Hamel, had been blown within a second of the planned time. And yet once again, Paul found himself wondering. On time; only why so early, ten full minutes before the infantry assault?

His aircraft's nose plummeted earthwards. Stay five miles clear, they had said. And they had very nearly got it wrong! Spiralling down he searched for the others. One machine was virtually upside down, but correcting: the other was rightside up, but passing out of sight behind Paul's upper plane. His own rudder, he found, was finally answering, and within seconds he was back under control, diving, and with the speed coming up nicely. He had reasonable faith in his own method of getting out of a spin but he had no wish to put it to the test in a de Havilland carrying a full war load, at such a low level, in the middle of an artillery barrage. He rolled to the horizon and eased out of the dive, coming back to level flight at about 2,500 feet above the ground. His compass was spinning wildly but his rev counter was steady and the Gnome had not missed a single beat. The oil level was good, at halfway up the dome. He cast a hurried look around, checking struts and wires and planes. And took a deep breath, easing the tension in his spine.

It was Dick Fisher who had been overturned but he seemed to be all right. Paul gathered from the corner of his eye that the boy had recovered by pulling into a dive, inverted as he was, and rolling to head-on-top flight. Peter was already closing on Paul's wing, waving and wagging his head as if to make sure it was still there. But full relief did not come until Dick pulled up alongside also. Then, realising that they too were a little shaky, he gave them a moment or so to settle before turning them back towards Beaumont-Hamel. The pall of smoke had reached a monstrous height, towering grotesquely above their heads to spew out dirt and debris in an obscene shower. It was a gruesome sight, the shattered earth returning to its own, taking with it what remained of who knew just how many hapless men.

Even engine noise seemed muted now. Paul took the section into a lazy orbit, gradually gaining height, watching the dirt settle and searching the terrain to left and right. For the most part the ridges remained unbelievably normal; green slopes unploughed this two years past with wide, rolling, unfenced fields rising up from the valley of the Ancre, breasting the slopes to the heights of Thiepval ridge and then holding their level, as he had remarked before, as an undulating upland plain. From here he could see Hunland stretching away into the distance, woods and villages and tiny towns folded into the vista in a serenity that must surely be unreal. He looked again at the slopes, wooded here and there where re-entrant valleys broke their flanks, yet for the most part billiard-table smooth. Only belying the normality and naked to the eye, heaped everywhere along the crests, the chalk-white spoil of German trenchworks laced and interlaced four and five rows deep, frowning down upon the tiny, wood-screened River Ancre.

For all that, however, little seemed to be happening, the woods and slopes appeared so innocent and still. Below him thousands of guns were shooting out tons of metal and high-explosive, churning the air so that at times he had to struggle to keep an even keel as some projectile surged past only feet away. And yet, in the main, the complaisant earth showed scant sign of any untoward offence. Here and there a shell burst in a flash of red fire, to be as instantly expunged, the thin plumes of smoke pulled ragged by the freshening breeze and seldom persisting once the leap of earth fell back. And all the time there was the mist, pooling in the river bottom, clinging in the trees, and holding to the lower slopes, mere early-morning gossamer the sun would soon dispel though presently lingering, pale and milky, screening much that man had already done in ravishing this tiny stretch of earth.

But now the natural screen was supplemented by a man-made mist billowing forth from smokeshells and canisters, streaming before the drift of wind from score upon score of points along the British line, thin at first but joining then in confluent sheets, the white smoke lifting under the breeze to climb towards the crests, thickening in places but still woefully thin. Paul could see the British lines clearly now, the trenches black with troops packed forwards for the off.

And stretching wide before them the broad, impassive, seemingly unbroken bands of tangled British wire.

Suddenly the barrage swelled and now Paul raised his eyes to the broad, red-brown brushwork that was the distant German wire and saw the earth leaping and falling, shimmering along the ridge like a dancing fountain, the ridge itself seeming to alter its form as the mass of shell went down. His scan ranged back and forth across the swathe of newly-pitted desolation that represented no-man's-land, deserted as yet, with only the occasional shortfall to disturb its stillness. He looked at his watch, seeing the minute hand hovering on the half hour.

And now, as if what had gone before was merely a prelude, the ridge before him disappeared altogether in a cataclysmic eruption of smoke and tortured earth. To Paul it was a muted eruption, its fury muffled by the engine's roar, but it was terrifying to look upon and to know that men were cowering for their lives beneath that soulless rain of steel. It might well have been too awesome to bear but Paul lifted his eyes – and there was the sky, and summery clouds that soared majestically to the heavens filling him with an overwhelming sense of unreality. He lowered his gaze from this calm and staggering immensity and found even the fury of the bombardment puny and insignificant in comparison: viewing it from his Godlike stance, it became a shabby spectacle, devoid of sound, and quite devoid of meaning, detachedness robbing it of all malevolence.

He waved his hand from side to side and as one both Dick and Peter rocked their wings and broke away, each to his own patrolling beat. Paul cocked the Lewis, hunching down, and firing off a testing burst, swiftly scanning within the cockpit to reassure himself that all was well. It was 7.30 ack emma on a glorious first of July. And below him, all along the line, the barrage died away.

That he could be aware of a cessation of noise surprised him, for he had been convinced that the Gnome was drowning all sound. He thumbed the switch, and as the engine note diminished, heard only the whining rush of air. Southwards, as far as the eye could see, the smokescreen rolled and billowed, not in an unbroken sheet, however, although it should have had sufficient time to spread, but tending to pool, here and there filling some hollow in the ground, shredding elsewhere to stream upslope as a thin and ragged drift of floss.

Then jets of earth began to spurt again, but erupting now beyond the smoke as the barrage laid down the first of its protective screens, out across no-man's-land towards the German front-line defences. And figures were emerging from the British trenches, in ones or twos, and then in clusters, swelling as Paul watched into thickening threads and braids of men as they spread uncertainly along the frontage of the lines, moles from the sunless depths, newly exposed to the glare of day. Gradually the minute figures began to distance themselves from their trenches, only to pause almost at once and begin to bunch as they approached the bands of British wire. There was a hiatus, and then a movement sideways as they found a channel and began to funnel through. Paul remembered what the Sopwith captain had said about the uncut wire and wondered if this was just the start: this was British wire, and supposedly under British control! But now the troops were moving forward once more, fanning out from the cleared lanes into extended line, advancing directly up the slope.

There was still an air of unreality about it all. These were not men surely, these thousands upon thousands of puny mud-hued dots straggling out from beyond the churned-up chalk: tiny clockwork manikins perhaps who did not like the surface of the playroom floor and who fell in rows refusing to rise again to rejoin the other onward-tottering toys – but never men? And yet he knew that somewhere down there were the South Staffs who had succoured him in the Salient …

Nowhere was the advance continuous for the figures would become still and remain motionless for moments at a time before moving forwards on their way; far fewer than before, but gradually making ground. Now they formed a distinct wave, separated both from their trenches and their barbed-wire. And now a second wave was emerging, bunching at the British wire again, but less hesitantly now that the access lanes had been made obvious: where bodies were heavily draped was wire, a mere scattering of bodies meant no wire. A fixed line of fire for Hun machine guns, of course. But a lane clear of wire.

Paul winged back across the River Ancre, climbing, aware that he was flying head-on to the British shells, registering the awareness, and discounting it. He reached three thousand feet again and turned once more towards the battle. The smoke was denser now across the German front-line trenches as shells rained into no-man's-land and the defences beyond in an unceasing deluge and as he neared the scene he saw the barrage lift, and drop again some fifty yards beyond, paving the way for the infantry to advance, just as they had practised – lift and drop, lift and drop –, the high-explosive curtaining their front. – And keeping the Germans head-down in their lairs?

The lines of dots were moving more slowly now, those that Paul could see between the shreds of smoke. Some had stopped even before the British wire, unable to find a passage across, and all the way over no-man's-land he picked out files, and ranks, and dots in isolation, and watched as they renewed their snail's-pace way. But inexorably the British guns moved on, lifting and dropping 'to a measured pace', steadily outdistancing the attacking troops, depriving them of their protection, and leaving them at the mercy of the German counter-fire! The lines wavered, and thinned, checking, and then, as if breasting a strong wind, gathering themselves and moving on once more.

But they were pitifully few, and dwindling; now braided cords of men, and then threads, then tiny clusters, and then but ones and twos, trickling up and through the German wire, fading in the smoke, then disappearing as they fell upon the first defensive line. Paul overflew bunched groups who could not penetrate the German wire, and watched as, enfiladed by machine guns long since up and at their bloody work, they parted like petals from a flower, collapsing outwards on the meshes.

And now all movement seemed to cease. What was left of the second wave had disappeared into the German lines. Paul dipped down towards the khaki-littered ground, sweeping back across the hideously festooned British front-line wire towards the river, holding low and feeling lower.

STORMERS IN ENEMY FRONT-LINE TRENCHES, he scribbled, HEAVY LOSSES DUE MGs. BARRAGE OUTSTRIPPING TROOPS. OWN AND ENEMY WIRE NOT RPT NOT WELL CUT.

He undershot the drop by some yards but saw a man retrieve the weighted, bright-streamered bag. At least they had the message, although what they could do about it now with the troops already committed Paul could not conceive.

A third wave had gathered on the parapets and at once, as if at a prearranged signal, the picture changed, and what had until now been a heavy fall of German fire erupted into a veritable maelstrom of shrapnel and high-explosive shells. Paul held three thousand feet again, but all he could see was smoke and a ferment of earth as the German counter-barrage intensified. Aimlessly, dulled in mind, he drifted back across no-man's-land.

Unbelievably, figures from the first and second waves of stormers were still emerging from the shambles to tumble over the deserted parapets and traverse along the German trenches, their progress marked by hand-bomb flashes well into the second and third defensive lines. Though few in numbers the stormers were obviously making their presence felt but support was vital or they would be swamped before they could consolidate their hard-won gains.

Paul circled back to check on the progress of the third wave and was staggered to find no sign of them – they had not even left the trenches.

But the reason for that was only too clear. From his bird's-eye vantage point Paul could now see the plan of the intensified German fire. Viewed from directly above, what had seemed a haphazard blanket-barrage resolved itself into three deliberate and well-ranged zones of shellfire. The nearest was playing across no-man's-land, holding back the advance of supports. The second was falling on the British front-line trenches themselves, and was smashing the mass of troops who were to have made the next assault. The third was bursting fifty yards further on to prevent reinforcement from the rear. There was nothing haphazard about it. It was a calculated firing scheme, allowing the first waves to come across and then sealing them off from supports. And the German gunners had the range to a nicety.

Hurriedly he printed out:
STORMERS IN FIRST, SECOND, THIRD ENEMY TRENCHES. URGENT NEED SUPPORT. GUNS SEALING OFF SUPPORTS.

A Sopwith flashed past Paul's front as he pulled up from the drop, startling him, and bringing to mind that it was long minutes since he had last checked the sky. Nor was there any indication that the Sopwith's crew had even seen him – perhaps they too were feeling stunned. He re-checked the instrument board and looked around the machine generally, reassuring himself that nothing was amiss. He scanned the sky, but the horizon was devoid of air activity and again he swept his eyes across the fields beyond the Ancre valley, unable to reconcile the tranquillity there with the agony unfolding only feet beneath his wings.

Troops were massing again despite the heavy fire, moving forwards to succour those who had gone before. They would be sorely needed, Paul reflected, for the stormers of the first two waves must already be running short of bombs. Around him the air shuddered sending the machine pitching and rolling a clear second before a shrieking rush blotted out the engine's roar. He steadied the craft, knowing that some large projectile had missed him by inches. Again, and then again, the machine lurched to the passage of similar shells. Dismayed, he looked back to see what was happening.

The British support trench he had just overflown had disappeared beneath a living hedge of earth and smoke: high-explosive designed to entomb the troops beneath their trenches! He faced the incoming fire, feeling for the survivors below, watching them emerge from the support trench only to see the forward trenches too disappear in showers of high-explosive. And, beyond that still, awaiting them across the largely uncut wire in no-man's-land, were shrapnel shells, flailing down upon the wounded and the living, equally as they did upon the bodies of the dead.

Paul climbed steadily, looking north-east, across the higher ground commanding every British objective. He had no need to check the map: the whole plateau, from Serre back to Bucquoy, and down the ridge across the Ancre gap to Grandcourt, was asparkle now with venomous points of fire. One hundred batteries at Bucquoy alone, Intelligence had believed; and here, the vindication of that belief. Yet still the troops had been committed!

And beggaring all belief those troops were actually on the move again, picking their way through the British wire and edging forwards up the slopes of no-man's-land. But stumbling and falling, dropping in clusters as the machine guns caught them, and remaining there as their fellows plodded on.

Paul dived steeply, engine off, to traverse the German front at a lower level than he cared to think about. To the rear the firefight was still going on as the stormers in the second and third enemy trenches battled it out. He dipped a wing towards the overrun front-line trench – and recoiled, unable to credit what he saw. The trench was once more fully manned – but with grey-clad troops! The stormers beyond were now cut off without a hope.

He pulled for height. More British troops were emerging from the smoke and plodding towards the German wire, the shrapnel now dogging individual groups, playing on them as they broached the curtains of ranged fire. And still they came. And still they fell. It was nothing less than ritual slaughter.

He was diving at top speed, conscious of his revs, switching off and swamping his senses with the noise of battle: the roar of cannon, the whiplash crack of shrapnel, the rattle of machine guns and the heavy thump of hand-thrown bombs. He switched on again, back to the sounds of his own familiar world.

Now he was sweeping over German lines bewildering in their intricacy and depth. They were wider and more extensive than any trench lines he had seen before, affording glimpses of deep dugouts with the tops of staircases leading even further down. The fighting was clearly bitter and few looked up to note his passage. He was low enough to differentiate between khaki uniforms and grey but all he saw was grey.

He sounded his klaxon and fired off a flare, looking for a response, and finding none. He caught a glimpse of distant khaki figures bombing their way up a slope towards Serre village and marvelled that any could have got that far. But their position was hopeless, there was no support, and there was nothing he could do to help them.

He winged back down towards the main fight, conscious of the Serre to Grandcourt ridge behind his back and of hostile eyes tracking his every move. He swept across the embattled trenches, signalling with his klaxon, but there was no response and he did not see a single flare. The piteously reduced wave of attackers was nearly up to the German wire, and coming grimly on.

From the corner of his eye he saw four grey-clad, apparatus-laden figures leave the trench and run out into no-man's-land, braving their own first line of falling shells. He watched in awe as they went to ground in the open, coming into action almost at once with a burst of enfilading machine-gun fire that cut swathes through the already depleted stormers. It was the sort of courage he could only wonder at but in sheer frustration he banked towards them, triggering his Lewis as it came to bear. He had no idea where his bullets ended up but he saw their startled faces as he swept across their heads and hoped that he had put them off long enough to enable the attackers to reach the trench. And then what?

He dropped his third message,
ENEMY RE-OCCUPIED FRONT LINE! STORMER REMNANTS TOWARDS SERRE. 3RD WAVE TOO WEAK.

He considered putting down at a forward strip to make a detailed report but decided against it. How the Germans had re-occupied the front line behind the stormers was beyond him. So there would be nothing he could add. He could only hope that the observers in the two-seaters had done better at interpreting the development. But it was high time to turn for home anyway.

He climbed gently, letting the machine follow its own devices as Doullens took form on the horizon. Then he levelled off and turned for Fienvillers, seeing with relief the other two de Havillands already parked outside the sheds. There were only two Sopwiths, he saw, but even as the handlers swung him into line he saw the missing pair settle down and come bumping across the field. He sat there, switching off and listening to the engine running down, still trying to come to terms with all that he had seen. The comparative silence was unbearable.

The pilots and observers were clustered together outside their squadron office with Major Lawrence and the recording officer seated at desks trying, amid the swelling clamour, to record the reports. At intervals one or the other would shout imploringly, 'Gentlemen, please!' and the babble would die away, only to regain its former intensity within moments.

Peter and Dick appeared from the direction of the mess with plates and mugs in their hands, having ordered for Paul too, and now all three of them stood apart, awaiting their turn in silence, perhaps because they were indeed three alone among many, gulping down sandwiches and hot coffee laced with rum. Eventually the recording officer beckoned them forward.

Paul listened as the others struggled to piece together the last two hours, trying to bring some semblance of order to their impressions. Around him he was aware of other conversations and he caught the tone of frustration running through them all, frustration and the sense of – he searched for the word he wanted, and found it – outrage: the sense of outrage that everyone felt. By the sound of it no one had anything but disastrous failure to report.

After Paul had concluded his own narrative Major Lawrence grunted. Nor did he speak before the recording officer had put down his pen and pushed the three reports across to him. He scanned them rapidly, then grimaced.

'Yes, gentlemen. It looks like the same story all the way along.' He raised his eyes from the papers. 'First things first. How did you go about it?'

Paul gathered his impressions. 'At first, sir, I held three thousand feet as an average, but it was too high for detail. I think it's only at about six hundred feet or so you can make out who's who.'

He saw the others nod agreement, and went on, 'After a while I came down, feeling they'd be too busy to bother overmuch about us.' He paused. 'The smoke made it difficult to see what was going on, particularly at first. There were no flares.'

'Or signal panels,' Peter put in.

'And the klaxon didn't draw any response, either.'

'I tried Very's cartridges too,' reported Dick, 'but got nothing.'

The CO nodded glumly. There was a footstep behind them and he looked up. 'Oh, Bernard –' He turned to the de Havilland pilots.

'You've met Captain Doughty?' he confirmed. 'The De Havs,' he said to the captain, 'report just the same. No identification signals at all.'

Paul turned to meet the somewhat cynical smile of the Sopwith pilot from the day before. So his name was Doughty.

'The poor sods,' Doughty opined, 'are obviously too intent on keeping their heads on their shoulders to bother about signalling,' He paused, and looked at Paul. 'Beautiful, wasn't it? Wire not cleared enough even on our side, ground so wet that a cat would sink – especially one with two tons of clobber in its knapsack –, and an artillery bombardment not worth a damn waltzing off and leaving the poor bloody infantry floundering on behind.'

'And the machine guns,' said Dick.

'The machine guns most of all, by the look of it,' said the major, shuffling the reports into a pile. 'We've been on to Wing, and had Army reports.' He pulled a watch from his tunic. 'It's 9.45. The attack's been on since 7.30. So what's that – about two hours? And it begins to look like a monumental bloody fiasco. Except that there's been little hostile air activity anywhere near the lines. Ossie saw a two-seater, didn't he, Bernard?'

Captain Doughty nodded. 'An Aviatik, but it sheered off before even crossing the lines with a whole horde of Army-Wing buses on its tail.'

'Yes, we've successfully swamped the sky by the look of it. But on the ground, as we feared, the guns haven't done anywhere near as much damage as it was hoped. All reports seem to suggest that the German wire was reasonably well cut in most places but that the dugouts weren't even scratched.'

He tapped Paul's report. 'This re-occupation of the front line. It seems that once our storm troops passed on into the second and third trenches the Huns came up from deep bunkers that've obviously been made both shell and hand-bomb proof, and let fly at their backs.'

'It's Würtenburgers holding the line over there, not Prussians,' Doughty put in, 'and they're no slouches. Ossie –' he glanced towards Paul – 'my observer, caught on to what they were doing and wirelessed it back. Army have just confirmed that they've pulled the same trick nearly all the way down the line.'

'It's a grim lookout for the men trapped over there,' said Dick feelingly.

The major grunted unwilling agreement. 'Incidentally, about the Serre guns,' he said, his voice expressively neutral, 'Army say that the German barrage was no heavier than expected.'

The captain let out a snort of disgust and at that the CO grinned thinly. 'It's the level of machine-gun fire that's surprised them. That's what's doing all the damage, they say.'

Paul told them about the machine-gun team running out into the open to rake the attackers from the side. 'If ever men deserve an iron cross, they do,' he added feelingly.

A sergeant handed the major the phone. 'Wing,' the major told Paul shortly, returning the instrument, 'want you to go out again. Take off at eleven, if your buses are all right?' He looked questioningly at all three and saw them nod. 'Good. Army are desperate to know where their forward troops are; nothing's getting through.'

Paul looked at the others and spoke for them all. 'We could get airborne for 10.20, sir.'

The major eyed them in satisfaction. 'Then, thank you, gentlemen. I'll let Wing know.'

The heat was building up and several of the Sopwith crews were sprawled in front of their machines, heads pillowed on their fur jackets.

'They didn't give you much rest,' Paul said to the captain.

'The dawn job was in the Cambrai area,' Doughty explained. 'They wanted it looked at before six. Then, while you were away, we got off again for three-quarters of an hour or so.'

'How was Cambrai?' asked Dick.

'Pretty quiet. Roads, railways, nothing unusual.' He grinned his cynical grin. 'Hardly surprising, I suppose. They'll have prepared for this months ago. After all, they've been given warning enough.' A mechanic intercepted them to have a word with the captain and Paul waited, leaving Dick and Peter to stroll on ahead.

'You say you fired at those machine gunners?' Bernard Doughty asked, rejoining Paul. 'Do any good?'

'I was still taken aback at seeing Germans in the front line,' Paul told him. 'I opened fire too soon – and I was skidding at the time, but I think it put their heads down.'

'Put the fear of God into 'em, I don't doubt, seeing a bloody great scout come hurtling down on them like that.'

Paul snorted as he thought how ineffectual his unpremeditated action had been. 'It was sheer frustration. But for just a moment I felt I was actually doing something instead of only spectating. I mean, what use are we to them? We're not even effective as a bloody diversion. Even our messages can't really help. It's sheer murder, of course, just as you said it would be.' He paused. 'All those men ... Hundreds ... Thousands ... I tell you – when I stopped the engine just now I could have sat there and cried.'

Doughty looked at him, and there was not a trace of cynicism about him. 'Could have?' he said quietly.

'We're going to have to go in lower if we're to do any good at all,' said Doughty.

Paul nodded. 'I'm not looking forward to it, but you're right. We're going to have to search for them. I can't see anyone willingly giving away his position by setting off a flare.'

The breeze brought the fury of the cannonade back to their attention from twenty miles away.

'Any idea how many went across?' asked Bernard. Paul shook his head. 'Nor me,' said the other. 'Let's just hope there's one of 'em left to light a bloody flare.'

Paul's machine had suffered no damage while inspection of Dick's showed just four tiny tears in the fabric of his left lower plane, easily and quickly repaired. Peter's, however, had developed a fuel leak and the best efforts of Flight Sergeant Morgan and his men failed to get it ready by the declared departure time. Accordingly Paul and Dick took off at 10.15 and flew in company to the rendezvous, receiving, on arrival, a valedictory wing-waggle from one of the two-seaters they were relieving.

Paul's brief was to locate the foremost stormers in the stronghold of Beaumont-Hamel village, Intelligence having reported serious opposition from that area. Only with knowledge of their positions, he had been told, would the artillery be free to carry out the bombardment necessary to stem the expected counter-attack. Hardly half past ten, and Army was concerned about counter-attacks! So much for the high hopes of the night before!

Cautiously Paul nosed towards the village at 3,000 feet, holding its crossroads slightly to his left in order to get an unimpeded view. From here he could see how the few white walls still standing rose from the skirting tide of brick-red rubble that had spilled across the roads. Beaumont-Hamel was a ruin, but far from deserted, for even now desultory light-calibre fire was coming up at him, although presenting no threat at this altitude. He fancied he saw movement in the ruins, but nothing that he could identify, although off to the north, where he had seen the furthest stormers, up near Serre, there was now a truck descending a chalky gulley. He grimaced. If the Germans still retained such freedom of movement between Beaumont-Hamel and Serre then there was little hope that those particular stormers had survived.

Further along, beside a tiny wood, a column of men had halted, waiting perhaps until he had gone, almost invisible in the shadows as he approached but betraying their presence by lifting their faces to watch him circling overhead. Paul marked in their position on his map.

He fired off a red, and watched it burble away, curving down until it fizzled out. He had fired without expectation of eliciting a response. And to that extent he was not disappointed. He raised his eyes from searching the ground. To find that off to the south, dim in the distance, the Germans had raised a solitary balloon: another nice job for one of the Army-Wing machines there. He pulled his shoulders down inside the nacelle, unable to put it off any longer. As he had known from the start, there was nothing for it but to go right down and see just where the storming troops had got to.

He banked away towards the British lines, then eased the stick forwards, feeling the air pressure growing on his chest. The wind rush was blotting out the thundering of the guns so that chalky plumes exploding in a quarry rose and fell in mime. He kept an eye on his airspeed, thumbing off the switch when revs and speed approached his self-set limit and pushing the stick even further forwards to compensate for the loss of engine power.

The German barrage was still playing heavily in no-man's-land but Paul forced himself to ignore the invisible rain of shells as he turned to climb with what gradient there was towards the village. The air buffeted his wings and once there was a jolt that made him think he had been hit, the machine checking and leaping, but responding then to firm control. Paul no longer dared even glance inside the cockpit. But he was too low now for his altimeter to be of any use and that alone meant that he was far too low for comfort, while the rate at which the ground was blurring past gave him all the speed clues he could use.

Despite his dive-enhanced speed it took a finite time to cross both sections of the German wire, his passage bringing for the first time real appreciation of just how thick the defensive bands had been and the havoc wrought where the wire had been left uncut. There were khaki forms everywhere, cut down in droves in the open, pinned amid tangles of wire, bundled on the muddy chalk and asprawl on the slopes of every water-brimming hollow. He held the speed with full power, lifting into a shallow climbing turn that brought him parallel to the line, banking this way and that so that he could lean over and see down into the trenches. More khaki here, heaped before the parapet, and tumbled in the bottom of the trench. But only field-grey figures alive and taking frantic cover as he passed.

Paul was under continuous small-arms fire now but there were tracers too, curling across his front, one stream so close that he flinched away. He eased towards the second row of trenches, dipping over a line of craters, to be rewarded by a solitary flash of khaki. Three or four men, he estimated, gathered just below a crowded German trench, hidden only by the parapet, and therefore, cut off and effectively beyond all aid. More tracer curved towards him from a ridge and he banked away, turning back across no-man's-land again.

He made another run, setting course a little to the north of the village and running into heavy fire the moment he approached. If any British troops had penetrated beyond here, he decided, then they must surely be among the lost. It was time to pass some information back.

He turned away, grateful for the excuse to do so, lifting over the shrapnel in its ceaseless scourge of no-man's-land. There were none of the extended lines of stormers now, only isolated groups of men trying to pick their halting way back, and dying as the shrapnel and machine guns sought them out. One group caught his eye, a stretcher party with a gathered tail of walking wounded, daubed in mud and chalk, groping their way between two flooded craters. He cursed. These were the men he would be letting down if he reported back without a closer look.

He climbed, making height up to two thousand feet. It was like pulling off a sticking bandage. Give it a jerk, and get it over with. Thinking about it simply made it worse. Paul gave his baser instincts no time for second thoughts but banged over the stick, banking hard and ruddering brutally into the turn.

He had never handled the machine so unfeelingly before and he knew a sudden sense of shame. For its part the scout resisted with a marked check before tucking violently into the turn as engine torque and instability allied themselves to pull it round: it wanted to turn, wanted to spin, and yet, as if sensing his contrition, responded at once to the softened firmness of his touch, straightening out when asked to and calmly regaining speed. Paul smoothed his glove across the outside of the nacelle in atonement. He could have destroyed them both. And his brutality had served him not a bit, the airflow having taken so long to recover from that initial check! He froze his nerve, and set course back towards the guns.

There were quarries around the village, deep storage pits, and caves, and undoubtedly cellars, in which the enemy might hold out for months, but he had to be sure that the attacking troops were clear before he sent a message sanctioning the letting loose of any further British shells. Again he was in the path of projectiles, coaxing altitude from the scout, but trying to keep a margin of speed in hand to cope with any upset. A black object barely registered on his mind before it disappeared. A howitzer shell, or a mortar perhaps, reaching its apogee and hanging there before descending on its way.

It was clear that the Beaumont-Hamel position was too heavily defended for him to make a frontal approach: information, after all, was no use unless it was brought back, and the defenders were tracking him even now. It was machine guns he would have to contend with, those and the scores of rifles brought into play. His advantage was that ordinary line troops would have little notion of leading a fast-moving target. The thought that many might be Würtenburger forester lads used to pigeon shooting from the cradle was yet another he pushed from his mind.

He widened his turn as he passed through three thousand feet, circling towards the smaller village of Hamel – presently in British hands, although still hotly disputed from all the evidence –, aiming to give the impression that he had lost interest in Beaumont-Hamel itself. Reaching three thousand five hundred feet, Paul turned east, to pass between Beaucourt-sur-Ancre and Grandcourt, the pair facing each other further up the cleft where the river Ancre wound through damaged banks to cross the lines. And now he found himself for the first time in range of anti-aircraft fire and he dived at once, but not before three quick and spiteful bursts had cracked above his head.

The ground was coming up fast for he was diving against the slope. Deceptively fast, Paul realised with a start, over-tightened nerves once more causing him to clumsily jerk the stick in his far too hasty rush to flatten out. The July day was living up to its promise and the air had become decidedly choppy. He held low, concentrating on the terrain, only too aware of fire being brought to bear in his direction despite the absence of tracer. The grass was streaming past him now and he pushed still lower until nothing was distinct but the view immediately ahead. On he forged, hugging the undulations, edging towards his objective, and taking aboard impressions as he hurtled by.

Troops along a farm track scattering as he swept overhead; a driver controlling four horses looking back over his shoulder, unable to decide what to do and doing nothing until the team panicked and spilt both him and his wagon against the sunken bank; trenches packed with grey-clad figures; a chalk-cliffed quarry, fringed with trees, shadowy and cavernous, with tracer streaming from its banks towards some target in the valley but swinging up and traversing without a let-up on the trigger to track him as he passed.

Paul banked to the left now, beginning the wide, left-hand loop that would bring him over the position, searching in vain for a flare, or a figure in khaki. There must be some survivors, he told himself. How many men had he seen go across this morning, forty thousand, fifty thousand? Some at least must have safely gone to ground!

For a heart-lifting moment he thought he saw what he was looking for on a sunken road beyond Beaucourt, a column of men unmistakably khaki-clad, making their way along a lane to Serre. Prisoners, he then saw, who waved dejectedly as he passed low overhead, marching under guard in the van of a convoy of Red Cross wagons. He felt the bite of bitter disappointment and held the turn hard left, still skimming the surface, lifting over what had been Beaumont-Hamel cemetery and running onto the village from the north. There were troops in plenty now, but field grey to a man; and fortifications to make the blood run cold all along the higher ground south to Grandcourt, and beyond.

There was firing wherever he turned his eyes, troops firing from the shoulder, leaping up onto the parapets in their eagerness to take a potshot, one man jumping up as he passed and tumbling backwards in surprise to find the scout so close, his rifle flying from his hand. Line after line of trenches packed with troops, expectant, ready, filing up from dugouts, seemingly prepared for all contingencies. Paul tightened his stomach as he bumped overhead, plywood alone protecting his loins. Shell-holes, gullies, folds in the ground, barbed-wire; each held its toll of khaki figures, but nowhere did he detect a sign of life.

He jinked across the ruins of the village proper, and away again like a scalded cat, machine-gun tracer seeking him from a half-dozen points. Now there were khaki bundles everywhere, littering the pitted ground down the slope and all the way back to the British start point. He crossed the German wire, averting his gaze as best he could, careless of the unceasing bursts and lifts of shell, running for home and coming under jittery fire from his own front line as he passed. He scribbled on his pad,

> BEAUCOURT TO BEAUMONT-HAMEL. NO SIGN BRITISH TROOPS. STRONG ENEMY IN ALL LINES. PRISONERS BEAUMONT-HAMEL-SERRE ROAD.

The black and white shuttered device began to wink and Paul shot a hurried glance around the sky to make sure that he was not about to run into anybody as he leaned over to interpret the message. 'Return base,' he read, and waggled his wings in acknowledgement.

He continued his turn and as now-distant Beaumont-Hamel passed before his nose so the first British shells began lifting dust above the rubble. He glanced at his watch. Less than three hours earlier the troops had walked out across no-man's-land towards the village. And now our guns were playing on that self-same ground once more – it was the surest admission of failure.

The assault on Beaumont-Hamel, intended as merely a stepping-off point towards the commanding ridge, had been nothing less than an unmitigated disaster. It had failed to gain a single inch. Nothing gained, and what a fearful price had been exacted!

Chapter Five

Peter, his fuel leak repaired, had just taken off when Paul reported back. Dick landed unscathed about fifteen minutes later, weary yet somewhat bewildered by his early recall. In the squadron office Major Lawrence drew them over to the sector map to take their reports.

'Army have tacitly decided that the attacks have failed in certain sectors,' he told them. 'They haven't said so in so many words, of course, but it's plain to see.' He pushed his finger against the map. 'Those fellows you saw near Serre, Paul. Apparently they were East Lancs, but they've disappeared. For the rest of that sector, both brigades of Thirty-One Division – what's left of 'em – are falling back on our own lines.'

'Even the Hawthorn Redoubt mine's gone sour,' said the recording officer. 'It's suspected that the 0720 blow was an error. Too early.'

'Mm! I wondered about that. Yet it looked colossal when it blew.'

'But it gave Jerry ten minutes, and he was already there at the crater when our chaps arrived. We're holding our side of it but the machine guns have the lads in flank and they can't hang on much longer.'

'Number Eight Div was brought up from reserve,' said the major, 'but that didn't lead to anything significant. So Army're preparing for counter-attacks.'

Paul nodded. 'People are jittery enough. I got fired on crossing our lines. Also, sir, we resumed shelling Beaumont-Hamel fifteen minutes ago. There's no sign of any substantial number of survivors. A few prisoners, and some wounded straggling back, little else.'

'It's stagnated over there, then?' asked the major.

'The whole Beaumont-Hamel area is nothing but quarries and excavations, probably cellars too,' Paul told him. 'The Germans look ready for anything and the lines are packed with 'em. They've obviously got shell-proof dugouts to duck into during bombardments.'

'I'll swear some of the dugouts have concrete entrances,' put in Dick.

The major nodded glumly. 'Anyway, Wing've moved the two-seaters to cover that part of the front – FEs and Sopwiths. Further south the situation's still unresolved, around Thiepval in particular. Thirty-Sixth Div – the Ulsters – are having a terrible time of it by all accounts.' He spanned Serre and Bucquoy with his fingers. 'As you well know, that's where much of the trouble lies. The guns up here totally dominate the area even beyond Thiepval.'

'They've obviously got every bit of terrain ranged, too,' said Dick.

'It looks that way and what with high-explosive cutting the telephone wires and machine guns doing for the runners Army are desperate to know what's happening.'

A signals corporal called across, 'A mate here, sir, says it's taken one lot six runners to get a message back – the first five was scuppered.'

The major pulled out his watch. 'The reserve brigade – Inniskillings and Irish Rifles – should have moved off by now to reinforce.' He glanced at each of them in turn. 'That's your next job. More of what you've been doing, I'm afraid. From here,' he stabbed at the map, 'just north of Thiepval, then south to Ovillers. Peter Mainwaring's overlooking the HLI and Fusiliers at present. There'll be other machines on patrol, so he's been warned to keep a good lookout.'

Paul studied the map, tracing the sector from a little south of the area he had just been covering, down to the Albert-Bapaume road.

'We might as well split it,' he told Dick. 'I'll stick to the Irish and the Highlanders around Thiepval if you'll take the area from Authuille to the Albert-Bapaume road.'

Despite the time of day neither Paul nor Dick found himself hungry, although the coffee and army rum went down well. They found a quiet corner beside the mess and stretched out in the sun. They spoke rarely, and then only in monosyllables, mostly as aircraft of other units arrived and departed. Their minds were too full to make light conversation and neither wanted to talk about what he had seen or about what lay ahead. Peter, still airborne, was much in their thoughts.

Dick broke the long silence as they rose to slip on their flying coats once more. 'And it's such a lovely day.'

Thiepval village sat on the brow of the ridge, perching above a smooth scarp which fell to the River Ancre, along this stretch winding its way sinuously through the wooded bottom of its shallow valley. Here and there woods clothed the slopes, some in German hands, some in British, but shell-torn and shattered no matter who their tenants, their splintered thickets affording a certain amount of concealment but little shelter.

As Paul now knew, the whole Thiepval ridge, running virtually north-south immediately behind the village, had been occupied by Würtenburger troops for the last two years, and what they had made of it was clear to see. Earthworks and entrenchments, broad bands of barbed-wire and menacing bunkers, with post after post of machine guns, presented a daunting face to any attacker. The whole fortified ridge was covered from the north by the guns around Serre and Bucquoy, and to the south by the Leipzig Salient which stuck down finger-like above friendly riverside Authuille to enfilade any frontal attack up the hill to Thiepval village. And that it really was a hill was in no doubt despite the general flatness of the area and the diminishing of the contours from Paul's vantage point of five thousand feet.

He circled to the south for a while, assimilating this new sector. He took in the Leipzig Salient, with its stern redoubt, then ran his eye due north along the ridge, over the fortifications of Thiepval village to where the brooding strongpoint of the Schwaben Redoubt could be seen crouching above hostile St Pierre Divion, itself frowning across the Ancre at hard won Hamel; two miles simply bristling with defences and everywhere overlooking the Ancre valley among whose woods the British stormers had massed for their attack just hours before.

Height and distance dealt kindly with the landscape but even from where he circled Paul could see the ravages of the bombardment in the pitted rings of light brown, chalky soil. He looked towards the east. The Thiepval area, seen from above, was revealed to be more than just an isolated concentration of fortifications, rather it was the focal point for a whole network of strongpoints and trench systems – also two years in construction – stretching back across the undulating uplands and far beyond the crest. The Irish and Scottish stormers had been set a monumental task.

The first fire came up as Paul spiralled down to 3,000 feet; a looping line of tracer that fell far short. But heavier anti-aircraft fire followed at once, two rocking bursts that forced him to veer, a near-fatal change of direction that took him head-on into three others before he could jink clear. It took him some time to collect himself, for the second group had been so close that his cockpit reeked of its discharge.

Settling, Paul saw that fighting had flared up to his left, to the north-west of the village, accordingly he drifted that way, seeing the fire-red flash of hand bombs. The attacking infantry had reached that far at least then, and were still battling it out. He peered down, firing off a flare and looking for an answering signal. He just might see a signal sheet spread across the ground, but he hardly expected it when the fighting was so closely hand-to-hand that grenades were being used.

More such flashes starred the smoke even further north and he slackened his turn, marking that area too on his map. The machine shuddered to another flurry of explosions and he banked over, diving away, and seeing the subsequent bursts flower in the sky above him. His concentration on the fight below had led him almost over the Schwaben Redoubt itself and fire was coming up at him from several points. He banked away out of range and took up an orbit, loitering watchfully until the interest in him died down before venturing in again.

While waiting Paul checked for signs of damage, for some of the bursts had been uncomfortably close. However, his breathing was the only ragged-running thing he could detect and only his nerves showed any sign of fraying. He looked at the marks on his map, trying to draw conclusions. It was hard to be certain, but it appeared that the Irish had been able to dent the defences by outflanking Thiepval village to the north, leaving it on their right. They might even have got as far as the trenches bordering the Schwaben Redoubt, although that would seem unlikely. But unlikely or not it was his job to make sure.

He headed back across the Ancre to circle to the north of St. Pierre-Divion, catching sight of another machine, crawling mothlike over towards Serre, the sighting making him feel just that little less alone. It also acted as a spur and he slackened the turn, easing north-eastish from St Pierre Divion, turning with the Ancre to overfly first Beaucourt and then Grandcourt. He circled Grandcourt's defences once, and then, cutting the switch, turned back to dive south towards Thiepval from the heights, putting his nose on the road out of Grandcourt with both St Pierre-Divion and Schwaben Redoubt now on his right.

He corrected towards a hand-bomb flash, and leant forwards to cock the Lewis, not managing it first time and cursing as he was forced to take his eyes off the pinpoint to complete the action. Looking up it took him a moment or so to relocate the spot, a mound of chalk spoil beyond a stretch of fresh plough. But no! – Paul revised his first impression: not freshly ploughed land, of course, but a vast double thicket of earth-hued barbed-wire. And suddenly he was flying over troops in khaki, small bunches of them waving up at him from shell-holes and from natural cover in the ground. He lifted over a deep trench filled along its length with British uniforms until the trench changed direction at a traverse to bring him face to face with troops in grey who raised their rifles and began to fire.

Paul broke right towards the downward slope, but held level then, and circled back, to make a better assessment of the situation. As if his presence had sparked things off the firing suddenly became general. He saw a dozen grey-clad figures rise from the concealment of a trench only to be met with a volley of lobbed bombs that left three of them kicking on the ground and sent the others scrambling back to shelter. He overflew another trench, little more than a narrow ditch, a communications trench originally, perhaps, now filled with British troops; and he found a further group of fifty or so, crouched under the bank of a sunken track some yards beyond. He estimated rapidly; at best he'd seen three hundred troops, no more.

He made one further pass and then turned back down the slope towards the river, the ground falling away almost as steeply as he could dive. Nowhere hereabouts seemed anything but flat, yet here, where the Germans had sited their position, the attacker was presented with a fearsome uphill pull. It was clear that Paul was following in reverse the path the Irish attackers had taken, for the slope was festooned with khaki-clad figures, some saffron-kilted, boots and bare legs asprawl, tumbled by the hundreds as the machine guns had caught them.

An arm waved from a shell-hole and once or twice Paul saw men making their way painfully down the hill. He passed low over one group of three who did not even turn their heads, a measure of just how far gone they were. And now the ponds of the Ancre sparkled below and he climbed away to make out his report.

Double-checking the co-ordinates on his map where he had seen the forward troops, he held the stick between his knees as he pencilled the figures onto his pad, noting then:

THIEPVAL – SCHWABEN REDOUBT. 300 TROOPS, STATIC. NO SIGN OF SUPPORTS. HEAVILY ENGAGED. BOMBING, HAND-TO-HAND. FIRST AND SECOND LINES HELD.

He supplemented both the map co-ordinates and the text with a sketch.

Having made his drop, and waiting only to see the message bag retrieved, he circled, climbing overhead, watching a Morane pull in below him and dive low over the signal panel before making off to the south-west. One of No.3 Squadron's, no doubt, heading off for Lahoussoye and home. Paul wished he could do the same, but there was the second part of the job to be done. He had seen the situation to the north of Thiepval, now he had to find out what had happened to the troops of the Highland Light Infantry who had attacked it from the south.

The troops Paul was looking for had made their initial advance against the centre and right of Thiepval, clearly coming under heavy fire the moment they left their starting points in the woods: this much was obvious from the bodies strewn outside the trees and up the slope towards the crest. He decided to bite the bullet and come in low, climbing up the slope the way the troops had gone, hoping to escape notice at least until he reached the top. It was a pitiful, painful, zooming sweep, overflying their casualties all the way, countless dead and but few wounded, as if 'no quarter' had been the order of the day, for machine-gun crews at least.

He marked an open area slightly left of his nose as singularly empty of bodies, and banked that way, finding, above the woods, a section of slope pulverised by shell fire yet without a casualty in sight. He circled, queasily intrigued, when a glance between the shattered thickets confirmed what he had begun to surmise. There lay the assault troops, shelled out of existence before they had even left the wood.

Intense fire was coming down from the outskirts of Thiepval village itself, from a tower reduced to little more than rubble. Paul passed over British troops tucked into a captured trench but showing no signs of being able to advance further. Gladly turning aside from the attentions of the gunner in the tower, he banked right, finding Highlanders at once, not just in the first trench, but in line after line towards the crest, their numbers thinning rapidly the further they had penetrated, clearly under heavy pressure still, but grimly holding on. Picturing the death-filled slopes behind him he could see no way in which they could survive, for reinforcements could not possibly reach them.

Shells were bursting thickly across to his right along the finger of the Leipzig Salient, shrapnel in the main but high-explosive too and he turned in that direction, climbing, of necessity, to lift above the bursts. A fierce firefight was going on in the very shadow of a large redoubt but close observation was difficult and although he circled overhead he was forced to constantly change his altitude to avoid fire coming up at him from all sides.

Grimly he pressed on, peering down through the smoke-rack, endeavouring to determine the forward limits of the advance, no longer even looking for flares or signal panels but simply for glimpses of khaki; and seeing only sprawling, dark-trewed dead. It was clear that the Highlanders had entered the Leipzig Redoubt itself but it was hard to be sure whether any still survived, and after circling once more the fire became so heavy that Paul was forced to turn away.

Although there seemed little chance of his discovering anything more definite the urgency of the situation, at least, was clear and Paul took advantage of the billowing smoke and hugged the slope as the swiftest way towards the river.

He broke into clear air again nose on to a fringe of woodland, to find tracer hosing into supports advancing up the hill. On impulse he skidded his nose towards its source, centralised the controls, and squeezed the trigger, sending almost a full drum towards the wood and shouting in exultation as the German tracer cut off short. His satisfaction was short-lived, however, for a moment later the machine gun opened up again and men once more began to spin and tumble to the ground.

Paul pulled away, crossing the river, searching the map for the machine-gun's position and finding it as he climbed through a thousand feet.

    TROOPS STATIC SOUTH FRONT THIEPVAL, he printed.
    TROOPS SOUTH-EAST OUTSKIRTS THIEPVAL HARD-PRESSED. FIRST THREE LINES HELD. URGENT NEED SUPPORT. SUPPORTS UNDER MG.

He appended the map reference, sketching that corner of the wood housing the machine gun. Then he divided the report with a line and resumed,

    LEIPZIG REDOUBT ENTERED AND HELD: SUPPORT URGENT.

Somehow the Highland troops had succeeded in entering the redoubt but without support they were likely to find themselves pinched off on either side. Paul secured the weighted message bag and held it poised for a moment before tossing it clear, seeing the yard-long, multi-coloured tail unwinding as it fell.

Repositioning, Paul pondered on the situation. From what he could make out virtually all the surviving attackers were falling back on their own starting lines, while those few still in possession of what ground they had taken were subject to fierce enfilading fire from all types and calibres of weapons and in imminent danger of being overrun. Nor, he imagined, would they be permitted to disengage even if they so decided. So that, pinned here, and with reinforcements being cut down by German machine guns the moment they ventured into the open, there seemed little chance of their survival. Certainly there could no longer be any talk about success.

The Thiepval sector, then, compared with Beaumont-Hamel, was only less disastrous to a degree. And this was what they had heralded for so long as, 'The Big Push'!

Peter Mainwaring was waiting for them when they landed. One of his rudder cables had been shot through but the recently-adopted squadron practice of separating the entwined double cables supplied by the makers to give what amounted to a duplicate set had paid off. Paul made a mental note to separate his own at the earliest opportunity, aware that, since picking up the machine from Hendon, he had not had time to get it done. On inspection Dick's machine proved to have some twenty tears in its fabric but no serious damage, although something hard and hostile had ricocheted off the engine mounting and only just missed the fuel feed. Paul's aeroplane, despite another hour's exposure to almost constant close-range fire, showed only two small rents in the left upper wing, a fact that caused Peter and Dick to enter into a side-glancing leg-pull as to just where Paul had spent his time.

'He probably visited a different war,' suggested Dick .

'If he did,' said Peter warmly, 'it could only have been a better one.'

They found hot meals instantly available to them, all the cooks on the aerodrome having been tasked to prepare meals whenever they were called for. They ate in the mess, not changing on this day of days but merely slipping off their heavy flying coats and finding pleasure in standing while they drank a beer.

They took off again at five o'clock, heading once more for Thiepval, flying over farmers toiling away behind beasts as unhurried in their labours as the sun which bathed them from above, a sun already dipping as if in salutation to any close of day in Picardy. Only near the roads did tranquillity give way to bustle for the traffic was even heavier than before with more Red-Cross-bearing vehicles than Paul had ever dreamt existed.

He carried out an initial reconnaissance at a reasonable height, fully aware that he would be forced to descend later in order to furnish a report of any value. Flares, and back-pack mirrors, and signal panels, would have been all very well if the breakthrough had been achieved. Now that the attack had gone to ground, however, the troops could not be expected to reveal their positions, overlooked as they were on every flank. It was the Inniskillings whose dead bore the saffron kilts, Paul had been told, and from the evidence of smoke and bomb flashes they, and the other Irish stormers, were clearly holding stubbornly to what they had taken.

Paul tested his Lewis, and even as he watched the Sparklet tracer pulse ahead of him he came under anti-aircraft fire himself and was forced to twist and turn until at last it let him be.

Once clear, he continued scouting the Thiepval sector, recording signs of conflict everywhere bar on the east, beyond the crest. Accordingly he set course in that direction, and ignoring one or two black shellbursts that blossomed wide on his right, overflew Thiepval itself, focussing upon an area to the left of the road running south-east to Poziéres where fire was coming from a clump of buildings. He glanced at his map, identifying 'Moquet Farm', and as additional fire began to lace towards him from a little further north, he snatched a glance at the red military overprinting. That nest of hate would be 'Zollern Redoubt', then. So – the farm and the redoubt; two more nasty places holding back the troops.

Paul turned, diving back towards Thiepval from the east, watching for the tower that had played him up before – the remains of the church spire possibly, although it was difficult to tell. The tower was still there, but distinctly more crumpled, and with not the slightest sign of occupancy now.

He headed down the slope, skirting the village, leaving it above him and to his left, seeing two lines of badly mauled trenches with masses of tangled German wire, and here, thinly manning both trenches, he found the Irish troops. Dirt drummed on the fabric as a shell exploded just in front of him and he cried out, shocked. But the Gnome continued its steady snarling and he ruddered, wheeling about. Then, a road, slightly sunken – and everywhere a scattering of waving khaki. Beneath the steepest part of the cutting he glimpsed a row of huddled forms, thirty or more, pulled up into shallow hollows with men bent over them, men who straightened, pointing to their charges as he passed them by. And then the uniforms below were grey once more, and he turned away downhill.

Paul scribbled his report taking especial care to confirm the location of the wounded, although short of a truce he could see little chance of their being brought out, and he reflected on the desperation of those in pain and shock, unable to fend for themselves, unable even to seek what little cover there was.

Five minutes later and he was back in the thick of it again, pulling up beyond Thiepval, jinking as tracer pursued him after another low-level pass, this time upslope, leaving the village to his right. There was no doubt that the Irish had gained a shallow toehold to the north, precarious though it might be. They still held the first and second row of German trenches but the Germans were fiercely contesting their continued presence.

The heaviest pressure was being brought to bear on those who were now dug in along the outer works of the Schwaben Redoubt. Not only were they under heavy fire from the Redoubt itself but they had Thiepval to their right rear, and lacking right-flank support were suffering badly from its enfilading fire.

Paul flew west of the Redoubt, and below it, finding a support trench with a sap leading off. The tee-junction so formed was being held as a strong-point by Irish troops, using sandbags in lieu of traverses, but even as Paul approached a soldier jumped to the parapet, momentarily displaying his Lewis two-handed over his head before tumbling back to cover. It was a gesture as eloquent as it was desperate – the gun was out of ammunition. Yet on the far side of the sandbags the German bombers were massing for an assault. The notion of dropping his spare drums of Lewis came to him; and died still-born as being impracticable. But he had to do *something*.

He brought the nose up, pulling over onto one wing, and turning back, tensing his stomach against the clutch of visceral fear. Speed built up quickly, although it could never be quickly enough, and he concentrated on firm movements of stick and rudder to bring the nose to heel. He had to get it right, better than before: get it wrong here and he would kill his own people. He steepened his dive, sensing the ground beneath his wheels, and now perfectly aligned with the trench, fixed his eyes over the gunsight with khaki streaming beneath his nose. Sandbags now – and open fire! Nose easing up slightly, triggering and then flattening out at parapet level, firing still, and praying that he was not about to fly himself against the ground.

He used half a drum before the trench bent back around a traverse, when he climbed, zoom-turning again, but struggling for speed, and staggering around, half-stalled, and fearing he had cut it too fine, but recovering and flopping down to make a second run, this time to take them from the rear.

He felt the smoke gritty beneath his eyelids and thought about pulling down his goggles but both hands were full and he continued firing, watching grey-clad figures falling before him, tumbling away, hammered back into the floor of the trench, or scrambling desperately to scale the walls. He saw one man leap up into the open and stand poised on the parados before collapsing, shot down by a British rifle from beyond. His own fire was snaking perilously close to the sandbag barrier now but the trench was almost clear and he swerved aside, expending the rest of the drum on a machine gun seeking him from a corner of the Redoubt.

The defences were stung to fury now and knowing that it would be foolhardy to stay any longer even if he could summon up the resolve, Paul made off down the slope, mentally lashing the de Havilland into its stride as he went. Only when he had safely crossed the British reserve lines did he begin to climb, reaching forwards and loading on another drum, then using his cuff to wipe his wind-chilled brow.

He licked at his pencil with dry lips, and printed, 1ST AND 2ND TRENCHES BRITISH HELD. FOOTHOLD SOUTHERN SIDE SCHWABEN. DESPERATELY SHORT AMMO. LOCAL COUNTER-ATTACKS.

Below him the signal was flashing a message but he missed it and used his klaxon to ask for a repetition. 'Avoid Schwaben', he spelled out. 'Recce Leipzig Salient Redoubt'.

Paul acknowledged, and continued to climb, turning his attention to the Leipzig Salient which overlooked the village of Authuille and was bordered in part by Authuille Wood. A light railway, he could see, had been built from the village into the woods, running along a shallow valley – 'Blighty Valley', the army overprint designated it. Neither it nor the screening wood could be very healthy places today, Paul reflected, a Blighty wound would be the very best one might expect up there just now.

A flurry in his peripheral vision, and a storm of shells smothered the far side of the Schwaben Redoubt. He watched, appalled at the thought of the carnage he had visited upon his fellow men and offered a silent prayer that at least the gunners should get it right. He had given the most accurate co-ordinates he could and the Irish needed the very closest of support. But just how close was close, he asked himself, with firepower as monstrous as that?

He climbed above Aveluy Wood, across the river from Authuille, circling in comparative safety while he took stock. German fire was falling heavily below the Redoubt at the north of the Leipzig Salient, denying the ground up which reliefs must come. The German gunners were again using curtain fire, supplementing this with specifically-directed shelling whenever supporting troops attempted to breast the slopes.

One such attempt developed even as Paul levelled out, a thin line of figures appearing and moving slowly away from the battered woods. He spiralled down overhead, horridly fascinated by the way they bunched together, willing them to find a way through their own barbed-wire before the guns found them. The British artillery was laying down covering smoke but it had started too late and the first thin eddies had hardly reached the wire before the German artillery opened up. The shrapnel spewed iron traceries upon the advancing troops, followed with hardly a pause by the high-explosive, great gushes of light brown earth rearing up and exposing the sub-soil chalk before collapsing back onto the sadly depleted supports below.

Incredibly however, the advance had not checked, and Paul saw the remaining troops continue to pick their way steadily up the slope, wandering here and there as the terrain led them off the direct line, but seemingly undeterred by the rain of fire. Other troops, heavily laden with supplies, had left the trenches now and were making their way past the bodies of the fallen, not going to ground – realising, no doubt, that the artillerymen were ranged-in to a metre – but threading through the wire and falling into the by-the-book 'artillery formation', the platoon-sized columns spacing out from each other by some fifty yards and steadily pressing onwards up the open slope. And it was in artillery formation that the machine guns caught them as they came into range, melting them away in the space of thirty yards.

Helpless otherwise to prevent or even lessen the debacle Paul located three machine-gun nests and flew back to call in the guns to deal with them. Then, without waiting to see what effect his call would have, he turned back towards Aveluy Wood. Having gained what height he could he steeled himself and fell into a dive, on course for the Leipzig Redoubt, aiming towards the sector where the continuing firefight seemed to be at its hottest. Again he could only hope that an aeroplane would be anyone's last concern, no matter what colour their tunic. He found himself too low to see things in perspective and he lifted up, flying at once into the angry spite of three quick-firer bursts that nearly floored him, but missed, so that he was afforded space to recover, and to be rewarded by the sight of British troops bombing their way down a debris-cluttered ditch.

A vignette, gone in a flash: two soldiers crouched behind a hummock, looking up as Paul passed, their dead comrade beside them, his head and shoulders covered in a cape which, breeze-ruffled, lifted heavily to reveal his tartan trews.

The Highland Light Infantry, then, were still in possession of their dead, and of this part, at least, of the Leipzig Salient. How they had taken it was more than Paul could fathom but they must be in desperate need of support, and he had just seen the fate of the latest attempt to bring it to them.

He kept his turn going, never out of sight of khaki, facing downhill towards Authuille with Blighty Valley on his left. There *might* be a supply route there, a narrow one, and enfiladed, but offering better possibilities than the forlorn hope that had just foundered! He circled again, noting the dispositions of the troops, and realising that here were the most advantageously-placed British forces he had seen throughout the day. If only they could hold out until nightfall when reserves could come up!

The fire slackened momentarily and Paul found himself flying along the line of two parallel, partly-covered excavations leading upslope from the woods – Russian saps! Narrow, *roofed* trenches, dug by sappers under the cover of darkness, no doubt, towards the Leipzig Redoubt's own trenchworks: that explained how the Highlanders had breached the defences, crawling forwards under cover and then springing at the defenders the moment the gun barrage lifted. One up to them! But unless they were relieved soon, they would lose all they had so dearly – and so artfully – gained.

He pulled clear, amplifying his report with a sketch map showing the wooded approach to the Highlanders' position. Almost undoubtedly the corridor would already be known to HQ but there was just the chance that neither runners nor signals had been able to get through. And the Highlanders deserved every chance there was.

The remainder of Paul's patrol he spent at a more reasonable altitude, finding no one at the rendezvous when the time came, and setting course for Fienvillers alone, climbing gradually to seven thousand feet. Settling there, he flew level for a space, content with the tranquillity of the clear, smooth air, gazing westwards the while to where the sun was making its own reluctant descent, savouring the stillness and finding in the pearl-grey cloud-tones the calmness and serenity he had last found in a woman's eyes.

At length he cut his engine and spiralled down in an easy glide. Sweeping over the boundary, his mind still dwelling on blue-grey eyes and the possibilities of mail, he misjudged his touchdown and bounced hard, blipping the engine to smooth out further bounds, before lumbering to an untidy stop outside the hangars.

'You were so late we thought you'd found trouble,' Peter told him. 'but when we saw your landing we knew you were all right.'

In the mess that evening emotions were mixed. Pilots and observers who had been engaged in contact and artillery work tended towards despondency, gathering in their own separate groups, talking in low tones. In contrast those who had flown on line patrols or bombing jobs, or on offensive patrols far behind the lines, talked volubly, gesticulating as they re-fought chases with their hands: and chases, rather than combats, it seemed, had been the order of the day, the offensive policy having gained that air supremacy upon which the whole outcome of the 'Big Push' might well now depend.

At Fienvillers the crews were in a better position than most to take the measure of the day. As 'special duties' units they had seen the new offensive from both sides of the lines, covering between them all the various jobs in which the RFC had been engaged. Those who had been tasked beyond the immediate land-battle front were patently dismayed to hear that the army was virtually bogged down on its starting line, although when fact-seeking officers from the staff at Advanced Headquarters joined them for dinner they were able to give just a little hope, reporting that things had gone better to the south.

That the day had proved a disaster – and an unimaginably bloody one at that – could not be doubted, although from the Flying Corps' point of view things could have been much worse, for the German Air Service had been firmly kept in its place by the Army Wings while, despite all the risks run, not a single aircraft of the Corps Wings had been lost flying contact patrol, a fact which made Paul shake his head in wonder.

Casualty figures were beginning to emerge for the troops, however, appalling figures that shocked even the airmen who had watched the cataclysm at close hand: 60,000 British casualties, they spoke of. 20,000 British dead! And so many in that opening hour! *20,000* British dead.

And not a thing to show for it.

Chapter Six

It became clear from the start of this second day of the offensive that the Germans had more time to spend on dealing with aeroplanes. Paul levelled the vic off at five thousand feet where the air became less turbulent and turned them to parallel the front. From this height it was hard to pick out detail with the naked eye but flashes tearing to shreds the sheets of gunsmoke showed that the bombardments had scarcely diminished. Maintaining height he turned towards the lines and almost at once came under anti-aircraft fire.

Both the others were watching him, waiting for his signal, neither looking unduly perturbed. He pointed downwards and began a gentle dive to lose three hundred feet, turning in a wide sweep over Thiepval and back towards the British lines before checking the descent. The bursts followed: ten, twelve, fourteen, he counted, but the manoeuvre had deceived the gunners and the shells continued to pockmark the sky well above.

Paul pursed his lips and leaned over the side. Even now they were too high to pick out much but he was loth to order the others down until he had tested the water. Unfortunately, the nature of the job was such that there was, in all conscience, little enough he could do for them.

He turned over Hamel, today's rendezvous-point across the Ancre from Thiepval, and pointed down, seeing the others acknowledge. A moment more, for a final search of the sky, then he waved them away to their sectors.

'And for Christ's sake, take care!' he muttered.

Thiepval was once again wreathed in shellfire and some isolated buildings, little more than ruins, were on fire. 3,500 feet: probably too high even yet. But again, far too low for comfort. Paul fumbled out the binoculars pushed inside his coat. By now the air currents were bouncing the de Havilland about the sky, helping to throw off the guns perhaps, but making it even more difficult for him to concentrate on picking out detail. He leant over the side of the nacelle and lifted the glasses. At once a bump jarred them against his nose, but his face was too cold to admit sensation and he simply clamped them harder into position. He had pre-focussed them for long-range use but the turbulence made it difficult to hold them steady, besides which, he discovered, it was almost impossible to bring them to bear on any one object long enough for the image to register.

He held the stick between his knees in order to use both hands and at once picked up a road, littered with debris, along which a gun limber was being manhandled by figures in field-grey. An instant later his left wing dropped sharply, the nose dipping in sympathy, not only sweeping the road sideways out of the eyepiece and out of his sight but forcing him to grab for the stick and let the binoculars take their chance on the retaining cord looped through a buttonhole of his coat.

Notwithstanding this, an experience that became only too much the norm, he persisted in his attempts to use the binoculars throughout a long slack orbit of Thiepval, ignoring the bumps and for moments on end allowing the machine to simply wallow. He would focus on a spot selected through the glasses and try to register an image: tracer rising from a ruined building; the flash from the muzzle of a heavy, firing through camouflage netting; or troops massed in a quarry. Almost invariably, however, before he could assimilate what he was seeing the glasses would be jolted from his face or a gust would threaten to upset the machine completely.

Even having made an identification, on lowering the eye-pieces he found great difficulty in re-locating the specific object he had been studying: had he been looking at the quarry there, behind the wood, or that one, with the building beside the entrance? A severe bump and the heavy glasses floated up from his lap and thumped against his right eyebrow. He swore in double frustration and pulled his goggles back into place. The glasses had been worth a try. But the lesson forced upon him yesterday still obtained. There really was nothing for it but to go down and see for himself.

Today's overriding task was to locate the surviving attackers, to see where they had moved to overnight, to determine whether they had pushed their way forwards under cover of darkness, or whether they had been able to extricate themselves, relinquishing their short-lived gains. Short-lived, Paul reflected, but how dearly won!

He studied the ground, leaning over and cross-controlling, stick against rudder, the better to see what lay immediately beneath, skidding and slipping crabwise across the sky, telling himself that this would make it difficult for the myriad muzzles below to follow him and not believing it for an instant. He looked for marker panels, for red Very flares, even for the flash of a mirror – and saw only the silent spurting of the shells.

'Put out your bloody panels,' he gritted. And in the same instant caught sight of one at last.

At least, it was a splash of colour, and he spiralled down, turning steeply on one wing, keeping his eyes fixed upon the spot, almost certain that it was a panel but desperately anxious to make sure. He cast one furtive glance around the horizon and then concentrated on the point again. It really was a panel! Lying along a narrow track, in a cutting, half-concealed in shadow. He squinted, wondering whether to bring out the binoculars again, but deciding against it. Now he fancied he could make out bunched figures, huddled into the shadow at the side of the cutting, but whether khaki or field-grey he could not tell: he would need to be much lower to determine that. But a Very was what he really wanted to see.

Tracks and roads in Picardy were often deep-sunken like this one, the banks offering welcome protection in a landscape where any eminence was a rarity. Paul remembered only too clearly peeping over the edge of the shell-crater when he had been downed and discovering how severely curtailed his field of vision had been. And with the memory it came to him once more that at ground level even the slightest eminence on these rolling, chalkland folds could give kingly command of the terrain: a matter of just a few feet and an infantryman's position no longer commanded, but was commanded: little wonder that identification signals were being so seldom used.

He circled, locating the position on his map, and scribbled down a message.

OUR TROOPS ALONG SUNKEN TRACK PARALLELING
MAIN THIEPVAL-ST PIERRE-DIVION ROAD TO EAST.

He estimated the distance from the road to the track and jotted down the area reference. The troops were in a perilous position, beneath Thiepval and the outer works of the Schwaben Redoubt, their every movement commanded by both fortifications. Perilous, that is, if they were indeed British. And before he dropped his message it was imperative that he make certain.

Except that, filling him with relief, at that very moment a red flare spluttered from the track beside the panel, not fired upwards, but horizontally, presumably in the hope that the banking would conceal it from ground observation. Almost at once two more flares appeared, one from a thin patch of woodland, one from a second section of trenches. Swiftly, hardly daring to believe that things were working out at last, Paul plotted in the two fresh positions. At least the three points gave some indication of a held and defended line. He levelled his wings, and fired off a red in acknowledgement. Now he could get his report away.

Again, it was peripheral vision that alerted him, and he ruddered fiercely, reversing the turn, his heart in his mouth. The German artillery was spot on. Five separate bursts merging one into the other, blotting out the cutting in an instant's eruption of red-cored earth and smoke. Paul turned a complete circle and the smoke cleared and there was no sign of the marker panel and the lip of the sunken track no longer cast a shadow. He levelled out, and climbed away across the lines, sick to the soul.

Why had he not made just a single pass? Instead of spiralling down on them for all the world to see? Had they finally tumbled the flare along the ground in desperation? 'Yes, we're here. You've seen the panel. Now, *please* bugger off before Jerry ranges in on us!' He finished his report and tore off the sheet.

And what did the report really amount to? A line drawn between three signal flares: who was to say that there were no friendly troops forward of the line, troops who were in too critical a spot to give away their position, who knew better, perhaps, than the ones whose response he had just been instrumental in rewarding with annihilation? He crumpled the message sheet and let the air-rush take it.

Under full power, and diving as steeply as he dared, the speed increased beyond all reason. The scream of the wind through the wires blotted out even the sound of the rotary, the laced fabric around the cockpit billowing and ballooning. Paul lifted his head out of the dubious protection of the windshield and the goggles were nearly torn from his head. It was bitingly cold at this speed, but he was not aware of the chill. The aircraft bucked and heaved, protesting against the buffeting but responding gamely, tucking its nose down as he momentarily blipped the switch and picked up his line.

He started his run just past St Pierre-Divion and the anti-aircraft gunners were on to him at once. A burst rocked him and he wrenched the scout aside so that the succeeding bursts went wide. Quick-firer tracer though, was already looping from his left to head him off. And more tracer from ahead and to the left. All from the left! So that was hopeful!

He picked up the track and swung to follow it towards Thiepval, having the Schwaben Redoubt at his shoulder and St Pierre-Divion at his rear – out of sight, both of them, but far from out of mind. For a brief space the track ran over turf, surprisingly unmarked, then it began to sink beneath chalk banks.

He made a sharp turn, directly towards the most threatening tracer – and then quickly back again, leaving glinting streaks angling away behind him. Swiftly re-correcting his line along the track he pushed lower, coming at once upon the shambles he had so irresponsibly brought about. Craters, smoking still, scalloped across the banks. Knots of men in khaki drab, looking up, but not waving, and a few ominously unmoving figures stretched full-length against the chalk. And then, the marker panel itself, muddy and torn, draped across the broken bank in mute but eloquent accusation.

He swept overhead descending still and banking right for the wood where he had seen the flare. He was down at ground level now and the tortured earth was streaming past: a cluster of three shell-holes, water-filled but with khaki figures crouching around the rims nevertheless; a section of trench, chalk-starred from heavy bombardment and in places almost obliterated; a group of six or seven men seemingly lying in the open but clearly taking advantage of some natural tuck of ground ... He saw a brief burst of tracer firing *away* from him up the slope towards Thiepval – clearly seeking his notice–, and abruptly cut off as if to conserve ammunition. And then he was clipping the wood, seeing the fluttering of some garment, a poncho, or a cape, and a khaki-clad figure scrambling back into the meagre shelter of the trees.

He turned away, skidding right, heading for the Ancre, and hugging the slope all the way down. There were lagoons among the woods, spreading between the trees along the broken banks, created no doubt as German counter-fire released the pent-up waters swollen from the recent rains. What in normal times must have been a pleasant, tree-lined, partly-canalised flow was now more like a swamp. It was about the only new development he had seen today he realised, and even then it was hardly favourable.

Paul drew deep breaths, climbing steadily now, turning and looking back over the line he had tentatively proven, seeking for yet more positive confirmation. He was almost sure that no German troops lay downslope of those forward positions he had noted, certainly all the tracer had been coming from his left. But *had* any of the attacking troops pushed forwards across the track, only to find themselves, like the other erstwhile stormers behind them, pinned down by enfilading fire, unable to get back, only positioned too close to the enemy to risk giving themselves away by signalling? That he had not yet determined.

He repressed the thought of the carnage the German guns had wreaked along the sunken track. He must make sure that our guns did not do even worse. Maybe he would be better advised to go back and drop the information already gleaned rather than risk another run first? It was a thought that had its own attractive logic, but he was well aware that much of its appeal lay in the fact that it offered him an easy way out.

The jolting was severe; if anything the gusts were getting worse, and Paul cast a careful eye over the structure. There was a slight tear near the upper-right wingtip but that was all he could see. Behind him the rotary was fruitily bellowing away, while the controls still felt positive. The ground vanished as cloud briefly closed about him but there were many gaps and he was able to maintain a check on his position, wheeling and taking full advantage of the misty cover while selecting a course that would lead him back towards the track.

Moments later the guns began to search him out, accurately ranged to just above cloud level, but bursting yards off to the right. Paul nosed his way deeper into the cloud, forcing himself to keep straight for a few seconds more. The mist gathered about him, robbing him of his visual cues and rolling tiny drops of moisture over the windshield, but for the moment he was content. If he had lost sight of the ground, then the gunners must have lost sight of him. Ostrich-thinking indeed, but it served to bring him comfort.

There was a sharp metallic bang, a brief red glow through the mist, a jolt that owed nothing to the turbulence, and a pungent burning odour. Paul's nerves leaped and he craned around to check the rotary, but in reflex only, recognising the breath of the shellburst. He faced front, blind in the mist but confident that he could maintain lateral control long enough to position for his run. He passed his tongue across feelingless lips, waiting for the right moment. Then he eased forward on the stick.

He came out of cloud diving much more steeply than he had anticipated and with the aircraft banked quite steeply to the right. He rolled wings-level, easing off on the stick to bring the nose up a degree: so much for his ability to maintain a wings-level attitude when flying blind! But he had emerged very close to where he wanted to be so that an instant later he had regained his bearings. He amended his heading a little, concentrating then on his chosen line, skirting the battered road from St Pierre-Divion and veering back upslope to cross the sunken track. His grip was firm now, forcing the machine to his will, pushing ever lower towards the surface rising up below him, counteracting the violence of the gusts as the speed built up towards the limit and the airflow raged about his ears.

Suddenly the grasses were streaming beneath him, the undulating slopes taking shape. The machine was bucking, heaving over bumps, and lurching down, uncomplaining although severely tried. Now that he was this low every instinct told him to get lower yet, to belly on down to actual ground level, but he needed height enough to see what was going on.

Tracer was snaking towards him now but the gunnery was wild, taken unawares by his sudden reappearance. Paul was aware that at this height he would be the target for every weapon that could be brought to bear and he flew a jinking course, thankful that only the tracers made their presence known. It was brought home to him too, that off to his left, at the highest point on his horizon, shells were wreathing the Thiepval ridge in smoke, the bursts flowering like phantom trees in some foul, ephemeral forest.

A patch of turbulence jarred the machine, lifting it to cramp him into his seat and then instantly dropping it again to grind the lapstrap hard against his groin. His feet floated up off the rudder bars and he cried out in alarm, panic tightening his grip on the stick and sending his other hand clutching at the edge of the nacelle. He cramped his stomach muscles tight, and forced the aircraft down towards the ground once more; bumps like that were the penalty for speed.

Ground fire was coming up from his left front, merely – damn it!– reinforcing his earlier conclusion that everything to the left was German-held. Which meant that chancing his arm – as he had been from the outset in making this extra run, he told himself – had been a total waste of time! Except that at that very moment a flutter of red light caught his eye, and a flare, thrown low, once more, no doubt, in an effort at concealment, came bouncing and tumbling off the ground towards him. And came from the left! Beyond the track, a full fifty yards to his left! Just where he would have called down shellfire! Gustily he vented his relief. The doubt that had forced him to do this final check had not then, been unfounded.

Figures below, clad in field-grey, a communication trench jammed to capacity with enemy support troops, frozen now into immobility, aware what his passage might mean. Banking right then, and yet another red, but slightly right, and merely proving the remainder of his line, and the first fresh glimpse of khaki, huddled in the shelter of a copse.

Confident of the line at last Paul banked away down towards the river, seeing khaki figures thinly spaced amid the welter of churned earth, but waving cheerily enough as he passed. Sudden shells threw up spumes of chalk and water for him to fly through, bursting ahead of him near the river's edge. A quick-firer, more persistent than the others, had followed his every swerve, and was rapidly closing in. He was racing now at flat-out level speed. But oh! for a motor twice as powerful. Although he took comfort from the fact that what there was of the Gnome was shielding his back. If he once crossed the river he would be safe! It was a charm and a wish, a mantra, and an oft-repeated prayer.

There was a sharp crack, and an impact that jostled the stick. A piece of fabric lifted from the nacelle somewhere above his right leg and he knew that the quick-firer had made its mark. But it seemed as if that was the best it could do, and now he was out of range. A flash of water as he crossed the Ancre, the shattered walls of Hamel – and he pulled for height with Aveluy Wood falling away beneath his wings.

The talc-covered map case had fallen back behind his thigh, its securing string entangled with the pencil. Paul tugged impatiently at the first bit of string he could find, yanking at it with his gloved hand until it snapped and the map came free. He cast one look around the sky, searching beneath the level of the cloud, and then began to plot the demarcation line he had determined. He pencilled a sketch, bowing the line east, out beyond the sunken track, marking then the communication trench where the German stormers were massed and targeting it for instant attention. He jotted swiftly:

> 50-100 OUR TROOPS AS SKETCH, AROUND TRACK N.E. MAIN THIEPVAL-DIVION ROAD. CRITICAL IF NO SUPPORT. OTHERWISE SMOKE TO COVER WITHDRAWAL. FACING IMMINENT COUNTER-ATTACK FROM SCHWABEN.

Three minutes after seeing his message retrieved the first shells began to burst. Too far north initially but quickly pulling back and onto target, for now that the most forward British troops had been located the gunners could go about their killing with deliberation. Paul climbed in easy spirals, watching as the bursts traced out the pattern of his sketch, shrapnel shells remote from the track, high-explosive nearer to the stalled attackers. And then the smoke, at first wispy and insubstantial but thickening with every smokeshell that arrived, the barrage intensifying in an effort to pin down the local opposition and give the remnants of the stormers at least a chance of breaking contact and withdrawing safely to their lines.

The lines that had not moved an inch since they had advanced from them – at a measured pace – so long ago the day before.

Enough fire-eating for one patrol, Paul told himself, and settled down to police his sector like a gentleman. He flew backwards and forwards tracing figure-of-eights and maintaining 6,000 feet, untroubled now by tracer and eluding any anti-aircraft fire that came too close by diving or climbing a little. Suddenly he felt superfluous. Clearly the battle in this sector had reached a stalemate as far as the British offensive was concerned and now that the line appeared to have stabilised there was little for a contact-patrol machine to do. Only if the German counter-attack developed and pushed the line back would there be any chance of giving direct air support to the troops.

The hate he had stirred up around the jam-packed German communication trench had died away, the smoke drifting downwind to reveal a tumbled mess of blackened chalk. That, he thought, looking down from the detachment of 6,000 feet, should make up in some small measure – some infinitesimally small measure – for the slaughter he had caused among the hapless British troops along the sunken track. He looked at his watch and with a sense of relief saw that his patrol had only five minutes to run. He was suddenly aware of how cold he was. And of how desperately close his bladder was to bursting.

Having made his report Paul took the opportunity of broaching the subject of the continued usefulness of the de Havilland detachment. Major Lawrence, he knew, hoped to be joined at Fienvillers by four more of his Strutters at any time, although the recording officer took a more jaundiced view.

'Even when they are allocated I'll bet we get lumbered with the Navy's leavings,' he ventured.

The major grunted, then returned to Paul. 'So you feel contact patrol isn't for single-seaters?' he prompted.

'Well, with things virtually static, it's more of a spotting or recce job. A job for a two-seater, really, sir, with wireless and an observer who isn't busy keeping rightside up.'

The major nodded. 'I take your point. The demonstrations beforehand were all very well, with dummy trenches and dummy creeping barrage and dummy battle objectives Even the dummy wire was cut. And the troops flashed their mirrors and laid their panels and fired off their flares: the demo I saw was like Mafeking night. But as you say, to all intents and purposes the front's gone static.' He raised his eyes. 'Any recommendations?'

Paul spread his hands deferentially but the major cut short his protestations. 'No, Paul, I mean it. There's a lot to re-learn. Let's just hope to Christ somebody up there learns it. But here and now you're the one with the expertise. So you recommend twin-seaters?'

'Well, sir,' Paul said. 'I honestly don't think we're earning our keep the way things are. But even if the troops had broken through I think a two-seater would have been better. There's no great difference in speed or manoeuvrability but with one man flying the machine and keeping his eyes about him the observer can concentrate on plotting positions. And if they do have to come down low to help out they'll have twice the firepower to bring to bear. Up higher, there'll be Archie, of course.'

'But like the poor, he's always with us,' murmured the recording officer.

'As you say, William,' said the major a shade reprovingly. He turned back to Paul. 'I think you'll find Wing will listen, Paul. But you've done a fine job, the three of you, and shown what can be done with single-seaters, although I can't help feeling we've been lucky.' He broke off and looked at Paul piercingly. 'That *you've* been lucky,' he amended.

He walked Paul towards the door. 'As it happens, I don't think you'll find Wing will object to releasing you. And Major Hallam's been on the phone twice already today, he wants you back, too. So I'll let you know the moment Wing make a decision.'

Flight Sergeant Morgan had been hovering outside the office. 'Spare us a moment, sir?' he asked.

'Of course, Chief. They don't want us again until 2.30,' Paul told him.

Several mechanics were standing expectantly around Paul's machine.

'Would you clamber in, sir?' Flight Sergeant Morgan asked. Paul smiled wonderingly and put his foot up onto the step.

'There! Look at that, chief!'

One of the air mechanics pointed at the leg of Paul's right flying boot. Paul held himself at half-lift, eyeing the razor-like slash running diagonally along the line of his calf. He lowered himself to the ground, and probed the gash with his fingers.

'It was almost certainly a quick-firer,' he told them. 'But I didn't realise it had done that.'

Robinson, he reflected, was a dab hand with a needle. Perhaps he would be able to do something with this. A prompt from the senior NCO, and as directed, Paul swung back up, and into the cockpit. A ginger-haired mechanic on a set of steps and holding a long metal rod stood poised above him. Paul eyed the man quizzically.

'OK, Ginge,' Flight Sergeant Morgan nodded. 'And watch Mr Cowley's leg.'

Paul watched, now intrigued, as the mechanic fed the rod carefully through the exit rent in the fabric, passing it down into the nacelle until it came into gentle contact with Paul's knee. The flight sergeant was crouched low on the left side of the nacelle peering up through another jagged vent.

'Could you just shift your knee around a bit, sir. So he can get the rod through? Perhaps if you'd push the joystick forwards a bit.'

Even so, with Paul guiding the rod past his knee and manipulating the stick, it took several attempts before the flight sergeant was able to catch his end of the rod. Now the rod traced the route of the projectile that had passed through the nacelle, entering below on the left and emerging at the top right. Paul frowned with sudden unease. He shifted his feet on the rudder bar, but wherever he positioned his leg the rod pressed uncomfortably hard on his calf. He moved his right knee but only by straining to the right in an impossibly uncomfortable manner could he bring his leg clear. Even then the stick fouled the rod in any but the most forward of positions.

'Well how the dickens did that pass through?' he asked in amazement.

'How the dickens!' agreed the flight sergeant. 'The very words I uses myself, sir.'

'Well, very roughly the words,' interjected an air mechanic dryly. And there was a general laugh.

Paul tried to lift himself out of the cockpit but the rod trapped him, actually snagging in the gash in his boot. So how the shell fragment had passed through without touching him was absolutely beyond understanding. The airman slid the rod out of the nacelle and Paul jumped down to the ground to look from the entry rent to the tear in his boot. He smiled weakly.

'I thought you'd like to see that, sir,' said the flight sergeant comfortably.

'Believe me, you thought wrong then, Flight Sergeant.'

The words, so obviously heartfelt, causing another general laugh.

As it transpired the recording officer's scepticism concerning the arrival of the squadron's outstanding Sopwiths was fully justified. It had been the delays in the supply of new machines and the desperate need for aircraft that had led to No.70 Squadron's piecemeal dispatch to France in the first place, their 'A' Flight having arrived in May, 'B' Flight not until late June, and still to arrive at Fienvillers. And now, as the recording officer had surmised, it had been decided that the outstanding 'C' Flight was to be formed from Royal Naval Air Service Strutters – when they became available. The news left Major Lawrence fuming but there seemed little he could do. Meanwhile the de Havillands were to return to their own squadron.

The Sopwith crews laid on a farewell binge that evening. Not that they had seen much of their guests, for the de Havillands had been operating as a separate flight, but their imminent departure was as good an excuse as any. Paul spent the evening avoiding the most excessive of the high jinks and maintaining an intermittent conversation with Bernard Doughty, the Sopwith captain, about the situation that had arisen following the virtual failure of the offensive. It was clear to them both that the offensive would have to be called off now. Accordingly, after a few more drinks, they turned to solving all the problems of the Corps, formulating between them a scheme for pairing off a two-seater and a single-seater scout, finding the idea so good that after yet more drinks they took themselves over to the office and forced it upon the major. That seriously cut into their drinking time but even so Paul was not too clear-headed when Robinson shook him awake at seven next morning.

'It's Major Hallam, sir,' the batman told him urgently, 'on the phone.'

'What does he want?' Paul heard himself snapping irascibly. He rolled from the cot and reached for his greatcoat. 'Sorry,' he apologised, 'I was half-asleep. And I don't suppose he told you anyway.'

'That's OK, sir,' the batman replied imperturbably, 'but it's my guess he wants you to stay on here for a while.'

'It's not a very good line, sir,' said the orderly room corporal, handing Paul the telephone.

That almost went without saying but duly warned Paul shouted into the instrument. 'Major Hallam, sir? Good morning, it's Cowley.'

'Paul?' The line was worse than not very good and the major had obviously had great difficulty in making contact. 'HQ have been on about the liaison you've suggested between a singleton and a two-seater. What's it all about?' Robinson had not been wrong!

'Well, sir –'

'What's that?' bawled the major.

Paul reverted to semi-telegraphese. 'The Strutter to make contact, our scout to keep heads down. The observer plots positions. Sort of contact-cum-close-support.' It took a while to get across but finally the major managed to piece it all together.

'It's pleased both HQ and Army apparently,' he shouted. 'And they'd like you to do a few sorties at it. But Mainwaring and Fisher come back right away.' He broke off at a particularly fierce burst of interference and when he resumed the line had become perfectly clear although he continued to shout at the top of his voice. 'Sorry about this, Paul, but we'll get you back as soon as we can. Just take care.' A fresh burst of static, and the line went dead.

'Want you to stay with us, do they, sir?' asked the corporal conversationally.

Paul grinned. The major had not been shouting as loudly as all that.

'That's right, corporal. But Mr Mainwaring and Mr Fisher will be going back today.'

'Yeh, that's what we thought, sir,' the man replied complacently.

Paul shook his head, wondering, not for the first time, at the efficiency of the bush telegraph, and made his way back towards the sleeping quarters to find Robinson already packing the kit of the others. The batman had not awakened them as yet so Paul took it upon himself to kick at the foot of their beds. This, at least, was an awakening they would welcome.

In the event it was another two weeks before Paul found himself back with his own squadron, two weeks in which there had been no let up in the job although in part, he had to admit, he had only himself to blame for that.

From Gommecourt down to Thiepval the offensive had stabilised with the British back in their old front-line trenches – indeed in places they had never been able to leave them – and with the Germans still holding their original commanding positions on the high ground. Reports from British stormers who had made their way back to their own lines spoke wonderingly of vast, reinforced-concrete strongholds painstakingly constructed by the industrious Würtenburgers; deep, cavernous warrens capable of withstanding any shell, luxuriously fitted out, often with electric light, and all bristling with machine guns.

Sending troops against unsubdued positions such as these had proved to be exactly what Bernard Doughty had said it would be the night before the off, Paul reflected grimly, 'Bloody murder'. What confounded all their expectations, however, was that despite the appalling losses and despite the lack of progress there seemed to be no thought given to calling off the offensive; indeed both sides appeared to be settling down to a stolid war of attrition by artillery fire. The British general staff, Paul concluded, must have very rarefied minds to see some gain in continuing the bloodbath. Ossie Temple, Bernard Doughty's observer, held the same opinion but was far more outspoken in expressing it.

As Paul had argued, with the northern front stabilised there was no call thereabouts for contact-patrol operations. Ground communications by runner and landline had been re-established and despite the continuous shellfire Royal Signals wiring parties kept communications open. For three days neither the Sopwiths acting alone, nor the team of Sopwith and de Havilland acting in concert, had any significant change to report. There was always the threat of counter-attack but until that occurred, or until a fresh offensive was mounted, it seemed that the requirement for close contact work had come to a temporary end.

In the southern part of the British sector the situation was more fluid, for not only had the gains of the first day had been consolidated but by the end of the second week the fighting was in places as much as one and a half miles forwards of the starting line. It was Paul who suggested, after the second day, that the pair of them seek permission to try out the new technique in the southern sector, operating on a roving commission. Bernard Doughty had looked at him sideways when he had first raised the subject.

'If we'd guessed you were such a fire-eater we'd have stayed well clear of you,' he had said.

Ossie Martin had sniffed, 'Wants to be another effin' Rees.'

For Major Rees – whose flight had escorted Paul to St Omer on the first leg of his Fokker ferry flight – was in the news. There were stories of an epic air battle on the first day of the offensive involving eight to ten hostiles. Estimates of how many Rees, flying a DH2, had engaged in person varied, although some days later *Comic Cuts* – more respectfully, the RFC's regular *Communiqué*, in this instance No.41 –, gave it as four. Rees had suffered a leg wound but first reports were that it was insignificant, certainly he had fought on after receiving it. Rumour had it that he had been recommended for high award.

Ossie had sniffed even harder at the actual workings of Paul's scheme.

'It's all right for you darting backwards and forwards like a kingfisher, we've got to sit and be potted at.'

They had all grinned, the Strutter being that much faster than the DH2. But as opposition had stiffened so being potted at had become something No.70 Squadron had been forced to reckon with. On 7 July one of their observers had died of wounds received in a fight with Fokkers over Cambrai while the very next day they had lost a Sopwith by a direct hit from, of all things, dear old bit-of-a-joke Archie, which had killed both its crew. All this aside the three of them had talked over Paul's idea, tossing it around until eventually Bernard had shrugged his shoulders, looking at Ossie and saying with a show of reluctance, 'Oh well, England Expects.'

'Expects too effin' much, most of the time,' had been Ossie's sour reply.

Ninth (Headquarters) Wing approved the suggestion and orders were passed immediately so that the Sopwith and de Havilland pair found themselves operating as an independent unit with the set task of developing a technique for close-supported contact patrol. For the purpose a small ground party was moved to the advanced landing field at Baisieux, just west of Albert, only minutes flying time from the thorny Fricourt salient, and here, from a strip even shorter than most in France, they found themselves carrying out between three and four sorties a day. Each evening they would fly their machines back to Fienvillers, returning again at first light.

The fighting in the southern sector was intense and although the gains were measurable, they were measured only in yards, with every yard paid for over and again by a hellish price in blood. Accordingly every day was akin to that first one of the Somme, with the battle lines too hard-fought to be easily defined and with troops in such close proximity to the enemy that they were understandably reluctant to reveal their positions by signalling to the airmen.

The ground over which the fighting took place, a landscape of woods, rolling fields, and tiny villages just a matter of days before, had by this time become an abomination. Every village had been made a stronghold and now only their sites remained, mere red, discoloured blots of brickwork spaced at intervals across the crater-studded plains. Only the woods retained their shape – until one flew low overhead when they revealed themselves to be the mere ruins of woods, with trees shattered and felled and barely a vestige of green leaf; thickets of destruction, fought over still, and daily becoming more deadly and more vile.

The composite pair quickly acquired an intimate knowledge of the area as the line moved painfully beyond Fricourt and Mametz: of the villages Montauban, Contalmaison, Bazentin, and Longueval, clustered together in little space, and of the woods: Caterpillar Wood, Mametz Wood, Delville Wood – the latter presently held fast like a meat-red bone between two snarling dogs – and Trônes Wood, where they watched helplessly as the Royal West Kents got cut to pieces and Paul remembered his first contact with Diane Cousins, and wondered if the twice-wounded Royal West Kent lance-corporal from her ambulance had returned to France and was lying now amidst their dead …

And brooding menacingly across them all, tumbled villages and lacerated thickets alike, still virtually untouched as the second week of this monstrous battle moved ponderously on with no sign of cessation, the square, dark, forbidding shape of High Wood harboured hidden death, and waited for its turn to come.

After the first day or so the roving pair began to look upon the southern sector as their own, so that every group of shell-holes, every mine crater, every track and trenchway became as familiar as their own aerodrome. At intervals throughout their sorties they would drop their messages, the Sopwith crew – notwithstanding that they were wireless-equipped – as well as Paul, and each evening they would collate their experiences and send in their combined report. They were not alone in the sky, of course, for as an independent unit they were merely supplementing the activities of the Corps Squadrons of the Twelfth Wing of Four Brigade, whose area of responsibility it was, and whose BE2cs and Moranes were rarely out of sight.

The pair quickly developed what they found to be a workable way of operating, with Paul positioned behind and underneath the Sopwith so that by initiating a shallow dive he could spray the ground ahead and to the side of the speedier two-seater with his Lewis. Similarly, at the first sign of tracer from a flank Paul would dive off towards it, firing continuously, while the Sopwith continued along its designated track, Bernard, with his forward-firing Vickers, taking over Paul's role of keeping heads down in front of them, and Ossie, the observer, leaning far out over the side, observing, plotting and recording without interruption, although always ready with his moveable Lewis, if required. Despite the lack of co-operation from the ground the results were impressive, especially as the three of them became more familiar with the sector which the daily-blooded army so expensively extended for them, inching the boundaries ever further north.

Certainly even Ossie was forced to concede that the results of his observations were far superior to those he had been able to record before they had paired up, when Bernard had been forced to throw the machine into violent evasive manoeuvres halfway through nearly every pass. Paul's presence could not save them from all the small-arms fire, but it did seem to make life easier.

And as the days went by the troops did, at last, begin to co-operate, gaining confidence in the ability of the airmen not only to render immediate assistance with their airborne machine guns but to bring down rapid and accurate artillery fire at the closest possible range. For the experiment had paid off in developing a technique that permitted the artillery to aid all but the most hard-pressed of infantry, Bernard flying the tightest possible circles over the exact target location while Paul flitted back to drop the 'assistance-required' message; the gunners taking range and bearing on the circling Sopwith. Ossie was not pleased at being used as 'an effin' target', although professionally impressed by the results. He was even less pleased, however, with the tight circling, invariably coming down a bilious shade of green.

'It's all very well for you,' he would tell Bernard, wiping clammy perspiration from his brow, 'and for your effin' sheep dog there.' – that was Paul – 'But you try hanging over the side head-down while some ham-fisted so-and-so tries his best to tip you into kingdom come and see how you feel.'

'And there speaks a volunteer!' declaimed his pilot reproachfully.

Paul kept in almost daily touch with the squadron by telephone, always intending to fly over and visit but never managing to get away. On occasion he spoke with Roly, the recording officer, and with Mike Carter, his flight commander, and they kept him posted with what was going on. Martin Bellamy, he learned, had been killed in a crash while flying, of all things, a Morane. How, and why a Morane, Mike did not say and Paul, shocked at the death of one of his own flight, forgot to ask. Dick and Peter, on the other hand, had arrived back in good shape with Peter being transferred to 'A' Flight and Dick to 'B.' What news he did not hear from Mike and Roly, Robinson more than made up for by regular communiqués culled from sources of his own.

By the middle of the second week of July the advance had slowed perceptibly and there was a brief lull while both British and French gathered strength to renew their offensive. The independent unit flew three last sorties as a team and then submitted its final report.

'Never to be seen again,' Bernard said cynically, sealing the brown envelope and handing it to the recording officer.

'Well, not unless they make a breakthrough somewhere,' Paul qualified.

'Then it'll have to wait until the next war. This one'll all be over by Christmas,' observed the recording officer blandly. 'Won't it?'

Chapter Seven

Major Hallam and Roly were away at Brigade Headquarters when Paul finally rejoined the squadron late on the afternoon of the fifteenth of July. 'A' and 'B' Flights had just returned from a job and the pilots, with Ken Evans, flight commander of 'A' Flight, in the lead, gathered around to welcome him back to the fold. Familiar faces pushed forwards to greet him and he was buffeted good-naturedly around the shoulders.

'So the wandering boy returns,' smiled Ken. He looked around him. 'I think you know everybody, don't you. No, hang on! what about Alfie here?' He pulled forward a stockily-built young sergeant who had been holding back at the edge of the group, smiling faintly. 'Alfie Cox. Alfie joined 'B' Flight just a day or so after you left on your travels, came with –,' he paused, searching for a name.

'Padden,' volunteered the youth.

'Ah yes, Padden, of course.' Ken pursed his lips, evidently remembering. He grasped Paul by the elbow and began to lead him away from the crowd. 'You'll get to know each other later.'

'Padden?' Paul queried.

'Keen as mustard, but foolhardy. Caught sight of a Hun two-seater on his first trip over and dived off after him. Straight down the gunner's barrel. First burst must have got him for he didn't fire a shot himself, just dived past the Hun and into the ground, flaming all the way. Didn't see the seven others up above, and they didn't even bother to come down, just sheered off when the flight turned towards them. Poor old Ralph was very cut up.'

Paul nodded understandingly. He could see why he would be. Like all good flight commanders Ralph Beatty of 'B' Flight prided himself on looking after the pilots entrusted to his care. The novice, Padden, had obviously thrown caution to the winds at the sight of his first enemy machine and paid the penalty accordingly. One new pilot, one relatively-new machine, both valuable, both expendable – both futilely expended.

'C' Flight arrived back while Paul was occupied with an engine run. The first he knew of their return was when Mike Carter tapped him on the shoulder to yell, 'Great to see you back, Paul.'

'How're things?' Paul asked, once he had switched off and after they had exchanged the usual greetings. 'How was Paris?'

'Bloody French place names. It was reading it on that bit of paper. If I'd heard it pronounced ...' Mike pulled off his flying helmet and ran a hand through his hair. He yawned, and Paul saw the tired circles beneath his eyes. 'You know we lost Martin?'

Paul nodded. 'Any details yet?'

Mike shook his head. 'No. There was a Morane here when we arrived. We made it the squadron cab. Martin was visiting Twenty-Four Squadron. Who knows what happened! No one seems to have seen anything. Some pioneers found the wreckage.'

They shook their heads, contemplating Martin's fate in silence. Rightly or wrongly, accidental deaths always seemed more futile ...

'And apart from that?' Paul asked at length.

'Not too bad. We've had the Hun outnumbered from day one. They're around, only they've been hanging back. We're keeping the pressure on – three and four sorties a day. But it's beginning to tell. The boys are getting a bit ragged at the edges. Getting careless. And from what you've been telling Roly on the phone, it's all been for nothing.'

'Well, even in the south the troops are bogging down. But you Army-Wing lot have been doing a great job for I haven't heard of much interference with us Headquarters Corps-Wing chappies.'

'Welcome back,' Mike said dryly. Then grinned. 'But it's nice to hear. At the moment, as you'll find, the Hun seems to be keeping his head down. But you can bet your shirt he'll not stay quiet for long. There're rumours they're regrouping.'

'Re-equipping?'

'That too, I'm sure. But something more. And we'll be the first to find out about it, mark my words.'

Paul did so, nodding. No matter how stagnant the fronts on the ground, things in the air were always changing. The Allies had made the skies their own at the beginning of the offensive but it was certain that the enemy would not simply accept the situation, particularly now that the much-vaunted 'Big Push' had foundered.

Major Hallam and Roly arrived back shortly afterwards.

'You've already heard, I know,' Major Hallam told Paul, having welcomed him back, 'that young Barton was treated well by your Uhlans. The Red Cross have done a special report on him.' Paul eyed him attentively, aware of a certain discomfiture, remembering both the CO's censure, and the subsequent recommendation he had put forward.

'Special report, sir?' he asked.

'He's not physically injured, it seems. But they think something's gone in the poor devil's mind. Anyway he's been recommended for repatriation.'

Paul was swept with a wave of compassion. He met the major's eyes and saw there the awareness they both shared, that death was not the worst evil.

'By the way,' the major said briskly, breaking the silence. 'Congratulations on your "Mention." But remember what I told you at the time – I need you, and I need your machine. Understood?'

'Understood, sir,' Paul smiled, 'And thank you.'

'Have you got the sheets, Roly?' the major asked. The recording officer passed a single sheet of paper across the desk. Next day's flying programme, Paul saw. 'I'm putting you back into "C" Flight as deputy flight commander, then. I've a feeling we won't be keeping Mike much longer – they're bound to promote him soon – so hold yourself in readiness to take over. And meanwhile pump him for all you're worth.'

'I'll certainly do that. And again, thank you, sir,' Paul assured him, saluting, and turning to leave.

'You're down for early patrol, Paul,' Roly told him as he completed his salute. 'How's your machine?'

Paul smiled widely, 'Well, despite a lot of dark mutterings it's been conceded that Flight Sergeant Morgan's boys haven't done *too* bad a job.' He held up his hands, oil-smeared having come straight from the hangar at the CO's summons. 'But grudgingly – they're still taking nothing on trust.'

'And nor are you, I see,' noted the major approvingly. 'Keep it up.'

For two days after his return Paul flew with Mike as his mentor, flying six sorties in all. As Mike had intimated, Paul found a striking change in the behaviour of the enemy, for although the de Havillands ranged far and wide along the length of the front, and penetrated up to fifteen miles inside hostile territory, only once did they encounter any opposition. And even that was nothing more than a brush with two *Eindeckers* who opened fire far too early to be effective and made no attempt to zoom and re-engage but continued their dive until they were lost in the haze. As Mike had said, there were enemy aircraft about, but they kept well back out of harm's way and showed no inclination to come to grips with any of the Allied squadrons who cruised early and late, prowling the sky.

Mike spent some time bringing Paul up to date with the ideas on formation flying they had been working on prior to Paul's leave. In the interim Mike had sought ideas from neighbouring squadrons, both scout and twin-seater, and had written up a paper on the subject which Major Hallam had submitted to HQ. The problem was a live one. Since August last, when the Fokker menace was at its height, the RFC had become increasingly aware of the need for protective formations and as late as January, just six months ago, had ordered all units to practise flying in formation.

The formation envisaged then, however, had been more or less a matter of flying in company in order to deter attackers. The aim now was to develop fighting formations in which aircraft reacting to a leader's signals, and employing previously-rehearsed tactics, could operate as cohesive units. Such fighting formations would ensure the maximum efficiency in both attack and defence, each aircraft having its responsibility to the formation as a whole yet losing none of its capacity for independent action when called for. It was an exciting concept, and now that Paul was back discussions with Mike took up a considerable amount of their off-duty time.

On several occasions, when other duties permitted, Paul went with Mike and some of the other pilots to continue the exchange of ideas with members of neighbouring squadrons. At times they were joined by staff officers equally eager to gather information and equally convinced that the Germans were about to produce something new in aerial strategy. Naturally a fair amount of drink was consumed in the course of such discussions but then discussion, like close formation flying itself, was hot and thirsty work.

One evening, in an *estaminet* in Amiens, they found themselves in company with a group of equally thirsty French aviators who had detoured up into the British sector having been on leave in Paris. It quickly became obvious that the French, by virtue of their experiences over Verdun, had decided views on the efficacy of formation flying, accordingly the British pilots hung on their every word.

'At least,' concluded a French officer swaying behind his wine glass, having described with graphic hand-manoeuvres the tactics they had found most effective, 'this we believe to be, for by it we have survive.'

'So far,' murmured the Frenchman next to Paul dryly.

Paul glanced across at him appreciatively, noting first the decorations on his tunic and then the amused curve of his lips. As a captain he was not the most senior French officer present but his long, sardonically-cast features and his calm gaze set him apart. Paul put him in his mid-twenties, somewhat older than he was himself, a tall man, immaculately dressed and with such an air of sophistication that Paul felt distinctly provincial in comparison. Paul raised his crossed fingers from beneath the table, and the Frenchman's easy laugh dispelled any momentary discomfort.

'You too, Lieutenant? You too feel it tempts fate, even to speak of having survived?' He held out his hand. 'Jacques Delcamp.'

Paul responded, uncrossing his fingers and introducing himself in turn. They already knew each other's units and aircraft; the French were all on Spads.

'But surely, flying the DH2,' said the other, 'you shake Fate's hand every time you fly. "The Spinning Incinerator", don't they call it?' He inclined his head. 'Is it really that bad?'

The captain's English was faultless, retaining just the flavour of an accent so that no one might mistake him for being anything other than French: Paul suspected the retention to be not wholly unintentional.

'No, it's not,' Paul replied, 'but they pared down the cylinders of the early engines and some broke up, causing a few fires. Even now the airframe is rather light for so much torque, but the De Havs've long outgrown their early reputation.'

'As they have outgrown the *Eindecker*. But not, I fear, the new Albatros.'

'The new Albatros? The D1?' Paul raised his eyebrows. 'We've been hearing about them but I don't know that anyone's met them yet.'

'We met a few over Verdun. But they were operating singly, like the Fokkers. Then the *Boche* seemed to withdraw them. We believe they've been preserving them, building up their numbers to redeploy them in special units under their top people. People like Boelcke, now that Immelmann's gone.'

'We've been hearing the same,' Paul nodded. 'And because of it, we've been concentrating on formation flying, for there doesn't seem to be much hope of our re-equipping in the foreseeable future.'

'I think you are wise,' said the Frenchman. 'But despite all you have just heard from my compatriot, we French still find troubles with formation. We have orders to formate in threes and sixes but although our pilots take off together they act as individuals once they get into the air. Some still consider it cowardly to band together, they say it lacks *élan* – er, dash? They consider themselves knights of the sky. But we are learning – gradually.' He turned down his mouth. 'From the *Boche*, as always.'

Paul smiled with him, sympathetically.

'A month ago,' Jacques Delcamp went on, 'I was in Surrey trying your new Sopwith Pup – very small, very beautiful in its handling – although perhaps a little slow. And certainly too late. For even that is months away and soon the *Boche* will be taking the initiative.'

Paul grunted agreement. 'And being perfectionists they'll fill the new units with their best men.'

'Leaving the rest with mediocre men and machines,' countered Jacques. 'But even that won't hurt them provided they can move the top squadrons quickly from sector to sector.'

Paul ran his gaze along the Frenchman's medal ribbons. The *Croire de Guerre* he picked out at once with its green background and thin, red, vertical stripes, and the *Medaille Militaire*, yellow with green edges. The others were unfamiliar to him.

'You seem to understand the Germans very well, *Capitaine*,' he observed.

'*Jacques!*' chided the other. 'On the contrary, Paul, it is our national tragedy that none of us have such an understanding, for if we had the *Boche* would not be doing his shit all over France.' His eyes were bitter. 'This is not the first time the *Boche* has overrun our lands, nor was '70.' He smiled, but thinly, and humourlessly, 'The *Boche* have a joke: they say we plant poplars along our main roads so that invading German armies may march in comfort in the shade.'

Despite himself Paul had to choke off a laugh but Jacques was not affronted.

'No. Laugh, Paul! For the joke is on us. But after all this –,' he flung out his arm as if, with the gesture, to blot out their immediate surroundings and embrace all the ugliness and desolation that war had brought to France, 'after all this we must be sure to learn to understand that German mind: so never to make the same mistake again.'

The sombreness of the moment was broken by a clamour for Jacques to lead his compatriots in a song, a demand he proceeded to fulfil with gusto, his dark eyes lighting up as he mounted a table to conduct the chorus.

The song he chose was clearly a favourite among the French airmen and drew scandalised squeals of protest from the women who, with their modesty duly attested to, joined with racy enthusiasm in the chorus. It was a simple, repetitive chorus which the English were soon shouting with the rest regardless of whether they understood the words or not – in Paul's case, the latter. When the applause had died down Mike was pushed to his feet to lead the assembly in a soulful rendering of 'The Dying Aviator', which was popular throughout the RFC, and by the sound of it, throughout the French Aviation Service as well. The evening had all the makings of a good binge, but a quarter of an hour later the senior French officer was reluctantly tapping at his watch and the impromptu party began to break up as the various groups came together to say their noisy goodbyes.

'Your name's been puzzling me – Delcamp,' Paul told Jacques as they made their way to the door 'You didn't fly in England before the war, did you?'

Jacques smiled sadly. 'My brother, Richard. He had a *Bleriot Bis Dix* which he took to Brooklands often. He was killed late last year. Over Verdun. But me, before the war, I never flew at all.' His grin became rueful. 'And yet given a little more time ...' The doorway was jammed with boisterous revellers, none of them over-anxious to leave. Jacques cupped his hand against the din. 'I built myself a *Bleriot*. Not to full scale, but big enough to support me.'

'And did it?' Paul asked.

'It should have done, but I had no experience. Possibly the elevator was too tricky, but I came down in a crash.'

Paul nodded understandingly. How many early aeroplanes might have been successful had their constructors only had the good fortune to keep them in the air long enough to learn how to control them!

'Did you rebuild?'

Jacques nodded. 'I started. But there was poor weather, and then there was the war.' He was amused by a sudden notion. 'Why not finish it for me when the breakthrough comes. If the *Boche* haven't smashed it, or taken it away, it will be still in the barn at –.' Between the noise and Jacques's fluid pronunciation Paul missed the name of the place.

'At where?' he shouted. Now they were having to bawl just to make themselves heard. Jacques tried twice more before giving up and scribbling some words on a piece of paper. Paul pored over the name and address but the location still meant nothing to him and he shook his head, 'Where's that?'

'Near the *Bois d'Havrincourt*, you know? – Havrincourt Wood?' In repeating the name Jacques smiled mockingly, deliberately giving it the English-style 'kort' ending. 'Near there.'

Paul frowned. All airmen knew Havrincourt Wood, just as they knew Adinfer Wood, and Ploegsteert Wood and Trônes Wood, but as pinpoints, not as real places.

'You mean, that's your home? Just over there?'

Much as Jacques had done earlier, Paul swung his arm towards the east. Jacques nodded, his features limned with weariness by the porch's shaded lamp.

'Home, family, friends, fiancée – all just over there. And that is what the *Boche* has done to us, Paul.' He indicated his companions, already beckoning from their transport. 'We are all from this area, that is why we come this long way round, back from Paris. Just to be close.' He held out his hand as the others called to him. 'Study the *Boche*, Paul. Fight him, and kill him when you can – hate him if you will –, but never underestimate him, or the workings of his mind.'

Paul awoke from a fitful sleep in the early hours, his head alive with concerns that *le Capitaine* Jacques Delcamp had brought welling to the surface. It was the first time that he had really considered the plight of the French populace, split as they were by a war zone that for nearly two years now had stretched, unbroken, from the Swiss mountains to the English Channel; for with the stabilisation of the fronts everyday life – behind the Allied lines at least – had to all intents and purposes returned to normal; the crowds of refugees had long since been assimilated and only in the most forward areas were civilians still disbarred from returning to their homes or going about their normal business. It was commonplace, even on the very fringes of the military zone, to see workers in the fields stoically bent to their labours, seemingly oblivious to all but the tending of the land.

The British troops in general, Paul was well aware, saw the locals as grasping and avaricious, and by and large, found their way of life different, and therefore suspect. How the locals saw the armies billeted upon them was a matter of conjecture; at best, Paul concluded, they must view them as a necessary evil.

Now he pictured an England divided as France was. And with that fancy the landscape-figures tending their fields beneath the very muzzles of the guns took on unsettling substance. Fleshed out, they were no longer anonymous, and in the instant he felt an unwilling kinship with them, as if their burden was his burden too. How much he would resent being denied access to what he considered to be his own! How much more so must these men of farming stock, born as they were to the care of the land!

How much worse must it be then, for those ensnared behind the German lines, similarly struggling to carry on their lives but beneath the oppressor's yoke? And what of those like Jacques who must suffer additional torment on behalf of loved ones held beyond their reach? Perhaps fliers could at least find comfort in the fact that they were carrying on the fight; that they could even, on occasion, snatch glimpses of the places, if not the people, they loved. Or did such tantalising proximity, Paul wondered, merely make the sense of loss more painful?

He was still awake when Robinson came to call him for the early patrol and as he stumbled around the hut in the half-darkness pulling on his gear he knew that the night had given little rest. Nights like that he could most decidedly do without.

Chapter Eight

The next few days proved particularly busy for the squadron as with clear skies and good visibility they were able to put in several purely training sorties in addition to their war tasks. The very fact that the aircraft were kept busy seemed to cut down the irritating faults that invariably developed during periods of bad weather. Probably moisture had a lot to do with such problems but it was generally held that the machines had feelings too and that they, like the pilots, preferred flying to sitting idly on the ground.

After each sortie and having made their operational reports, the members of the flight would gather to discuss the lessons learned in the course of the job. For some, especially for those officers recently seconded to the RFC from regiments where young officers were to be seen – if absolutely necessary – but never heard, the free and open discussions were a novelty. Such officers found it equally novel to find no taboo placed on 'shop' talk in the mess.

'The hangar doors are open again, it seems,' the elderly armament officer would say disgustedly to Paul, folding his newspaper resignedly and moving off as if to leave the room. Yet invariably he would be found, only moments later, in the midst of an animated group of pilots half his age, arguing the merits of the Spandau over the Lewis or the morality of using incendiary and explosive ammunition against aeroplanes.

Such an atmosphere stimulated discussions which ranged right across the rapidly expanding spectrum of military aviation; discussions in which both personal and apocryphal experiences were blended together and seasoned with rumours, theories, and fanciful ideas before being tossed into a common pot where they simmered away giving off vast quantities of vaporous hot air; but, on occasion, producing the good solid stock of new and valid techniques.

'C' Flight had just landed from escorting a FE2b on a two hour artillery shoot during which close-formation practice had been the order of the day.

'It's all very well, Mike,' complained one of the recent replacements, 'but I never saw the Fee once: the Huns could have been doing cartwheels around him for all I know. It took me all my time trying not bump into you, or miss a signal.'

Mike laughed. 'Well, if it's a matter of choice I'd prefer you to miss a signal. But you're coming on. Very soon you'll find station keeping as easy as riding a bike. Then you can take care of the Huns.'

'I broke my wrist learning to ride a bike,' said the other dolefully. 'But I suppose you're right.'

'Of course I'm right,' Mike told him, 'I'm the flight commander.' He turned to a tall, lanky youngster who was standing on the fringe of the group dejectedly rubbing one flying boot against the other. His name was Whitehead and he had come to the Flying Corps straight from school, arriving on the squadron just two days before. 'Any problems, Chalky?'

The other coloured bashfully. 'Well,' he swallowed, 'it was all right at first but –' he looked unhappily at the ground, fearing ridicule, yet finishing gamely, 'then I kept losing it.'

Paul felt for him. It was clear that it had cost him a lot to make the admission in front of the others.

'Oh! then there was nothing personal in it?' Mike established with mock relief. 'Once or twice there I thought you were deliberately trying to swat me with your wing.' There was a general laugh, but it was friendly laughter and it seemed to reassure the boy for suddenly he grinned and began to laugh along with the others.

'No,' Mike told him, 'you were just getting a bit too tense; we all do the same – ain't that so?' He indicated the assenting nods. 'There! It really is just a matter of practice.'

'What happens,' he went on, 'is that you're all concentration. You get the bottom edge of my top plane, just so, and my tail just there in the corner of your eye. And when my bus moves you make the necessary corrections. The trap we fall into – *all of us*,' he stressed again, casting a glance about the gathering, 'is to make a correction and then forget to relax again. So from then on we're getting tighter and tighter, and all our movements get jerkier. This gets tiring and we lose concentration, and we correct later and harder than we should – and so it gets worse.'

'That's right,' the boy agreed, relieved, 'That's exactly how it went. I *knew* I was overcontrolling but the gentler I tried to be the stiffer I got.'

Mike ignored a sotto voce comment that drew a gust of ribald laughter from those of the group within earshot and went on encouragingly, 'Believe me, knowing the problem is half the battle. Tensing-up's a bit insidious – it creeps up on you. When I find I'm tensing up I mutter, "Relax Chump, and fly the bloody aeroplane!"– 'cept that chump isn't the C-word I employ – and that seems to do the trick.'

'And every now and again,' put in Paul as the chuckles died down, 'just ease out a little – that'll help.'

The boy nodded, clearly much happier. 'I thought it was just me.'

'Far from it,' Mike assured him. 'And while we're on the subject,' he wagged a finger at Simpson, the other new boy, a cheery youngster, bursting with keenness and breezy self-confidence, 'When I signal you to open out and relax, just open out, and bloody relax.'

'But I was relaxed,' the other protested.

'Then next time open out and let me relax. And now, Chaps –,' Mike held up a hand to stifle the groan that greeted this old chestnut, 'let's break it up: back here at one-thirty. Take-off at two. You'll get your instructions then.'

For the next three days 'C' Flight flew an average of four jobs a day without once coming within firing distance of a German machine. The other flights reported the same state of affairs. Anti-aircraft fire, in contrast, markedly intensified, corroborating intelligence reports that the Germans had moved new mobile anti-aircraft units into the area, some sources holding that they were those no longer required in the Verdun sector, although most suspected that the slaughter over that particular charnel house would get worse before one side or the other decided that enough was enough.

The uncharacteristic timidity of the German Air Service, however, was viewed with extreme suspicion by the more experienced members of the flight who found it wearing in the extreme, and Paul soon realised that he was not alone in searching the skies harder than at any time since his arrival in France.

At least the lull in air fighting gave the new arrivals time to settle in, although Mike was concerned that it might breed complacency. On several occasions flight commanders had been driven to discipline over-enthusiastic youngsters who clearly showed that they were becoming careless. In one case a young 'A' Flight pilot, named Winthrop, dived away to pounce on what proved to be a Spad. The Spad pilot, seeing him coming, and recognising him as supposedly friendly despite the tracer spewing from the de Havilland's Lewis, simply pulled beneath him and sat on his tail. Winthrop twisted and turned until the Frenchman eventually got bored and allowed him to scoot for home where he was found shakily but proudly filling in an air-combat report. The supporting members of his flight, hurrying from their machines, gathered about him, grinning over his shoulder, but Ken Evans, his flight commander, delayed by his mechanic, was not grinning when he arrived. Nor, moments after that, was the would-be ace.

Not that straightforward training flights were less subject to the malady as 'B' Flight discovered when one of its new pilots started skylarking during a formation turn and touched wings with his leader. Both pilots came to earth safely, the miscreant at base, where he made a classically-perfect, three-point touchdown, Ralph Beatty at an emergency landing ground close to the lines where he bounced and damaged a wheel. The white-faced and penitent young man had to kick his heels for a full two hours before a tender arrived carrying an irate flight commander whose fuming ill humour was not assuaged by the praise fulsomely heaped upon the novice's textbook landing by all the pilots of his and the other flights.

Both incidents could have happened during any flight, of course, for the risks of mis-identification and of collision were just two of the many hazards inherent in war flying; and indeed it had to be accepted that under the pressure of inculcating 'Offensive Spirit' into pilots of such limited experience, accidents were bound to occur. Striking the right balance between enthusiasm and restraint, of course, posed a difficult problem for squadron and flight commanders alike and although, in these instances, the lessons learned sunk home, it was not unknown for recalcitrant pilots – as with those failing to make the grade – to be returned to Home Establishment for re-assessment, or disposal.

The mere threat of this extreme measure, however, was normally sufficient to make the individual see the error of his ways, for invariably the problem lay in overkeenness rather than the reverse. As for nurturing the required mix between keenness and discipline, natural competitiveness and inter-flight and inter-squadron rivalries were actively promoted. The time was gone, it was felt, when an individual could regard himself as anything other than a member of a team, notwithstanding the fact that within the team in question there was scope and to spare for personal initiative; indeed such initiative was a prerequisite of team membership. All very complicated and prosy when spelled out, but with good example and leadership, and helped by some – frequently drink-based – riotous relaxation, it was surprising how simple it all became.

And as the weather changed, the clear skies giving way to masses of summer cumulus, so the German Air Service suddenly made its reappearance, taking full advantage of the cloud cover and once again employing decoys. Now, however, they were found to be using, on occasion, up to three layers of protective scouts above the lure.

On their first encounter with the newly-aggressive Hun, Mike's signal nearly caught Paul napping, coming, as it did, as he was eyes down checking his cockpit. He looked up from his instrument board and glimpsed a two-seater passing from sunlight to shadow behind a patch of cloud some three thousand feet below. By now Mike was gazing upwards, shielding his eyes against the sun and already beginning a turn. Paul saw the hostiles an instant later, four scouts, noses down, and coming very fast.

After the days of waiting his initial reaction was a compound of relief and alarm, with alarm predominating, drying up his mouth. He was aware that Simpson was slower than usual in following the turn: clearly startled by realising that this was the real thing. But it was only a momentary hesitation and did not affect the lad's handling so that the flight turned almost in unison, curving in against the dive to frustrate the attack.

The attackers, a mixture of types, one Fokker *Eindecker* and three Pfalz, realised that they had lost the element of surprise and made only a half-hearted attempt to press home the attack. The leader had singled Mike out for attention but opened fire too early and Mike turned inside him and as he passed, stood on one wing to follow him down, firing as he went, leaving Paul to guard his tail. A Pfalz shot across Paul's nose and he pressed the trigger, but too late, and his unbalanced turn threw his tracers off to one side.

The attackers had too much of an advantage in dive-speed and although Mike led the flight after them for some thousands of feet he eventually eased up and began to climb back towards the north-west, signalling the flight to reform. Paul had a careful look about him for the two-seater, almost certainly a decoy, but saw no sign of it.

Although it had been an inconclusive encounter it had livened them all up and on landing Mike professed himself well satisfied with the way they had handled themselves. He reported strikes on the German leader but thought he had caused only minor damage at best. The other three members of the flight were very full of the experience and astounded at the speed with which the attack had developed. It was a salutary lesson in wakefulness for it was clear that had the Germans not been seen when they were there might well have been a very different outcome.

The next few days saw many similar encounters, with 'B' flight claiming to have sent an LVG two-seater out of control into a cloudbank. In the fight one of their pilots suffered the loss of his engine but managed to glide back to a forced-landing. It was later found that a bullet had severed his fuel feed allowing petrol to spill back over the hot engine, incredibly, without catching fire. On one occasion Paul's flight had four encounters in the course of a single patrol, the last a melee with five Rolands in which no one could get the advantage and which had settled into a stalemate situation until the arrival of two Sopwith Strutters sent the Germans packing.

On the following day Mike was posted home to form and take command of a new squadron, his promotion to temporary major, as the order said, becoming effective on his arrival in England. Major Hallam appointed Paul to the command of 'C' Flight, with his promotion to the temporary rank of captain to follow the moment it was approved by HQ. Mike's orders required him to move at once and so the squadron were unable to give him a proper send off but all those not on duty turned out to see him go. Paul and the remaining three members of 'C' Flight were stood down from mid-afternoon to enable them to accompany him to Amiens but he refused to allow them to come as far as the station.

'We'd be standing there hunting up small talk and that gets embarrassing after the train's first few false starts.' He contented himself with shaking hands all round and accepting a bottle of wine and a slit salad-loaf of French bread, arranged by Paul, for the journey: Paul had never forgotten the meal-in-a-loaf his landlady on the eve of his Fokker-ferry flight, had given him for his own journey.

'Look after them, Paul,' Mike said finally, 'I know you will.'

It was a theme Major Hallam returned to that evening when he spent half an hour going over Paul's new duties with him.

'Mike had a fine record with the squadron,' he said in summation. 'He is credited with destroying five enemy aircraft but his real strength lay in the way he looked after his flight. I've watched the way you've been helping him work up the new lads since you got back and I'm very pleased. I know they'll be in good hands.'

Possibly it was the look in the major's eyes, or something in his voice, but it suddenly came home to Paul that a squadron commander's must be among the most difficult of military appointments; as closely involved with his subordinates as any regimental officer yet forbidden to lead them into action or to share in their perils. The squadron commander could not accompany his pilots into their ordeal but he was the one to meet their eyes as he gave them their orders, to see a whitening above the cheekbones, or a tensing of jaw muscles that did not mask the sudden fear; to see calm-eyed acceptance in many, wry fatalism in some, or cheerful flippancy, and what might be hardest of all to bear, eagerness, particularly in the young, and in the newly-fledged. He could wave them off and watch them out of sight, but he could only stay behind: that was his ordeal.

The squadron commander would be with his men as they clambered bulkily into their machines, his was the hand that signalled them on their way. He would be there to welcome back the first flight after dawn, and the last before dusk. Paul had watched the way Major Hallam's gaze followed a departing flight, and had studied his face as he stood, hours later, waiting for the last of his aircraft to return. Like all squadron commanders, whether of single- or twin-seater machines, his lot was to be there to welcome his pilots back, to help his wounded from their splintered cockpits, and on occasion to walk, grim-faced, beside silent and blanketed forms.

Later it was his part to inspire the binge, to lead the singing in the mess, to umpire riotous games, and see that none was left too much alone; to watch his young men unwind as whisky and wine and comradeship eased their wire-tight nerves.

And later still he would pen the letters, working long into the night, trying to imbue the hollow words of sympathy with a sense of his own sorrow, yet unable to indulge that sorrow: for the Aircraft Park was still refusing to replace that low-revving engine from 'A' Flight, while the mechanics detailed for that electrical course would leave 'B' Flight short-handed for two days, and HQ were hopping mad about the apples stolen from that farmer's orchard ...

With Mike gone 'C' Flight comprised Paul himself, Chalky Whitehead, the irrepressible Simpson, and Alfie Cox, and was, therefore, one man short. Whitehead and Simpson had been with the squadron only nine days and Cox – quiet and rugged-faced, and despite his slight build and shy manner, an ex-drayman from Leeds – only a few days longer. Accordingly Paul applied to have either Dick Fisher or Peter Mainwaring appointed as his deputy flight commander. He had taken their measure during his detachment with No.70 Squadron and knew that either would fit in well. In the event Major Hallam gave him Dick Fisher, Peter presently being employed as deputy flight commander of 'A' Flight owing to the official deputy's sickness.

That the brief respite in the air war was well and truly in the past soon became very evident, with every patrol providing fresh evidence of the revitalisation of the German Air Service. In his first two days as flight commander Paul's flight had seven skirmishes with enemy machines, all of them inconclusive but proving useful in putting an edge on everyone as they settled to the new order. Despite this, on the third day they were nearly caught out at the very start of their patrol by three Rumpler C1 twin-seaters who pounced from the rear just as they approached the lines. The German anti-aircraft gunners must have been equally surprised at three of their own diving from the west for their shells continued to burst even as the Rumplers closed, forcing the attackers to run the same gauntlet as the attacked. Possibly this unlooked-for hostility from their own guns put the Rumplers off for they continued on without firing a shot, the leader diving almost vertically past Paul's nose, his two companions passing well underneath. The German gunners belatedly recognised their mistake but the cessation went unnoticed by 'C' Flight as they followed Paul into a headlong, power-on dive.

Paul had reacted on the instant as the enemy leader plunged past him, pushing forwards on the stick and ruddering after him. The German was already pulling away but Paul squeezed off a burst, cursing when his Lewis stopped abruptly after three rounds. 'C' Flight had not yet warmed their guns for they had still been over friendly territory when the attack developed so the stoppage came as no real surprise. He banged the mechanism with his left hand, wincing despite the numbing cold as the cocking handle dug through the leather of his glove. But it did the trick for his next burst clattered away without a hitch, the cordite fumes excitingly acrid. It was a snapshot with the stick hard against the instrument board and the nose tucking ever more steeply towards the ground, but there was no deflection to worry about and the Rumpler, silver, with red wing tips, was no longer drawing away.

Paul ruddered straight and felt the machine snap back into balance. The airspeed was 120 mph and rising, with only his gunfire sounding through the wind. His tracers were going home to the right of the cockpit, but as he saw no signs of damage he pressured his nose to the left. And then, in an instant, a major section of the top starboard plane of the Rumpler lifted cleanly away from the body of the machine, the pilot futilely reaching out as if to pull it back. Paul stopped firing and watched as the Rumpler rolled swiftly to its right, maintaining its integrity until it was upside down when the remainder of its wings broke off and the fuselage, tail high, plunged earthwards, dragged down dart-like by the madly-revving engine.

Carefully Paul began to ease away, mindful of the tumbling wreckage. Beside him Dick Fisher was waving congratulations and he raised a hand in acknowledgement. But now it was the others he was worried about. Alfie Cox was swinging in from wide to port with Chalky below. Of Simpson he could see no sign – but off to his right an ominous trail of smoke disappeared into a patch of cloud. He bit his lip, sick with sudden apprehension. And then, with a surge of relief, he saw Simpson's machine, thousands of feet below, but already clawing upwards to rejoin the flight.

Paul struck a complicated balance, continuing to climb back towards patrolling height – but only slowly –, carrying out a slack turn towards the straggler to allow him to catch up, and permitting an eastwards drift as he did so, taking the flight deeper into Hunland but away from the violently renewed anti-aircraft fire. And all the while he was aware of a knot of discomfort that had formed in the pit of his stomach and now refused to unravel. This, though, he pushed from his mind, redoubling his efforts to avoid any further surprises, twisting in his seat the better to ensure that the sky about them really was clear.

Simpson caught up with them at last, holding up a thumb and wagging his wings exuberantly as he approached but once he was in position settling to his station steadily and without fuss. There were still one and three-quarter hours of the patrol to go and although they met no further opposition Paul was conscious of the new alertness that had come upon them. As far as the flight was concerned he was satisfied that the recent training had paid off. As for their flight commander's dozy showing, well, that was an entirely different matter …

There were congratulations all round when they returned, for the action had taken place in full view of the front-line troops and reports of the fight had been telephoned back. Simpson was over the moon for although none of the flight had seen him shoot down the second Rumpler the gunners had verified it beyond question. Nevertheless, in a sudden burgeoning of maturity he was ready to admit to all and sundry that it had really been a matter of luck.

'I couldn't believe it,' he said, grinning. 'I think their own Archie put them off because my man pushed down below us to avoid a burst. Had he just kept going I couldn't have touched him, but he lifted up straight in front of my nose. I didn't have to aim or anything. I gave him a short burst, and he caught fire.' He looked across at Paul. 'I probably shouldn't have followed him down,' he said contritely, 'but it all happened so fast.'

They filled in their reports and made their way back to the hangars to chat over the engagement with the ground personnel who were, as always, eager to hear what had happened. None of their aircraft, it seemed, had been damaged and it was established with some amusement that while Paul had fired off a full drum to achieve his kill, Simpson's 'short burst', had expended just five rounds, an economy in ammunition which delighted Simpson.

'Not even a burst,' he crowed, 'a mere squirt.'

A remark which cost him dear, for by next morning he found himself known to one and all as 'Squirt' Simpson.

Paul accepted the congratulations with mixed emotions. He was delighted at the flight's success so soon after its reshuffle, and was equally pleased at his own victory, although both as an engineer and as a pilot he was appalled at the ease with which the Rumpler had come apart. His performance as a flight commander, however, filled him with misgivings.

He could accept the fact that the attack had taken him unawares and that only the distracting influence of the German ground fire had saved them: that was just one of the quirks of air warfare. What he could not shrug off was the guilt that had burdened him from the moment he had been unable to find Simpson.

The fact that Simpson had not been the flamer had no bearing on the matter. For Paul knew that as the Rumpler had dived past him he had reacted in reflex, following without a thought for what might have been above! For all he knew there might have been scores more hostiles just waiting to come down. And not an upward glance had he given to make sure! His first real action as a commander, and what concern had he shown for his men? Yet now he was forced to listen to their congratulations knowing that he could have cost all of them their lives. The fact that they were proud to lionise him as the author of their triumph, seemingly oblivious to his shortcomings, only added to the burden of his guilt.

That evening after dinner a whole crowd of them, officers and sergeants alike, piled into a tender and went bounding noisily into Amiens to celebrate. It was a good party and even Paul, regarding the proceedings somewhat morosely, could not help but admit that this afternoon's performance had done wonders not only for the flight but for the squadron as a whole. On the way back the journey was prolonged by several impromptu stops as wine and whisky were voided in one way or another. A companionable fug built up within the canvas confines of the tender, warm, but far from odourless, and at the last halt, a mile or so short of the aerodrome, Paul elected to walk the rest of the way.

It was a comparatively clear night and chillier than he had realised, forcing him to walk more briskly than his mood allowed. A few clouds high over the horizon flickered as if with lightning, but it was man's thunder, rather than God's, that came disquietingly on the wind. Hearing a brook nearby he walked aside to peer into its waters. It was not wide, but its banks were steep and rush lined, and when the carrying breeze died away, as it did at intervals, its tuneful rippling quite drowned out the muttering of the guns.

He leaned against an ancient, pollarded willow, grasping one of the smooth new shoots, but only tentatively at first, for the roots had been exposed by the high spring floods and did not look too safe. The breeze rustled through the branches overhead and some way downstream a fish leaped, splashing silver in the moonlight, the disturbance quickly stilled amongst the gravelled flurry of the shallows. He shifted his body to favour his right leg, letting the night close around him, forgetting for a while the chill and the dull ache in his knee that was rarely absent when his mind and body were fatigued.

The lads of the flight, it was clear, were more than happy with his performance, as was Major Hallam. Yet supposing the three Rumplers had indeed been merely decoys? Suppose he had led his flight straight into a trap, diving as he had with no more thought than Winthrop careering off after his Spad? Supposing it had been Simpson dead, and not only Simpson, but the rest of them? What then? His omission, he told himself in an agony of self-recrimination, had been criminal; at very best a grave error of judgement. But could a flight commander be permitted to make such errors of judgement when lives depended upon him?

The fish leaped again, closer now, almost at his feet, the slap so loud and unexpected that he jumped, and looked around in quick embarrassment. And on the instant the worry fled his mind! He laughed, self-deprecatingly. For he was not really asking, 'Can a flight commander be permitted to make mistakes?' But, 'Can *I*, Paul Cowley, be permitted to make mistakes?' He shook his head wonderingly. What a charlatan he was! The breeze was freshening and he was getting cold. But the burden of guilt had gone, leaving him clear-headed and objective once again. He had made a bad mistake. There was no denying it. But there was nothing to be gained by wallowing in self-recrimination.

And yet, even as his mind eased from his surface burden, he became aware of a subtler and far less worthy relief, a tension hitherto unacknowledged, but deeply-felt notwithstanding: he had got away with it, therefore there would be no criticism and no censure. How much of his guilt, he wondered now, had been for fear of ridicule, or reproof?

He put that train of thought aside. Firmly. In the future there would be other mistakes, but now he had the measure of the problem. After all, common reasoning told him that if he had wasted an instant this afternoon the Rumpler would have made good its escape. Equally, unless the flight, honed by their recent training, had followed him without hesitation, Simpson would not have got the second Rumpler. He could only do his best, he knew that now, and try to learn from – and pass on – his experience.

He tossed a pebble, but it brought no response from the fish, and after a moment he turned and strode resolutely back to the road, aware of the chill but with spirits high, his knee no longer troubling him.

Chapter Nine

By dawn next morning warm air had moved across from the southwest bringing with it vast masses of cloud which hung in dull, unbroken sheets across the whole of northern France. 'A' and 'C' Flights had been detailed for an early patrol but in view of the low cloud base Wing called for a weather check before deciding if the flight should go ahead. The major and Roly had left before first light for a conference at HQ so Paul and Ken Evans, tossed for the task.

'Tails, you do it,' called Ken. The coin spun with a faint whirring sound, teetering for a moment before toppling over to reveal the King. Ken cursed. 'Best of three?' he proposed, without hope.

Five minutes later Ken exchanged places with his air mechanic, Hoskins, who had been warming up the engine for him. The assembled pilots stood about waiting, some with only dressing gowns over their pyjamas despite the chill, but as Ken let the engine run to full power against the chocks, there was an outburst of irreverent protest and a general movement back towards the mess.

'I'll see if I can get through to the tops,' Ken shouted down.

Paul frowned, looking dubiously at the clouds, but Ken was the senior flight commander and he felt constrained not to question his judgement. 'It looks pretty solid, Ken – watch it,' he restricted himself to shouting back. Ken held up a valedictory thumb, and waved away the chocks.

The prop wash lashed the dank air into a minor gale so that Paul staggered, thankful for the knee-length leather flying coat he was wearing. Alfie Fox came from the direction of the kitchen to hand him a steaming mug of dark, strong tea and he took his hands from his pockets to cradle its warmth gratefully. Ken circled the field, coming back overhead and levelling his wings as he passed over the windsock so that he was climbing directly into wind. They saw him wave and they waved back, cheering ironically, but with sober eyes.

'About eight hundred feet,' said one of them, as the aircraft ghosted through the lowest layer of cloud.

'More like seven,' said someone else.

The machine appeared just once more before the cloud swallowed it whole, muffling its engine in enveloping vapour although leaving it audible to the watchers as a steadily receding purr.

'Do you think he'll really try and climb through this lot?' Alfie asked. Nobody responded.

'You wouldn't attempt it, would you, Paul?' asked Chalky Whitehead.

Paul found that a grunt was the only response he could offer. A grim-faced grunt.

Eyes aloft, he reflected. Before entering cloud, Ken would have settled his machine into as stable a climb as he could. Now he would be climbing wings-level. With luck the wind would not alter much with height and he could be reasonably certain that the aerodrome would remain pretty much at his back. Ken would have started the timing from setting course overhead the field and would be schooling himself to fly relaxed, striving to apply the very minimum of movement to any control.

Flying in cloud would, of course, deprive him of his visual cues, but he was not entirely without aids. Any extreme change in pitch attitude would be reflected in a corresponding change of engine revs. Then again he would have been climbing at a steady speed as he entered the cloud and any change in pitch would also be reflected in a corresponding change of airspeed. So, with careful manipulation of the stick, the two together, engine and airspeed, would enable him to assess and regulate his nose-up, nose-down attitude.

He would also be helped by his compass, and by the seat-of-the-pants muscle sense, which together with his inner-ear balance organs, would be sending continuous signals to his brain. Ken would be well aware that the senses could send unsettling signals, to minimise which he would be moving his head as little as possible.

All this, Paul knew, would be sufficient to allow a pilot of Ken's experience to penetrate any reasonably thin layer of cloud. The problem was that today's layer seemed as if it might be very thick indeed. Certainly there was no sign of the sky brightening, only the dull grey overcast oppressively blanketing the earth. There was also a dampness in the air suggestive of rain in the offing, and that too spoke of thicker rather than thinner layers above.

'Washout,' someone muttered, and there was a general murmur of agreement. There was little chance of this clearing up.

Paul looked at his watch. Once Ken broke cloud above he would assess the upper sky, looking for layers which might prove workable. If he was unable to find any then he would put the wind behind him by turning through 180 degrees and then, relatively sure of his position, and knowing that he was heading pretty well towards the field, drop down into the overcast once more.

The trouble would come if he found himself unable to win through to the tops. Then he would be faced with turning back in cloud, which as everyone present was aware, was a procedure fraught with peril. In that event he would undoubtedly stop his climb, settle, and then rudder gently around in a flat turn back towards the aerodrome before letting his nose drop into a descent, solicitously endeavouring not to upset his wings-level state.

The problem was that no pilot flying blind in cloud, no matter how experienced he was, could hope to maintain his aircraft on an even keel for more than a matter of minutes. After that his senses would begin to play him false. Deprived of visual guidance, the very mechanisms of the body that normally help to provide a sense of balance would start to send unsettling signals to the brain; signals so disorientating that despite the natural stability of his machine he was almost certain to lose control.

And when gravity took over – and that it eventually would was the only certainty – then all a pilot could hope for was to be given time enough to regain control once he broke cloud and could visually assess the attitude his machine had adopted. Regain control, that is, before he ran out of sky.

In cloud flying it helped to keep a cool head, to relax and make the very tiniest of movements, to trust to the aircraft's built-in stability, and to keep the imagination well in check, containing nervousness and holding panic at bay. For since primeval times Man had been accustomed to rely upon the messages from the brain, so to endeavour to ignore them now, though life itself depended upon so doing, went against nature.

'Listen!' Paul held his breath the better to catch the sound.

Ken had been airborne for more than twenty minutes now and in the meantime pilots had drifted off in ones and twos to dress. Few had changed into full flying kit for there seemed little chance of the patrol being called and so the flights stood reassembled in an extraordinary assortment of clothing. Although most of the newer arrivals were dressed in standard RFC flap-chested jackets, leggings, greatcoats, and headgear, many of the older-stagers sported outfits that collectively reflected their various pre-Flying-Corps military backgrounds; regimental tunics resplendent with collar badges, slacks of various styles and hues, and one Glengarry bonnet, defiantly retained despite all edicts from above.

'It's him,' exclaimed Simpson, only to be hushed into silence.

There was a whisper of sound from the west fading a little as the breeze lifted and then becoming momentarily more audible. It brought a buzz of anticipation and Peter Mainwaring, now officially confirmed as deputy flight commander of 'A' Flight, showed his relief in a sudden expulsion of breath.

'Began to think the old bugger had got himself lost.'

As Paul was aware, such language, coming from Peter, betrayed the depth of his concern. Standing beside him Paul strained to the sound a moment longer and then grunted and shook his head.

'Premier,' he said quietly.

The sound swelled until there could be no mistaking its source.

'Don R,' said Chalky, in disgust, as with a blast on his horn to the sentry at the gate the motor-cycle dispatch rider sped past on his errand, the sound of his passing drowned in the wave of restlessness that spread through the waiting pilots. Paul looked at his watch, calculating times and distances.

'He's got quite a bit of fuel left,' Peter murmured abstractedly. 'He's probably come down to have a look about underneath.'

'Probably,' agreed Paul.

Dick Fisher moved over to speak to Peter, enabling Paul to take advantage of the interruption and leave the group. Head bowed now, he made his way across the cinder apron to the hangars. The air mechanics had stopped work and were gathered just inside the hangar, out of the breeze. He walked thoughtfully to where his own machine was standing.

'You're not thinking of going up, sir, are you?' Flight Sergeant Moss, the squadron's technical senior NCO greeted him, 'It seems to be coming down properly over there.'

Paul had been almost unaware of the spots of rain but now he saw that the fields were beginning to lose their definition, a veil of drizzle hanging in ragged folds to create an amorphous fusion of earth and sky. A corporal and an air mechanic had detached themselves from the others. Paul recognised them as Evans' ground crew.

'Nothing from Mr Evans yet, sir?' The corporal put the question lightly but Paul detected the anxiety in his voice.

'We was expecting him back long before this, sir,' Hoskins put in, aggrieved.

It was Hoskins, Paul remembered, who had shown such perception in summing up the value of Andrew Barton, the pilot Paul had tried to pick up from Hunland. A bony individual, his liking for the local *vin ordinaire* kept him in constant conflict with the 'SWO-man', the squadron warrant officer. He was rarely out of squadron disciplinary orders and whenever Paul found himself on duty officer Hoskins was invariably among the defaulters. He was the scruffiest mechanic on the squadron, and without any doubt, one of the best. Had it not been for his record of bad conduct he would undoubtedly have been a sergeant by now, his technical reputation was so high. Equally, had it not been so high, the Corps would have got rid of him long since. Paul, like the majority of the pilots, had a lot of time for him.

'No news yet, I'm afraid. He's probably found a hole somewhere and dropped down for a spot of breakfast.'

The corporal nodded, none of his anxiety allayed.

'Wing want their effin' arses kicked,' Hoskins growled. The expletive, used in front of an officer, would have landed him in yet more trouble had the squadron warrant officer been within earshot but Paul was well aware that it too was a genuine measure of his concern for his pilot.

Flight Sergeant Moss stepped forward.

'Never fret, lads. Mr Evans's probably looking for a blower right now. He'll be all right. Meanwhile how about giving Captain Cowley's chaps a hand?'

Corporal Metcalfe and the crew had anticipated Paul's intentions and were already preparing to push his machine onto the apron.

'What do you reckon, sir?' asked the flight sergeant as the others hurried over to help.

Paul pursed his lips. 'I'd like to have seen him back sooner,' he admitted. His crew, he saw had just finished chocking the wheels.

'Run her up, sir?' asked Corporal Metcalfe. 'She's topped to the gunwales.'

'Please,' Paul requested. 'I'll be back in a few minutes.'

It was significant, he thought, that the group of pilots had drifted towards the squadron office. They had now been joined by pilots of the off-duty flights. As he neared the office the telephone began to ring and at once there was an expectant craning of heads. He pushed his way through the doorway. The clerk was just replacing the receiver. 'Ration returns,' he said simply.

Peter Mainwaring and Dick Fisher were intent upon the wall map, Peter measuring along a line with a rule, a grease pencil stuck behind his ear. Ralph Beatty and Paddy Rawlinson of 'B' Flight had arrived, unshaven, having just got up.

'Maybe he's put down into Beauquesne,' Peter conjectured. 'Or Vert-Galant.' Both were in line with Ken's intended track.

'Or Fienvillers, even,' suggested Dick.

'Give 'em a call,' said Paddy Rawlinson.

Mr Slattery, the squadron warrant officer, came out of the CO's office.

'I've just finished a general ring around, gentlemen,' he reported. 'None of the local squadrons have anything. We've asked the lads on the network to keep ferreting, but nothing yet.'

They heard the Gnome of Paul's machine misfire twice, coughing explosively, only to choke, and clank to a stop. There was a pause, and then it burst abruptly into life as all nine cylinders caught, roaring away to full revs where it steadied, adopting the characteristic blurt of the rotary, cutting and surging as Corporal Metcalfe brought it under control. Nobody spoke until the engine note stabilised as the fine adjustment was carried out. Then Ralph Beatty moved back from the window.

'You think it's worth having a look already?' he asked Paul.

Paul walked across to the map. 'He should have made contact by now.'

Peter Mainwaring indicated the narrow, fan-shaped segment he had drawn on the map. It originated at the aerodrome and splayed out on each side of the south-westerly course Ken had taken up, its far end bounded by an arc. Paul spanned the distance to the boundary arc with thumb and little finger. Against the current wind, twelve-minutes flying time at the most.

'If I came too,' suggested Peter.

Paul shook his head, the negation coinciding with the first flurry of rain against the office window. 'It's getting a bit thick out there,' he demurred, 'and with two of us floating about it'd be pretty fraught.'

'I suppose so.' Clearly Peter had already reached that conclusion but waiting was always the hardest option.

Dick Fisher was pointing to the map symbol for a wireless aerial. 'You'll have to watch this, Paul. A hundred and fifty feet above ground level. It's right on the edge of the sector.'

Paul peered closely, double-checking that the map was a British overprint with the height in feet, and not a French original showing metres. That sort of complication could make life difficult. And abrupt.

'You're not going to try getting above cloud, are you, Paul?' asked Paddy Rawlinson.

'I am not,' Paul told him categorically. 'I think about twenty minutes there and back, no more.'

'Are you going to tell Wing, sir?' Warrant Officer Slattery, had been busy on the phone again but now he leaned through the hatchway, the instrument still in his hand.

'It might be an idea,' Ralph Beatty put in.

Paul hesitated. The thought had been in his own mind. He completed signing-out and put down the pen. If Wing agreed to authorise the search, well and good, but if they refused ... 'Ring them once I'm airborne, Mr Slattery,' he said.

'Very good, sir.' The warrant officer pulled at his waxed moustache. 'And take care, sir.'

'Thank you,' Paul acknowledged.

He got airborne in another flurry of wind and drizzle, but it was evident that the precipitation had not yet become general and conditions were better than he had expected. As Ken had done thirty minutes before Paul circled back over the aerodrome, picking up his line to pass over the windsock on the same south-westerly heading, not climbing full-out but content to allow the machine to find its own way up towards the cloud.

The first foggy tentacles reached out for him at 600 feet but he let the aircraft continue its drift upwards. At 700 feet the flight commander's pennant on his outer interplane strut vanished momentarily in the mist and at that he eased down to 550 feet where he had good forward visibility and the best ground contact he was likely to get. In places the rain was falling vertically in thick dark columns like pillars in some vast cathedral nave, in others it hung in sheets, indistinguishable from the clouds. There was no definite horizon, just a leaden opaqueness where the fields lost colour and merged mistily into the drizzle. Beyond the rainy areas the visibility was quite good and what vague horizon existed receded as he flew towards it so that for the present he could see no problem in completing his search.

He skirted the first patch of rain, bumping through the eddies gusting from its base and noting with satisfaction that he could still see the earth through the downpour. There was a hamlet on the fringe of the precipitation, little more than two farmhouses with their buildings close together and a dirt road winding away into the mist. There was no movement on the road itself but a farmer trudged head-down behind his team on the far side of a field, as unimpressed by the de Havilland as he was by the weather. It was a reasonable bet that nothing untoward had disturbed his concentration recently.

Paul swung back on course, varying his height as the terrain undulated, circling every patch of woodland he came to, checking its perimeter and then descending spirally towards its core, peering down into its depths before switching on his engine and climbing up again towards the next.

Even this far from the front line there was more evidence of military activity than he had seen since the beginning of the July offensive: horse lines, vehicle parks, tented and hutted camps, equipment dumps; and in one instance a whole column of steel-helmeted infantry breaking ranks and scattering into the fields, heads down, at his approach; on a training march, he suspected, and welcoming the relaxation his appearance afforded them. At every actual military site any off-duty men looked up and waved; but casually, and this showed him clearly enough that they too had no news of Ken's machine.

Away from the main roads the farms and villages were dotted neatly in a landscape quite unvisited by war; a grey and depressing landscape in the present season, but ordered and well cared for, passively awaiting winter, and the ensuing spring. The fields were smaller and narrower than English fields and lacked the familiar patterned hedgerows, but there was the same enduring quality about the land, patiently accepting what Nature cared to bring and unlikely to be moved by any passing urgency of war.

A village appeared at the bottom of a slope running down to his left, and above the hill beyond it, rising out of a wood, Paul saw the slender framework of the wireless mast, its topmost sections shrouded in the mist. He eased to the right across his mapped-out sector, quartering the ground with anxious eyes. Now he was halfway along the search area and the weather was bidding fair to clamp down on further progress: already he was meeting the lowest base at just about 400 feet. There would be little flying today, he reflected, if everywhere was like this, and that would displease the powers that be.

He breasted a slight ridge, lifting over the poplar-lined road running along its crest – and saw at a glance, and with a sickening jolt of the senses, that his search was at an end.

Three khaki-drab motor lorries were parked close under the trees. Beyond them, fifty yards or so out into the field a crowd had gathered. Paul swept low overhead and saw faces lift towards him as he passed. It was a large, flat field, he noted, with a good surface, and he made a circuit at low level. On his second pass he saw that one of the roadside poplars had lost its top and he slowed to his minimum safe speed as he overflew the site, crabbing, stick holding off bank, to give himself a better view.

There was little left of Ken's machine, a scatter of bits a few feet beyond the trees and then the main pile around which the troops had gathered. Paul saw splintered spars and torn canvas but nothing that looked remotely like an aeroplane any more. There were no impact marks along the way, and no signs of fire. Men were busy at the very centre of the heap and none of them looked up as he passed. That must be where Ken was.

As he began his third pass an officer ran clear of the crowd, and judging his moment until Paul was only yards away, shook his head, sweeping his arms in front of his chest in a horizontal, criss-crossing motion, palms down. The message was unmistakable. Wash out! There was nothing to be done.

Dully, Paul climbed away, battling with his emotions. It was only what they had all expected, but now there was no longer any doubt, no lingering trace of hope. He made one final pass, rocking his wings in acknowledgement, and then set off back to base. There was nothing he could achieve by landing, except to run the risk of damaging his own machine, and besides, the others would be waiting. It was best to get back and report their common loss.

Five minutes later he touched down, having arrived at the aerodrome on the fringes of a veritable squall. He sprinted from the machine to the shelter of the squadron office, easing his way through the glum-faced crowd. His watch showed that he had been airborne for just fourteen minutes. Wing had got their weather check, at least.

The news had reached the squadron through the army net only minutes after Paul had taken off and Peter Mainwaring and a party of aircraftmen had already left for the crash scene. Meanwhile, in view of the weather, Wing had cancelled flying for all units for the rest of the morning. The SWO held out the phone.

'It's Major Hallam, sir. I told him you'd just landed.'

The concern in the major's voice was evident. Ken had not only been his senior flight commander but his personal friend. They had come to France in the early days, and along with Roly, the recording officer, had flown together through the Retreat, so that when the major had been given a squadron, he had applied for Ken as flight commander. Further, they knew each other's families, having been in the same regiment before the war, and their wives lived close to each other in Surrey. All this Paul knew, and heard in the major's voice, but there was no comfort he could offer, only that Ken had died quickly, and that there had been no fire.

But beyond concern for Ken, the circumstances gave the crash significance. Death and crashes were an everyday part of war flying and were accepted as such. Other accidents could be attributed to causes that had nothing directly to do with war but to carelessness or inexperience: landing badly, bouncing or misjudging the approach, stalling, or overstressing the machine; or getting lost. Others still came under the category of hazards inherent in aviation: the unexplained structural break-up, or engine failure in flight – both happily less common as reliability improved; or bad weather: fog, and heavy rain, and high winds.

But there was a different category still. Every airman wanted to see the boundaries of aviation pushed back, and each, within the limits of his own capability, applied his knowledge and his experience and his enthusiasm for flying to furthering the quest, venturing on every opportunity that presented itself just that little further into the unknown in a science – or pastime – scarcely fifteen years old. The problem was that such advancement – like the creeping artillery barrage of recent unhappy memory – all too frequently outpaced that which had to follow on.

Engines, for example, were being built to carry machines to 22,000 feet, and higher. And yet after patrols at only 15,000 feet perfectly fit young fliers would habitually land with headaches, or filled with an elation akin to drunkenness. Then again people were even now talking about the 200 mph scout. And yet there were times already, on pulling out of steep dives at only just over 100 miles an hour, when the vision drained away and the mind lapsed into momentary unconsciousness. So it was that progress was made; but so too was the stage set for accidents.

A few years earlier the bogey had been the sideslip, until Lieutenant Parke, whirling out of control in a nose-down sideslip and facing certain death, had decided not to continue trying to pull away from the swiftly-nearing ground, but to push the nose even more steeply towards it instead – and had recovered. Now, even though the mechanism of the spinning nose-dive was still not fully understood, and although pilots were still failing to recover from nose-down spins and killing themselves, others of their breed were looking towards the crossing of the Atlantic and to girdling the world with air lanes. Machines had flown non-stop for more than twenty-four hours, and speed and height records were being broken every few weeks. Aeroplanes had been flown carrying enormous numbers of passengers, and already cartoonists, at least, saw ocean liners giving pride of place to liners of the sky.

There were the ever-present problems of taking-off and landing in poor visibility, or in strong winds; in landing over obstructions on too-small, too-narrow fields with no way of steepening the glide without increasing the speed, and with no effective means of stopping short having landed. But looming large above all others was the problem of maintaining control when orientation was lost in cloud, or in bad visibility, or on a dark night. It was a problem that stood in the way of progress. And because Ken had crashed in attempting to remain orientated in cloud, and because it had killed him, and because they knew it for a problem that had to be solved, his crash became significant in its own right.

'A sad business, sir,' Paul agreed down the line.

Beside him Ralph Beatty waved the assembled officers and NCOs to silence. From the butts came the stutter of a Lewis as a de Havilland had its gun sighted, and closer to hand outside the hangars, a Gnome roared into life, and ran for a few minutes, as an adjustment was made. The life of the aerodrome had not come to a complete stop despite the accident and the foul weather.

'It looks as if Ken clipped the top of a tree and began to break up, hitting the ground vertically about fifty feet further on.' Paul was forced to raise his voice to get his message across, the assembled audience reacting to this first witness-confirmation of the crash each after his own manner, some shaken, some embarrassed, most set-featured. Later there would even be grisly humour.

'Returning low, perhaps?' the major queried, his voice threadlike down the line.

'From tree to impact, that'd be the wrong direction, sir,' said Paul. 'Besides, there was no sliding. It looked as if he came down in a pile having zoomed. Low-flying you'd lift up well before the ridge; it would be too steep a pull-up otherwise. At least, that's how it struck me.'

'I see.' The major's voice was hollow. 'Well, we'll see what Mainwaring comes up with. The troops might even produce a sensible witness. Although that's asking a bit much. Anyway,' his voice strengthened, 'I hope to be back by six.'

He broke off, and when he continued his voice was hoarse and low. 'Thank you, Paul, for going out after him. Perhaps you'd have his batman gather his things.'

The court of inquiry was presided over by the Officer Commanding No.32 Squadron, a major newly appointed to replace Major Rees, whose Victoria Cross – awarded following his epic attack on four machines of a ten-machine formation on the first of July – had been gazetted less than two weeks before. Major Rees – who had been sent home, his leg wound having proved more serious than first reports had suggested – had been a highly respected squadron commander and a very experienced DH2 pilot, and had done much to allay the early fears surrounding the machine. The new major was, by all accounts, proving a worthy successor. On the appointed morning, he drove down from Treizennes, getting the inquiry under way with the minimum of fuss.

Peter's party had established that Ken had lost both right wings in slicing through the top ten feet of a poplar, that his aircraft had next struck the ground thirty-eight yards further on, with no sign of forward motion. The detached right wings had been found, together with the severed treetop, some fifteen feet from the tree. Various other pieces of debris had come to earth before the final impact point but none beyond it, making it certain that the machine's final plunge had been almost vertical. A subsequent strip-down examination of the engine showed that it had been running at full power up to the moment of impact with the ground. There was no other sign of malfunction.

As for witnesses, four army vehicles, it transpired, had been halted for a break by the roadside and the troops had been sitting around, brewing up and smoking, when the crash occurred. They had run to the scene but on finding that nothing could be done to aid the pilot, the officer in charge had sent a vehicle to report. Five of the witnesses were present at the inquiry, including the officer who had signalled to Paul. As was to be expected, their accounts varied widely in detail, particularly since few of them had ever seen an aeroplane up close before. The essentials, however, were clear.

They had heard a 'whooshing' noise in the clouds, although one, a driver, claimed to have heard an engine shut off before the sound became pronounced. The machine had broken cloud very low down and was turning quickly around its nose 'like a dart', going straight for the ground. Then it had come towards them, and four testified, when asked, that the pilot had been sitting 'rightside up'. At about the same time the engine had come on; one soldier had seen a cloud of blue smoke and still maintained that the machine was on fire. Some, watching from the far side of the trees, thought the machine had landed, for it disappeared below the level of the ridge, but they realised their mistake when it appeared again, showing the whole of its underbelly as it soared over their heads.

All expressed amazement at the way the wings had come off 'like paper' when they touched the tree. They had expected an aeroplane to be much stronger and to brush through the thin upper branches like a lorry through brush. Losing the right wing had not stopped the machine from flying though, they were all agreed upon this. Indeed it had seemed to climb to an enormous height, immediately above them. And then it had stopped, and hung there, before simply dropping to the ground in the middle of the field.

Medical evidence was produced to show that Ken Evans was killed instantly on impact; that there had been nothing wrong with him prior to hitting the ground.

'It looks as if you were right, Cowley,' said the president as he pushed back the last of the papers. 'Evans got disorientated in cloud, lost control, and either spun or got into a tight spiral. He broke cloud still rotating but although he regained control his heading on recovery was such that he was facing the ridge head on. He hadn't time to turn and had no option but to try and zoom over it. Unfortunately he was already too close and hit the poplar on the way.'

'Just for the lack of ten feet,' said Paul bitterly.

'Or ten degrees,' the president nodded. 'If he'd only come out on a different heading, over flat ground, or where the ridge was lower.'

'If,' said Major Hallam heavily, '*If*. But then, isn't it always.'

Which brought a general nodding of heads.

'We can discount low-flying,' said the president. 'And the machine itself is beyond suspicion which,' he inclined his head towards Major Hallam, 'we never doubted for a moment. There will have to be a finding, but I think we'll be able to put it down to active-service conditions. Provided –' he looked up from under his eyebrows, 'that as pilots we know where the trouble really lies. We can't fly in fog, and we can't penetrate really thick cloud. What we'll be able to do this time next year, is neither here nor there. For now anyone who tries it's a BF.'

But the understanding in his eyes took away the censure in his words.

'The sort of bloody fool,' murmured Major Hallam, 'that takes on ten Huns with one De Hav.'

The president acknowledged this with a smile. They all knew that Major Rees – VC – was a close friend. 'I suppose so,' he conceded. 'And the same sort who must try to match the De Hav against the new

Albatros and Halberstadt. Losses are bound to increase. That's yet another reason why a man like Evans will be so sorely missed.' He gathered the rest of his papers and handed them over to the corporal clerk to place in a file. Then he pushed back his chair and stood up. 'Gentlemen,' he said to the assembled members, now on their feet around the table, 'let's all learn from this tragedy.'

The bad weather settled in for the next four days, intensifying the gloom that hung over the squadron; days of blustery winds and rain and low cloud, a weather pattern that was bound to persist until drier air moved in to clear the skies. Around the field the ground had become a quagmire, the vehicle tracks brimming with rainwater that was reluctant to drain away. Even tons of cinders proved unequal to the task of preserving the manoeuvring area in any fit state. Paul wondered what it must be like up in the trenches. If this was a fair taste of what was to come then autumn and winter seemed set to prove very unpleasant indeed.

Various outings were organised to fill in time, with visits to nearby towns, and to other squadrons and to army units both in and out of the line. There were football matches, deemed more suited to the state of the ground than cricket, and a boxing tournament in which Hoskins, released from defaulters' parade for the occasion, demolished a bruiser from the London-Scottish with a venom that suggested that he found in the bout some gratifying release from emotions pent-up since the loss of his pilot.

There were binges in the evening, and parties, but it was an unwelcome cessation from flying for it gave people time to brood. It was a time when the flight commanders had to be particularly alert. For many men — most, perhaps — it was a time for sitting around and playing cards, or listening to the gramophone, or simply sitting back daydreaming, or gazing out of the window at the incessant rain and wondering if the weather would ever change. But it was a time when a man might withdraw too far inside himself; when war-taut nerves might suffer too much stress. Some went walking in the fields and orchards, or pottered around their machines until they made a nuisance of themselves around the hangar where the aircraftmen too found time hanging heavily on their hands.

Another football match was organised, but cancelled for lack of interest, and tempers became short. Hoskins, the hero of the hour after his boxing triumph, was returned from Amiens – rather the worse for wear – by the Military Police. Having resisted arrest he was lucky not to be in detention, but the moment he arrived back he became involved in a brawl with another aircraftman over a mislaid screwdriver and both finished up on defaulters. Depression settled like a pall over the whole squadron and despite all the efforts of the flight commanders and the senior NCOs, morale plummeted.

It was useless to compare their lot with that of the troops only a few miles away, suffering the same weather but in flooded ditches, for each fighting-arm had its own tensions. An operational squadron was as tightly wound as a watch spring and when there was no flying the unrelieved strain quickly became intolerable both for those who flew and for those who normally kept them flying.

On the third morning Major Hallam carried out a full inspection of the squadron, starting with the aircraft sheds and continuing through the quarters, the stores, the vehicle park, and all the various messes, squelching through the mud where the cinders had disappeared. He began the inspection grim-faced and as it progressed his displeasure became more and more evident. He made no comment as he went his round, but his tour completed, he called all the officers and senior NCOs into one of the Bessonneau hangars and addressed them in chilling tones.

'Gentlemen,' he began, as rain drummed against the canvas sides of the shed, 'in 1914, it was in weather just like this that the Germans made their breakthrough.' He looked around the assembled throng. 'Some of you will remember those days.' He scanned their faces and picked out a man here and there. 'You, Sergeant Corbett, and you, Sergeant McKenny.' Beside him, Paul noticed, Roly nodded. He would remember. Mr Slattery, rigid at the CO's heels, remembered too.

'For weeks on end,' the CO went on, 'we never spent two nights in the same place. Wherever we settled, the Germans were on our heels, and it was, "bags packed and off we go".' He paused. 'There is no reason at all why the same thing might not occur again. But,' his voice rose, 'from what I have just seen I don't think we'd be ready for it, or for doomsday itself. A few days of inactivity and we have fallen into a state of sloth.' He looked at his watch. 'It is now eleven ack emma. At two pip emma I shall carry out a second inspection. Gentlemen, if at that time I am not satisfied that my squadron is no longer stagnating in lethargy, then I shall order a practice move.'

There was a gasp of dismay, followed by a sotto voce outburst of scandalised comment. He allowed it to continue for a short while and then held up his hand. 'Gentlemen, you have three hours.'

Amid a deathly silence he left the hangar, followed by Roly and Mr Slattery.

Nobody was in the least doubt as to what a practice move would entail. There would be the same upheaval that had accompanied the squadron's most recent move, south from Ypres – except that the equipment would simply be driven in a circle and then put back again.

'He can't do that,' agonized one of the pilots. 'Can he?'

'It's absolutely bloody pointless,' burst out another. 'What'll it prove? What good will it do?'

What it could do, and did, was to set the whole squadron on its head as the senior NCOs reported back to their sections and told them of the CO's dictum. There was an immediate and furious reaction to the news, leaving officers and men alike sulking and scowling. It was unfair, and uncalled for, and childish, an unwarranted insult to their intelligence! They were not a bunch of footsloggers, but RFC: clerks, and technicians, and pilots; and they did not deserve such treatment! Nor would they stand for it. And when Wing heard what the CO had done to them ...

There was much cursing and muttering with animated gesturing and figurative slamming of doors. But hot resentment was overcoming apathy and officers and men, grudgingly at first, but then with better will as they swore their anger away, threw themselves into their various tasks, mainly of a housewifery nature, and wry laughter began to take the place of fury. People began to skylark as the job got under way.

'A practice move? Not effin' likely,' Paul heard Hoskins telling his late opponent as they staggered beneath a pile of oily rags towards a bonfire. 'Not if I can bleedin' help it.'

The bustle and confusion went on until one-thirty when a halt was called and the men repaired to spick-and-span billets to tidy themselves up after their labours. The hangars were spotless, the machines glistened, the shed floors were clear of the slightest trace of oil or waste, and even the sky seemed a trifle brighter.

At two precisely, Major Hallam left the squadron office and began his second tour of inspection, stepping dry-footed across cinders newly-raked across the mud, his keen eye missing nothing as he made his way from section to section. Nothing had really changed with the weather but the mood of the squadron had totally altered, and even the rain could no longer dampen their spirits. There were cheerful grins whenever a word was passed and at the end of the inspection, when the CO declared himself satisfied with the turn-out, there was a spontaneous cheer. That evening all who could be spared from duty piled into any available transport and made for Amiens and a glorious binge.

Hoskins and his fellow-in-crime, as defaulters, were preparing to carry out picquet duty as Paul paid a final visit to his machine before setting out.

'Do you think the Old Man would really have done it, make us move?' he heard Hoskins's companion ask.

'Course he would,' came the reply. 'But he knew fine well he wouldn't 'ave to. Cunning old sod.'

Chapter Ten

During the last weeks of August and on into mid-September it became evident that the build up for the next phase in the battle was under way. It was like a repeat of the build-up for the First of July offensive and effectively, on just such a scale, a fact readily appreciated by the airmen as they watched the rear areas become steadily more glutted with all the placement of men, machines, and materiel necessary for the prosecution of modern warfare. Vast new areas of hutted and tented camps sprang up overnight, yet more railway sidings and spurs spirited themselves away into the cover of woods, convoys of lorries were discovered parked beneath camouflage netting along roadside groves, while heavy artillery edged steadily closer under cover of darkness despite the increase in captive balloons which had been resurrected on the German side of the lines.

Columns of fresh troops arrived by the trainload until at times the airmen wondered dispassionately where they were all coming from. Few, however, doubted where they were going to: where else, if not to their graves? It was hideous, but familiarity – and the detachment of several hundred feet of altitude – made many airmen cynical. Yet as they skimmed overhead at anything up to a hundred miles an hour even the least cynical among them turned a jaundiced eye upon the growing concentration of horse-lines as the cavalry were moved up yet again.

Late one rainy evening, returning from Amiens, the squadron's tender halted to give passage to a unit of the Deccan Horse. The turbaned lancers, with steel helmets slung and heads hunched into caped shoulders, turned their bedraggled horses through the muddy entrance to their lines. Back in mid-July, in company with the Dragoon Guards – and with the help of an aeroplane –, they had carried an advanced position with lance and sabre, holding it until the infantry had caught up and relieved them. It was hailed as the first blooding of the cavalry since the early months of the war: and how they had bled!

'God, when you remember what things are like in India, what must they be thinking of all this?' wondered one of the pilots.

'What must Haig be thinking of all this,' returned another. 'Lances and guidons and gas capes against high-explosives, barbed-wire, and machine guns.'

As the second week of September drew to a close there were ever more frequent calls on the squadron, as an Army-Wing squadron, to carry out long fighting patrols aimed not only at preventing the German scouts from interfering with bombing raids against their re-supply routes, but also at preventing them from clearing the way for their own reconnaissance machines.

Behind this screen of Army-Wing squadron activity, the Corps-Wing squadrons, like No.70, were busy from dawn to dusk, spotting, ranging, and photographing every inch of the new line running south-east from Thiepval.

Thiepval itself still showed no sign of falling, although the Leipzig Salient had been snipped off. Moquet Farm – now, perhaps inevitably, 'Mucky Farm' –, the strongpoint Paul had disturbed, continued to pass from hand to bloody hand, while High Wood, now of murderous notoriety, stood obstinately half-and-half across the line. Running further south-east still, Delville Wood – Devil Wood – had been taken at enormous cost. But from Thiepval to the north not an inch had so far transferred hands.

Looking down as he passed overhead their ground-hugging machines, Paul could vouch for the fact that the neighbouring Corps-Wing squadrons were invariably in evidence whenever the weather was in any way fit. Intriguingly, nor was their activity restricted to daytime, for as the momentum grew so they were tasked to fly at night as well, droning up and down the lines as directed by Brigade, although whether to disturb the sleep of the shell-weary German troops or simply to demonstrate the RFC's air superiority by night as well as by day nobody in the Army-Wing squadrons seemed able to say.

As an Army-Wing unit on the prowl the Squadron had several sharp clashes with enemy scouts, notably a fight over Flers in which 'A' Flight shot down one of six Roland scouts it encountered just at the end of its patrol when petrol was getting short. Next day, as if to balance this success one of the 'B' Flight pilots was attacked by a lone and obviously very audacious Fokker monoplane which nobody saw until it had carried out its attack and dived away into the shelter of a cloud. The de Havilland's engine was put out of commission but the pilot was able to glide safely back to base. On landing, however, he crashed badly and, although unhurt himself, damaged his aircraft beyond repair.

The renewed offensive opened on the fifteenth of September and found the squadron busy from first light. For the last two patrols of the day 'C' Flight flew in the high position at 14,000 feet and whether because the intense patrolling was beginning to tell on him, or because of the enervating effects of high-altitude air-sickness, Paul found that he was suffering severely from the cold. It seemed to require an ever-greater effort of will to concentrate on the job in hand while floating suspended in space with hands and feet numb and eyebrows frosting despite his face-mask and a liberal coating of Vaseline. His eyes were sore and prickly but he was loth to use his goggles, fearing, as always, that they would cut down his vision.

At times now, he was aware, he had to literally force himself to turn in his seat to carry out his periodic check of the other members of his flight. He found it difficult too to keep a proper sense of perspective. Once on the ground he soon felt more at ease and obtained some doubtful comfort by noticing that the other, younger, members of the flight seemed to be suffering just as much as he was. Doubtful comfort though, because as a flight commander he had responsibilities they did not have, minimal as these might be. Moreover, he was chronically tired, for there was little respite between patrols and by the time the last machine was put away at night he was always more than ready for his bed.

Throughout that first day of the renewed offensive the weather had been good and the squadron had been able to provide a maximum effort with all three flights combining in a stepped-up formation to carry out a whole series of offensive patrols east of Bapaume towards Cambrai in an effort to smother the aerodromes of Lagnicourt, Vélu, and Bertincourt. Anti-aircraft fire was intense but they saw only scattered signs of enemy air activity and despite several long-distance chases they were unable to bring any German scouts to bay.

Employed as they were to the north of the new offensive, and ranging several miles over the lines, the squadron saw little of the ground fighting, although the reports seemed to suggest that considerable progress had been made in the south. Casualties were reportedly heavy but that had become so normal a part of war on the Somme that it raised little comment.

On one occasion, emerging from the latrine during a refuelling stop away from base following a distant patrol, Paul found the rest of the flight gathered around a contact-patrol pilot who had just forced-landed after being damaged by ground fire. The man was evidently highly elated at the way things were going generally and simply buzzing with excitement at the introduction of what whispers had been referring to for some time past as 'crawling strongpoints': a variant term which had intrigued Paul.

'They're called "tanks" and they're incredible!' the pilot was enthusing as Paul came within earshot, 'They only crawl along but nothing seems to stop them. One of our chaps saw three of them in Flers, two knocking houses down on the outskirts and one just walking up the main street. But I saw them myself, trampling the wire and taking no notice at all of the machine guns.'

'How many were there?' asked Paul.

'Well not that many,' admitted the pilot. 'But they were certainly making things hum.'

The others pressed around him anxious for more details of the new weapon and he was only too glad to oblige.

'They've got caterpillar tracks and were crossing trenches and pushing walls aside, with the infantry simply following on behind. They've got guns too. The one I saw had two cannon, one on either side, but they say some have machine guns.'

'Then there's nothing to stop them,' burst out Simpson excitedly. 'They can just roll up the German flank.'

For the first time the visitor looked a little doubtful. 'Well, I'm not sure of that. During my last job I saw one over on its side – direct hit, I imagine. And there was another halfway across an open field – maybe it had broken down, but the guns had it ranged, and it was on fire when I left.' He brightened up. 'But how they work! I saw one rooting away at a machine-gun pit like a truffle hound.'

The others clamoured for further information but the pilot knew little more, although he was able to clear up one mystery.

'The night before these tanks were sent in some of our two-seaters were up half the night patrolling their approach routes to cover up the noise of their engines.'

Paul grunted. So the recent night patrols had not been just to keep the German troops awake. Yet, impressed as he was by the enthusiasm engendered by this first-hand report, he found himself remembering the technical shortcomings that had been so evident when he had chauffeured General Cousins to the tank trial in Lincoln.

Nor were his doubts allayed in succeeding days, especially after a staff officer told him just how few tanks had been sent into action, for he remembered the passion with which General Cousins had pleaded that the new weapon should be reserved until it could be introduced into a battle in such numbers that it would prove decisive. As things were, the tanks seemed to have achieved only local successes – and now the element of surprise had gone for ever. Yet the task of achieving a breakthrough, as Paul could see for himself, faced the staff with what might well prove an unfathomable problem, the German defences in their amazing complexity and in-depth strength stretching back for between three and five miles beyond the present front line.

It soon became clear, however, that the offensive which had opened in mid-September – unlike that of July the First, and those lesser shows subsequent to it – had made substantial progress. High Wood, brooding perhaps – or possibly even gloating – over the appalling losses suffered within its bounds, was now firmly in British hands, although tanks had been unable to penetrate the tumbled chaos of its interior. On the right, nonetheless, and showing what might have been, tanks proved instrumental in achieving the capture of Switch Trench – between High Wood and 'Devil' Wood – and indeed of Flers itself, when seven out of the ten deployed had not only penetrated the defences but spent the whole day cruising around and causing havoc.

Even so, Paul found, exactly how much the tanks were judged to have contributed to the success of the offensive depended upon who was telling the tale, some divisions swearing by them, others at them. What they would have achieved had they been deployed in hundreds rather than in scores, he decided, must always remain a matter for conjecture. Of one thing he was certain, General Cousins and his adherents would have no doubts at all that a golden, one-off opportunity had been simply frittered away.

Nevertheless, people did sense that a battle had at last been joined which might well result in a positive conclusion before the end of the year. For by the close of the month Martinpuich, Courcelette, Flers, Lesboeufs, and Morval were in British hands, together with Combles – where a handover to the French had been effected –, and even Thiepval was coming under pressure. Perhaps, after all, there would be a reward for all the incessant carnage? Perhaps there would, allowed the airmen, always provided the Autumn weather held!

But the weather did not hold, indeed from the eighteenth low cloud and heavy rain had begun to make conditions difficult both on the ground and in the air. Where the Flying Services were concerned it was the old story, nothing could be expected to remain stable for very long, their 'lines' were fluid and infinitely variable and there were always changes in the wind. News of the latest came to Paul on the day the weather also altered for the worse. The news came in the way such news so often comes, a whisper from the orderly room, an overheard word on the headquarters net, a query from a shopkeeper, an excited buzz across the table in a café in *la Rue des Trois Cailloux* in Amiens. Nobody knew anything at all, and then suddenly everyone knew, and no one bothered any longer about the source. Robinson knew.

He was pottering about the hut when Paul returned from patrol, lingering, Paul realised later, both to impart the news and to get Paul's reaction at first hand.

'Awful business about those bom-bing planes, sir.' Robinson always sounded both Bs in the word 'bombing'.

'What business was that?' Paul asked dutifully.

'It seems they was bombing Cambrai this morning, twenty of them. BEs. And a great crowd of Fokkers came out of nowhere and shot 'em all down.'

Paul considered the news, subsiding onto the bed and gratefully accepting the batman's assistance with his flying boots. As Paul had anticipated, Robinson had indeed found a contact in a nearby army cobblers and the slash in the right one was now barely visible. Idly Paul fingered the residual scar in the leather. That shell fragment had so nearly taken away his calf!

'Where did you hear all this?' he asked finally.

It didn't really hang right; rumours rarely did in their raw state, but the gist of the thing seemed plausible enough. Certainly, this could be what they had all been anticipating for months, and actually waiting for in the weeks since the German Air Service had first shown its renewed mettle.

'Oh, it's all over the place, sir. They were from further north.'

'BEs, you say, bombing Cambrai?'

The BE2c was slow and stable: too slow and far too stable by all accounts; indeed Paul doubted if they would cruise at more than 80 mph. Cambrai was a normal enough target but they would be a long time over enemy territory, and longer still coming back with the wind against them. Certainly it would feel longer. They may well have been unescorted, too, for it was becoming policy on the longer-distance jobs for the bombers to set out alone on their tasks while the scouts aimed to hold the enemy fighting scouts over their bases and miles away from the raiders. As a concept, Paul agreed with it wholeheartedly, but not with the types currently employed as bombing machines.

Not that a BE2c formation would be totally defenceless. Each machine had only one Lewis, admittedly, but the observer in the forward cockpit was able to move his gun to a variety of positions, choosing the one which gave him the best field of fire as an attack developed. True, he had to be careful firing back over the head of his pilot towards the tailplane, likewise forwards over the top of the propeller. Then too he was completely blind to attacks from underneath and from behind. But the formation would be holding station, with every machine providing covering fire in protection of another's blind spots. There was no doubt, however, that the now antiquated BE2c – the original 'Fokker Fodder' – was nowhere near up to the job.

Paul was dubious too about the attackers being Fokkers, for by what Robinson was saying the hostiles had attacked in large numbers and it seemed unlikely that Fokker monoplanes would have been regrouped into packs when they were outclassed by so many current Allied scouts. Unless they were the new Fokker biplanes No.24 Squadron had reported recently?

'Which squadron was it?' he asked.

Robinson gave Paul's tunic a final flick with a clothes brush. 'Eleven Squadron, they say.'

'Eleven don't have BE2cs,' Paul pointed out. 'They're all scouts. And a mixed bag.' But No.11 Squadron were off to the north, all right. An Army-Wing squadron with Three Brigade. At Le Hameau, up near Arras.

Robinson handed him his shoes and Paul smiled appreciatively; a lot of spit-and-polish energy had gone into that shine. No, not Le Hameau, he corrected himself, but Savy, further north. Fees and Nieuports. They had been one of the first to get Nieuports, he remembered, back in the spring. He picked up his cap and Robinson took a rearward pace, giving him an appraising once-over.

'I'll have a word with Mr Clarke before dinner,' Paul said, as Robinson, satisfied that all was well with his officer's turnout, and equally satisfied with the reaction to his news, held open the door for him.

Roly was working on the programme for next day's jobs and carried on doing so until Paul had finished checking the patrol report he had left for typing. Then he passed his pen across the desk, spreading his elbows to ease his shoulders.

'Tired?' asked Paul, signing the report.

'Old age, old boy,' the other told him, and they both grinned.

Roly made a final addition to the flying programme and looked up again, pushing aside his papers. 'What's on your mind, Paul?'

'What do you know about a fight up north this morning, Eleven Squadron and some BEs?'

Roly picked up the paperwork, added Paul's report, and passed the whole pile through the hatchway.

'Bad new travels fast, doesn't it? Mind you, good news probably travels just as fast, only there's never so much of it.' He opened a drawer and pulled out a file. 'Not this morning. Yesterday. The seventeenth.' He crossed to the wall map and pointed to the north of the squadron area. 'They were raiding the railway station just here, at Marcoing.'

His finger was indicating a place just south-west of Cambrai. Paul nodded acknowledgement. Both the station and its junction were key points in the railway system which brought German supplies and reinforcements to the Somme.

'There are loose ends,' Roly went on, 'but it seems that they sent out eight BEs from Number Twelve Squadron at Avesnes to do the bombing, with six FEs from Eleven Squadron to look after them.'

Paul waited.

'The BEs dropped their bombs,' continued the recording officer, 'but then, as they were leaving the target, they were set upon by some biplane scouts they'd seen circling overhead. Either Fokkers or Albatroses – one s, or two, or should it be Albatri?' He did not wait for illumination but went on: 'Biplanes, anyway. Apparently it was something of a massacre. It sounds a bit exaggerated – we'll get the real story later, I suppose. Anyway they say all six scouts were lost.'

'*All* of them?' cried Paul, incredulous. 'What, *six* of them?'

'And some of the bombers too.'

'How many?' pressed Paul.

'First reports said four but now they're saying it was three. There's not much doubt about the Fees though.'

'But that's what, nine aircraft?' said Paul. '*Nine*? I just don't believe it.' Don't want to believe it, he amended inwardly.

'It sounds unbelievable,' agreed Roly. 'Let's hope it is.' The door of the inner office opened and Major Hallam came into the room.

'Ah! you're there, Paul.' The major turned to Roly. 'I've just had another call from Duffy at Brigade. I heard you telling Paul. The majority of the Huns were Albatros Scouts and very hot. Nobody seems to know just how many there were, but apparently halfway through the fight more turned up. Survivors estimate about twenty Huns all told.'

'All Albatros Scouts?' Roly asked.

'Apparently not, but they couldn't tell me what they were, except that they were biplanes.'

Paul had accepted the news now and his mind was wrestling with the ramifications of the event. This had to be what they had all been anticipating!

'You say they circled. Waited until the BEs had actually dropped their bombs?'

The CO nodded. 'Yes, it doesn't make sense, does it? The whole purpose should have been to stop them reaching their target.'

'Unless ...' Paul mused.

Roly slid the file across the desk.

'Roly has a theory,' the major explained. 'And it looks as if Intelligence have come up with the same thing.' He opened the file and flicked over some of the enclosures. There were several newspaper cuttings among them. 'Look at this.'

It was a cutting from *The Times*, date-lined Amsterdam, June 20.

Roly skimmed through it aloud: 'Captain Boelcke, reported to have been killed ... is in good health. He says we are brave and tenacious sportsmen. German papers, he states, speak badly of British airmen so often brought down behind German lines. He says, on the contrary, that is the best proof of their intrepidity.'

Paul smiled grimly, remembering reading the passage while he was on leave. It had been interpreted by many as damning with faint praise the RFC's policy of offensiveness at all costs.

'Yes, I saw that.'

'Well that's virtually the last we heard of Boelcke.' Roly eyed him. 'Intelligence now think the German High Command took him off active service in case he went the way of Immelmann.'

'With morale in mind, of course.'

'Well now, since about three weeks back his name has appeared in several German communiqués.'

'There was a De Hav lost a couple of days ago,' said Paul.

'And that's not all.' Roly turned back to the last addition to the file. 'The De Hav was Boelcke's twentieth kill. Yet here it's talking of his twenty-*fifth*. There's no doubt he's back. And operating on the British front.'

'Running a special unit?'

'One whose sole purpose,' said the CO, 'seems to be to shoot down other aeroplanes regardless of their role.'

'Because they didn't bother upsetting the bombing,' Paul supplied, 'just got into an attacking position. A sort of Independent Command of fighting-aeroplanes with Boelcke heavily involved.' Across the yard the mess corporal began to beat upon the suspended shell-case to indicate that dinner was served. 'There was a Twenty-Four Squadron report some days ago.'

The CO and Roly exchanged wry grins. Roly reached for another file, already open. 'I said you'd cotton on to that.'

The file was open at a Flying Corps communiqué dated the last day of August, just over two weeks before. DH2s of No.24 Squadron, it recorded, had encountered some new single-seater biplane types that had, seemingly, totally outclassed them. They had described the new machines as having large and rounded tails and streamlined propeller bosses. Nobody had known what to make of the report at the time. But something different had obviously been let loose at Marcoing.

'The new Albatros at last?' Paul hazarded, with a long release of breath.

'It makes you wonder, doesn't it?' Roly replied. He reached around to tap at his injured back. 'As for returning to flying,' he grinned thinly, 'all of a sudden I'm feeling all over poorly.'

The figures for the actual casualties suffered at Marcoing gradually filtered through: six RFC machines had been lost; two of No.12 Squadron's BEs and four of No.11 Squadron's FEs. This may have been the first sign that things had indeed changed, but there were plenty more on the way.

The squadron's initial exposure to the new order came when 'B' Flight dived to attack two Albatros single-seaters. Instead of running for home the Germans zoomed up, guns spitting, leaving 'B' Flight more than a little rattled, as their leader, Ralph Beatty, readily admitted.

'I expected a chase. Not to find the buggers coming at me with mouthfuls of guns.'

'Proper put us off our stroke,' confirmed Paddy Rawlinson, his deputy. 'Great cloud of blue smoke as they put on power, but instead of disappearing into it they just lifted their ugly great noses and started spitting.'

'They out-turned us, outmanoeuvred us, outclimbed us, and outgunned us,' Ralph took up the tale once more.

Paddy nodded. 'Tied us up in knots.'

'Then three Nieuports came along, and we sloped off,' said Ralph.

'Haven't lost any Nieuports today, have we?' asked Paddy innocently.

'But you were eight to their two,' pressed Simpson.

'And still we managed to get away,' Paddy boasted.

The very next day 'B' Flight, again – as if singled out –, came upon what they reported as a lone Halberstadt, evidently of the latest mark, and cautiously stalked it, suspicious of decoys. Instead, the Halberstadt too, turned towards them and proceeded to lead them all around the skies, simply climbing away at the end with a waggle of his wings leaving them roaring in frustration.

'I'd have rammed the bugger,' snarled Paddy furiously, 'if I could have caught him.'

'Faster than the Albatros?' asked Paul.

Ralph Beatty shook his head. 'It's difficult to say. It's a lovely looking, slim thing, but it doesn't seem that powerful. And yet, as Paddy said, when he finally let us go we were left standing, like until then he'd only been using part-throttle.'

Paddy Rawlinson turned to the clerk. 'Corporal, get me Major General Trenchard on the line.' He turned to the others. 'I'm going to use my influence with "Boom" to get myself a private Nieuport like Ball's, then I'll show 'em.'

The corporal, who had merely grinned and carried on typing out the combat reports, looked up. 'They say the general has asked for naval Pups.'

'High time,' said Paddy. 'If the Hun keeps up this aggressive business then sooner or later he's going to bloody kill someone.'

Prophetic words, for next day 'A' Flight came back badly shot up and missing one of their number. They had been escorting some BEs when they were set upon by what was afterwards confirmed to be units of Boelcke's newly-instituted *Jagdstaffel* – *Jasta* – chaser-hunter squadron. There had been five enemy machines, they had reported, all new D-type Albatros Scouts, already said to be the most deadly scout yet built, very fast, very manoeuvrable, very handy – and from this encounter evidently, very aggressively handled.

The DH2s had done their best to protect the BEs but had found themselves so hopelessly outclassed that they had rarely been able to put in an attack of their own. True, their tactics had enabled the BEs, fighting spiritedly, to withdraw in good order but with their job only half done. Then, as the defending force had approached the lines, with the BEs diving for home, three Rolands had come down out of the sun. They had kept on going but had left a stricken de Havilland to trail fire and smoke before breaking apart and scattering its burning wreckage across the German lines south-east of Serre.

Understandably it was a shaken 'A' Flight who trooped into the office to make their report. Peter Mainwaring felt the loss of one of his men keenly, and blamed himself for not having seen the Rolands. The fact that his flight had escorted their charges safely home did nothing to ease his mind and although, in accordance with Major General Trenchard's long-established rule of 'No empty place at breakfast', a replacement pilot arrived that night, it was clear that Peter would grieve long and deeply for a gap so filled.

That evening Paul received a letter addressed to '*Le Capitaine Paul, RFC, Escadrille DH2, Amiens*'. The army postal branch had done well, for the frank was only two days old. The letter was from Jacques Delcamp, the French pilot of the Amiens bar. Delcamp wished Paul well and wondered if, by now, he had met the new Albatros. Jacques was in good health and had shot down two more *Boche* and was now an official ace: although he reported an ongoing squabble – 'among those who cared' – over how many downed Huns gave ace status. He had only found time for one flight over his home near Havrincourt Wood and he chided Paul for the British army's failure to break-through and re-unite him with his fiancée. And would Paul please ask young men in DH2s to desist from attacking his Spad when he was in the course of such a home visit, there being quite enough *Boche* to go around?'

It was a chatty letter, lightly-written, and veined with a fine thread of cynical humour, and Paul was pleasantly surprised to receive it. For one thing it cleared up any mystery attaching to Winthrop's trespassing Spad: trespassing, that was, into 'British' territory. Paul was particularly amused by the way in which Jacques, with five accredited 'kills', had ridiculed his new 'ace' status, writing of a French sniper who had painstakingly cut a notch on the butt of his rifle for each of thirty-five *Boche* shot cleanly through the head. Far from being made a seven-times-ace, and being decorated accordingly, Jacques related, the private had been charged with damaging army property and had lost all privileges for a month!

Paul read the letter twice through, standing by the window against the darkening sky, smiling a little sadly as he tucked it into his writing case. Even now he could not report any personal contact with the new Albatros. Nor would he be able to tell Delcamp that Winthrop had been duly chided for attacking innocent Spads. Winthrop – 'Spadman', ever since –, impetuous, and as keen as mustard, was the 'A' Flight pilot who had gone down in flames over Serre that morning.

Paul soon had personal experience and to spare of the Albatros, and at least the spirit of the Boelcke *Jasta*. Three mornings later 'C' Flight had just turned west over Adinfer Wood at 13,000 feet when Paul saw five machines climbing hard from the east. They were mere dots but they looked suspiciously businesslike and after a swift assessment he turned the flight towards them and began to climb. It took an age but eventually he reached just over 14,000 feet. It was clear, however, that both Simpson and Alfie Cox were having great difficulty in holding that altitude so he descended until he was satisfied that all the machines were as comfortable as could be expected so near their ceilings.

Paul had been keeping a close watch on the approaching scouts and had known for some minutes that his first contact with the new D-Class Albatros was at hand. It was a contact he could well have done without, but the patrol duty was only halfway through and although they were close to the lines he could think of no reasonable excuse for diving back across them.

It was a grim cavalcade clawing up at them, stylish, colourfully-painted killers with sinister black pattée crosses, the machines the latest and best from the German factories. Paul flung a final glance at his own de Havillands, frail and outmoded, mere stringbags in comparison, even their roundels dull against the squadron's khaki-green.

The five German scouts seemed likely to continue to climb before making their attack. They had the benefit of both performance and firepower, accordingly Paul had to act before they could get the additional advantage of height. He waggled his wings and dived, getting the nose down as low as he dared. Even then, casting a hasty look behind, he saw the tailbooms writhing under the strain, the sight so unnerving him that he promptly faced his front once more. The revs were screaming and when he glanced aside to check that the flight were holding position he saw wing fabric bowing up across the point of greatest curvature where pressure was at its lowest.

He was closing the distance rapidly. The enemy machines had not yet reached 13,000 feet but their leader had seen Paul's tactics and was turning now in an attempt to force the British machines to overfly his command and so put themselves at a disadvantage. Paul countered, adjusting his bank. The German matched him, and so they closed at a combined speed of nearly 200 miles an hour, each seeking to out-think and out-position the other.

What would have happened had the fight been prolonged became a matter of conjecture for suddenly the Albatros leader broke away, banking sharply off to the east and taking his patrol with him; but banking, at that, no sharper than Paul, who, seizing the instant did not wait to discover the other's future intentions but disengaged 'C' Flight by diving flat-out for the west. Minutes later and well clear, he found himself pumping breath as if his lungs were bursting and wishing that he could get down out of the sky and think about it. If this was the way things were going to be from now on there seemed little future in it!

There was a certain amount of jubilation when they landed thirty minutes later. The rest of the patrol had been uneventful and even Simpson seemed to be thankful for it.

'D'you think that was Boelcke?' he asked.

Paul shook his head. 'Unlikely. Our man let us catch him off balance. Boelcke would've got the height before letting us get within range.'

'They really are hot buses, anyway,' said Dick Fisher grimly.

Comparing notes they found that none of their machines had suffered damage. But nobody claimed hits on the Germans, either.

'I kept firing bursts,' confessed Alfie Cox. 'I just hoped that someone would fly into one.'

'Preferably one of the Albatri, I hope,' said Simpson.

Paul was subdued. The new German machines so far outclassed the DH2s that at the moment he was at a loss to know what they could do about it. Fortune had favoured them on this occasion but they could not depend on luck all the time. It made him feel no better when the flight insisted upon talking of how successful his tactics had been. Even if it were so, there was nothing in the quiver for next time. And there was certainly going to be a next time.

In the following three weeks there were many 'next times', all of them exciting, and none of them enjoyable. The tasks went on as before, although for the squadron the emphasis changed from escorting artillery spotters to escorting BEs on bombing jobs. The newly-equipped and revitalised German Air Service was always much in evidence and within only a few days everybody was harking back to the near-halcyon days of midsummer when contact with an enemy willing to fight was something to write home about.

'C' Flight made it by a hairsbreadth, sweeping into the German formation with no more than a two-hundred feet advantage of height but diving at top speed against machines who were hanging on their propellers. Paul saw fish-like bodies, pointed spinners streamlining the noses, single-bay wings with only outer interplane struts, and large, powerful, part-cowled engines; noting the details with one section of his mind while computing speeds and angles with another. But the de Havillands were in the ideal position, blunt noses down. Now was the moment. And he opened fire.

The leader jinked aside, but Paul ruddered after him and kept the burst going, seeing the tracer snake and whip. For a moment it hovered over the German's top plane and Paul felt excitement course through him, but then knew that he had missed. He banked and pulled, even in that extremity initially easing the nose into motion but heaving after that until he felt the first tremble of the stall, infinitesimally relaxing then and knowing that he was turning at the maximum possible rate. From the corner of his eye he watched the leader, wings near-vertical now in a might-and-main endeavour to reverse the order of chase. Other members of the flight were wheeling and zooming, desperately swamping the Germans to prevent them accelerating away when their superior performance would permit them to re-position and attack.

Intelligence, Paul remembered, had reckoned the D-Scout's level speed at some 110 mph, at least fifteen miles an hour faster than the de Havilland, and with anything up to three thousand feet better ceiling. How manoeuvrable they were was anybody's guess, although by the way the leader was coming around they were no barges. Add on the two synchronised machine guns and a DH2 caught without some edge would be in bad trouble.

It was the early sighting and Paul's tactics that saved the day, that and the weeks of team training. For though essentially a case of every man for himself, the de Havillands' overall aim was to support each other, one zooming as another dived, so that for the first few vital moments the Germans were separated and confused; wherever they turned it must have seemed that there was a de Havilland in their way causing them to swerve aside and even reduce power to avoid a collision. It took only moments for the de Havillands to lose their artificial, dive-enhanced speed but it was enough to disrupt the German patrol and prevent them from using their superior performance.

As they entered October so the weather began to deteriorate with days of mist interspersed with days of high winds, low clouds, and driving rain. For the troops on the ground it was the beginning of a purgatory that would only get worse as the weeks went by. For the airmen, although there were few days when the weather totally grounded them, such conditions, while workable, made the job more difficult. It was on the clearer days that they grew to know the Albatros.

It was strange how the various types of hostile could be picked out one from the other, and long before their shapes were recognisable. Even close at hand the Albatros D-type was not all that different in appearance from the Halberstadt, sharing the same lack of dihedral and the same square-tipped wings. What made the Albatros so easy to identify, however, was the way its tail seemed to be dragging down its nose in the climb. And it was the D-type's climb they saw most of, for it was seldom that the Germans first appeared from above unless the cloud had favoured them with cover during their approach.

The DH2s took nearly an hour to reach their effective ceiling at around 14,000 feet. The German machines, on the other hand, tended to get airborne only when warned, having long since cast aside the time- and fuel-wasting strategy of mounting a barrage – or standing – patrol. Consequently it was invariably a case of watching the sharp-spinnered hostiles swim up from the depths, holding themselves laterally out of reach as they did so until reaching an altitude of between 16 and 17,000 feet; a case then of the De Havs waiting as the now overflying Albatros scouts sidled closer, of keeping one eye on the dependant bombers below, one eye on the fuel gauge, and both eyes on the enemy scouts up above – of waiting for the moment when the wings of the high-hawks dipped for the stoop.

They quickly came to recognise individual aircraft in the Albatros *Jasta* although they could never be certain which of the Germans they read about in the press was flying which. Most of the German machines were painted in uniform colouring, greys or greens, but almost all would have some distinguishing feature, a patch, or an oil stain, or at times some personalised splash of colouring on wings or tail or fuselage.

For days on end, it seemed, Paul found himself engaged at some time or another with a machine with yellow wingtips. In the middle of a melee he would find himself circling with it, neither of them able to get the advantage. Its pilot was clearly not of the first rank for he could so easily have broken off and zoomed for a fresh attack when his firepower, twice that of the de Havilland, must surely have told. As it was he seemed content to whirl around, causing Paul to pull out all the stops merely to keep him off his tail. Oddly, Paul never gave the machine another thought afterwards, not until the next time combat was joined when suddenly, there it was again, with wasp-sharp nose and yellow tips, like a nasty, recurrent dream.

Now, within weeks, the DH2 pilots found themselves in the unenviable position of being outgunned and out-performed by nearly every enemy scout they met, whether Albatros D1s, the newer Albatros D2s, Halberstadt D2s, or Fokker biplanes. They knew themselves to be no worse off than others before them, and hoped to survive until the Spads, Pups and Nieuports came into more general supply. Out of necessity they quickly accepted the fact that they would be continually fighting on the defensive, aware that they must seize any chance on the instant, that any mistake they made would be their last.

It was not themselves, however, but the BE crews they felt sorriest for, plodding along below, accepting the fact that their machines were museum pieces and easier prey than ever for the new German scouts. The Squadron's days were often spent at high level above the BEs, at anything up to 14,600 feet if the engine was feeling that well, peering around the sky, and waiting for the attack to develop.

For from the moment the British were sighted over the lines German observer posts would be sending constantly updated reports in order to predict what the bombers' target would eventually be. At their leisure, and when it best suited them – and only then –, with the attacking force committed, and being helped eastwards by the prevailing wind, the enemy scouts would come up to meet them, Albatros Scouts and Halberstadts in the van. The DH2s would then move to get between them and the slower, heavily-laden bombers. And then it was cat-and-mouse as the Germans steadily climbed above them, holding, as always now, safely out of range.

It was hard for the de Havillands, constrained as they were to manoeuvring below, to prevent the swift-diving Germans from breaking through. Most often it became a case of popping off the single Lewis and belatedly diving in their wake, futilely hoping to distract them. The BE2c gunners, with twin-Spandaus intent on blowing them from the sky, were understandably reluctant to stop firing at an attacker merely because a de Havilland was vainly straining to catch up to the hostile's rear. Frequently, therefore, the de Havillands found themselves ducking British tracer and wondering just how many enemies they were fighting.

By the end of the second week in October Paul counted himself fortunate that he had not lost a single pilot from 'C' Flight. Peter Mainwaring was looking increasingly drawn, 'A' Flight having lost two more, one of them the replacement for Winthrop, the Spadman, the other a more experienced pilot who had been with the squadron for nearly three months. 'B' Flight had lost the use of a pilot who brought his crippled machine down in Allied lines but was then hospitalized in England.

It was all very much a case of watching each other's tail and darting full pelt at any German aircraft that came their way. Always with an eye for any who sought to break off and get through to the bombers. And despite the de Havillands' best endeavours the bombers suffered heavy losses, 'C' Flight alone witnessing two of them fall to the guns of the *Jasta*. Losing any of their charges inevitably saddened them all and accordingly they were touched towards the middle of the month to receive a letter from the BE2c squadron commander thanking them for their efforts and assuring them that the bombers valued their assistance.

The letter both comforted and humbled them, but left Paul even more incensed at the powers that be, at Trenchard and those whom Paul saw as the soulless men like the commanding general, who persisted in sending such outmoded machines on bombing raids so far into enemy territory. Paul had not for a moment lost his conviction that the real job of the aeroplane in this war was to carry the fight to Germany itself. But the aeroplane had to be right!

Paul saw it as a case parallel to that of the tank. Why not wait until the right machines became available? Wait until night-flying instruments and improved bomb-aiming sights enabled the bombers not only to find their targets, but to actually hit them? And to hit them hard enough to do more than superficial damage. Surely results alone must show Trenchard what criminal butchery it was to expend machines and crews as he was doing? Cold, statistical results, let alone his conscience!

Could Trenchard not see that the BEs were too slow and too lightly-armed to defend themselves effectively, and that, limited by their bomb-aiming equipment, they were forced to fly low over ever-more-efficient ground defences? It would, after all, mean scarcely more than a few months' delay, for it could hardly be that long now before the new bombers became available; the new DH4 from Airco, the DH9, also from Airco – and for which there seemed to be high hopes –, and the giant Handley Page that Frank Taylor was monitoring at Cricklewood, a veritable monster of a machine, it was said, specifically designed for just such independent action.

Surely Trenchard was not such an egomaniac that he could not afford to wait for just a year and cut the present senseless, bloody waste of human life?

So Paul fulminated! If only to himself.

Chapter Eleven

Late October brought deceptively light winds on the ground with strong westerlies aloft, making it only too easy to rush across the map with the wind sweeping them along, lured onwards by some tempting target just a tiny bit further east, losing sight of the fact that on turning for home they would stop like moths pinned on a board, puttering away into sixty mile an hour winds and making, at best, a speed of thirty miles an hour over the ground. The time they spent actually recrossing the region of the lines themselves, virtually hovering over the anti-aircraft batteries, seemed interminable, and they could only wonder at so much hate being expended to effect only the loss of the occasional strut or flying wire.

The strong winds brought mainly clear skies and the German Air Service took full advantage of the conditions. The squadron lost one more pilot, and a noteworthy one at that: Paddy Rawlinson, the deputy flight commander of 'B' Flight and one of the Squadron's most experienced pilots. Paddy was caught napping when three Albatros Scouts dived out of the sun.

'From what we hear,' gritted Ralph Beatty, the flight commander, 'the Huns had been mixing it with some of the Eleven Squadron chaps and had their noses put out of joint for once. They'd just broken off and were heading for home when they came across us.'

He was, understandably, more than normally cut up for he and Paddy had long been inseparable and between them, in their months together, had built up a first-class team.

'It was my fault,' he declared heavily, 'I'd just checked that wretched bit of sky too. Then I had a quick look at my watch to see if it was time to start heading back. When I looked up, it was all over. The bastards were diving for the deck and Paddy was just sitting there. They must have smashed a strut for his top plane crumpled and he went down like a stone. I simply missed them.'

There was an instant outbreak of dissent.

'But Ralph, I was covering that sector. I'd actually got my hand up,' protested a pilot, demonstrating how he had peered through splayed fingers to screen out the sun. 'And even I didn't see anything. They came of the centre of the sun. You can't blame yourself.'

'Then who the hell else can I blame?' snarled Ralph. 'Don't be so bloody stupid.'

And he stormed off out of the office and over the cinders towards the fields beyond.

Paul laid his hand on the younger man's shoulder. 'He didn't mean it.'

'He did,' said the other, 'and he's right. Words are worse than useless. But God if I'd only seen the beggars! And heaven knows, I was looking!' He left the office in his turn and Paul saw him moments later walking head down, swinging his flying helmet listlessly as he made his way towards the hangars.

Ralph and Paddy had seemed like institutions around the squadron, and with the partnership broken Paul was suddenly brought face to face with his own vulnerability. He wondered how long it was since he had had a leave, and he knew the answer to that – no matter how long ago, it was too long. He wondered when he would get another. And unbidden the thought came to him that with Paddy gone he would be one place further up the leave roster. Provided he survived long enough to claim his place when the time came.

They were all aware that the casualty figures had soared with the advent of the new German machines and rumour swelled the facts that came their way. But despite their own involvement it was No.11 Squadron to the north who seemed to suffer most, probably by virtue of their proximity to Boelcke's base. Only two days after the debacle over Marcoing Boelcke's Albatros Scouts and others – over twenty, it was reported – had hit them again. No.11, in company with No.60 Squadron, had been tasked to carry out a reconnaissance near Quéant, north of Bapaume and almost overhead the *Jasta's* base at Lagnicourt. The attack was so fierce that the British aircraft were forced to break off the job before it was anywhere near completed and to fight every inch of their way back home.

But worse was to follow this humiliation. In early October twenty more enemy scouts, reportedly led by Boelcke's chasers, had set about one of No.11 Squadron's patrols engaged on a photo-reconnaissance task at Mory, near Bapaume, and as Paul first heard it, had shot them all down. Later it became known that just two of the No.11 Squadron machines had been lost but by that time rumour had done its damage to morale. Then, only days after that, following a period of bad weather, six of No.11 Squadron's machines were on a reconnaissance to Douai when they came under continuous attack by some thirteen German scouts. Only two of their number returned to base intact. Taken in all, it was a savage series of maulings for any unit to face.

On the bright side Naval Strutters and Pups and Nieuports had indeed been released to help stem the tide, although the effect had been negligible so far. Other machines that might have been of use also appeared on the scene, but these were not always effective. The BE12 was one such, having – as the squadrons put it – to be taken from the sky by the RFC before they were literally blown out of it by the Huns. Meanwhile the pressure on out-classed types like the BE2c, and for that matter the DH2, was growing increasingly severe.

Brief hope of relief came at the end of October although – probably to their chagrin – long-suffering No.11 Squadron were not involved. 'C' Flight were airborne at the time and might have been involved, but that circumstances forced them into adopting the role of mere spectators.

It was the twenty-eighth day of a long and tiring month. Paul was leading a cold and weary 'C' Flight through a cloud-filled sky, heading back from an offensive patrol along the line of the Bapaume-Cambrai road, when he saw a fight in progress off to the south. It was some miles away nevertheless he gave the signal and dived his five machines full-out towards the melee.

As 'C' Flight closed, so the dots took on form, and Paul saw that there were Albatros Scouts among the combatants. Six, he counted, against two FEs, with six more Germans diving in to take their places at the kill. It was gusty, choppy weather and he bounced against his lapstrap as he steered between the clouds. Ah! Not FEs, he saw now, but DH2s – at such a distance the similar twin-boomed configuration had deceived him. Their own 'A' and 'B' Flights were on the ground, and it was unlikely that machines of No.32 Squadron would be this far south. So, No.24 Squadron then – and set for a pasting.

Machines were wheeling and zooming, climbing away in elegant chandelles and diving again, meeting and matching in perfect counterpart as the de Havillands fought it out. Wings flashed in the sun as they banked and turned, chasing and being chased, spiralling together and breaking away, in conjunctions as brief and wild as a mayfly courtship. But there was no time for fancy. Paul checked his gun. He had test-fired only a few rounds and the drum was nearly full: no need to risk changing it then, when bumps like these they were experiencing might jar it from his hand back into the propeller. He eyed the sky above the engagement, satisfying himself that it was clear. Although already he doubted that they would make it in time.

The de Havillands were fighting so gamely that their attackers were having to jostle each other to get their shots in. Their steam was running out, however, and the superior performance of the swarm was beginning to tell. The engagement was still agonisingly far off and Paul found himself rocking against his lapstrap as if to spur himself on. He thought of General Cousins, a cavalryman born and bred: and here he was himself, with a hundred horses powering him on, and still not enough speed.

Two Germans suddenly wheeled and dived, converging like barracuda on the same de Havilland. Paul screamed a warning: the DH2 had but moments to live! And Paul was powerless! Powerless to warn, powerless to aid! His finger moved to the trigger – as tracer lanced forwards from his right. It was Simpson, acting on the identical impulse! But it was hopeless, as they knew, and they saw Simpson's Sparklet charges arcing down far short and burning out. Any second now and an Albatros must open fire.

Paul found himself hypnotised by the doomed de Havilland, dispelling the converging Germans to his peripheral vision. Yet suddenly he perceived that they had staggered and were drifting apart, and instantly he gave them his full attention, at a loss to know what had gone amiss for them. Certainly they were no longer attacking, and even as he watched one of them began to spiral slowly down into a cloud. At once the other turned to follow, the rest – not one or two, but all of them! – immediately breaking off the engagement and following suit. The first machine re-appeared briefly through a gap and he distinctly saw part of its wing flutter clear. The second machine was circling anxiously around its stricken companion, and then they fell back into cloud and the whole gaggle was lost from sight.

Paul expected the de Havillands to make off at top speed, thankful for their reprieve, but either the members of the world's first all-scout squadron were made of sterner stuff or they were dazed by their luck, for initially they turned as if to give chase. But they were already outdistanced and as the last of the German scouts vanished into cloud, so they banked around, totally unaware of 'C' Flight's vain attempt at succour, and began to sink away west towards the lines.

Paul waved 'C' Flight out of their dive. At least the two scouts were safe. He looked behind him, beyond the flight, and to a sky that was empty of aircraft. He checked his watch and set his nose into a climb. By the time they reached the lines their stint would be up. He began to select a route through the anti-aircraft bursts, furiously wondering what had caused the break up. Had a de Havilland got in a lucky shot, or had damage suffered earlier suddenly taken effect? Had the German simply overstressed the machine in his eagerness to down the de Havilland and pulled himself to pieces, or had the enemy scouts touched each other? All these were possibilities, but what tantalised him most was the way in which the whole crowd had immediately broken off the engagement ...

The sky looked a little less hostile over to the left so Paul banked the flight in that direction, hugging the edge of a cloud for protection. Aircraft had broken apart before, and undoubtedly would again. And they would probably never know what had caused the break up in this case. Just as well then, to put it from his mind ...

But Chalky had seen the whole thing, and came running over before his prop had fairly stopped. 'Did you see? Slap bang into each other.'

Alfie stamped across and he had seen it too. 'It looked as if one clipped the other with his wheels. He was so fixed on getting that De Hav he didn't see his chum.'

'Too greedy by half,' said Simpson, 'I bet he feels a bit sick.'

'I'll bet they both do,' said Alfie.

Dick Fisher said reflectively, 'It was a bit far off to be certain, but I thought I saw something fluttering from that poor devil's strut.'

'I wondered about that too,' said Chalky.

'And the whole crowd peeled off to follow him down,' mused Paul. 'Although by then they had the De Havs cold.' A silence fell, while they pondered the significance of this.

'They were definitely hot stuff,' said Simpson thoughtfully. 'You could see the way they were handling themselves. They had to be Boelcke's bunch.'

'Where're Twenty-Four Squadron living?' Paul wondered aloud, 'Still down at Bertangles?' Nobody answered, but there was a concerted move towards the office, and the phone.

The news that it was Boelcke himself who had fallen, killed in a midair collision with one of his hunter-chasers, went around the Royal Flying Corps with quickfire rapidity. When Paul first got through to No.24 Squadron, however, he found them inclined to caution: it was always possible that a 'cub' had been flying leader's pennants.

But confirmation came quickly enough: Boelcke was dead. The man who had instilled new life into the German Air Service and was said to have shot down something approaching twenty RFC machines within a month had been killed by a momentary lapse of concentration, although whether on his part or on that of his colleague, nobody seemed to know. The German Air Service had suffered a grievous blow. A double blow, indeed. Immelmann first. And now Boelcke. And there was wide speculation that they would never again find a man of the same calibre to take his place.

'Brave and tenacious fighters,' Boelcke had said of the Corps' pilots and crews. Now, a few days after his fatal collision, the RFC repaid the compliment by dropping wreathes and messages of condolence to the German Air Service. Boelcke and his brood had struck severely at the RFC but he had been a brave and tenacious fighter himself as well as a talented leader of fighting scouts; above all he was a fellow airman, and for all these things they saluted him.

But any hope that his death might relieve the pressure on the Flying Corps was short-lived. It was said that Boelcke had been given his pick of the German Air Service in selecting his pilots – his hunters – for his new *Jagdstaffel*. The last few months had shown how well he had chosen and with nearly sixty victories already attributed to them it was clear how his leadership had brought them on. So it was that when Boelcke fell from the race there was any number of his followers to pick up the baton; men such as Voss, Mueller, von Richthofen; not least the unfortunate Hoehe, who had killed him; men whom the squadrons read of almost daily in the German-source summary of *The Times*.

Boelcke's prowess had inspired German aviation generally and his passing brought the German Air Service pride and increased activity rather than grief and withdrawal. It quickly became clear that until the new machines arrived there was to be no let up on the hard-pressed RFC.

Chapter Twelve

The first few days of November were dull and overcast with gusty, rain-bearing winds at ground level and heavily-laden skies aloft. The lower cloud hung in sullen sheets, layer upon layer from 600 feet upwards, until at 8,500 feet the main body presented a solid face so thick that it defied further penetration, effectively blotting out the sun and shortening even more the seasonally-attenuated hours of daylight. Each individual layer below the main cloud base was no more than a veil of mist, scarcely perceptible as the flight lifted through it but combining with those that lay below so that after a while the earth was curtained from sight, making observation from the air virtually impossible but promising some degree of protection against the keen-eyed guns below.

'C' Flight had been detailed for two sorties and although they weaved backwards and forwards across the lines at only 8,500 feet they saw no sign of anti-aircraft fire during the first sortie. There was equally little sign of German air activity, although whole fleets of aircraft might well have passed each other unseen between the layers. As flight commander Paul had his work cut out keeping track of their position, holding a compass course from the moment the ground disappeared from view, timing their passage from the last recognisable feature and hoping that the cloud would part once in a while to provide him with further pinpoints.

There was no doubt that the whole air mass was in an unsettled state. Paul would lead the flight into a hopeful-looking cloud avenue only to find floor and ceiling merging before him, forcing him to change either height or direction, and often both, in order to pursue his course in clear air. At times the sides of a cloudy corridor would close in upon them, gradually at first, and then suddenly, so that he lost sight of the outside machines and had to manoeuvre carefully to get the flight back into the clear. If they ran into German scouts, Paul told himself, it would be by chance alone. It was cold, boring, and unproductive work, and they landed in high hopes that the second sortie would be cancelled. Their hopes were quickly dashed.

Roly passed the signal slip to Major Hallam with a lift of his eyebrows. Having scanned the paper Major Hallam excused himself and went into the inner office from where they could hear his tones raised in what could only be protest on the phone. After two or three minutes he returned and put the paper firmly on the desk. He was clearly annoyed but nothing of it showed in his face.

'The squadron is required to drag a cape, so to speak, in front of Bertincourt and Lagnicourt. Take-off in twenty minutes.'

Paul and Dick looked at each other, and grinned. Bertincourt was just south of the Bapaume-Cambrai road, and Lagnicourt just north of it. Lagnicourt, where Boelcke's old *Jasta* still had its home. The chances of enticing the *Jasta* up in such conditions were negligible so they could only presume that somebody on the staff wanted to demonstrate that neither the recent maulings nor the present bad weather could dampen the RFC's offensive ardour. It was a fair bet that the major's phone call had been to protest the futility of the job.

Ralph Beatty, as senior flight commander, stepped back and saluted for them all. 'Twenty minutes it is, sir.'

'You can bet Boelcke's orphan boys aren't fairying around in this little lot,' grumbled Simpson, when Paul broke the news to the flight. 'Their machines will be tucked away in the sheds and they'll be gathered around a big log fire drinking beer.'

'Schnapps, old boy, not beer for German officers,' objected Chalky.

'They can drink hot cocoa for all I care,' retorted Simpson. 'But they won't be wasting their time in this. And if they actually hear us overhead they'll laugh their cotton socks off.'

They got airborne at just before four o'clock. Wing had wanted a combined squadron show in stepped formation but in view of the poor weather the major had exercised his discretion and dispatched the flights separately on short, widely-spaced beats. Accordingly, 'A' Flight took off first, detailed to patrol Adinfer Wood then head for Hébuterne. 'B' Flight was to set course towards Bapaume and turn north for Lagnicourt. 'C' flight was to follow five minutes later on the same initial course but then turn south to Bertincourt. After overflying their respective objectives all were to return to base by different routes.

'Let's hope we see something this time,' said Simpson.

'Let's hope we don't,' said Chalky.

Although the air above three thousand feet was smoother than on the first sortie there was still a chaotic churning of moisture and temperature throughout the atmosphere which blended the layers into ever-changing labyrinths of cloud. The main base had altered too, lowering, and they met it at only 4,000 feet, far too low in normal weather for a prudent crossing of the lines but safe enough today, Paul decided, with the flight screened from the ground by the layers below.

Safe enough, that was, based upon the experience of the first job. But the moment they approached the vicinity of the lines Paul discovered that the same situation no longer obtained. It was immaterial how the gunners had obtained the height of the cloud base – from one of their balloons, or from one of their aircraft; or even from sighting on bursts through gaps – but they had the range to a nicety. Paul not only saw the first burst but heard it as well: a fire-cored eruption as big as a house, followed by a metallic report, flat and spiteful above the din of the engine; then a hot, pungent stink, like train smoke in a tunnel, and billowing brown fumes as his de Havilland jolted through.

Then bursts all around; a maelstrom of steel: high-explosive shells, shrapnel shells, phosphorus, possibly gas; and smoke of all colours; a multi-hued palette of hate against which Paul tightened his buttocks and drew in his breath. There was nothing else left to draw in, with only the fabric and wood of this drab-painted, wind-puckered and wholly insubstantial shield to protect him from so many shards of jagged white-hot steel.

He blipped the switch – no time for the niceties of the lever – and dived three hundred feet, the flight keeping station on his wings. Most of the bursts were peppering the air above them now, frustrated by their sudden change of height and falling further behind with every dry-mouthed breath he drew. He levelled from the dive, nerve ends tensed, with nothing for it now but to wait as time and distance strained to draw them clear.

Two shocks, like mallet blows on the structure behind him, and an instant later a single shellburst, seemingly only feet above his head. Paul craned around, desperate to see what damage it had caused. To find nothing untoward. Nothing that he could see, at least. The controls felt normal while the Gnome roared on untroubled, its nine, oil-laced cylinders a full power blur, whirling the propeller blades between the quivering tail-hung booms. He faced forwards and looked intently at the instrument board: pitot pressure hovering just above ninety miles an hour, revs 120, perhaps a trifle more, and steady. He chewed his lower lip, glancing up. Fuel-pressure fine; oil, well up the glass: no trouble anywhere evident. He checked the wings and as much of the tailplane as he could see. No signs of torn fabric or damaged spars. No broken wires. He tried the stick, and the rudder, rolling, yawing, and pitching a little. Still no handling difficulties. But *something* had caused those blows!

'Oh dear, what can the matter be, Archibald, certainly not!' Puzzled and grim-lipped, he extemporised tonelessly into the airflow, marrying the nursery rhyme and the George Robey song with which No.5 Squadron's 'Biffy' Borton had, seeming ages since, christened 'Archie'.

He checked around the flight and saw their thumbs go up. Nothing was wrong with any of them. Nor was anything wrong behind him, he told himself, but imagination would have you falling out of the sky if you let it. Forcibly Paul put the possibility of damage from his mind and began instead to wonder where they were.

A gap in the clouds, unexpected but more than welcome, opened up to the right to show a cluster of buildings where a section of straight road ran at an angle to their line of flight. The Albert-Bapaume road, he reasoned tentatively.

A rapid check of the compass, rocking in its bowl about a north-easterly mean, gave the lie to this snap deduction; the road down there bore too much to the east: they must have passed Bapaume and this then, must be the Bapaume-Cambrai road. At that point cloud perversely shuttered off the view but not before Paul had seen the railway curving in from the left. He ran his thumb across the map: Frémicourt, or Beugny? No, not Beugny, the railway was not right. It must have been Frémicourt. So, with Beugny coming up, or rather, falling behind them now, it was high time to begin the right turn.

He straightened out on a southerly heading. Three minutes to Bertincourt aerodrome and nothing to see but cloud. He would fly on, maintaining altitude, he decided, and see what it looked like. Then, with a bit of luck, they could all go home.

A sudden movement caught his attention and he looked up. Dick Fisher had pulled alongside and was urgently pointing downwards. Paul leant across, squinting through the rush of air that battered at his eyes.

They were just visible, but disappearing fast behind two layers of cloud some three thousand feet below: a vic of three. Two Rolands, led by another machine. They had passed out of sight before he could identify the leader's type, but they had been flying straight. So, if they would only hold their course!

A hurried, clearing glance above. Nothing but cloud. A hand signal, instantly acknowledged by all, and engine off, he pushed the stick as far against the board as it would go.

Grey-white sheets of stratus floated up to meet them, tilted, became momentarily opaque, and flicked past to vanish wraithlike overhead, peeling away one after the other like a houri's veils. 'Salome, and the dance of the seven – stratus sheets.' Dismissing the whimsy, Paul checked the Lewis. This was no dance of seduction, here the discarded veils were shrouds, and 'C' Flight, icy-dealing Death. Or they would be, if the Germans held their course. 'Please, Salome, don't deviate,' he muttered.

If it had indeed been a prayer, then it was answered. For a moment later the Hun trio swam into sight through the mist, only five hundred feet below – but almost on his nose! In the dive the de Havillands had outstripped them and were now too high and too close. Fortunately – but then so much in this game was a matter of luck rather than judgement – there was a clearer area to the right, affording him space in which to lose the height. Hastily, Paul banked the flight towards it.

The leading aircraft, he saw now, was either an Aviatik or an LVG. He curved back, diving further, to position himself directly behind the left-hand Roland, holding his breath as if to conceal his approach and forcing himself to breathe out and then swallow, his ears clicking as the air pressure equalised.

The leader was definitely an Aviatik, Paul decided. And now they had been seen! A puff of blue smoke from the Aviatik as its pilot put on full power, and another from Paul's Roland. The Roland's gunner was firing now and Paul's stomach tightened as the tracers leaped towards him. Both Rolands turned at once to escape the danger but turned towards each other in their haste and came to within an ace of colliding. They swerved apart, avoiding catastrophe, but the hiatus proved equally fatal for it unbalanced their gunners. Paul saw the tracers run wild and altered his plan of attack. He had intended to dive under the Roland and pull up into its blind spot, but with the gunner unable to bear he eased off the dive to attack from above. The pilot was casting alarmed glances back over his shoulder for now Paul was only fifty feet away, and closing rapidly. Coldly Paul eased the pressure on the stick and allowed the nose to come up, the gunsight travelling forwards along the Roland's fuselage to encompass both cockpits. He waited until he felt a tingle of alarm. Until he was far too close. And then he began to fire.

The gunner disappeared from sight and in the same instant the Roland fell away onto its nose: perhaps it was simply nose-heavy, or perhaps the pilot had fallen forwards on the stick. The tail reared in front of Paul's face and, fearing that he might fly into it, he lifted hurriedly out of harm's way. But the leading machine, he saw, the Aviatik, was now directly ahead of him, and slightly below, its gunner leaning over the side trying to bring his gun to bear on another of the flight. Paul clicked his tongue. If he could only get his nose down in time he was in a perfect position for another attack from above!

Spiritedly, he pushed forward on the stick, the sudden reversal of forces throwing him against his lapstrap as the nose went down and the Aviatik swung up neatly into his gunsight. His finger tightened ... But it had been brutal controlling, jerking the weight of the aircraft, as he had, from the flying wires onto the landing wires. As was to be expected, dirt and loose objects rose from the cockpit floor and blew into his face while the map holder, caught by the airstream, tugged hard at the end of its thong.

But totally unexpectedly, a full drum of ammunition broke loose from its stowage and sailed upwards. Letting the stick fend for itself, Paul grabbed out frantically with both hands, desperate to stop the drum flying rearwards, and knew an instant of intense relief when, having snatched it inboard, he had it secure against his chest. An instant, but no more, for relief died as there came a bang from the rear, as the engine raced, and the machine went wild. Clearly something else had come adrift and this *had* struck the propeller! And suddenly he was in serious trouble.

Chapter Thirteen

Paul saw the cause at a glance: amid the tight-racked row of Very-pistol flares, the blank space glared like a skull's eye-socket. A Very cartridge, thrown from its rack, had been caught by the wind-blast and slammed back into the propeller whirling behind him. He had secured the heavy eight-inch diameter drum of Lewis ammunition, but missed the lighter signal cartridge! And there was little to choose between them. He had known many things shatter a propeller: long grass, a pair of goggles, a peaked cap – one not circumspectly reversed pre-flight –, even a pencil. A brass-based Very cartridge had been more than enough to do the same. Now the prop was vibrating as if to tear itself to pieces; soon it would wrench the motor from its mounting; in which event the motor would not leave much of the airframe: the old-old DH2 story.

Paul had reacted as if by instinct, jabbing his thumb on the button to cut the ignition and then reaching over to turn off the petrol tap. And already the Gnome was choking into silence behind him. He looked back as the cylinders shivered and were still, the propeller disc spoking and slowing in unison, kicking once and then hanging motionless. The vibration ceased and he gently eased up the nose in a meagre trade of speed for height. Then he strained rearwards, pulling himself round on the coaming in a bid to determine the extent of the damage.

Craning to see over the rear of the nacelle, he could make out the whole tip of one, gratifyingly undamaged, blade. Another blade-end was partially visible and appeared to be whole but the remaining two had come to rest out of sight. Undoubtedly however, one, or both of these, had suffered a fair amount of damage for the vibration had been extreme. He recalled the thuds after crossing the lines and wondered afresh if there was shrapnel damage as well. Or impact damage, if he really had been hit by a shell on its way up. Too late to worry about that now, but he would keep it in mind and fly as if there was indeed extra damage: vibration like that would have done the structure no good at all.

Paul had the machine back onto an even keel now, gliding as slowly as he dared, the needle hovering at 60 to 65 mph. He looked about him, taking stock. His cavortings in the last few moments had carried him off through several different bands of cloud and now he found himself alone. Some dance that! Some seductress!

The fight already seemed remote, although less than two minutes had elapsed since he had opened fire on the Roland. He had a vague recollection of it spinning away with Dick following it down, and of Simpson and Chalky paired off against the other hostile. He had not given another thought to the Aviatik but now he realised how lucky he had been that its gunner had not been wider awake; possibly Alfie had held the fellow's attention and seen the machine off. For the rest he must hope that Dick would be able to gather up the flight and take them home in some order. He had his own predicament to sort out.

His altimeter was reading just over 4,000 feet and he was miles over the wrong side of the lines with a strong westerly to help keep him there. He brought the speed back a little lower yet, assessing the rate at which the altimeter was unwinding. There was the rush of wind through the wires but other than that his world had become uncannily quiet. He adopted a south-westerly heading towards the lines, keeping clear of all but the thinnest layers of cloud. 3,600 feet already. Not so good; he had hoped for a better glide.

Paul did a rapid calculation. At this rate he would barely make five miles, especially with the wind against him. His mind turned heavily to the last time he had suffered such damage, when he had finished up in the shell-hole: at least this time the aircraft was not likely to break up around him. But right now that was cold comfort. For this was not to be a case of history repeating itself. On that occasion, five months ago, there had been every chance of making it home. Now there was none.

He ran his finger over the map, calculating his chances. He had passed Bapaume and dived the flight south-east after the German trio. Assume then that he was halfway between Bapaume and Bertincourt! He swung his finger in a five mile arc south-west from his supposed position. Towards the British lines, towards Flers, Lesboeufs and Morval, he would be short by a good two miles. Towards the French zone, further south towards Sailly, probably just as far. There was simply no question of making it this time. He gazed at the map as if for inspiration. He had to make up his mind what to do.

2,200 feet indicated, and he caught his first glimpse of the ground. He could not reach the Allied lines. That was certain. And the area of

Hunland immediately behind their lines was bound to be swarming with German support units. His mind was racing now. Bertincourt aerodrome must be down there to the left: land there and they would be on to him before he could shake a leg. Away from the lines, on the other hand, the Germans were bound to be thinner on the ground ...

The decision was made. He banked to the right, lowering the nose to maintain the speed, curving around to the north-east, using what was left of his height to distance himself from Bertincourt aerodrome, and the lines. 1,900 feet and steady on his new course. Any moment now and he could expect to begin breaking cloud.

Had he downed the Roland? He had not fired a single shot at the Aviatik, what with his pulling and pushing and letting go, but maybe the rest of the flight had finished it off. Paul grunted aloud, mildly surprised at himself. Maybe he was becoming a fire-eater, after all! Then he recalled his present predicament and rephrased the thought: maybe he *would* have become a fire-eater ...

He concentrated on gliding for maximum range, easing the nose down to maintain what he had, long since, determined by both calculation and experiment to be the optimum speed, striving to keep a straight course. In his mind's eye, now he gave thought to it, he could picture the flight forces in a glide: gravity, lift and drift – or gravity, lift and *drag*, of course, nowadays: nothing stayed the same for very long in aviation, even its basic terms. Nothing, but gravity.

All his training and all his experience told him that lifting the nose would only serve to steepen the glide but his visceral instincts pleaded with him to do so. Surely, they urged, the more you hold off the longer you will glide? The trite lines of a mess refrain came into his mind, one he had last bawled out shoulder to shoulder with Jacques Delcamp in the *estaminet* in Amiens,

> 'And this is the reason he died,
> He'd forgotten that twice iota
> Gives the minimum angle of glide.'

Trite but true. And Paul grinned as he pushed the nose down to regain the optimum gliding speed, wondering what his old mentor, Lanchester, would think of a student who could only resolve an aerodynamic conflict by having recourse to a popular song. Strangely enough he rather thought the eminently practical aeronautical theorist would heartily approve.

He peered over the side, and seeing nothing, sat back in his seat, the discomfort growing as it began to be borne in upon him what the future held in store. For the present, however, he was powerless to do anything but wait for the earth to appear, to hold his speed, and to listen to the sound of the wind humming through the wires.

700 feet, on the clock. at least, and unless the weather had deteriorated beyond all expectation he must break cloud soon! The flight had entered cloud at 600 feet on the climb, not all that far off to the west: the base could not be that much lower over here. So with no appreciable change in ground level – no more than a hundred feet or so – he was unlikely to run into any mountains; although a surviving tree would be enough to do for him! And the altimeter was little use in this situation, it was only a barometer after all. Although the pressure would hardly have altered much since take-off. Just the same he tried to put from his mind the thought of what might be looming up below ...

300 feet on the clock. He was beginning to get decidedly twitchy. If he failed to break cloud very soon he would have no time to manoeuvre no matter what he found himself facing. Or at what real altitude.

200 feet on the clock, and suddenly the cloud shed itself from his wings and he was looking down – on swiftly moving ground! God! How far out had his altimeter been! His visual faculties did a rapid reassessment. Not two hundred feet above the ground then, but far less than bloody fifty!

The light was much worse here below the clouds, and filtered yet more by mist. Paul cast a swift glance around for a horizon, but drizzle curtailed his view. No sign of buildings, or roads, just rolling downlands with narrow chalk-strewn fields, tree-bordered and seemingly untouched by war. He looked at the terrain skimming directly below. Undulating in the main, and taking shape as he sank inexorably lower. To the right it sloped up to an unnaturally flat-topped embankment, to the left it flattened out, to be bordered by a wood running wild and woolly into the mist. He banked that way, eyeing the surface. Ploughed, but not too deeply furrowed and with only the occasional gleam of water glistening in what troughs there were. He still had most of his fuel on board and he did not fancy cartwheeling.

He guided the machine to where the ground seemed firmest, parallel to the edge of the wood. Then he rolled his wings level and deliberately put his nose down, discarding height to gain that extra bit of speed. And now he held off, using the extra mile an hour or so he fancied he had stolen to choose his own touchdown point, the treetops blurring at the periphery of his vision. The machine touched lightly, struck a rut, and bounced. He held the stick where it was, and let the bounce sort itself out. Then, just too late to do anything about it, he realised that the ground fell away more sharply here, sloping down to the left in a grassy ramp towards the wood. He kicked at the rudder but he no longer had way enough to pull the nose around. There was nothing he could do but let the de Havilland run on.

He was slowing somewhat, although not so rapidly now that he was on the grass and clear of the plough. Then, seeing that the left wings were bound to crumple against the first of the trees, he unfastened his lapstrap and drew back his feet from the rudder bar. As he did so the right wheel hit a rut and slewed the nose around before bumping itself free with a jerk that threw him hard against the coaming. But the smash with the trees was averted. A final rumble or two, more gentle now as the slope lessened and the speed died away. And all at once there was a total lack of sound. The de Havilland had stopped, and he was down.

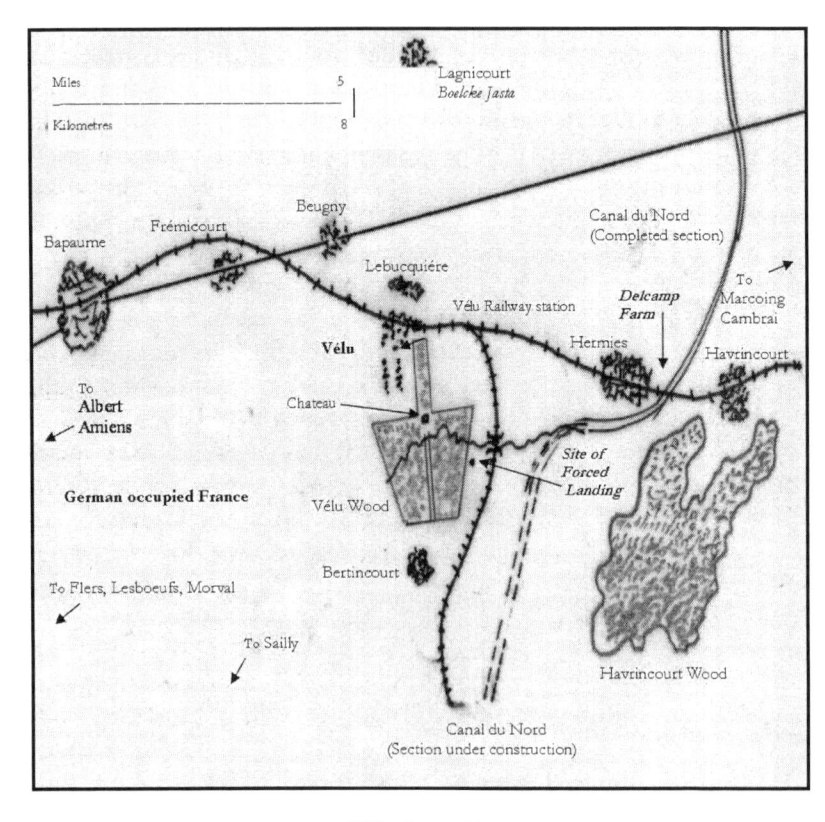

Vélu Area, 1916

Chapter Fourteen

He was not just down, but in one piece. Only there was not a moment to waste. Paul scrambled over the side, awkward in his flying gear, poising on the foothold to lift the Very pistol from its stowage. He selected a cartridge from the rack, easing it out with a chagrined thought for the one which had not been so well-fitting. He hesitated, took a second flare in case the first did not suffice, then jumped to the ground.

It should have been a significant moment. Now he was on enemy-held soil with no chance of being picked up. The other members of the flight had no idea where he had gone down and in these conditions there was no way in which they could find him even if they had. It should have been significant but the full implications had yet to come home to him, for more than part of his mind was still re-living those last few frantic seconds of the glide. Besides, he had only limited time available, and none to waste in metaphysical reflection.

He broke open the signal pistol, pushed in the first cartridge, and snapped the barrel back up to the butt. God, how it went against the grain! And yet it had to be done. The Germans might indeed have captured DH2s coming out of their ears, but that was not the point. Only how like shooting a trusting horse! Grimacing, he took a pace backwards, and in one movement, cocked the action, pointed the pistol at the nacelle, and squeezed into first pressure –. Only to pause.

A moment passed. Then, still pressuring the trigger with his forefinger, he lowered his arm, and turned, pondering the slope down which he had rolled. An old logging track, perhaps, grass covered, its wagon ruts shallow, ill-defined, indeed almost obliterated by the passage of time ... Behind him, and as far as he could see in both directions, stretched the trees, with dead leaves soft and thick beneath the boles, and the sweet wet scent of Autumn mingling with the faintest hint of pine.

He had anticipated immediate capture and was surprised to find himself still alone. And it struck him that to set fire to the aircraft now would merely draw attention to his presence before he had formulated a plan of action. He took his finger off the trigger and lowered the Very pistol, leaving it cocked, just the same. Then slowly, looking back nervously every few steps in case someone should appear from the wood and cut him off from the machine, he began to walk back up the slope.

A scan of the ploughland ghosting away into the nothingness of near-dusk showed him that he had come to rest at the bottom of a shallow, saucer-like hollow, some twenty yards from the edge of the field. The logging track, he registered, showed little sign of the de Havilland's passage although the bracken had suffered where the machine had left the edge of the plough. Reaching the start of the track Paul eyed the wheel marks in the chalky mud. Then, with sudden resolve, he made off into the field.

The plough itself was harder going than the grassed-over slope but he soon came to the end of the wheel tracks, his final touchdown point, walking on then to where he had bounced, and finally to the first touch. In all, it had been a surprisingly short run. He looked around him. For as far as the fading light would let him see there was no movement. There was no sign of life, no livestock, no people, no buildings. There was just the mist, and the drizzle, and the deepening dusk.

Paul turned back, to consider the field itself. Chunks of pale rock littered a surface that, while skimmed with creamy chalk, was far firmer than he might have hoped. He realised too that the gradient taken by the logger's track was slighter than it had seemed from the cockpit. Nevertheless he saw now that, shallow though the hollow was, when viewed from his present vantage point it concealed all but the de Havilland's upper wings. Thoughtfully then, he began to make his way back towards the wood, pushing at the wheel ruts with the side of his foot and looking around to assess how successful he might be in covering them. His breathing was shallow, his heart still pounding with nervous excitement, but now he was beginning to settle down.

He had a critical decision to make. He was in enemy territory, but he was not yet in enemy hands. And he knew that he did not want to spend the rest of the war in captivity. He wanted to be back with the squadron, back where leave would soon be a possibility. Leave, when he would seek an understanding with Catherine. For welcome as her few letters had been he had been puzzling for weeks to fathom why, being so warm of nature, she should write so coldly. Although he had conceded that, given the alarums and excursions of the life he was leading, his expectations might have been running altogether too highly. Then he forced such considerations from his mind. Now, before they picked him up, was the time to make his plans. He uncocked the pistol, but left the cartridge in place, simply easing the hammer forwards against the cap, leaving it ready to incinerate the de Havilland at the first sign of intruders.

It was unlikely, he reasoned, that anyone had heard his gliding descent. It now looked as if even his sudden appearance from the clouds might well have gone unnoticed, while the fact that both the drizzle and the growing dusk had combined to lower the visibility was very much in his favour. Even the breeze that made him thankful for his leather coat was not a clearing breeze and would only cause a thickening of the mist.

Reckoning it out then: he must be about seven miles behind the lines, somewhere between the Bapaume to Cambrai road, and Bertincourt. He held the map against the fading light. There were several woods shown, but one, singular in shape, stood out, just north of Bertincourt. He climbed to the cockpit to consult the compass. His wood ran almost due north – and so did the wood on the map. He jumped down. That was good enough for a beginning. Now to formulate a plan of action while the adrenaline was still flowing.

One option was to walk west and hope to cross the lines. Alternatively he could set out to the north, beyond the limit of the ongoing offensive, find a quiet sector, and try to sneak across there. Or, he might reach the sea: and swim past the coastal barriers? He envisaged wading along the shallows when the tide was out, avoiding any obstructions by swimming around them under cover of darkness. But it could hardly be that simple.

Then again, he might consider walking north-east away from the lines altogether, travelling by night, until he eventually reached neutral Holland. That would be possible with care and determination. But the best it could bring him would be an extended period of internment that might be little better than prisoner-of-war detention. The same applied to walking south, towards Switzerland. He had several choices. And none of them appealed.

Paul drummed his fingers on the taut fabric of the wings, eyeing the de Havilland speculatively. He cast another searching glance into the woods. Then, pistol in hand, and ready for any eventuality, he began to walk around the machine, eyes intent, prodding it here and there with a gloved hand, examining the vertical inter-wing struts for damage and testing the tension of the landing and flying wires, just as if he were making ready for flight.

Paul soon satisfied himself that there was nothing wrong with any of the flying surfaces. The nacelle was undamaged, and although the tail had a few tears in it there was nothing of significance. He made a careful study of the solid-tyred landing wheels, scraping off the mud until he was satisfied that they had suffered no ill effects from their rough-field landing. It was when he came to inspect the four tubular-metal tailbooms that he brought up short.

The bottom-right tailboom had been shot through about mid-way along its length! The damage had been done between the two vertical struts, meaning that the boom had been playing its part in supporting the tailplane with less than a third of its normal thickness remaining. Hurriedly Paul switched his scrutiny to the one immediately above it. It too showed signs of damage, certainly nowhere near as significant as the lower one but sufficient to have called for immediate grounding back at base. All of which explained the thumps during the shelling!

Now, assessing the weakened members, Paul recalled the way he had handled the machine when trying to attack the Aviatik, and quelling only with difficulty the visceral discomfort this brought him, breathed a heartfelt prayer to Mr Geoffrey de Havilland for designing a structure with so much built-in strength. Finally, having put it off until last, he turned his attention to the rear of the nacelle, to the engine, and to the propeller.

Paul saw at once that the damage was confined to one blade of the propeller, not two as he had feared. The last six inches of the tip – protected against incidental debris-damage on this four-blader with doped cotton rather than a brass sheath – had completely disappeared while the new end, bearing a deep indentation where the cartridge had struck it, was raw and ugly, and sharp as a broken tooth. It was no wonder that the vibration had been so violent.

The other blades were completely undamaged, the mathematical perfection of their proportions seemingly enhanced when compared with the unnatural asymmetry of their damaged fellow. Leaving them,

Paul returned to the damaged blade, running his hand over the surface. Below the break there was no sign of splitting, and although it was difficult to estimate what strains might have been set up by the impact, he assessed the remaining structure as sound. For a while longer he stood gazing at it, deliberating. Then he turned his attention to the Gnome.

Gingerly pushing the Very pistol into his belt, he concentrated upon looking for damage caused by the cartridge. Such damage, he thought, was unlikely, the engine being largely shielded by the rear of the nacelle, but not impossible, considering the vagaries of airflows. Certainly the thin, tubular push-rods and their rockers seemed to have come to no harm and he took that for a good sign. He was more concerned for the cylinders themselves. The working barrels of the nickel-chrome steel cylinders, he knew, were only some sixteenth of an inch thick, and it would take very little to distort one of them. The close-set integral cooling fins, left on during machining, provided extra strength, and he used them as a practical guide, reasoning that any external damage to a cylinder must first have broken or distorted a fin. Gradually he worked his way around all nine, finally running the back of his thumbnail along each cylinder in turn and listening to the deepening of tone as the fins lengthened towards the combustion-chamber ends. Finally he nodded, satisfied that there were no obvious signs of damage to cylinders or motor.

He took hold of an undamaged propeller blade, and with great care, eased it through a full revolution, breathing a sigh of relief when there was no unnatural restriction or grating of metal. Not that he was too surprised, for he had switched off at the first sign of trouble and had judged it unlikely that the motor itself had come to any harm; nevertheless, it was a relief to obtain even this degree of confirmation. Next he turned to the far side of the engine, to the components of the ignition assembly, examining each ignition wire and the cap of every sparking plug, although damage was even more unlikely on this rearward-facing side of the engine. He straightened up, and was at once agreeably surprised to see how much the mist had thickened.

Taking a moment from his task Paul made his way into the woods to relieve himself, and with that off his mind set-to to make a brush of broken branches. Armed with this he returned to the field and backed his way from the initial touchdown point, side-kicking clay over the worst wheel marks and then brushing away all signs of the disturbance.

Back at the aeroplane he used a jagged branch to gouge out the earth behind the left wheel, afterwards putting his shoulder to the tail until the wheel rolled into the hole he had made. Then, with the left wheel effectively chocked, he lifted the tail-skid and walked the machine in a semi-circle until it was facing nose out of the wood. Finally he channelled a ramp to free the wheel again.

Moving the machine bodily backwards was harder, but after an effort he managed to roll it the final few yards back towards the trees so that when he walked up into the field again he was unable to see even the top surface of the wings. There was a reasonable chance then, he told himself, that a casual observer might well walk past without seeing it. A reasonable chance.

Returning to the De Hav he shrugged, and climbed into the cockpit. The partly-used drum from the Lewis, and the three spares, he carried back into the woods, concealing them under a pile of leaf mould. Hopefully he had glided far enough from the lines for civilians to be going about their everyday lives; the ploughed field strengthened that hope. Best to ensure then, that nobody, and children in particular, stumbled across a live machine gun.

In the last of the light he pored over the map, leaning against the leading-edge of the wing, well aware that he was taking comfort from proximity with the machine. And why not? It was the only thing for miles around that was familiar and friendly. Everything else, whatever lay beyond the woods and fields, was strange and hostile, and he was loth to move from where he stood. But time was passing. He had been lucky, landing unseen in an area presently free of German forces. Now he must build on that.

His must be Vélu Wood, taking its name from a village that was both station and junction on the railway running from Bapaume, via Marcoing, to Cambrai. Of course, with the junction being regularly visited by bombers of the RFC, one must suppose it would largely in ruins by now. But Vélu also had an aerodrome with, if Paul remembered correctly, at least two hangars. He tried to visualise the juxtaposition of airfield and railway junction but failed, although he rather thought both must lie diagonally across the wood from where he was standing.

He was probably closer to the bigger German aerodrome at Bertincourt, immediately to the south. Closer than he might have hoped, indeed, for he saw from the map that it must be only a mile or so away, possibly even less. In fact, the boundary of the aerodrome might well be the southern end of the very field he had landed in! It was a stunning thought, and this too he put firmly from his mind. It simply meant that time was even more pressing.

Turning to the map he decided that Vélu Wood resembled a bucket with a handle. A bucket viewed side-on, its base to the south, its wider, open top, to the north. The wood then extended further northwards in a narrow band: so forming the handle. Running lengthwise from south to north through the wood proper, dividing it, was a narrow track which ended abruptly at the northern end. Perhaps at a building, but it was hard to tell on this scale of map. Vélu village lay to the north-west: at the top left-hand corner of the bucket. The railway, he now saw, lay beyond both the village and the handle, again to the north.

Paul was on the eastern edge of the wood. Along the western edge, a road hugged the wood along its length, coming from the south, from Bertincourt, and into Vélu village. Its existence simplified things, he decided, for all he had to do was strike off north-west through the wood until he came to the road, turn right, and follow it to the village. There would be no need to unship the compass, a measure that had been in his mind.

But before anything else, and before formulating any deeper, arguably pie-in-the-sky plans, he had to guard the Gnome against all this moisture in the air. For want of anything better he draped his silk scarf across the back of the nacelle to protect the ignition harness, covering it with his leather gloves and weighing down both with his makeshift brush. Finally, he patted the side of the nacelle. 'Don't go away.'

He had walked for fifty yards or so into the gathering gloom of the woods before he remembered the Very pistol. It was pointless carrying it so he stopped beside a tree that had been partially toppled in some storm and pushed both pistol and spare cartridge into a hollow between its roots, covering the cache with leaf mould. It struck him that he was becoming very squirrel-like in his behaviour and the thought lightened his mood. Then, without a backward glance, he set off on what he reckoned to be, at the very most, a trek of one and a half miles across the woods.

Despite the poor light it was not unduly hard going but flying clothing made the journey more laborious than it might have been. There was nothing Paul could do about his boots, which soon felt as if they were made of lead, but within ten minutes he had unbuttoned his leather coat, and not long afterwards, he took it off altogether. The trees fended away most of the drizzle but now and again a splash exploded against his face, startling him and bringing home to him just what a state his nerves were in. He could rationalise the situation and tell himself that anyone in like circumstances would be equally nervous but he knew that the double shocks of the forced-landing and of being here in enemy territory were merely incidental, that the root cause lay in the months of war flying.

He knew too that he held the remedy in his own hands. All he had to do was turn left into Bertincourt. He imagined presenting himself to the German sentry at the aerodrome. *'Ich bin ein Englisch Flieger Officier,'* he would announce. He wondered if the Germans were any more tolerant towards attempts at speaking their language than the French. They must be, surely? No nation on earth could be less so. *'Mein Gott!'* the sentry would exclaim. *'Kommen sie in, Tommy.'*

Certainly such a course of action recommended itself as the least hazardous way of becoming a prisoner of war, for the camaraderie extended by both sides to fellow fliers was legendary. No danger here of falling into the hands of front-line troops who might have a grudge to settle, merely a pleasant interlude of wining and dining in the mess before being sent on his way – and the remainder of the war for a rest cure. It was certainly something to think of.

He was only playing with the notion, of course, but the sobering thought came to him that had the situation been only a little different he might well be doing just that. Had he been wounded, or had the machine been hopelessly damaged on landing, or had he been forced to seriously face the prospect of days of marching and evading hostile forces in the illusory hope of reaching Holland, or Switzerland, or the Channel even, then what might his attitude be? As it was, he had a reasonable chance of getting back into the air again. Provided he could find the simple tools he needed, and get the job done before the Germans found the aircraft. He would need luck, and continued poor visibility. But the weather, at least, seemed set foul for as long as he would need it and as for luck, well, the next few hours would settle that.

Paul came upon the central divide he had seen on the map – a ride, it transpired – a good five minutes before he expected to, stepping around a clump of bushes to find himself in the open. Hurriedly he jumped back into cover, but the ride was both overgrown and deserted, and after a pause he ran across into the shelter of the woods on the far side. He could see nothing to the south due to the mist and an undulation in the ground, but looking up towards Vélu he fancied he could make out the loom of what looked like a sizeable house, a chateau, perhaps, facing down the ride. He was tempted to follow the cleared way up past the house but in the end he decided to stick to his original plan and to make his way diagonally through the woods to strike the road.

He found it eerie walking in the half-darkness among the trees but he put it down to his nerves and the awesome hush. At this time of day there was no birdsong, and no sign of life, and only the distant guns and the stirring of the breeze to break the silence. It was a settled wood, a demesne, no doubt, similar in size, by its appearance on the map to that of General Cousins, in Derbyshire, neglected perhaps because of the war, but otherwise quite untouched by it.

He paused to rest, hearing now the patter of actual droplets on the leafy carpet underfoot. Would the time soon come, he wondered, when Vélu Wood must take its place with High Wood, Trônes Wood and Delville Wood in the grim arboreal register of death? If it did, then in years to come there would be eeriness enough, lingering here among the glades.

Paul ran over his requirements in his mind. A good saw, and a plane – or a rasp. That was the minimum he could do with. A spanner that would fit the sparking plugs would be a bonus. Or an adjustable wrench. And rope – to find wire cable was more than he could hope for. A mallet and an axe for cutting pickets. A couple of mild-iron straps. He grinned thinly in the dusk. Might as well say two tailbooms and a new propeller. But essentially, just the saw. And first, to decide how to go about getting it.

The big house would seem the obvious choice, but it might well have been commandeered by the invaders. The meanest of the village houses, on the other hand, although more likely to offer succour than those further up the social scale, might not have the tools he wanted.

His best bet would be to look for a small farm with its own workshop, ideally, one remote from the village. He peered at the map, but was now unable to read what detail there was, even by holding it to the sky. He gave up the attempt. To a large extent it would have to remain a matter of chance.

His left heel had become sorely rubbed, and he felt the first twinges of discomfort in his right knee. He came upon a stream, but it was not that deep, although he had a certain amount of difficulty in negotiating the far bank. Once he tripped over a root and fell full-length, burying his chin in the mud and cursing through a mouthful of leaves. And now, as he neared the edge of the wood, brambles snared his legs, the undergrowth proliferating where trees had been felled. A dozen times he thought he was coming to the road, only to find more trees rising up before him. He took off his helmet, soaked with the constant dripping from the trees, and turned his head to listen. There was the sound of men's voices, and a sudden laugh, and he edged forwards, taking care to remain under cover. There was the tinny rattle of a bicycle, and another laugh. And all at once Paul found himself looking down into the road, his face only a matter of feet from the heads of three German soldiers.

Chapter Fifteen

The three were moving down the road towards Bertincourt. The one nearest Paul had a bicycle and was riding it slowly, employing exaggerated wheel angles to keep to the pace of his companions. The other two were skylarking, trying to upset the cyclist's balance. They were dressed in grey, high collared tunics and wore the pork-pie hats that until now Paul had only seen in photographs. Whether they were fighting troops or aircraftmen he had no idea. As far as he could see they were unarmed. And it struck him as unreal that he should be standing in such close proximity to the enemy, almost close enough to reach down and touch them. Suddenly the cyclist put on a burst of speed, racing away down the road, and at once the others gave chase, voices raised amid bursts of good-natured laughter.

The encounter gave Paul fresh cause for thought. Evidently there was a bar in the village where Germans were accustomed to drink; even a military canteen, perhaps. He would have to take great care from now on. He satisfied himself that the coast was clear, and jumped from the low banking down to the road. At once the going was easier, and within minutes he found himself where the road divided at the northern extremity of the wood. One branch turned and ran at ninety degrees to his right along the top edge of the wood – the rim of the bucket – towards the entrance to the chateau. The other ran straight on towards the first houses of the village – more a hamlet in English terms, he judged. Taking post at the very corner of the wood he climbed the bank, and settled down to observe.

The road running on ahead sloped down into a shallow gully, reemerging flanked by buildings with, some considerable way beyond, on the crest of the rise, the spire of a church. Stepping into the better light beyond the trees, he peered at the map – the church belonged to the neighbouring village, Lebucquiére, just beyond the railway line. The bulk of Vélu, he now realised, lay off to the right of where he crouched.

His nostrils had grown used to the scents of the woods; now they were assailed by the smell of fresh dung, the hallmark of every French farmhouse. He still found it inconceivable that people should willingly pile manure outside their own front door, yet every farm conformed to the custom as if to an immutable law. Now and again he saw a chink of light as a curtain was disturbed, and once a door opened, and closed again. A dog barked, but there was no other sign of life.

Paul looked at his watch, craning to read off the dial. He would wait for fifteen minutes, he decided, before venturing out beyond the wood. Back in the mess they would be sitting down to dinner. Robinson might already be packing up his things and the major would be shuffling the flight. Had any mail come for him in the evening's delivery, he wondered? Had Catherine written? Even one of her brief, infrequent, no-frills notes? More business reports than love letters, he reflected wryly.

It was time, Paul decided, although scarcely ten minutes had passed, but he could stand the inactivity no longer. Leaving the bushes he followed the side road, off to the right, walking in the shadow of a towering red brick wall, undoubtedly the boundary of the chateau. He kept to the shadows, his eyes wary, finding that the closest part of the village was built on two parallel roads, both eventually running uphill towards the railway station and its environs. Moving in cautious fits and starts, his flying boots scuffing softly over the damp pavé, he came upon pillars at the end of the wall and checked to his right, seeing the pile of a mansion, set amongst the trees. As he had foreseen it was just the sort of place to be commandeered by the occupying forces and he ducked back and retraced his steps until he found himself peering along the second parallel road. There were still no signs of life.

Cautiously he crossed the road. He passed what looked like a farm but decided against trying it, then passed two more darkened buildings before lamplight brightening a curtain showed that someone was inside. It was not the farmhouse with a workshop he had planned on seeking out but he decided it must do.

Suddenly dry mouthed, he knocked on the door. There was a lengthy pause, and he was about to knock again when the door opened and a man stood looking out at him suspiciously.

'*Je suis*,' Paul began, and was immediately aware that he had nearly said, '*Ich bin*'. Ah, well! his French was better than his German. He started again. '*Bonsoir, Monsieur. Je suis* an a*viateur Anglaise.*' The man gazed at him without a change of expression. He made not the slightest attempt to reply, merely stepped back and closed the door.

Paul was taken aback. He had never given a thought to the reaction he might expect on this side of the lines. Suddenly he felt very isolated. And aware of how cold it had become. But after a while he collected himself and moved along to another house. Here nobody answered, although a curtain moved. He made two more calls and at each received a curt, practically wordless rejection. Perhaps they thought he was German, trying to trap them? At the fifth house he fared a little better. Here the lady of the house joined her husband. Having looked him over from head to toe the man shrugged his shoulders and turned back into the house, taking the oil lamp with him. The woman, however, stepped past Paul into the street to point back down the way he had come, indicating a turning he had missed, and a house set back off the road.

'You think, there?' he asked. And then, searching his memory, '*Je vous me remercie ...*'

But she had already turned away, still without a word, the door closing firmly to behind her.

He was very wary now, edging to the corner. '*Rue de l'Eglise*', he made out, looking up at a shadowed wall plate. He hesitated before the house the woman had indicated but then, with sudden resolution, pushed through the gate and entered the short drive. He kept a close eye on the houses he had already tried, but saw only blank darkness.

The door opened to his second knock. The inevitable lamp, and the same non-committal scrutiny. The man was on the lower borders of middle age, but the face was thin and lined, and the hollows around his eyes were only partly cast there by the lamp. The eyes themselves regarded Paul steadily, not with suspicion, but with weariness. A weariness that Paul had seen before. In the wards, in the eyes of men made old before their time by sickness and the constant fret of pain.

'*Bonsoir, Monsieur, je vous prie,*' Paul tried. '*Je suis* an – *un* – *aviateur Anglaise.*' He paused, and supplemented this with, 'English, *pilote.*' And moved his hand, swooping it through the air.

The man's eyes followed his hand and then studied him overall, his gaze finally falling to dwell on Paul's boots. Paul looked down and saw the moisture seeping onto the scrubbed porch, the leaves caked on the insteps, and the mud around the welts. God, he must look a real tramp! He began again, '*Je voudrais, s'il vous plait ...*' But the man, without a word, stepped back into the hallway and beckoned him inside.

In silence Paul followed down a stone-flagged corridor into what was obviously the main sitting room of the house. It was vastly overfurnished to the English eye but bespoke quality and taste. There were damask drapes pulled to across the windows, with tasselled pelmets of the same material forming shelves on which were displayed figurine groups in dust-proof glass domes. The well-worn furniture appeared comfortable, if too bulky for the room, while the ornate clock taking pride of place in the centre of one wall seemed as if it had been jammed into place between ceiling and floor. There was a log fire in the substantial hearth and even from the doorway Paul could feel its heat upon his face. There were more logs piled high beside the fireplace with sparkling brassware on a stand. He had an impression of glass-fronted cabinets full of ornamental plates and dishes, and shelf upon shelf of books. A red lamp burned beneath a statuette of the Madonna and child, the infant beckoning with outstretched arms towards the family portraits massed along the mantelpiece.

Apart from his host there were two other people in the room, a lad sitting in a wooden chair drawn up to a corner of the fire, and a girl, kneeling in front of the blaze rearranging the logs with a pair of long, brass tongs. Both looked up expectantly, but before either could react further the man walked to the hearth and spoke rapidly in a tone too low for Paul to catch. Paul noticed that he kept his back turned, presumably imparting in private what had transpired on the doorstep.

The man spoke separately to the girl and by his manner seemed to be giving her instructions. Paul looked uneasily at the second door, standing slightly ajar and possibly leading towards the rear exit, but the girl made no move to leave the room, simply put the tongs back on the companion set and sat down in an armchair where an opened book suggested that Paul's arrival had interrupted her in her reading. Paul was struck by her dark good looks but she lowered her eyes and took no further notice of him, her lips moving slightly as she began to read, her head turned a little, the better to catch the light.

The lad, on the other hand, had evinced deep interest from the first, jumping to his feet and examining Paul intently throughout the hurried exchange. He was scarcely more than a boy, with a shock of dark hair that would break the heart of any sergeant major, and he moved from foot to foot, eyes eager, clearly excited by this unexpected visitation.

But as the man spoke, the lad's features stilled, although as he sat back slowly on his chair his eyes never for a moment left Paul's face.

The man turned abruptly, and seemed surprised to find Paul still standing in the corridor. '*M'sieur.*' He beckoned him further into the room. Paul pointed down at his muddy flying boots and pantomimed his reluctance to venture spoiling the polished wood-block floor. The man smiled slightly, overriding his protests with a sweep of his hand.

'Thank you,' said Paul, '*Merci, M'sieur.*'

Gladly, he made his way closer to the warmth of the fire, and stood for a space, watching the steam begin to rise from the knees of his trousers. The clock was silent, either broken or left unwound, and the quiet was disturbed only by the crackle of the flames. The girl was a slow reader for she had not yet turned a page.

'*M'sieur?*' his host's voice was politely interrogative.

Paul straightened up and stepped away from the fire the better to keep all three of them in sight. The man was regarding him impassively, not pressing him, simply waiting for him to explain himself. Paul took out his RFC identity card and proffered it. The man looked at it closely, turning it over in his hands before passing it to the boy.

'*Je suis un aviateur Anglaise,*' Paul tried again. '*Mon –*' Hell! what was the word for aeroplane? *Machine volante?* His mind went blank. '*Mon* Spad,' he said finally, '*Est panne. Je tombe –*' he pointed in the direction of the woods. '*En arbre.*'

The silence lengthened. The man and the boy looked at him attentively. The boy had not even dropped his eyes to examine the card.

'*Je voudrais ascende,*' Paul struggled on. '*Je voudrais outils –*' What on earth was the word for 'saw'?

And suddenly he was exasperated with the whole situation. What was the matter with these people, they looked bright enough, so were they simply being obtuse, being typically bloody French?

'I'm English,' he burst out. '*Le Guerre.* I am your friend, your bloody Ally, damn it!' He caught himself immediately and inclined towards the girl. 'Pardon me! *Je prie –.*'

The girl looked up from her book and laughed softly. 'I think he really is, Papa,' she said in virtually unaccented English. 'No *Boche* would speak such execrable French.'

She lifted to her feet and came towards Paul with outstretched hand and at once the atmosphere changed. Suddenly there were smiles all around. Paul let out his breath, and felt himself beginning to grin.

'Well,' he said finally, 'well.'

'I am Angele Basquin,' the girl introduced herself. 'This is my father, *Monsieur* Louis Basquin, and this is my brother, Henri.' Her handshake was firm and warm, and her dark eyes smiled up into his. '*Monsieur* – ?'

'Paul Cowley,' he supplied. 'And thank you for taking me in.'

'Where is your Spad, *Monsieur*?' The lad was fingering the sleeve of Paul's leather coat. 'Are you an acc? Have you shot down many *Boche*?' The questions which came spilling out were so heavily accented that Paul had difficulty in understanding them but the girl laughed and spoke rapidly to her brother in French. The lad looked crestfallen and dropped his hand from Paul's coat, but hurried off through the far door which Paul now saw led into the kitchen.

'Henri is very excited,' Angele smiled. 'He would like to be a soldier and to be an aviator would be his heaven. His English is not so fine, but he is a good boy. I have sent him for coffee.'

She led Paul across to her father and watched as the two men shook hands. Louis Basquin stood several inches taller than Paul, a handsome man, still supporting a full head of thick, black hair. He was big-boned and held himself erect but his features were gaunt and lined and his frame was strangely wasted. Beneath his dressing gown his shoulders showed thin and narrow, shaking painfully when he broke off the handshake to cough into a handkerchief.

'*Pardon, M'sieur*,' he excused himself, and having caught his breath, went on at once as if to forestall any reference to his infirmity. 'You are welcome in our house, *Monsieur* Cowley. I must apologise for your reception, but you will understand that it is necessary to be cautious.' His English was not nearly as fluent as his daughter's but he spoke slowly and clearly and Paul had no difficulty in understanding him.

'Papa means the curfew.' The girl had moved to link arms with her father and now looked fondly up at the older man as she went on. 'Father was an officer in the – the reserves. He was wounded on the Marne and the tribunal would not let him continue to serve. He was allowed to return home to recover but the *Boche* do not like him and they watch him all the time. And I must watch him even more closely for he is too proud to – to – conceal, his own dislike.'

Basquin smiled, his eyes lighting up as he looked down at his daughter's head nestled against his shoulder. He murmured something into her hair and she looked up at Paul in protest.

'He says I am a *babillar* – a chatterbox. You see, he thinks I am still a child. But he should not be so haughty with the *Boche*.'

Her father spoke again, smiling at her proudly, and she rounded on him, turning then to Paul. 'But he is a man, and this they do not forgive. For a girl, I tell him, it is easy.'

Basquin held up a hand. '*Monsieur* Cowley is wet and will soon be cold,' he pointed out. 'He should dry out his clothes while we discuss what is to be done.'

The girl, clearly annoyed at her own remissness, went quickly from the room. A moment later there was the sound of movement overhead.

Paul faced Basquin worriedly. 'I had forgotten the curfew.'

Yet it was common knowledge that the Germans had imposed stringent curfew restrictions throughout all the occupied territories. Penalties for curfew breaking were said to be severe. Harbouring or otherwise assisting fugitives would be even more seriously viewed; indeed it was rumoured that in some areas the death penalty had been exacted for aiding escaped prisoners of war. And not solely for people as exceptional as Nurse Cavell. True, it could be argued that Paul was not technically a prisoner of war until they caught him, but that would make no difference to the punishment meted out to anyone who helped him. The sudden realisation that he was putting at risk the very lives of these people filled him with alarm. He had begun to unbutton the flap of his tunic, now he hastened to fasten it again, and picked up his coat and helmet from the table.

Basquin shook his head. 'They are not strict about the curfew in these parts. Your airmen drop bombs on the railway station and on their aerodrome and some people have been moved away, but we are not bothered much by the Germans. There are no soldiers billeted in this end of the village. There is – toleration. When the Allies break through, of course, it will be different.'

He drew Paul closer to the fire and indicated once again that he should remove his wet clothes. Henri backed through the kitchen door bearing a coffee tray while at the same moment Angele, cheeks flushed with the exertion of running up and down stairs, re-entered the room, her arms laden with clothes and towels. She dropped them on a chair beside Paul and at once busied herself with pouring out the coffee. Henri, freed from the tray, hurried to take the tunic from Paul, and held it against himself, eyes glowing, looking expectantly at Paul. The lad said nothing, but when Paul smiled, he seemed satisfied that some request had been granted, and slipped the tunic over his own shoulders.

'I knocked at other doors before a lady suggested I came here,' Paul said, suddenly remembering. 'Maybe someone will report it?'

'No,' Basquin told him, 'it will go no further.'

Paul turned to the girl. 'I was saying to your father that I am putting you in danger by coming here.' Basquin said something Paul could not catch, but both Henri and Angele laughed appreciatively.

'My father says that as an Englishman you have already put yourself in greater danger just getting here,' explained Angele. She went on, 'Now you must not protest. You must put on this gown, and sit close to the fire while we talk.'

Paul found that his leggings and the tunic had kept out most of the moisture, but his boots were of soft leather and the fur inners had become soaking wet. Angele insisted that they be removed, tugging at the right one herself when he found difficulty in getting it off.

'You are hurt? Wounded?' She had seen him wince.

'A motor bike,' he told her. 'Long ago.'

'Don't tell that one,' she said conspiratorially, indicating Henri, who was now trying on the helmet in front of the mirror and looking pensively at the boots which his sister had just put out of his reach to one side of the fire. 'To fly an aeroplane is to be admired; to own a motor cycle is to be worshipped.'

Monsieur Basquin and Paul took their coffee by the fire while the girl and her brother prepared a meal. It was plain wholesome country fare and Paul suddenly found that he was ravenous. He had no idea what rationing might be in force and he tried to partake sparingly but there was no hiding from the combination of Basquin and his offspring and when the meal was ended and the plates cleared away he could not have eaten another morsel.

Throughout the meal he had faced a continuous barrage of questions from Henri, only half of which he had understood. They did manage an exchange of sorts, however, at the close of which he became aware that he had gone down several pegs in the boy's estimation: he was not an ace, and he did not really fly Spads. Clearly a DH2, or indeed any English-built aeroplane, was nowhere in the reckoning beside the Spad.

For his part he had found out, mostly from Angele, that Louis Basquin was a widower, an accountant in peacetime, and a captain in the infantry reserve. He had been wounded in the chest by a trench-mortar bomb in 1914 and had lain untended in the marshes of St Gond for three days and nights before being found by a stretcher party. The wound, and the infection he had picked up, had left him with weak lungs. It was expected, according to Angele, that he would eventually recover, but it would be a long process. She had wanted to get permission from the Germans to move him south to the mountains but he had refused to let her approach them.

As for the boy, Paul learnt that Henri had been brought up largely by his sister and had no ambition in life other than to join the army in some way or another and fight the *Boche*.

Angele, Paul discovered, had spent a year or two in what he gathered was some sort of finishing school in England – in Kent – and after that had begun to work at a dress designers in Paris, returning home just before the war when her mother finally gave up the struggle against ill health. There had, it seemed, been an opportunity for her to get back to Paris even after the Germans came, but with her father being wounded she felt that her duty lay in looking after him. She did not wear a ring but she considered herself affianced to her childhood sweetheart, who was away at the war.

Despite Paul's learning all that, still the girl seemed reluctant to elaborate on the personal side of her life, except as it concerned her family, and he did not feel inclined to press her. It had been a hard and very unusual day. Two flights, and then all the subsequent trauma. And with the warmth of the fire soaking through him, and the replete feeling of the meal below his belt – his first home-cooked meal for who-knows how long –, he was beginning to feel decidedly drowsy. Abruptly, realising this, he sat up, and looked at his watch. It was getting late, another hour had slipped away. It was high time he got down to the business in hand.

Louis Basquin immediately perceived Paul's renewed sense of purpose. 'You mentioned tools, Monsieur Cowley.'

Paul had already explained that he had broken his propeller and had glided down beside the wood. Now he drew a sketch of the de

Havilland's location, making it a much larger scale than that of the map segment he carried with him. There was an animated buzz of discussion between Henri and Angele neither of whom was conversant with maps. Basquin put in a few words of explanation after which it was quickly established that they were both familiar with the spot where the machine lay. Henri moved his finger down the edge of the wood to its southern boundary and then about as far again off the end of the paper.

'It is close, the *Boche* aerodrome. Aerodrome?' He looked at his sister for confirmation of the word, and then repeated it again, 'Aerodrome.'

Paul nodded. 'I thought it must be.' He spoke directly to Basquin 'If the weather stays the same and I can get the machine repaired by first light tomorrow, then I hope to fly back to my army.'

'*Monsieur* Paul,' Henri had followed the sense of Paul's words. 'You take me. Then we fight the *Boche* together.' Angele spoke sharply and the boy looked sullen, but she patted him on the shoulder and in a moment he was smiling again.

'What tools do you need to carry out the repairs, *Monsieur* Cowley?' she asked. 'And is it possible to correct it in the fields?'

He answered her last query first. 'I believe I can do it.'

Pulling the paper towards him again he drew the shape of a four-bladed propeller. 'This is made of wood. This portion here, about six inches – say, fifteen centimetres –, is broken. If I saw the other tips off too, I can make it balance.' He sketched in the cuts he intended to make and all three nodded their understanding. 'It will not be happy,' he smiled. 'And it will not be efficient.' In fact, he admitted to himself, it will probably be bloody unhappy, and bloody inefficient. Aloud he said, 'A saw is the most important tool I need.'

Basquin spoke at length to the girl, and it seemed that she demurred at something he put to her for the discussion went backwards and forwards for some minutes. Finally Angele nodded acquiescence and turned again to Paul.

'What else – what other tools?'

He went through the list, sketching here and there where the technicalities were beyond her English vocabulary until in the end she took the pencil from him and wrote out a list of her own. This she read over to her father, making comments as she went. Basquin asked a few questions, and then fell silent, considering the matter. Paul waited quietly, content to leave things in their hands. He did not have to wait long. Father and daughter held a further consultation at the end of which Angele turned to Paul.

'It is probable that we could get nearly all the things from the village, only the sparking-plug one we do not have. But tell me –,' she turned over the paper and pointed, 'This part?' She pointed to the centre of his sketch of the propeller.

'The hub?'

She nodded. 'Is this part the same on all these? If so, there is one of these, and all the tools, not far from here.'

Paul looked at her in astonishment. He jabbed his finger on the sketch. 'A propeller? Like this? And other tools?'

She nodded. '*Oui* – yes. Many others.'

'But how?'

She looked across at her father. 'Before the Germans came there was an interest in all things: cars, motor cycles, bicycles, and aeroplanes. And these things will still be there.'

'Not confiscated by the Germans? Not taken away?'

She shook her head vigorously. 'They are still there. In a barn in the farmyard.'

'And would the people let me use them?'

'Yes, they are my friends,' she said simply.

Henri had been following the conversation as far as he was able and at this he yelped with laughter, repeating her words in a tormenting manner, plainly teasing her. Instantly she turned on the boy, colouring up and beating her clenched fist upon the table, a reaction which only fuelled her brother's mischief until Basquin himself intervened, '*Chut! chut! silence, Henri!*'

'But he *is* her lover,' the boy protested, appealing to Paul. 'She kiss at his picture every night.'

Again the two began to wrangle, affording Paul space to turn the information over in his mind.

It was unlikely that the propeller Angele knew of would fit. But there was always the chance that its hub would match his engine's nave: the Gnome was French, after all, and many propellers were designed around it. His present intention was to cut down the undamaged blades of his propeller to achieve a balance, something he had to admit would be virtually impossible to achieve with the propeller mounted as it was on the engine. At best the result would be inefficient, at worst it would produce a vibration that would rip the motor from its fastenings; either that or complete the fracture of the damaged tailbooms, tearing the machine to pieces in the air. Yet nearby, it would seem, was a workshop where he might well find all the tools he needed. Possibly even materials with which to strengthen the damaged structure. And if there really was a compatible propeller, then so much the better.

But the time element!

Paul had envisaged borrowing a saw and making a simple cut through the propeller tips, swinging the engine, and taking off before the Germans knew he was there. Only now that there was an alternative to consider he was forced to admit that it would be pointless finishing up in a smouldering heap at the end of the take-off run, and even more so finishing up in a splintered mess three miles away when the tail fell off. It was politic then to reassess the whole problem.

The chances were that he could unship the propeller and get it to this workshop, carry out the repairs, balance it, fashion the splints he needed for the tailbooms, and still be away before his presence was discovered. But it would need the co-operation of several people, each of whom would be risking the death penalty in assisting him. Even then it would need a lot of luck and another morning of misty weather to minimise the chances of the Germans stumbling over the machine before he was set to go. There was a lot to consider.

Paul's initial reaction was to stick to his original plan, trusting to luck and getting under way at first light. On further reflection, however, every engineering principle warned him that it would be foolhardy to attempt to take-off without doing everything possible to ensure that the attempt would be successful. Besides, technical considerations apart, enough people were already in jeopardy. If he presented the Germans with a pile of wreckage to sift through then more might come under threat. If, on the other hand, he got away successfully then he would take the evidence with him. And no one else would suffer.

'How far is this place?' he asked.

Basquin pored over the map. 'It is here.' He pointed. 'From your machine, about six kilometres. Just beyond Hermies, our market town.'

Paul eyed the map. Directly across country then. He grunted, musing: the squaw on the Potomac is equal to the sum of the squaws on the other ... – say about three and a half miles. Say four miles. It was feasible – it would march! But first, the sparking plugs.

'Have you a spanner like this?' he asked Basquin. He sketched an adjustable spanner. Basquin spoke to Henri who at once got up from his seat and left the room. A moment later, hearing the back door close behind the boy, Paul turned in alarm. 'But the curfew!'

Angele touched him on the arm, lightly, but imparting a comradely warmth. 'It is safe,' she assured him. 'He only goes two doors away. Many villagers even go hunting at night.'

'Poaching' Paul suggested, a little mollified. And both Angele and her father laughed aloud at the emendation.

'You think it would be best to go to this place?' Basquin asked.

'Thank you, yes,' said Paul.

Carefully he went over his reasoning, stressing his dread of implicating anybody who had helped him. Enumerating, on the other hand, the considerations which had then led him to decide that to hurry into things would be irresponsible. Angele, he was well aware, had begun to frown.

'Then we are agreed,' nodded Basquin. 'Angele was afraid you would not want to wait,'

'There is a risk,' Paul admitted, 'for if the Germans find the machine first –'

'Then at least you will still be alive,' said Angele as if to cut short any other objections.

'What we suggest, Monsieur,' Basquin diplomatically interposed, 'is that you rest here tonight. Then, when the curfew permits, first thing in the morning, Angele will take you in the – *charrette anglaise*?' he applied to his daughter.

'Dog cart.'

'Yes. The dog cart. To pick up the tools and the new propeller and take it back to the aeroplane. If you need more assistance, then it can be arranged.'

'And if you need to make other journeys to the workshop,' Angele put in brightly, 'I can drive you.' She smiled. 'You see, *Monsieur* Paul, it is all arranged.'

Before Paul could reply the back door opened and closed, and Henri came into the room, breathless in his anxiety not to miss anything, a small wrench in his hand. He handed it to Basquin, who immediately passed it across to Paul. 'It is correct?' It was an adjustable spanner that would open up to about an inch.

'It is ideal, thank you, Henri,' said Paul.

'They have many spanners at the farm,' Angele observed, her eyes not leaving Paul's face. And then, 'You do not approve of our plan?'

Paul shook his head, and specifically addressed himself to his host. 'It is a good plan, Monsieur Basquin, but I must beg leave to change it.'

Must beg leave! He sought to take himself in check. It would be, '*ow do you say*? next. He hurried on. Anything to avoid the girl's eyes.

'To go in the cart with *Mademoiselle* Basquin would be to put her in too much danger.' He ignored the girl's splutter of protest, and carried on. 'There is a safer way, which will save time, if you agree.'

'*Monsieur?*' Basquin inclined his head, and waited to hear what Paul had to say. That there would be an element of danger for Angele, no matter how slight, he could not deny.

'*M'sieur*,' Paul began. 'If as you suggest, I could rest for a while –,' he embraced both Henri and Angele in his request. 'Then at dawn I will return to my aeroplane, remove the damaged part and take it across country to the farm.' He pointed on the map to where the farm was shown beyond a minor road leading out of the neighbouring Hermies.

'If your friends were told of my coming then I could enter the barn and do the work without them being involved. If the weather stays foggy, I would leave again, and fly my aeroplane away. If not, then the machine will almost certainly be discovered. Then I would wait until nightfall and walk from the area. That way, nobody will be put at risk.'

It was clear that Basquin had not followed everything Paul had said but the girl had missed nothing. And it was obvious that she disliked what she had heard. She turned to her father and let loose a seemingly ceaseless torrent of French. Basquin responded now and then, but sparingly, as if overwhelmed by his daughter's passion while Paul watched in bewilderment as the girl held forth, pushing back her chair at one stage and actually hammering on the table with clenched fists. Her cheeks were flushed, her breast heaved, and the one glance she flung at Paul was dark with fury.

She did not raise her voice but raged on vehemently in tones that quivered with anger. In other circumstances Paul would have been struck by the picture she made, now he felt only embarrassment, fully aware that he had caused the outburst, but without being entirely sure how, and utterly lost to find a way of making amends. Henri, when he could get a word in, seemed to be taking his sister's part although his face, framed as it now was by Paul's flying helmet, was more eager than indignant. At length Basquin brought the discussion to a halt. He shot two or three sharp questions at the girl, each one cutting across her tirade and forcing her to a short, grudging answer. And out of the silence that ensued, Basquin began to speak.

Paul followed little of what Basquin said but it was clear that as the head of the household he was pronouncing upon the issue. At no time had he raised his voice any more than his daughter had, and now he spoke in tones of calm authority, as one who accepts it for a surety that his children will obey him without further question. And so it transpired, for Angele resumed her seat and sat with downcast eyes while Henri began to grin. Whatever the matter, it had been settled to the boy's satisfaction at least.

Basquin turned his attention to Paul without apology or explanation for the altercation.

'It is arranged, *M'sieur*. And it shall be as you say. After curfew tomorrow morning Angele will drive over and make the arrangements, then return here. But can you carry the propeller without a cart? Although to fly in the air a machine must be light, but –.' He raised his eyebrows.

Paul thought for a moment. The monosoupape Gnome gave a nominal one-hundred horse power. He dragged a formula from somewhere in his mind. 'Two point five times the square root of the horsepower': but was that for two-, three-, or four-bladed propellers? He raised his eyes and unintentionally met those of the girl. Angele may have acquiesced to her father's ruling but she was still far from reconciled to it and her eyes reflected this. Indeed Paul was so thrown by her manifest hostility that he actually reached for pencil and paper to work out two and a half times ten! So the seven-and-a-half-foot propeller should weigh not more than twenty-five pounds.

'Yes,' he replied. 'I can carry it easily.' This time he avoided looking at the girl. 'It should weigh about twelve kilos.'

'But when you return – all the tools and other things?' Basquin pressed. Paul turned it over in his mind: the metal straps, if he was lucky, the wooden stakes, and some rope. That was all. It could all be bundled, and slung.

'It will weigh very little more. And first, at the aeroplane, I shall need only the spanner.' He was struck with a sudden thought. '*Monsieur*

Basquin, do you have a screwdriver?' The word was beyond Basquin but the girl had been following the conversation.

'*Un tournevis*,' she muttered.

'*Ah, oui*. Yes, *M'sieur* Paul.'

'Then, thank you, that is all. Oh! perhaps a knife, for the rope.'

Basquin nodded. 'All that can be done. But, as you have said, it will be many hours before you can return to your machine. If the Germans find it, then they will trap you. So Henri will take you to your machine. I have told him that he must wait where he can keep watch without being seen. He will stay until you return. If the worst happens then he will meet you and warn you not to come closer.'

Paul mulled this over. 'But if he is seen out early, or found in the woods?'

'There is no risk,' interjected the girl brusquely. 'Many times we –' she broke off and shot a glance at her father, '*He*, goes out at night, hunting.'

'Poaching, we settled upon?' smiled Paul, relieved that she seemed to have recovered at least some of her goodwill towards him.

'Poaching,' she agreed, stony faced. 'The Germans do not picquet the wood.'

'And can you start the machine alone?' asked Basquin.

'It is normal to have two people,' Paul admitted, 'but I can do it.'

'Then thank you for your care, *M'sieur* Cowley. But now I think you should rest. Angele already casts doubt on your leg, for you have much walking to do.'

Paul looked inquiringly at the girl, but her objections having once been overcome Angele had clearly decided to make the best of things and made no further comment but went upstairs to prepare the spare room for him. Henri was sent into the kitchen and came back brandishing a knife and two screwdrivers which he tendered for Paul's approval. One had clearly seen better days but the other was useable and Paul put it with the knife alongside the wrench. His knee was throbbing with fatigue and he was glad when Basquin indicated that it was time to go to bed. And yet he paused, frowning. Something had been tugging at his mind for minutes now.

He unfolded the map segment fully, to beyond the limit of his patrol's brief, and pored over it, suspicion rapidly becoming a certainty. The farm where the tools and propeller were, Angele had said, was outside Hermies. But only the *Canal du Nord* separated Hermies from the *Bois d'Havrincourt*! The village woman who had directed him to the Basquin house would have known of the girl's connection with the distant farm. And with the aviation interest there. And how many farms hereabouts, or anywhere else, for that matter, were centres of aviation interest?

'The farm,' Paul asked now, 'is it the farm of *Capitaine* Jacques Delcamp?'

The astonishment on Henri's face was a joy to see.

'But only a few days ago,' Paul told them, 'I had a letter from *Capitaine* Delcamp. You will be glad to know that he is alive and well.'

Basquin gazed at him for just a moment longer, then began to smile. 'Angele!' he hailed.

There was a distinct pause, almost a deliberate pause, and no verbal acknowledgement, but then the girl's feet could be heard clumping grudgingly down the stairs.

Later, following Henri up the narrow stairs to bed, Paul paused and pressed his face against the landing window. There was no sign of the stars, and even when his eyes grew accustomed to the darkness he could see nothing towards the woods but the pale afterglow of the mist. He crossed his fingers and breathed a prayer that the weather would hold. There was nothing else he could do.

Chapter Sixteen

Paul slept well, dropping off the moment his head touched the pillow, yet when Henri aroused him he was reluctant to leave the bed and face the chilliness of the pre-dawn day.

'It is good,' the boy told him, grinning. 'It is fog, very fog.' He had brought with him a steaming jug of hot water and one of his father's razors, newly honed. 'Angele says breakfast will be soon.' He seemed inclined to linger but Paul shooed him out and he left, putting one finger up alongside his nose in an urchin's farewell.

Wryly, Paul reflected on the previous evening. If he had expected the revelation about his friendship with Jacques to placate the girl he had soon been disabused. For the most part it had been the others who had put all the questions; by and large she had remained icily silent. But she had taken in everything he could tell them about Jacques, of that he was convinced. And remembering how friendly and partisan she had been before their still-unexplained falling out he took her silence for a measure of just how much he had upset her.

They said their farewells in the passage. *Monsieur* Basquin regretted being unable to accompany Paul in person but he had to travel to Bapaume to chair a civic committee which negotiated with the German authorities to ensure that local interests were kept to the fore. It was largely as a result of his uncompromising line on such committees, Paul gathered, that the Germans continued to treat him with suspicion and as a man who would bear watching. *Monsieur* Basquin shook his hand warmly, and smilingly forbore from embracing him. Angele made not the slightest move towards embracing him but said goodbye civilly enough, although most of her attention was on Henri.

The boy, Paul saw, was kitted out with a rucksack into which Angele had packed bread and wine to sustain him during the course of his long vigil. Basquin had insisted upon Paul taking a pair of his sturdy ankle boots, refusing to listen to any protestations, and in truth, remembering his rubbed heel of the night before, Paul had not welcomed the overland trek in his flying boots. Now he followed Henri out into the dark, mist-shrouded street. There was a low '*Bon voyage!*' from Basquin, and a marked silence otherwise, before the door latch snicked behind them.

They set off on their way, Paul profoundly unsettled by the girl's sustained hostility. Yet puzzled too, for from the first he had been aware of a mutual regard. And distressingly, he had no idea what offence he had committed to so suddenly rate her hostility. Further, to leave on such poor terms with someone who was risking so much for him seemed unmannerly in the extreme and he paused, half-decided to turn about and set matters right. Henri, however, seeing his hesitation, beckoned him on. And a moment's more reflection told him that nothing was to be gained by further involving the Basquins in returning to the house.

That Henri harboured no doubts about Paul's proposed way of going about things was plain, for he led the way without a further rearward glance, past the church, set back amid the trees, and up the slope, swinging his arms light-heartedly. Paul looked back just once, but the house was in darkness, and he lost sight of it altogether as they rounded the first corner. Moments later, and before he could steal as much as a glance in the direction of the railway station – that frequently visited RFC target –, Henri stopped and beckoned him over a broken wall. Paul followed, scrambling on tumbled bricks and jumping down a foot or so, to see the boy's shadowy figure entering the outer fringes of the wood; the top section of the handle of Paul's bucket!

It soon became obvious that Henri was in his element in the woods, for dark as it was, the boy found his way unerringly. Paul had the impression that they were leaving Vélu Chateau to their right, receiving confirmation a short while later when they came out of the trees and he sensed open ground rising off to the left. Ahead, along the border of the wood, the mist clung to the branches in filigree, delineating the trees, transforming them even in the darkness into pale, translucent shades; to the left, over the yawning, unseen gulf across the fields, the mist seemed to take on a different quality, its bland opaqueness intensifying the gloom so that until his eyes grew accustomed to the illusory prospect Paul found himself edging closer to the wood, away from what felt like the brink of a void. Schooling himself to ignore this delusion, so reminiscent of flying in thick cloud, he found the going easy, a wide and grassy margin having been left unploughed. His borrowed boots were comfortable, and above all he was fired with a new sense of purpose after his lack of resolve on awakening.

They made good time, Paul's stumbling progress through the woods the night before taking on, in retrospect, a nightmarish quality. But then he had been tired and uncertain. Now he was fresh, and he had a positive course of action mapped out which offered every possibility of success. Abruptly Henri slowed, and Paul realised with sudden concern that, unwittingly, he had let the boy lead him to the very edge of the hollow.

Henri was thrown into a state of high excitement at the sight of the aeroplane and started forward eagerly but Paul, vexed with himself for not having realised just how far they had come, grasped urgently at the boy's arm. He had intended to go ahead and reconnoitre long before this. As it was, he cursed himself for endangering the boy, although in the same instant he accepted the fact that Henri, having proved himself a natural in the woods, was probably more than capable of deciding if danger lay ahead. That, nonetheless, did nothing to relieve Paul's sense of responsibility towards the Basquins. Accordingly, as a sop to his conscience, and despite the boy's repeated insistence that the area was clear, he forced down his own impatience and insisted that they wait and watch for a good five minutes. Only then did he release Henri's arm and give him free rein to run the rest of the way towards the machine.

Working together, they unpacked a lantern from Henri's haversack, adjusting the flame and then shuttering it down so that it would not draw unwelcome eyes. Paul, with a final scrutiny of the woods, then turned his full attention to the aeroplane.

He began by walking slowly around the machine with the lantern held close, eyes and fingers reassessing the work to be done, going over every step in his mind. It would be senseless not to do a thorough reappraisal now that he was rested, for when he arrived back here it would be rather late in the day to discover that he was short of something or other. Wherever he turned, however, the boy was there beside him, peppering him with questions, twanging at wires or trying to put his foot through the fabric. Finally Paul sent him off to scout towards Bertincourt, promising that he could sit in the cockpit once the work was done.

It took Paul twenty minutes of painstaking examination but at the end of that time he was as certain as he could be that he had overlooked nothing in his calculations. The inspection and reassessment complete, he summoned Henri, and started in upon the work.

Like all RFC machines the de Havilland was maintained in top-rate condition and undoing the centre flange nuts securing the propeller hub presented no problem. Paul removed the last of the nine nuts, enfolded it in a piece of rag with the others, and buttoned the lot into a pocket. After which he lifted the propeller off the nave and manoeuvred it, not without difficulty, sideways beneath the lower tailboom and through the bracing wires into Henri's eager hands.

Next Paul turned his attention to the sparking plugs. There were nine of these to contend with too. Plugs were notoriously troublesome components in the Gnome and he wanted to ensure that they did not let him down after their night's cold soak in oil and moisture. He lifted off the makeshift broom, and the now-soaking scarf and gloves, then set about carefully disconnecting the uninsulated brass wires leading out from the ebonite ring of the magneto, checking each for damage before stowing it neatly in a finger-wrapped coil.

A somewhat trickier task was to withdraw the sparking plugs themselves, a process with demanded infinite care for fear of straining the skin-thin walls of the cylinders. Fortunately the plugs stood proud of the fins and he had no trouble in obtaining purchase with the wrench, so that apart from the inevitable one that was stiffer than the rest and brought his heart into his mouth before it came free, he soon had all nine unscrewed. He wrapped each plug separately and stowed the whole bundle in one of the larger pockets of his flying coat.

In addition to the rags, Paul had procured a sheet of oilcloth from the Basquin kitchen and now he spread this over the magneto and the ignition wires to protect them from the moisture filming every surface. Once again he replaced scarf, gloves, and branch. And finally, having checked that the oil and petrol had not unaccountably drained away overnight, he stood back, knowing that he was ready to begin his trek. Already there was an appreciable lightening of the sky to the east.

First however, he had to honour his promise to the boy. True, doing so raised qualms in him but he reasoned that this, after all, was the time of least risk, for it was still quite dark and there was little likelihood of anyone being up and about. Moreover, unless Henri's eagerness was satisfied now Paul had no doubt that the boy would unpremeditatedly gravitate towards the machine during his hours of vigil: its very presence would act as a magnet – and such a temptation was too big a strain to load on any lad.

There followed ten minutes of pure joy for Henri who seemed to forget all the English he knew in the excitement of fastening the six-inch-wide lapstrap and donning the helmet he had only reluctantly given up the night before. He grasped the stick with both hands and pushed it and pulled it until Paul began to fear for the control surfaces. Henri flung himself from side to side, nose up and nose down, darting through the clouds and skimming the ground, pilot of a Spad – an ace – chasing the *Boche* from the sky with what he imagined to be all the appropriate noises and facial expressions. The only fly in the ointment was Paul's refusal to re-install the ammunition drums.

'Then I shoot the *Boche* when they come,' the boy pleaded, pointing in the direction of Bertincourt.

Paul shook his head. 'When the *Boche* come,' he said firmly, 'you will be there.' He pointed to the woods.

It was an interlude that Paul enjoyed quite as much as the boy, but it was only an interlude and he kept a close eye on the approaching dawn. He was uncomfortably aware that he had broken strict faith with Basquin in permitting Henri to become so involved but he was determined to make the boy understand how vital it was that from now on he stayed clear of the machine. At the end of the ten minutes, however, he discovered that Henri was already fully sensible of his role for the lad nodded at once and gave his word that the only move he would make from now on would be to warn Paul. And then it was time to go.

Paul climbed up into the cockpit and prepared to unship the compass. The first screw was recalcitrant and after a half-hearted attempt to release it he put Basquin's screwdriver back in his pocket. The compass was bulky, and despite the mist he thought he could manage without it.

'I'll try not to be too long, Henri. But it will be afternoon at least,' he warned. Whatever happened it was bound to be a long, cold wait for the boy.

'It is no matter, Paul,' the boy replied. 'I walk a little with you?'

Paul shook his head. It was light enough now to see each other's features. 'It is time,' he said, and swept his hand towards to the woods. As if to give point to his words the distant guns erupted in a morning hate, muted by distance and the light wind but menacing enough to destroy the fragile illusion of security engendered by the mist. Paul bent down and hefted the propeller. It was unwieldy, far too long for comfort, and rather heavier than he had expected; indeed it took him some time to discover how best to arrange it across his shoulder so that only the damaged tip was likely to strike the ground. He held out his free hand, '*Au revoir, Henri,*' he said.

The boy took his hand shyly. '*Au revoir*, Paul,' he returned. Then, his shyness forgotten, 'The machine-gun bullets?'

'*Au revoir, Henri,*' Paul repeated firmly. But he saw the gamin grin on the boy's face and he was smiling himself as he swung up the slope and out of the woods. He stopped and looked back before he took the first step onto the ploughed field but the boy had already disappeared into cover, and Paul hitched up the propeller, and set off into the mist.

Having studied the map Paul knew that it was far from a featureless tract he had to cover. The first landmark, running directly across his front after only a matter of yards, was a minor road, followed shortly afterwards by what was probably a light railway, although whether it was a permanent civil track or a temporary military construction, he had been unable to determine from the map. A stream was marked, however, running from the wood parallel to his initial line of march and that, if he found it, would help him to positively orientate himself.

The first few yards were tough going but after that the gradient eased and he soon began to get into his stride. The mist lay heavy in all directions and the compass would have been a comfort but he pressed on, confident in his ability to assess and correct any tendency to wander.

It was the road he came to first, in fact little more than a cart track, and he reached it far sooner than he had expected: the aviation map, understandably, was not as good as it might have been for his present purpose, but hopefully it would suffice.

Fifty or sixty yards further on, across the main area of plough, a wooded embankment loomed up, clearly the flattened mound he had seen just before touchdown the evening before. A substantial railway then, and civil, not military. Paul hesitated, shifting the propeller on his back, and peering up through the trees. It would be a steep pull, and slippery, and he was not all that keen to embark upon it. Besides, the stream shown on the map had to cross the railway somehow. He listened, straining through the ascending shrill of what he took to be a mounting lark, and after a moment's hesitation, walked off to the left.

Within just a few more yards he was rewarded by the ripple of water, and he paused, aware of a discontinuity in the side of the embankment: a solidly-built stone-arched tunnel admitting the stream to the fields beyond. Mentally Paul gave thanks to the far-sighted railway engineers who had sited the tunnel so very conveniently to his purpose. Moreover, the map actually showed the intersection of stream and rails. So now he had a positive fix as a starting point!

The ground beyond the railway, not having been that recently ploughed, presented an easier surface for walking, the light, clayey soil firm underfoot although churned here and there by cartwheels to a muddy cream. He kept the stream on his right, holding his line as it meandered away from him, hearing the murmur as it curved to his feet again, rush-bordered and somewhat marshy, until finally it sang itself off again and vanished for good, its gurgling lost in the enveloping mist.

Paul had expected to encounter a track leading left away from the stream but it failed to materialize, and he faced into the blankness and set off, blindly now, across the flint-strewn fields. Paths crossed his way at odd intervals but all angling off in the wrong direction and none of them marked on the map. Once, some red object in a puddle caused him to pause; a spent shotgun cartridge, he saw. And there had been others, less colourful, scattered among the furrows back by the railway embankment. So the hazards to be expected hereabouts were not all of Teutonic origin, for this was evidently a hunting area, even in these unsettled times. As he was reminded ten minutes later when, halfway across a mist-wreathed field, a game bird lifted from beneath his feet, exploding with heart-stopping suddenness into whirring, ground-skimming flight amid a flurry of feathers: pheasant, partridge, or jabberwock? Whatever it was – and though, in afterthought, reminiscent of grouse on Peakland moors – it unnerved him and he laid down the propeller and stood, breathless, peering around him into the blanketing opaqueness.

After a while he recovered, and walked on, now shifting his burden from one shoulder to the other every two hundred paces and, whenever a propeller tip scraped the ground, wishing – not for the first time in his life – that he was two or three inches taller. Eventually, however, there came a time when he stumbled down a steep bank and found his feet crunching on gravel, at which point, finding himself facing another bank just feet away, he knew that he had come to the first of the series of country roads leading left into Hermies, the town he was skirting. He lowered the propeller gratefully to the ground. The light was much brighter now and it was probably foolish to sit on the side of the road like this but he would only rest for a moment. He consulted the map. By the look of it he was already just over halfway there.

Paul rubbed his shoulders, realising even as he did so that the formula he had dug out the night before was for two-bladed propellers, not four-bladed. He was not carrying twenty-five pounds then, but nearer fifty! No wonder it was such heavy going! And then he grunted. Fifty pounds was still a lot lighter than the standard infantry-stormer's burden – and Paul had no steel hat, rifle, or bayonet. Nor was he trudging upslope through barbed-wire, mud, and shellbursts into machine gun fire. He lifted to his feet, heaving the propeller onto his back once more, no longer feeling quite so heavily burdened.

From time to time, heaped by the side of the fields, Paul passed vast mounds of root crops, sugar beet, at a guess. The roots, though bulbous, looked somewhat shrivelled, and he wondered if they were awaiting collection or if they had simply been dumped there.

From now on he had no fear of losing his way. His destination lay between the main road passing out of Hermies to the east and the gorge of the *Canal du Nord* curving down from the north. He had seen the precipitously-sided canal from the air only days before, welcoming it then as a landmark before climbing once more to the immunity of the clouds. Now he staggered a little, brushing past some gossamer-rimed bushes that fringed the road. During that last pause, brief as it had been, his right leg had begun to stiffen, and becoming aware of the fact, he caught himself favouring it. And cursed. If he did not stop pampering himself he would fall into the habit of limping and be walking like a cripple by the time he was forty!

He crossed a second road, and shortly afterwards a third, all running into Hermies like spokes to a hub. He was more cautious now, peering left and right before venturing to cross, bearing in mind that had it not been for the mist it would have been broad daylight. If he ran into trouble now he might not have to worry about what happened when he was forty.

He changed shoulders although he had only completed seventy paces. He was grateful that the mist was so thick but he would have welcomed just one glimpse of his more distant surroundings. The map showed that he had passed across the southern fringes of Hermies to parallel the railway line from Vélu. He spelt out its routing: Bapaume, Vélu, Hermies, Marcoing, Cambrai.

Marcoing, he reflected; that place of such bitter memory to the Corps! For no matter how long the RFC existed Marcoing must remain a name to conjure with: six aircraft lost in one engagement! Perhaps some day the Corps would follow the age-old army tradition and weave the name into a flag to be paraded now and again to ginger up recruits; that is, before being blessed and stowed away to rot in some church or other when it got too tattered to be decently flaunted abroad.

He laughed at such an ironic fancy: war at one hundred and twenty miles an hour fought at 15,000 feet – and battle honours laid up in a musty country church! Could anything be more incongruous? Unless it was the spectacle of an erstwhile God-of-the-Air, complete with crucifix, acting the part of a human shrine – a mobile calvary –, trudging across the French countryside like any unhorsed drum-follower down the ages. He laughed again, hearing the hollowness of his laughter through the mist.

'*Monsieur le Capitaine* Cowley amuses himself?'

The voice came from the bank to his left, startling him so much that he had to clutch at the propeller to prevent it thudding to the ground.

'How many kilos does your windmill weigh now, *Monsieur*?'

She was right to mock him, of course. For in the last few hundred yards he had been reconsidering the formula yet again. Not two-and-a-half times the square root, more like two-and-a-half *hundred* bloody times.

'And *Monsieur* is – halting.'

'Limping,' he offered. 'And only very slightly.'

Angele was standing on the banking by a large clump of bushes where two paths came together. She was dressed in a voluminous coat that came nearly to her ankles, her face framed in a scarf that she had pulled on over her hat. A sensible mixture of colours, Paul registered grudgingly, both for the season and the task she had undertaken, autumnal browns and russets that merged with the still-leafy hedgerow against which she had posted herself. For he had no doubt that she had been there for some time, waiting for him to come along.

She scrambled to the ground. 'Shall I take that for you for a while?'

He shook his head. 'No, thank you. It's quite all right.'

He changed shoulders once more and seeing this, she reached up and unwound the scarf from her head. Beneath the scarf she was wearing a broad-brimmed bonnet, its green band, now revealed, the brightest colour in her whole ensemble. Pulling off the scarf had left the bonnet slightly askew, allowing a tress of hair to escape and hang loose across one eye. Impatiently she pushed it back, and pulled the bonnet straight. Her all-enveloping coat was shapeless but the figure and the vitality he had marked the night before were evident in every movement as she folded the scarf end over end into a pad.

'Here!'

Obediently he let the damaged propeller tip rest gently on the ground, watching her as she came close and stood on tiptoe to take hold of his lapel. She pulled aside his greatcoat, sliding the pad into place over his right shoulder, between coat and tunic. Paul looked down into her face held close to his own, at her eyes, long-lashed and fixed intently upon the task in hand, at the frown of concentration across her brows.

Her skin smelt cold and fresh and from the moist-red rimming of her nostril he knew that she had indeed been waiting for some considerable time. He reached out with one finger and lifted another fugitive strand of hair back behind her ear. He could see the faintest down across her top lip and the set of her mouth as she tugged and adjusted, full lips compressed together, the tip of one white tooth just visible as an earnest of her determination to set the pad just so.

She sniffed suddenly, and stood back, a trace of heightened colour in her cheeks as if she sensed his awareness of her. Her eyes, nonetheless, when they lifted to his, were cool and remote.

'That should be better, *M'sieur.*'

'Paul,' he said reprovingly. He had not been fully aware of the discomfort his burden had been causing him but Angele had been rather more perceptive – and infinitely more practical – and the moment he shouldered the propeller again he realised what a difference the adjustment had made. She accepted his thanks with a lift of her head, but coldly and unsmilingly, waiting until he was ready before turning wordlessly on her heel and leading off up the track that now opened up before them.

Paul took some time to get into his stride, to overcome the stiffness, but he was determined not to favour his knee. And still he was at a loss to understand why she was so upset with him. He fixed his eyes upon her, now yards ahead. Her shoes were clumsy and low-heeled and her ankles below the hem of the coat were heavy and inclined towards thickness.

She'll have legs like tree-trunks before *she's* forty, he thought gracelessly. And suddenly he was angry. The arrangement had been for her to leave a tramp's sign at the entrance to the farm when all was clear – and then go home. That way no one but him would have been involved.

'You were to leave a sign – not to stay and meet me,' he snapped at her back.

As if she had been waiting for some such reaction she whirled in her tracks, lips thin with fury.

'You and Henri, and your silly broken-branch signs. *Merde!*'

She stopped short, and on the instant the flare went out of her eyes. Paul caught up with her, then paused, and they stood for a while facing each other in the drifting mist, and he felt his own anger draining away in turn until it was almost as though it had never been. Angele's face softened and she stepped up to him and took his free arm.

'There is too much tiredness behind your eyes, Paul,' she told him softly. 'I saw such tiredness when Papa first came home.' She led him onwards once more, not physically pulling him, but somehow drawing him along, as if by her presence. 'It is the war-tiredness that makes your shoulder sore, and your leg so limpy.'

He choked back a chuckle and she shot him a glance, divining that the word was a solecism. 'Not limpy,' she corrected herself, 'limp.' And suddenly the tension was gone completely and they were laughing together and he knew that they were friends and allies once again. He broke free from her arm and hugged her one-handedly to his side.

'Thank you for coming,' he smiled. 'But your father will be concerned.'

She grinned at him sideways and it was the same gamin grin Henri had given. 'Papa knew from the start I would come.' Suddenly she turned and grabbed at his shoulder with both hands, shaking him violently. 'This is *my* war too. And the *Boche* are *my* enemies too.' She let him go then and stood back, her face proud and defiant, reminding him suddenly of Catherine, and her abhorrence of war mongers and war profiteers. There was nothing he could say but he tried to smile his understanding.

After a moment Angele took his arm once more and they walked on in silence, coming to a metalled road and turning along it for some yards. At length she stopped, and pointed. 'Through here. I shall go ahead and make ready.'

The old farm gate hung wryly on its hinges and he steadied himself against it, watching until she had disappeared into the mist.

'The house is straight ahead,' she called back lightly. 'You can't miss it.'

Chapter Seventeen

The drive was deeply rutted, with grass and weeds flourishing along the borders and between the hoof-prints up the centre to suggest, as the gate had done, that the farm had seen busier, and almost certainly better, days. Cattle were lowing in a field off to the right and a misty shape that Paul had initially taken for a bush lifted to its legs as he passed and began to amble interestedly towards him.

'No *manger* here, I'm afraid, Old *Vache*,' he told it, and saw it lose interest and turn away. So, a bilingual cow!

The farm itself came into sight a few steps further on, built to a characteristic pattern with the drive leading to the main house through a gateway between enclosing barns. There were hens and black ducks scratching for seed, and the resident cockerel atop the midden.

Paul hesitated at the gateway, reluctant to go closer. He was uncomfortably aware that he should not be involving these people. It could be that he was being overprotective. And yet, as he reminded himself, *he* ran no real risk: whether the Germans liked it or not it was his duty to evade capture, and if possible, to try to escape. They knew it, and for the most part, he did not doubt, would respect it. It was the people lending assistance who would suffer. He placed a hand against the chipped and decaying brickwork of the barn, fresh doubts assailing him. Such a wall would have been the last thing the Belgian girl, Gabrielle Petit, would have known, just seven months before. And Englishwoman Edith Cavell before her.

He looked out into the mist. If he went back now no harm would have been done. He could throw away the borrowed tools and nobody would be any the wiser. The Basquins would be disappointed, particularly the younger ones, but at least they would be at liberty, and unmenaced; for surely nothing was worth the lives of people such as these. Paul took a half-step back the way he had come, only to stop short as Angele hailed him from across the cobbled yard. If she sensed the renewal of his doubts she did not show it but beckoned with her head. In her hands she held a cloth-draped tray.

'I thought you had got lost without your map to guide you,' she smiled. But her eyes, as he closed with her, were concerned, and he knew then that she was, indeed, fully aware of his doubts. With a jut of her chin she indicated the barn to the left. 'I will show you the workshop. Then you will see.'

Paul followed her past a lofty-sided wagon – much wider than most, and half-loaded with timber piled high at the far end –, past more questing chickens and two lean and slinking farmyard cats. From the barn on the right of the courtyard came the thud of a hoof, and a horse snickered. There was a dog, too, further off but it was intent on eating, its nose and both front paws deep in a bowl, and it took no notice of him. Smoke was rising from the main chimney of the house and not too far away there were some geese. Angele pushed open the door of the barn with her foot and beckoned him past her.

It was a huge, cavernous building, far bigger than it had appeared from the courtyard, built on two storeys with traps and hoists to the upper floor. Paul's nostrils were assailed by the odours of the stable, by fresh hay and dust, by leather and old manure, and by the pungent, far-from-pleasant reek of stale urine. He wrinkled his nose, and sneezed. At first sight the ground floor appeared to be full of bales of hay but as his eyes grew accustomed to the filtered gloom he saw that a space had been left clear against the far wall where a cobweb-grimed window grudgingly let in light. A workbench ran the whole length of the wall, central to which a man waited, stooping a little, and facing them. He looked older than the barn itself.

Angele smiled at him, 'Alphonse, this is *Monsieur* Cowley.'

Paul found himself facing a slightly-built man of something like sixty-five or seventy. There seemed to be nothing of him but skin and bones draped in a smock that one of Constable's rustics might have disowned long since. He had pulled a beret from his head and now stood twisting it between his fists. Paul leant the propeller gently against a bale of hay and held out his hand, but almost immediately withdrew it a little, seeing Alphonse's sudden frown. There was a quick exchange between the old man and Angele, but then the girl smiled, evidently brushing some objection aside as she beckoned the two of them together. Mollified, it seemed, or at least, overridden, for the present, Alphonse grunted, and obediently held out a hand, shuffling forwards through the ankle-deep hay.

The back of the hand bespoke a long labouring life with its mottle of yellow-brown liver spots and its veins and tendons knotting and cording as if to string together the gnarled, misshapen bones. The fingers trembled and Paul saw the calluses on the palms and the dark moons of ingrained dirt beneath the nails. He took the hand gently, fearing to fracture it with too tight a grip – and found himself clamped in a veritable vice! He winced, barely able to suppress a cry.

'*Pardon, M'sieur.*' The old man released his grip instantly. And Paul stepped back, rubbing his hand and grinning sheepishly.

The girl laughed and moved forwards to stand beside Alphonse. 'Alphonse lives in Hermies. He came with me this morning.' She held up her hand to forestall any protestation. 'He knows that you are not to be here.'

She pointed to the bench where an ancient toolbag of cracked leather lay open beside a large wood-vice. 'Alphonse is a carpenter – no – more than a carpenter – he does fine work.' She looked to Paul for assistance.

'A joiner?' he suggested. A cabinet-maker, even. To his eyes the tools laid out on the bench were museum pieces, but they had the patina of constant use, and each finely-honed edge showed the recent touch of a craftsman's care.

'A joiner? Maybe. But he does fine work. All sorts of work. He has worked here and in the villages all his life. He has never been further than Arras or Cambrai. In Paris he could have been a rich man.' She shrugged her shoulders. 'I know that you must work fast. So Alphonse can do the wood. You can work with metal. It is arranged.' Clearly, she loved arranging things.

'But first.' She took the cloth from the tray and revealed a bowl of soup, with freshly-baked bread-rolls and a pot of coffee. 'If we went to the house you would have to sit and be polite. This way, you can eat as you work.'

'Angele,' he told her, suddenly aware that he was ravenous, 'I think I am falling in love with you.'

She laughed, pleased, and poured out three cups of coffee, indicating that he get busy with the soup. Alphonse, the moment the introductions had been made, Paul noticed, had lifted the propeller from where it had been deposited on two of its tips, placing it instead, horizontally across four of the bales. There was an implied criticism in the action which, together with that recent frown, set Paul wondering.

He watched as the old man ran his fingers over the blades, examining every inch of their surfaces, repositioning them now and then, and turning them this way and that to take advantage of the light. Alphonse turned then to the hub, examining, it appeared, the spacing of the holes, grunting then in apparent satisfaction. At length, treating the propeller as if it was feather light, he carried it across to the widest section of the workbench where he stood regarding the broken end, rubbing at it gently with one thumb.

He called, and Angele put down her cup and hurried over, hoisting herself up to sit, legs dangling, on the workbench top beside him. Her calves were not that thick after all, Paul conceded.

The old man spoke for some while and at one stage, when the girl seemed to be out of her depth, he sketched in the dust with his finger. She nodded comprehendingly, and beckoned. Paul crammed a last fragment of bread into his mouth. Now he was fit for anything.

'Alphonse says that it is walnut wood from America. He could fit new wood and make it weigh the same, like this.' She pointed to the tracing in the dust, a representation of a dovetail joint.

Paul nodded. 'Tell Alphonse,' he said regretfully, 'that it must be strong not only in this way –' he showed how the end would tend to fly off under centrifugal force, 'but also in this way,' and he showed the motion forwards and backwards where the thrusting force of the blade would be felt.

'Yes, Alphonse said that,' Angele told him calmly, 'but he would make such things,' she pointed to the sketch of the dovetail, 'in both directions.' Paul considered the old man with growing regard. 'But,' the girl went on, anticipating Paul's next objection, 'he says it would take time. So, if you wish, he will now cut.'

Paul grinned wonderingly. Most propellers were indeed built up of either American walnut or Honduran mahogany and they had to be treated with respect. He said speculatively, 'He didn't like me leaning the propeller end-on against the hay.'

She laughed. 'He told me that it was – naughty of you.' Paul gathered from her hesitation that the old man had used an earthier expression and he laughed in turn. Angele held up a restraining hand.

'Shall he cut, *M'sieur* Paul?'

In answer Paul strode across and took the old man's hand. 'There're a lot of things I'd like to ask you, Mr Alphonse,' he told him, smiling down into the faded old eyes, 'but for now, please cut. I'll leave it entirely up to you.'

'Yes,' said Angele dryly from behind them, 'there may be time for questions later, but for now there is all this to sort out.'

'All this', was a pile of coiled ropes of various thicknesses with, beside it, a number of sharpened stakes, each about three-feet long. Close by were two, one-foot long, wooden pins. There was a billet of wood shaped to serve as a mallet, and several lengths of mild steel, half of them cut from flat material, half from angled. Off to one side was a reel of baling wire and laid out in a neatly arranged row beside it, a selection of tools – pliers, hacksaw, files – even a sheet of emery paper. Paul stared at the array, dumbfounded. He turned to the girl.

'It is all arranged?'

Angele laughed. 'There is no strong wire cable,' she pointed out. 'It is possible, but not today.'

'Angele, this is magnificent.'

Hardly crediting what he was seeing, Paul cast a rapid eye over the assembled items, checking them off in his mind. From all the evidence the barn had been used for many things in the past, so that finding what he needed would have been a daunting task. Having everything collected together like this had saved him hours of hunting about. He straightened with sudden suspicion. 'But when did you prepare all this?'

'Alphonse cut the wood and metal, and found all the tools. I looked for the rope.'

'That's not what I asked,' he told her. 'When did you leave home?'

'The curfew,' she flared, 'is your concern, not mine. This is France, and I am French, and I come and go as I wish.' She faced up to him defiantly, but he raised open palms. What was done was done.

'Angele,' he said fervently, 'I cannot tell you how grateful I am to you and to Alphonse: to all of you. But you must be careful. If the Germans harmed you, or your family, or your friends, because of me then I could never forgive myself. Don't you see that?'

Although conceding this with a turn of her head she was unwilling to make any further concessions.

'Alphonse has already begun to cut,' she said pointedly. 'Which of the metals do you wish?'

Paul turned to find that the old man had indeed settled to his work. He had started on the damaged tip, had already sawn it into shape, and was now setting-to with chisel and plane. Again Paul reflected on the lucky chance that the tips of this particular propeller had been guarded against damage from workaday debris by a winding of doped cotton, rather than by a brass sheath. Even so, wood was a recalcitrant agent where Paul was concerned and even the adage of 'measure twice, cut once' never saved him. As a consequence he had an unbounded admiration for any skilled woodworker; and it was obvious that Alphonse was in the first rank of craftsmen. Paul would have liked to watch the old man at work but he suspected that Alphonse would not thank him for hanging over his shoulder. Besides, there was no time.

Turning to his own task, Paul chose one flat and one angled length of mild steel for each of the damaged tailbooms, measuring them off in handspans to the length he had decided upon and cutting them at a metal-worker's vice further down the worktop. His intention was to bind splints around the damaged tailboom sections, so strengthening them against up-and-down and side-to-side motion. The tailbooms themselves being of tubular steel the mild steel substitute was better than he could have hoped to find on the farm.

Fore-and-aft motion he could do less about. He had intended to supplement the bracing wires with something approaching the original strength of the tailboom; now, in the absence of wire cable, he would have to make do with tensioned rope. He was well aware that a DH2 had recently returned with a tailboom completely shot through, one of the bracing wires having taken over the damaged member's load. All his own bracing stays, happily, were still intact, but with suitable materials here to hand it would be foolish not to utilise them.

The splints cut to size, Paul turned his attention to the rope, sorting out a suitable length for the restraining system he would use for starting-up and getting away. Rope to supplement the half-ton bracing wire was a more difficult proposition. A normal safety factor for cables would be six or seven times the maximum load anticipated, but using rope picked up haphazardly like this it would be a matter of guesswork. However, that part of the job was not of primary concern; he might not even bother with it in the event, but rely on the splints and the existing bracing wires alone: he could make a final decision on site.

Setting his chosen rope lengths aside, he checked over the stakes, and the club-like mallet, identifying Alphonse's hand in the fashioning of both. Adding these to his little pile he stood back, nodding his approval, satisfied now that he had everything he needed to see the job through.

Next he turned his attention to the sparking plugs, carefully unwrapping each one and laying it before him on the bench. Alphonse was now working on the other ends of the propeller, sawing away confidently and steadily while Angele busied herself picking up the ropes and the finished splints and carrying them out of the barn.

Paul ran a swift eye along the plugs, not anticipating any problems. They were the standard Gnome plugs designed to avoid distorting the cylinder wall; extra light, therefore, but sturdily constructed to ensure that they stood up under centrifugal force and did not break down under the effect of the lubricant thrown out by the characteristically oil-extravagant rotary. He wiped each one carefully, carrying it over to the window to inspect the points and the insulation, finding, as he had expected, that all were new and in good order. One was, perhaps, a little too oily but Angele, after a brief discussion with Alphonse, disappeared beyond a partition, to return just moments later with a can of petrol. Paul used a small measure of this to wire-brush the points, grinning as the girl at once walked off to replace the can. A neat and tidy mind, quite obviously, and like any woman he had ever seen around a house, not satisfied unless she was clearing up and putting things away no matter that the job was only halfway through. He found a slight burr on another of the electrodes and in the absence of a magneto file used the blade of the knife and a piece of the emery paper to rub it away. But he was only painting the lily. The plugs were fine. Now it was up to Alphonse.

The old man had put aside his saw and was making delicate stroking movements with a chisel. Paul watched him for some while without disturbing his concentration. Angele brought in another tray of coffee but the old man had still not touched his first cup, nor apparently, would he stop now. Paul finished wrapping the plugs and put the cloth bundle carefully on the bale of hay beside him.

'Are you finished here?' Angele asked. She pointed to the vice and the filings and the discarded scraps of metal.

'Only the propeller now,' Paul said. Then watched with amusement as she began to brush around the vice, collecting the filings in a dustpan and depositing them in an old sack. He anticipated her by bending down and picking up the discarded pieces of metal from the floor. These too went into the sack. Without a word the girl then walked over to a remote brick buttress and began scooping dust from the floor, returning with her dustpan piled high. Motioning Paul to stand clear she jerked it sharply upwards immediately above the vice, stepping back smartly as the black dust billowed out and began to fall softly all around the area where he had been working. Abruptly Paul's amusement faded. He cast a look around the barn. Apart from the coffee tray and the area where Alphonse was standing there was no sign that the barn had been especially used for theirs or any other purpose.

'And I accused you of being careless,' he said penitently.

'Never, with the people here.'

He nodded understandingly. 'I should have known.'

She smiled. 'Jacques' parents have gone to the market. They will not return until mid-afternoon.'

'Then who is in the house?'

'Old Maria, the housekeeper, and Suzanne, the maid. They know someone is here. They do not know who.'

'You arranged this market visit this morning?'

She merely nodded. Then, as if to forestall any compliment, said abruptly, 'Now that you have finished, come.'

She made off through the low door in the partition separating their part of the barn from that nearest the house. This second part, Paul could see at a glance, was just as long as the first, but with far more vertical space, having no loft. Also, rather than hay, it was given over to machines. And what machines! He came to a halt, gazing around him, and exclaiming aloud in astonishment.

There were none of the machines one might have expected to see on a farm. This was an enthusiast's collection of motor vehicles, some new, some old, and all in various stages of disrepair. There were vehicles Paul was familiar with and others he knew only from periodicals, but which made his mouth water.

There was a very early Maybach Mercedes, regrettably without wheels and with even its distinctive bonnet half-concealed beneath a dust sheet. And in the corner furthest from the large double doors, now closed, but opening out away from the courtyard, a delightful 850 cc Peugeot *Bèbé* – minus its bonnet and radiator grill. Pushed away into another corner, its front end a sorry mess, was what appeared to be the mortal remains of a V6-engined Delahaye which could only have been weeks old at the time of its demise.

Paul was not surprised to find a Model T Ford chassis just inside the doorway but he was intrigued to discover that it was an English import, Manchester-made. There was a Morris, and an Italian roadster, and three motor cycles crammed one beside the other along the wall with not a front wheel between them. All in all, and despite the fact that not a vehicle was complete, it was a fascinating collection, and in other circumstances, one he could have spent hours examining. As it was he saw only what registered as he passed. For from the outset his attention had been caught by the aeroplane wings suspended from the ceiling at the far end of the barn.

Paul threaded his way down the cluttered central aisle, negotiating most obstacles that littered the floor but stubbing his toe against a transmission assembly and stopping abruptly as the pain flamed in his right knee.

On the instant Angele was at his shoulder. 'Are you all right, Paul?'

He moved a palm, dismissing the pain, but dared attempt no other answer until the nausea had receded. Instead he forced himself onward to the machine, recognising it for what it was at once.

As Jacques had told him in Amiens, it was a Bleriot-type design but built to a reduced scale, and looking now at the standard of joinery evidenced through several rents in the fabric, Paul was convinced that Alphonse must have had more than a little to do with the actual construction. It had employed, he saw, leaning close, a 25 hp Anzani, three-cylinder, fan-type engine to drive a six-and-a-half foot twin-bladed pusher propeller, presumably the one which was presently laid upon a wooden platform jutting from the wall. A belated precaution this, by the look of it, for it had warped badly. Examining its laminations Paul could see that it was not a commercial product, but it was beautifully made. Alphonse's work again, he wondered?

Angele was watching him, still eyeing his knee with concern. Now she followed his eyes.

'It is the propeller I spoke of. But Alphonse says Jacques left it too long on its end. Also, he is surprised that yours too is for pushing. He understood, he says, that modern aeroplanes were to be pulled.'

Paul appreciated that she was giving him time to recover, so merely murmured in acknowledgement. He looked at the elevator. Splintered as it was it still appeared absurdly small even for a machine of reduced dimensions: no wonder the baby Bleriot had proved difficult to control!

Possibly it was just as well Jacques had not got far off the ground otherwise the almost inevitable loss of control might easily have killed him.

Now he managed a weak grin, only too well aware that it taken much longer than normal for the pain to subside into the throbbing ache he had become accustomed to live with. Was that too, he wondered, to do with the strain of war flying?

'Your leg is really giving you trouble, Paul,' Angele insisted solicitously. 'You must not try to walk back, not with all this load.'

'It's only because I banged it,' he argued.

'But Paul, why not –' Only before she could register her next objection Alphonse hailed them from the far end of the barn.

In order to test the now-modified propeller for symmetry, Paul found, the old man had clamped a balancing apparatus into the vice. Again, it had not been commercially produced, but it was incontestably well up to its purpose, utilising a sturdy ball-bearing spindle bolted to a right-angled extension-piece – presently held securely in the vice – well long enough to ensure that the blades cleared the ground. The ball race, Paul noted appreciatively, could be set into a variety of propeller naves and it was evident that Alphonse had already fitted one that matched the de Havilland's propeller. Working now under Alphonse's mimed directions, Paul presented the propeller hub to the nave, holding the blades square while the old man stood on a milking stool to fit the centre flange nuts to the nave, tightening them in meticulous sequence.

At the old man's signal, Paul stepped back, and watched the gnarled fingers steady the blade until certain that it was motionless, then lift clear. At once the blade began to rotate steadily, drawn downwards by what had been one of the undamaged tips, now distinguishable from the others only by the reference mark Alphonse had inscribed on each blade. It was only a very slow rotational movement and the old man repositioned the propeller for a second time before stepping forwards to make an adjustment with a chisel.

He seemed merely to stroke the wood, taking off little more than a sliver. So little, in fact, that Paul itched to grab hold of the chisel himself and cut off a decent-sized chunk. Did the old lad, he wondered, suddenly irascible, think they had all day? Alphonse stepped back and the irrational niggle of irritation melted – there was not a hint of movement from the propeller, it simply hung there, a model of symmetry, in perfect balance.

Paul grinned, feeling foolish, and more than a little shamefaced. Alphonse had done a masterly repair job, and now the propeller looked just as if it had come from the manufacturers, shorter by six inches or so, square-tipped, and lacking a bit of varnish, but a real and serviceable propeller once again.

Seemingly satisfied, the old man reached up, braced himself, then spun the blades full force, sending them whirring and flashing to stir up dust and hay from the floor, running so sweet and true, and with such a total absence of vibration that for a while they appeared set to run for ever.

Paul moved to the side, and picking up Alphonse's wooden rule, eased it out from the bench until each whirling tip just brushed the scale's brass-capped end. An eighth of an inch wobble between tips would be acceptable by any standards; these bettered that. Next, with Alphonse's approval, Paul stopped the rotation, and more for interest than anything else, measured each blade from hub to tip. Even the book would allow a sixteenth of an inch or so variation: Alphonse had been satisfied with none – the blade lengths were identical. Paul shook his head admiringly.

Behind them he had been aware of Angele brushing away the shavings. Now, as he stepped back to congratulate the old man, he saw that she had left the barn altogether, carrying the coffee tray with her. There were still question marks hanging over the propeller but Alphonse had given him every chance. He could never have done as good a job himself. Particularly with time pressing.

The old man had finished putting away his tools and now stood looking up at Paul smiling and pointing to the propeller and talking away nineteen to the dozen. Paul grasped his outstretched hand gratefully, wishing Angele would come back so that he could express in words the thanks and the admiration he felt. It was incredible luck to have come across a craftsman who was not only experienced in aeronautical joinery, but who was one of the old school. A voluble one too, once he got under way, for his speech and his gestures became increasingly more animated until Paul, overwhelmed by his sheer Frenchness, simply gave up trying to understand what he was saying and just stood there grinning encouragingly.

Moments later the penny dropped. Or more literally, the franc. Paul delved into a pocket and pulled out his wallet. At which the old man beamed, and on the instant lapsed into expectant silence. Paul looked inside doubtfully. He had little money, only a few francs. So perhaps he should offer an IOU?

'The King and Major General Trenchard Promise to Pay Alphonse so many francs, *apres la guerre*'.

In the end he took out all the notes he had and laid them on the bench for the old man to make a selection from. It did not take long. Alphonse made a scooping gesture, the smock lifted and fell, and not a note was left in sight.

Moments later Paul watched the old man's almost jaunty exit from the barn. Only the elation, he found, had vanished, leaving him with a distinct feeling of let-down, and not a little regret. Somehow he had looked upon old Alphonse as a comrade-in-arms, motivated by loyalty, and patriotism, and a sense of their Allied brotherhood against the common enemy. Now he stood revealed as just another avaricious French peasant out for whatever he could get, like all the farmers and shopkeepers and petty officials on the unoccupied side of the lines.

And what about the girl, and her father, Louis Basquin – and Henri? Were they the same, and would they expect payment for their services? It was an unworthy thought. Paul knew instinctively that they would not, nor even accept it if it was offered, that their motives, like his own, were of a higher order. So where was the difference, or was it, after all, merely a matter of class?

It was a train of thought that persisted in running its course as he unbolted the propeller, and one that forced him to look more closely at his own reaction to the old man's greed. What was it he felt? Contempt for the old man specifically, or for French peasants generally; or for any civilian who did not conform to his own notion of what was due in wartime? It was difficult to say.

Difficult to say? Paul undid the final flange nut and grimaced wryly. Now that he was being honest with himself it was not at all difficult to say, merely disagreeable. It was unpleasant to be brought face to face with one's prejudices and to discover how deep-rooted they were. For the moment he was glad he was alone; at least his blushes were spared and he could cover his discomfort in the physical activity of lifting the propeller clear of the nave and settling it – flat this time – on the hay bales. For hours now he had been thinking noble thoughts about keeping these people uninvolved, knowing that in their patriotic zeal they were risking everything by helping him. But where Alphonse was concerned there were other considerations.

Alphonse might be ready to risk his life if need be, but if that sacrifice was not called for he still had to live, and at the very least he had given up a morning's work and a morning's income; given up, in all probability, his only chance of making ends meet for the day. Life for a country carpenter of undoubted talent but only limited ambition must be hard enough even in peacetime; how much more so with all the restrictions and shortages brought about by war and by the Occupation! It was all very well Paul feeling disappointed but he had to face the fact that the old man had not disappointed him, but merely upset his arrogant expectations. Surely under these conditions the labourer was even worthier of his hire?

Alphonse re-entered the barn and began busying himself packing away the balancing apparatus. Paul clapped him on the shoulder, smiling. How many English craftsmen would have turned to at a moment's notice in the circumstances? Even braving the curfew. And how many would Paul have expected to work for nothing? How many war-workers on wage rates hitherto undreamed of would refuse all pay above the new norm, or go without pay even for one morning 'for King and Country' the way Alphonse had done? Or deign to work at all unless the money was forthcoming?

Paul remembered Catherine's diatribe against those who perpetuated the war for gain, even those, she had insisted, who manufactured aeroplanes. How many industrialists would refuse their knighthoods, Paul asked himself now, or the personal profits brought in by inflated wartime orders, or accept less advantageous terms on a contract because it was for England? He searched through his pockets and finding a few odd coins pressed them into Alphonse's eager hand, grinning as he did so. Would either the King or 'Boom' Trenchard honour an IOU if he wrote one out? They ought to. He would certainly look into it when he got back.

If he got back! He looked at his watch. Time was slipping past, for it was already getting on for eleven o'clock. Alphonse scanned the barn, then beckoning, turned out through the door, leaving Paul to heft the propeller and follow him. Out in the courtyard it was impossible to tell what the mist was doing because the gateway blotted out the view but the weathervane above the barn roof was still and that could only be a good sign. Angele was nowhere in evidence but Alphonse was waiting beside the broad-beamed cart.

Paul saw now that the singular, one-ended piling of timber in the cart left considerable space on the wagon bed. Space enough, he realised with growing suspicion, to easily accommodate the propeller lying flat! Grinning, Alphonse pulled back a tarpaulin to reveal a second nest among the bulkier lengths of timber in which reposed the ropes and pickets and the small roll of tools where it was evident that Angele had deposited them. He now gestured towards the wider cache, indicating that the propeller should be set down as well. Ignoring Paul's shake of the head, he mimed on, showing that with the propeller safely stowed it would be covered by the tarpaulin and concealed beneath lighter, piled timbers. Clearly it had 'all been arranged'.

Paul shook his head firmly. He pointed to the propeller over his shoulder and made as if to walk away. The old man pulled at the propeller and again urged him towards the wagon and for a few moments they squabbled wordlessly, Paul showing his determination to walk, Alphonse equally determined to get the propeller into the wagon. An impasse indeed! But not for long. The old man clearly did not intend to be denied. He stepped away, and then, pretending to balance a load on his shoulder, strode off, staggering on his right leg in grotesque mimicry. After a few steps he turned, and pointed at Paul's knee. Paul grinned and raised a hand in acknowledgement, but shook his head. He was determined to risk these people no further.

He walked back into the barn and once more laid the propeller on the hay. He would unload the other equipment and string it into a convenient bundle. Then, with a final word to thank Angele for all she and her family and friends had done, he would be on his way, leaving them in the clear.

'*Boche! Boche!*'

The alarm came as a clarion call from the house, followed swiftly by Angele, arriving in a rush of heightened colour having scattered chickens and cats before her as she came. Momentarily she checked beside the cart to yank at the heaped timbers and spill them back over the cached equipment. Then she seized Alphonse's arm and dragged him with her into the shelter of the barn. Paul leaped to slide the door to, but she stopped him. 'No, Paul, leave it open.' She whirled to face Alphonse and spoke to him rapidly. The old man listened intently, nodded and then, without a word, turned and walked slowly out towards his cart leaving the door ajar behind him.

'Quickly,' the girl pointed to the ladder rising to the loft. 'Up there.'

Paul paused, to pull at the stacked hay bales, shouldering them aside to topple them across the propeller. It took six bales to conceal it completely, but fewer seconds. Then he sprang for the ladder.

'Wait!' Angele pointed to his boots. 'Take them off.'

Paul glanced down. The wet mud, still caked damply beneath the heels, would be fatally obvious on the rungs. Obediently he kicked them off, toe against heel, cursing silently as the left one decided to stick. It came off at last and he gathered them up, and sprang for the ladder. The rungs hurt his stockinged feet but he pulled up strongly with his free hand until he was just below the trapdoor. Then he stopped, and peered down. Angele was standing behind the barn door, an eye glued to a crack, but sensing that he was still on the ladder she looked up and angrily waved him on. Clearly he could do nothing but obey, and push on upwards through the trap.

He found an extensive loft covering the whole of the first section of the barn. There were the loading bays he had noticed from below, their doors shuttered and bolted, and at least one other hatchway in the floor. Most of the space was taken up with hay and what little light there was came through cracks and knotholes in the end partition. Walking on tiptoe he made his way towards the partition, and selecting a spot where the light was dimmest, pushed behind the bales stacked there to make himself a space. Up here it was dustier and dirtier than down below so having done all he could to conceal himself his next concern was to take precautions against sneezing. Hurriedly he knocked apart one of the fresher bales and spread the hay across the floor, then, still in haste, but moving as quietly as he could, he stripped off his heavy coat, his tunic, and the bulky, fleece-lined leggings, and spread them, in turn, upon the hay. Finally, gently, his ears pricked for the slightest sound, he laid himself upon the hastily contrived couch, used the leggings as a pillow, and tried to still his breathing, powerless to do anything about the pounding of his heart.

Was this it then? He supposed it was. But if Angele kept her head, then there should be no problem. She had every right to be here, as had Alphonse. If the Germans had discovered his aircraft, as they must have done, and were searching the area for him, then it was only a matter of time before they came scrambling up the ladder with their bayonets at the ready. All he had to do then was to stick to the story that he had met nobody, that he had headed off across country and come upon the barn in the night. They were unlikely to search the barn once they had found him and he could always claim to have partially dismantled the machine in order to deny its use to them, employing tools from the aircraft and hiding the propeller in the same way as he had the Lewis drums and the Very pistol.

He had no thoughts of offering resistance. For a start there was nothing he could use as a weapon, and even if there had been, resistance would only complicate matters. Besides, by no stretch of the imagination could he see himself as that sort of a fire-eater.

Gradually his alarm died away, and his heartbeat settled, allowing him to hear the sounds around him once more. The dog barked from the yard, and the chickens had begun to settle. Back in the gloom there were unexplained rustlings in the hay and becoming conscious of the thick, black skeins of cobwebs in the darkened rafters above his head he shuddered and tucked in the neck of his shirt.

The door of a vehicle slammed, breaking the comparative silence, and as the dog began to bark more heartily, so there came the sound of many footsteps in the courtyard. There was a brief lull, and then a murmur of voices, too muffled for him to catch. Someone whistled for the dog, which at once stopped barking, an obedient response which might have been unexpected, for it seemed to bring a burst of laughter. Then more laughter, and he heard the footsteps moving off towards the house. How many there were he could not tell but clearly they intended to start their search up there. Angele had assured him that the servants knew nothing about him and he was thankful for that. But as he lay there dry-lipped, the thought of the risk he had so selfishly put them all to brought him a vilifying sense of self-condemnation. And suddenly he was sickened to the soul.

Chapter Eighteen

Paul lay there for what seemed many minutes, listening as the normal farmyard sounds reasserted themselves again after this latest interruption. Then he heard nothing and later wondered if he might have dozed. For when he came to it was to find Angele beside him, placing her finger over his lips.

'Hush, Paul!' she breathed. 'It is all right.'

He struggled onto one arm and half-rolled to face her. She must have had cat's eyes to have discovered him back here in the shadows.

'But they've found my aeroplane.'

He saw her shake her head. 'No, it is nothing. They come to see.' She pointed down to where the vehicles were housed. 'They are *pilotes*, like you. Like Jacques and Richard. Others have been before.'

He took that in, relief sweeping over him. And it made sense. 'Richard was well-known in England before the war,' he told her.

She nodded. 'Richard did not like the farm. But he loved cars, and flying machines. Most things of his are in the barn across the yard. These below, belong to Jacques. Today, the *Boche* say, it is too foggy to fly, and so they make a pleasure outing.'

'You speak German?' he asked.

'They are German, and they are in France – so they speak French. It is only our British Allies,' she said simply – and waspishly –, 'who cannot bother learning to talk to us.' She paused. 'They said all this to Alphonse. Now they have gone to the far barn. Later they will come here. Then they will go to the house and have coffee.'

'And you?' he pressed.

She hesitated. 'Maria, the housekeeper is not young, and Suzanne, the maid, is very dull. When they have seen the machines they will have coffee, and they will not stay.'

'And if they met you, then they would.' He nodded understandingly. 'But you should not have taken the risk. If they find you at the farm now it will look suspicious.'

She bridled at once. 'Is it your wish then, to spend all day here?'

He put his hand on her arm. 'I know what you say is true. They would want your company. It would be the same with us, on our side, with our men.'

'It would always be the same with men.'

They sat there in silence for a while, Paul edging aside to make more room for her.

'Tell me again, about meeting Jacques,' she demanded suddenly.

And so, as he had the night before, Paul went over everything he could remember. Only now he told her of the reflections Jacques had left with him – of the realities of having a conqueror in one's land. And seeking for a lighter note, of Jacques' benign handling of the lad, 'Spad' Winthrop. He told her too – in detail – of the letter he had received subsequently, but he withheld the poignancy of Winthrop's untimely death. Instead, thinking to please her, he enlarged upon Delcamp's incursions into the British sector, and his fleeting airborne visits to his home.

She said little, and asked few questions, although he felt the tension in her when he touched on the dangers Delcamp ran – and thereafter he steered away from that side of things, as he did from the war-weariness in her fiancée's eyes, playing such matters down, speaking admiringly instead of his sophistication and *élan*.

'*Élan!*' she spat the word fiercely. 'His brother Richard had élan, and now he is dead. There is too much *élan* in France.' She pushed her face into Paul's. 'You are English, so you cannot truly understand what it is like to have the *Boche* in your country. Also, you are a man, and you can fight. So you cannot understand what it is like to have to sit and do nothing. And when you came last night it was my chance to do something against the *Boche*, and last night and today you wish to take it from me.' She seized him by both shoulders. 'But you shall not, and when you have flown away, I shall be able to spit at them in their faces and say, "*Boche*, I, Angele Basquin, have sent him back to kill you and to rid this place of you!" You shall not take that from me ...' Her hands dropped from his shoulders, and the fierceness went out of her voice. '*Élan*,' she said again, but forlornly now, '*Élan* is not what we need.'

Paul felt her head droop, and he put his arm around her shoulders and pulled her comfortingly towards him. And as if taking refuge in that comfort she came to him, but her body was racked with sobs, and he sat there awkwardly, patting her head, but powerless otherwise, unable to find even a word that might assuage her sorrow.

Neither of them spoke after that until they heard the Germans crossing the courtyard and entering the barn below. They were a noisy, boisterous bunch, laughing and shouting, and calling excitedly to each other as they ranged among the vehicles. One of them found a motor horn and cheerfully set about drowning out the noise of all the rest. There seemed nothing to choose between them and any other group of young, off-duty men, and had it not been for the unfamiliar gutturals Paul might have fancied himself lying here seeking a moment's privacy on a dud-day's outing with his own flight. The similarity intrigued him, and he slid gently from the girl's side, lowering her onto the greatcoat and working forwards on his hands and knees towards a peephole that would look down upon the far section of the barn.

There was more light than he had expected but then he realised that the double doors facing the house had been opened up. He could not see the nearside of the barn from where he knelt but the Ford and Jacques's dismantled aeroplane were well within his field of view.

Three of the German flying officers were gathered around inspecting the machine and Paul saw with no real surprise that Alphonse was in attendance, pointing out some detail or other. And moments later, though now with a certain sense of incredulity, he watched as the old man directed their attention to the warped propeller, turning it about on its shelf then shaking his head and waving his finger as if he were giving them the same dressing-down about maltreatment that he had previously aimed at Paul. The three pilots laughed delightedly, their laughter drawing two more who had previously been below Paul's line of sight. It was relaxed and unrestrained laughter suggesting that they were getting the maximum benefit from their enforced day out of the air. Further, the exchange gave Paul yet one more insight into the workings of the old man's mind; what a sense of intrigue, he must have! And of humour. And what a sense of business too! Laughing like that they were bound to leave a handsome tip. He must certainly see about that IOU!

A door, half-hidden by the stacked wings – unnoticed until now –, opened to reveal a figure in a maid's costume. Paul could not see if she was really as dull as Angele had maintained, but she was obviously a welcome sight to the young Germans for they crowded after her into the house, six of them, seven, and finally, with a last reluctant toot on his horn, an eighth. Alphonse took his time in leaving. He did not so much as glance at the loft, but as he passed through the opening he raised an arm in ironic salutation. Then the door closed behind him, and once again only farmyard noises broke the silence. Paul stole an anxious look at his watch. With luck, and if Angele was right about Suzanne, it would not be much longer now.

He crawled back towards his hide, feeling for the edge of the coat, blind after the brightness streaming through the knothole. The thought came to him that now might be a good time for getting under way, while the Germans were busy in the house. Then reason argued that they probably had an airman driver with them who would be killing time outside, kicking his heels and looking for a quiet place in which to have a smoke. Paul could hardly risk running into him, for that would put everyone in jeopardy. Certainly, if he were found trying to leave – or even seen as he made off – Angele would immediately be implicated, for she would be hard put now to explain why she had not come forward before. He could only hope that she had not maligned Suzanne, and that the young Germans would get on their way sooner rather than later!

Angele appeared to be dozing for he found her motionless. At least she had stopped crying.

'They've gone to the house. Alphonse is with them,' he whispered.

He had intended to whisper into her ear but he misjudged the distance, and felt their cheeks touch. He turned his head and the wetness of her tears was salt against his lips. Her hair was warm and soft and he savoured its perfume with his nose held close beside her temple. She moved, and her eyelids flickered beneath him, tickling his chin, and he knew that she was awake.

He leaned closer, supporting himself on his knees, cradling her face in both hands, gently brushing her eyes with his lips and kissing away the tears. He heard the sudden intake of breath as her face lifted to meet him, and he lowered his mouth onto hers. Her lips were cool, and wet, and slack with crying, and the tip of her nose was cold. She snuffled softly against his cheek, and then she was kissing him back.

He met her tenderly, guided by her sweetness, and felt her lips begin to firm beneath his own. He moved his mouth and brushed aside her hair to kiss her ear. She pressed her lips against his throat and when he kissed her next her mouth had come to life, pressing and seeking in its own right. He heard a rustle in the hay and felt her arms lift around him pulling him down towards her. Her tongue, rich and full, thrust itself demandingly between his lips, and suddenly he was aroused and he kissed her hard, fighting with her tongue and covering her body. She turned swiftly, facing him before his weight could trap her, and he felt her thighs part softly, thrusting at him, and moulding to his hardness.

And then it was her breasts, and lowering his lips, and the coolness of her hands working dextrously to bring them both together until she had them free, first him, and then herself; and then she was opening to him, and she was warm, and moist, and ardently generous, and she met him, and met him, and met him, and grew fiercer and fiercer and suddenly it was the summer house and what-might-have-been, and it was none of those things and it was all of those things, and time meant nothing, and he wanted it to go on and on for ever ...

And suddenly they were clinging together, both explosively spent, and he felt her shaking, and thought she was crying but then realised that she was laughing and he began to laugh with her, waiting for the sadness to come, and when it failed to, laughing again with the wonder of it.

'Are you happy?' he breathed softly.

'Content,' she whispered. 'But who would have thought it of you, my cold Englishman?' He thought he knew what she meant, and he writhed with self-reproach. It was as if he had betrayed a trust.

'Jacques?' he said. And yet there was no sense of guilt. It had all been too swift, and too unpremeditated, and too – innocent. He tried to withdraw from her but she held him tight until he relaxed and settled where he was. She found his lips and closed them with her finger, musky now with the scents of love.

'Not Jacques,' she murmured. She laughed softly. 'But how English still!'

She refused to tell him what she meant and they wrestled playfully, restraining each other now and then to stop and listen. But outside the barn the farmyard noises continued undisturbed. Suzanne could not be all that dull, it seemed!

Paul leant across and held his watch to a gap in the boards and was dumbfounded to find how little time had passed.

He nestled beside her again, and they lay and talked. He told of his accident, and of Mrs Cossey. And he told her of Diane. And of Harry, her fiancé, in the Rifle Corps. She questioned him about other girls he had known, and he told her of loves from his student days, of a Maureen, and a Cynthia, and she pretended to be jealous. But he would not speak to her of Catherine, although his reticence shamed him. Nor – with Jacques in mind – did he speak any more of the squadron, or the war. But he told her of General Cousins, and of Mary and Tom, and caught her interest with their involvement in the land.

'It is all things, the land,' she told him passionately. 'Not *élan*, not courage. Courage comes from the land.' She turned to him, suddenly fierce. 'I would kill for this place, even for the cars below. In his shed in Hermies Alphonse has all the missing parts. To prevent the *Boche* being greedy. Everything must be held intact. And yet until I am mistress here there is little I can do. The old man and the woman have lost interest, and Richard had no interest, ever. Jacques has little interest, but he will listen to me once he is my husband, and he will build and race his cars, even fly his aeroplanes, and I shall stay here and make this place grow.'

He heard the fervour in her voice as she went on to speak of fields daily falling vacant, of ownerless fields adjoining the property, of untenanted farms ripening for merger; and of her plans for the future – when the war was over and the *Boche* had gone.

'Why don't the Allies come?' she complained vehemently. 'Then I could go to Jacques wherever he was. And we would marry, and then whatever happened the farm would be secure.'

Paul smiled. *She* would be secure, was what she meant. He teased her with the charge, gently, but she was not in the least contrite and made no bones about it.

'If Jacques were here where you are now,' she told him, 'I would go down to the *Boche* and say, "*Le Capitaine* Jacques Delcamp is in the hay. Take him now and put him away safely for me until this war is over." As it is, all you tell me is that he has *élan* and that he risks to fly here when there is no need. One "pouf!" and he is gone. One "pouf!" and all is gone. It is a foolish thing, this *élan*. Bravo *élan*! "Pouf!" And the farm will go for sale. And I ...'

Her voice tailed off and there was bleakness and desolation in her silence.

Paul had no more than passing knowledge of French air losses, but operating to the same offensive policy as the RFC they could hardly be much lower than those of the Corps. 'He'll get through, all right,' he comforted her.

She must have realised how hollow his reassurance was yet she nodded, and pressed her face into his chest. But moments later, when he put his hand beneath her chin, and gently raised her head, and they kissed, he knew by her lips that she was grateful and that her spirit had found renewal.

'It is this war,' she told him simply.

'And this?' He indicated the two of them, lying in each other's arms. '*C'est la guerre*, also?'

She shook her head vigorously, and sinuously slid her arms around his neck. 'No, Paul, *c'est cela Vivre!*' she told him. 'This is Life!' And she pulled him fiercely down towards her, and again all time stood still.

It was fast approaching midday when they heard the sound of voices in the yard. It was a repeat of what had gone before, talking and laughing, and the sound of many feet. There was a light-hearted chorus of guttural, '*Au revoir! Madame, Au revoir! Mademoiselle – Au revoir! Mademoiselle ...*'

'Not-so-dull Suzanne!' Paul said slyly. And was elbowed for his pains. A vehicle door slammed again, the engine started, and moments later a clash of gears – Diane's style, he thought, unkindly – announced that the visitors were on their way.

They came to their feet as the tyres crunched on the cobbles, not hurriedly, or awkwardly, but calmly, and at ease with one another. And they fumbled in the dark, helping each other dress, and so taking rather longer than they might have done. The noise of the engine died away, and his approach heralded by a scuff of his boot, Alphonse hailed them from below. Angele called back, and moved into the light from the trapdoor to finish brushing down her dress. Paul, booted once again, shook the flying coat and struggled into it, shrugging his shoulders into place. He moved towards the ladder intending to help Angele down but she stopped him short of the hatchway, to pull him close. And once more he felt her arms around his neck.

'Who is Catherine?' she asked.

He was stunned. He remembered, in London, playfully pretending to Diane that she had uttered her Harry's name in passion in the summer house, but this was repayment with a vengeance! For he had deliberately not mentioned Catherine, not even her existence, let alone her name, and he sensed that Angele knew why. 'She's –' he began, confused.

She pressed her mouth on his to cut him short. 'No matter, Paul,' she said softly. 'I understand.'

'But when –?' he insisted, still unwilling to believe that he had, even unconsciously, blurted out Catherine's name.

'When,' she told him, enigmatically. Her lips brushed his ear and she whispered softly. 'Soon you will go back to her. Give her this from me.' And she kissed him on the lips, tenderly, and with just a hint of renunciation.

'And this.'

Suddenly she pressed her body hard against him, holding him fiercely, and forcing her tongue deep inside his mouth to meet his own. Then her hand, snake-swift, slid down to stroke and fondle, and he reached for her, but she sprang from his arms with a mischievous laugh, turning to face him only as she gained the ladder. Her finger wagged admonishingly.

'The energy, maybe, *Monsieur le Capitaine* Paul Cowley, but the time you do not have.'

Chapter Nineteen

Paul climbed down the ladder to find Angele already in animated conversation with Alphonse. Unwittingly, he must have favoured his right knee for he saw the old man glance significantly at the girl. She too had noticed and shook her head.

'Alphonse says you will not use the wagon. But you must, Paul. You know I would not risk these people so you must trust me.'

This time she took his acquiescence for granted and nodded to Alphonse. Grunting with satisfaction, the old man went outside.

'Alphonse will load the propeller,' she told Paul, 'but before we go Maria insists upon meeting you.' She held up a hand, forestalling his objection. 'You have brought news of Jacques, and Jacques is the apple of her eyes. The *Boche* will make no trouble for Maria.'

Paul allowed her to lead him back through the barn and past the vehicles to the doorway the maid had used. Angele reached for the handle but at once the door swung back and a stout, motherly woman in bonnet and apron stood beaming up at him. She caught his hand in both of hers and wrung it, shaking it up and down and pressing it to her bosom, talking volubly the while. Then, she lifted to her toes and flung her arms around him, planting warm kisses on both his cheeks.

'Paul, meet Maria,' laughed Angele.

The housekeeper smelled of flour and freshly-baked bread and Paul recalled Mrs Cossey at her baking in the cottage, and swept away by the genuineness of the Frenchwoman's emotion, he hugged her fondly, telling her that Jacques was fine and well and sure to be home soon. Angele translated what Paul said and Maria responded with another smothering embrace. At length she set him free and flashed a question at Angele. The girl shook her head, setting off a spate of protestation.

'Maria wants to feed you,' she explained. 'But I have told her that there is no time. You join Alphonse, Paul. I'll pick up food.'

Maria's protestations increased but the girl overbore her with an easy manner, pushing her laughingly down the corridor, the capable young mistress-elect of the house she one day hoped to call her own.

Alphonse had worked quickly. The propeller was stowed and out of sight and as Paul arrived, he was completing harnessing up a medium-sized cart-horse which stood in patient submission, turning its head docilely to regard the newcomer over its master's shoulder. Paul stroked a finger across his palm and grinned at the old man.

'*Boche, bon?*' he asked.

'*Comme ci comme ca,*' Alphonse shrugged, and spread both palms, but he grinned widely, showing brown, stained teeth.

'*Bon! bon!*' returned Paul, pleased with his own easy fluency. Only our Allies cannot converse with us, indeed!

Angele rejoined them at the gate, a cloth-covered bundle in her hands. – *A bundle!* The sight of it jogged Paul's memory – jolted it, rather – so that, cursing in alarm, he scurried back into the barn, heart pounding anew. And there, on the hay bale, where he had put them, was the precious bundle of sparking plugs – left in plain view! Had he remembered them any earlier, he knew, and in particular, at any time in the loft, his blood would have run cold. And deservedly so.

'What was it, Paul?' Angele paused in the act of boarding the wagon.

'I'd left the sparking plugs near the bench,' he told her grimly.

The expletive she uttered was unfamiliar to him but it was clearly heartfelt, explosive, and pithy, for the old man looked at her admiringly, while even the horse twitched an ear. Flustered, Paul waved towards the house, where Maria stood at the doorway, holding her apron to her eyes. Above her, on the first floor, a curtain moved, and Paul pivoted towards it, raising his eyes, smiling towards Maria, then smiling yet wider at the window, and waving more widely still. But there was no response. So maybe Suzanne was as shy as she was dull. Only he was sorry not to have met her.

The roads were virtually empty of military traffic and what local vehicles were encountered passed with a greeting from their occupants but without undue notice otherwise, certainly without a second glance. The fields were woolly with fog, and mist still clung to the hedgerows, while the faintest of drizzles lent credibility to the tarpaulin sheet Paul wore to cover his head and shoulders. The arrangement was that if they caught sight of a German roadcheck – an eventuality both Angele and Alphonse thought too improbable to consider – then Paul would slip over the back of the seat and lie down under the tarpaulin when timber, especially piled as for the cache, would be spilled on top of him. It was an arrangement he viewed with misgivings but it satisfied both Alphonse and Angele and for the moment he had given up protesting.

Hermies proved to be typical of a modest farming and market town, its red-brick houses with their distinctive frets of ornamental brickwork below the eaves showing no signs, as yet, of the war. A white, stone-built church with pillared bell tower and a many-windowed dome of rich black tiles rose upwards into swirling mists which drowned its topmost portion. There were off-duty German soldiers here and there in the streets but none of them paid the slightest attention to the wagon. Shapeless black-clad women went about their shopping, while groups of ancient men stared from the dingy windows of a bar. A child in high buttoned boots sent its hoop spinning across the road, causing the horse to docilely step aside. Smilingly, Angele tossed across an apple and the child stood there, solemn-faced, apple in hand, the hoop oscillating into stillness as the wagon passed on by.

Angele had left her dog cart in Alphonse's yard, down one of the side streets, Paul discovered, to be collected after they had seen him off. He learnt too that it had been Suzanne, appointed to a sentry post at that first-floor window, who had given warning of the Germans, hearing their transport turning up the drive minutes before it had loomed into sight through the mist. And he remembered waving his farewell, and was even gladder now that he had done so.

He asked where the German airmen had come from, but neither the old man nor Angele could say for certain. Most likely, they thought, from Lagnicourt, some six kilometres up the road. Which would mean, Paul reflected, that they were from Boelcke's old *Jasta*. In which case it might not be all that long before he saw them once again!

They ate as they went, the old man noisily and with great gusto, Angele zestfully; Paul, however, constrained by taut-strung nerves, was unable to do more than merely pick. Although having passed the town the roads were even quieter. Indeed the only warlike thing they saw was a heavily sandbagged troop-train chugging its way west towards Bapaume; an encounter that, far from further alarming Paul, heartened him, for he took it as proof that the mist must indeed be widespread if the Germans felt they could risk a daylight troop-train this close to the roving Army-Wing squadrons.

But it was clear that a change was already on the way. The breeze had freshened noticeably even since they had taken to the road and now the drizzle had grown to perceptible proportions so that puddled wheel ruts beside the metalled road were patterned with intertwining ringlets.

Approaching Vélu, they crossed the branch line at a level-crossing, getting a wave from the keeper's cottage. Angele waved back and called a greeting but Alphonse ignored the keeper and Paul followed suit.

'The railway station,' Angele announced, just moments later.

Paul looked up to see a tall, three-storied building in the area's ubiquitous red brick rising beyond a concentration of rolling stock and storage sheds. A stone slab high up below the eaves window had the word 'Vélu' inscribed in proud, handsome lettering. Half-raised in his seat, he peered about more closely, mystified.

Two of the windows facing the platform were boarded up, and the middle-storey window at the gable end was bricked in, but apart from this there was not the slightest evidence of bomb damage. He frowned, remembering yet again how often the Corps had visited Vélu.

'The aeroplane bombs make noise,' Angele told him, interpreting his puzzlement. 'But they do not make much harm. There were three trains here earlier this month when the bombing aeroplanes came but when the smoke cleared there was little damage. That store hut was burned down.' She pointed to some charred remains that had escaped Paul's notice. 'But once the aeroplanes have gone away the Germans set men to work. The carriages off their road are lifted back and the trains rail – roll, again within hours.'

He grunted. That repeated bombing raids could have so little effect gave much food for thought. But not for digestion right now …

The cart turned left, leaving the road before it entered the village proper and heading south along the track towards Vélu Wood. They bumped along the rutted surface as it bore away from the narrow spur of wood – Paul's bucket's handle again – to clip the wood at its northeastern corner – his bucket's top, right-hand rim. Beyond the corner the track ran on to meet the embankment at the stream-access tunnel Paul had found earlier, while the wood itself angled back towards Bertincourt, and if all was well, towards Henri and the de Havilland. It was at the top corner of the wood proper that Paul drew the line.

Both Alphonse and the girl protested but now Paul was adamant. So far the girl had been right in her assessment of German activity but from this point on there was no question that to be found nearby – however things turned out, and whether now or later – was to be implicated in his presence. Paul peered through the mist down the wide grass verge he had walked along with Henri, then out across fields that by daylight looked so solid and unthreatening. Then, forestalling further opposition, he swung from the cart and seized the horse's bridle, refusing to let it budge another inch.

It must have been clear to both the others that they could not sway him further for Angele gave up her protestations while the old man, though growling dissent, and after a further moment's hesitation, biddably looped the reins and clambered reluctantly down, to begin pulling aside the wood from the cache. The girl dropped nimbly to the ground.

'You are right, Paul' she said softly. 'But you know I would like to see you safely away.' Then she smiled, and taking his arm, walked him to the back of the cart.

Working together, they tied the ropes to the propeller. The stakes and the metal strips they formed into a separate bundle with a loop to pass over the neck. It might not be the most comfortable of arrangements, Paul thought, but if it came to the pinch he could always stash the bundle and come back for it. Satisfied that all the equipment was duly packed, Angele reached in under Alphonse's driving seat and pulled out Paul's flying boots. He shook his head in exasperation.

'Angele! You should have burned them,' he chided. 'It was an awful risk to have them with you.'

She merely wrinkled her nose at him and they struggled together to change his footwear without wetting his socks on the soaking grass. He parcelled up the remains of the food and tucked it into his tunic.

'For Henri,' he said.

He shook hands with the old man, determined that he would look into that IOU. Or find out if some form of compensation was envisaged for the future.

And then he turned to Angele.

Looking down he saw the moisture on her eyelashes. To say, 'Thank you!' was inadequate, and neither Trenchard nor the King could begin to repay her for all she had done. She divined his difficulty and smiled through her tears.

'*Au revoir, Monsieur* Cowley,' she said softly.

He muttered something but it caught in his throat and he turned away. Then a thought – appalling in its ramifications – struck him, and in sudden consternation he swung to face her. Back there, in the barn, they had acted utterly without care!

'Angele,' he cried, 'what if ...?'

Clearly she was well cognizant of what it was he had, this belatedly, realised, for she shook her head.

'No, it is not to be worried of.' Her hand reached up and stroked his cheek. 'I would not be unhappy, Paul,' she told him softly. 'Only it will not be.' She looked out across the misty fields but he knew that her eyes saw nothing but the future, and the farm she carried in her soul. 'Perhaps before this war is over I shall wish ...'

In the silence she took a deep breath. Abruptly her head came up, and she lifted on tiptoes to kiss him lightly on the lips.

'Go to your Catherine,' she told him. Then she turned away and sprang aboard the wagon. 'And for her sake, Paul, and for mine,' she called back as Alphonse shook the reins, 'no *élan*!'

The old man raised his whip and waved, grinning, but the girl never once more turned her head. Paul looked after them as the sound of the wheels faded in the distance, wishing above all that he could feel more pride in the way he had handled things. But the breeze, he realised, was stirring the branches of the trees and he fancied that he could already see a little further across the fields. And then he could no longer hear the cart and suddenly, refreshingly, knowing that Angele and the old man were now truly out of all harm's way, relief washed over him. Only then did he become aware of the strain he had been under on their behalf. He took a deep breath. And then another. High time indeed, that he got under way!

Paul eased the rope-burdened propeller onto his shoulder, becoming aware at once that as neither he nor Angele had remembered a pad he must brave out this morning's bruise. For a while he struggled to lift the secondary bundle to his other shoulder but found it unbalanced him and eventually he settled for tucking it one-handedly under his left arm. The first drop of moisture pooled on his brow to trickle down his nose and he blew at it, only then acknowledging that the drizzle was turning into rain. The sooner he got the machine back together again the better it would be.

He stumbled a little until his knee warmed up but within a few minutes he fancied he recognised the spot at which Henri had led them out of the woods. The new bundle was far too awkward, however, and he stopped, putting down the propeller and passing the loop Angele had fashioned around his neck. The makeshift sling was better, but still uncomfortable, only it was not worth bothering about now, with so little distance to go. At which thought he began to walk more circumspectly, remembering how suddenly he and Henri had come upon the de Havilland earlier.

To the left the mist had drawn back so much that Paul could pick out the ploughed furrows more than halfway across to the railway embankment, and despite his concern, he smiled as he remembered teetering along here in the darkness, edging away from some purely imaginary chasm. Now, a few short hours later he might have been a different man. It spoke worlds for how tensed-up his nerves had been back then.

Henri exploded from the bushes, virtually at Paul's feet, and in such a rush that Paul actually cried out and all but cast the propeller from him the better to – to flee? Certainly not to fight. But assimilation was instantaneous and he sought to cover his agitation by bending down and placing both his burdens gently on the ground. Henri, however, had noticed nothing, he was so excited to see him back. He bounded like a puppy, wriggling, and wreathed in smiles, pulling at Paul's arms, bending to half-lift the propeller, testing it for weight. He kept up a constant chatter until finally Paul had to calm him down with a firm hand pressed on each shoulder. Paul saw now that in the best *Boy's Own Paper* tradition – there had to be a French equivalent – the lad had smeared dirt on his cheeks, to avoid being seen.

It took a while to get Henri's full report but as it was evidently safe to proceed Paul let him talk while they carried on down the verge, Paul with the propeller and the boy with the bundle of pickets and splints struggling to match Paul's stride and unconsciously aping him every step of the way.

It had been a long and uneventful vigil, it seemed, and Henri had seen nothing. As Paul had suspected Henri had long since got through the food and welcomed the supplement Paul produced from his tunic. After that, with his mouth full, the boy was harder to understand than ever. But nobody had come along, it seemed, and the '*De'avillan*' remained undisturbed where Paul had left it.

The news brought a fresh flood of relief and with it, a renewed awareness of the rare state of tension he was under. Angele had said it showed in his eyes, and remembering other pilots he had seen around the squadrons, and particularly in the revelatory light thrown by the shock of the boy's volatile arrival just minutes before, Paul no longer doubted that he really was somewhat stressed.

Henri would have walked blithely on and down into the hollow but Paul had his bearings now and held up a restraining arm, turning off into the woods to approach the machine from cover. He picked his way cautiously, keeping to the bushes, and knew a stir of excitement as he sighted the red of the roundel on the nacelle. He insisted then on waiting, to listen, eyes and ears alert, but Henri proved as good a scout as ever and the continued silence testified that the place was indeed deserted. Only then did Paul relax, and wave the boy on, laughing as the lad capered about the machine, and with Paul's nod of approval, climbed up and settled himself into the cockpit once again, donning the helmet as he did so. Five minutes, Paul decided, but after that, Henri must go.

Paul got down to work swiftly now, unlashing the ropes and setting them to one side. He carried the propeller over to the machine, laid it flat, then slid it beneath the lower tailboom, stepped through the bracing wires himself, and finally shoulder-eased it up into position on the nave. The nuts he hand-tightened to hold the propeller in place then, taking the spanner, tightened each in the approved sequence, evening out the strain. The truncated blades themselves still posed problems and he reviewed them in his mind as he worked, planning the next move.

For a start, even assuming that the engine had suffered no internal damage, the propeller, being six inches shorter than hitherto, would now push less air than it had before. Whether that would adversely affect the revs on the Gnome, causing it to overspeed, was hard to say. Propellers were a compromise at best, needing a fine bite at the air for slow speeds – as at take-off – and a coarse one for fast forward speeds. In the modern propeller the simple airscrew had become very sophisticated in design so that whether in losing the tips Paul had lost high- or low-speed capability, and how much of that capability he had lost, remained to be seen. He could almost certainly expect less performance on take-off and must therefore anticipate a longer run, especially with the muddy, essentially-ploughland surface he had to use. Once airborne – always providing he managed to get airborne – what he got from the propeller might go either way; he might even find performance enhanced. He doubted it, but he might. Even theory might not supply all the answers where so much was trial and error.

Paul tightened the last nut, and checked over his work, remembering, as a student, becoming increasingly dissatisfied with the scarcity of information available on propeller theory and the pleasure of discovering from Duchêne's *Flight Without Formula* – read as late as 1914, in translation, of course – that he was not alone in feeling that much more needed to be done. He wondered what advice Duchêne would give now? 'Get on with it', more than likely, for the eminent French authority, like Lanchester and so many other aerodynamicist pioneers, was above all a very practical experimenter.

Paul started as a branch fell, and heart pounding, ducked clear of the aeroplane to peer into the woods, waving Henri to silence. But the sound was not repeated, and after a while he turned away. Nonetheless, it was a forcible reminder that the time had come to send the boy back. In all conscience, he should never have let him come this far but after the lad had been standing sentry all day Paul had not had the heart to send him home right away. Now, however, he walked over to the cockpit, seeing Henri's face fall as he approached. The boy proved a true soldier, however, and climbed to the ground without a word of protest.

Paul held out his hand, and Henri took it shyly, smiling bravely, not wanting to show his hurt. Docilely he handed over the flying helmet and Paul hovered on the brink of presenting it to him. But it could prove a lethal gift and straight-thinking prevailed. In the end, he stepped back, and formally came to attention. Then he threw the boy the smartest salute he had ever managed in his life. He felt ridiculous and wondered fleetingly how Catherine – or Angele – would have viewed such martial histrionics, but it struck the right note with the boy for he braced, and gravely snapped back a French-style compliment. Then he turned on his heel, and marched smartly away without a backward glance. After a few yards however, he could no longer hold back his feelings and Paul could see his shoulders shaking as he broke into a run, to disappear moments later among the trees.

Chapter Twenty

Paul found that he was a little snuffly himself, but it had been wrong of him to allow the boy to come anywhere near the machine once he himself was in evidence. For only now, with Henri gone, were the Basquins absolutely in the clear. He looked up the incline towards the fields and realised that he could see to the top of the embankment. What had previously been mist was now lifting into low cloud under the freshening breeze. A little more, and the squadrons of both sides would be ordered into the air to make up for the loss of the morning.

Paul extracted two of the mild-steel strips from the bundle and carried them to the rear of the machine. Placing a right-angled section along one side of the starboard upper tailboom he then opposed it with a flat section to form a triangular box-like splint extending a foot or so on each side of the damaged area. The edges of the opposing sections did not quite meet but that was ideal, for forming a loop of rope around the splint and using one of the wooden pins as a windlass, he wound away until they almost met, finally lashing and re-lashing the splint with baling wire until it was as near solid as he could make it.

The lower tailboom was by far the most badly damaged of the two and here he had to bang the jagged metal back into place with Alphonse's mallet before he could position the splint. When complete his lashings lacked seamanlike neatness but they were locking the metal splints firmly over the damage and Paul was confident that with considerate aircraft handling on his part they would prove adequate to the task.

The next problem was to arrange things so that he could start the engine and get away single-handedly. In normal circumstances, of course, there would be a mechanic to remove the chocks once the engine had started. As things were Paul could not use chocks, for the Gnome, once started, would run flat-out to full revs and push the wheels hard against them, preventing him from pulling them out. In his abortive attempt at rescuing poor Barton he had partially – and utterly unsatisfactorily – chocked the wheel on a turf. This time he had to come up with a better solution.

In the past he had known people to start single-handedly without chocks, relying on soft ground to brake the wheels. For the most part they had ended up with their aeroplanes running off, or running over them, or running into hedgerows before they could clamber aboard. It always made for a good laugh, but not when you were personally involved, and not here, with only Germans to share in the joke. He had turned over several ideas already, discarding most before making his decision.

The tail of the aircraft was already positioned down the slope within feet of a stout tree. If, therefore, he tied the rope to the tree and then looped it around the tail-skid, securing it with a slip knot, then the aircraft would be held against the pull of the engine until he could get into the cockpit. Once seated he could pull the end of the slip knot and simply let the machine draw itself free.

The problem was to lead the pull-rope clear of the rear-mounted propeller. Paul had planned to sink stakes off to one side of the machine, beyond the wingtip, leading the long, free end of rope from the slip knot out and around the stakes and back across to reach the cockpit. It was only now when he came to put the plan into action that he began to have doubts.

For a start he wondered if the stakes were that practical an idea. He raked back the leaf mould and dug his heel into the soft ground. It would probably be solid enough a foot or so down but he doubted now that the mallet had the weight to drive the pickets in far enough to take the sideways strain that would be called for. Not only that, by the time they were embedded firmly enough they would be shorter than he had envisaged. In a word, he had misjudged it. Wood would never be his medium! And even then the stakes would be left to tell a tale. More damning still, Alphonse was too much of a craftsman to half-do a job and he had smoothed them and shaped them so well that nobody finding them would believe that they had been roughed out in the woods by a downed pilot working alone.

There was the rope, too; that should be retrieved, and for just a moment Paul wondered whether he had, after all, been too cautious in letting Henri go. But, of course, there was no question about that, and if it came to it he could always take a chance and trust to luck that he would make it to the cockpit before the aircraft got under way: it was facing uphill, which would slow it down ...

Time was passing, however, and for the moment Paul shelved the problem while considering his next move. It had been his intention to unship the Lewis in order to shed its twenty-pound or so weight, but now, in for a penny, he decided; if the propeller would get him into the air it would get the Lewis there too. There was nothing rational about the decision but somehow it seemed to have become a matter of pride, and he put aside the voice of scientific reason that warned him that he was adversely loading the chances.

Making his way into the woods he had to cast around at first to find the tree root where he had cached the ammunition drums – a pretty poor squirrel, after all. But after that it took him only a few moments to retrieve the drums and brush them down. They would add a few more pounds of weight, but with a touch of bravado he stowed four, including the partially used one, snapped the remaining drum onto the gun, and cocked the action: now he was a fire-eater again. But only if an enemy came at him head-on down the slope!

Paul's original intention of crossing the lines at the first sign of a clearance had been frustrated by the morning's developments. Now he had to re-think. Once airborne he had to anticipate handling problems, and being unable to climb very high, so that dusk would now be the safest time to attempt the crossing. But he had to weigh that against the risk of being discovered in the interim. For now that even the rain had stopped it was more than likely that people would soon be about. A few moments ago two birds had flown over at a height which showed how rapidly the mist was lifting. Clearly they thought conditions good enough; in which case other fliers would soon be thinking the same.

Having stopped worrying about the chocking problem, the solution came to him unbidden. He could simply utilise a tailboom which, of necessity, ran outboard of the propeller and would hold the pull-cord well clear. By fashioning a series of rope loops along the boom – to act like the rings on a fishing rod – he could then run the pull-cord through them, passing the end forwards and into the cockpit.

For a while he considered the angles involved and decided that there was nothing to choose between using an upper or a lower boom. Arbitrarily, he plumbed for the lower right. He further realised, in the course of fashioning his loops, that he could also improve upon his original picketing scheme.

Acting on this he passed one end of the rope first around the tree, then around the tail-skid. Next, pulling up slack from the other, much longer portion of the rope, and after a moment or two of fingers and thumbs, he tied a bow. The bow fashioned with the long end would form the slip knot. That on the shorter end he simply pulled through. Then, having tightened the knot, he began threading the long end – the pull-cord – through his boom rings, finally passing it forwards outside the inner vertical strut of the right wings and dropping it into his seat. After that it was not without some pride that he took his place in the cockpit, and gave a tug.

The knot came free – but with something of a jerk. Paul muttered a curse. It had resisted pulling free, yet he had hardly tightened it. Frowning, his smugness somewhat dented, he walked back, and on re-tying the half bow, put all his strength into it. Now, clambering back into the cockpit, he found, as he had feared, that although the knot initially slipped, it then jammed, resisting all further efforts to free it.

All traces of pride quite dissipated, he stamped back to the slip knot and gave it a straight pull. This time, with the pull no longer taken around tailboom and wing strut, the loop slipped clear– if with an effort at the end. Grunting, Paul retied the half-bow yet again, then fell to studying the knot, seeing, after just a moment, where the trouble lay.

By design, the single, tightening strand of the knot strangled the two side-by-side strands forming the bow's loop – a stranglehold which tightened the more it came under strain. Just the same the sisal strands slipped easily enough as long as they ran side by side. When they swelled out in the final bend of the bow, however, they jammed against the tightening strand, locked, and simply refused to be pulled free. It was just possible to free the loop now, using a perfectly straight pull, but under the full power of the engine, with the release pull coming from an angle, the tightening strand would act like a vice.

Paul wondered if greasing the strands would do the trick and to that end he looked around the wheel axles and control runs for a spot of grease. Drawing a blank he pondered for a while more and then began to search around for a fallen branch, breaking off a foot-long billet that he judged to be somewhat thicker than the combined side-by-side strands of the bow. Next he retied the half-bow, this time sliding the billet under the tightening strand. He grunted. Now when he put the knot under strain the tightening strand still carried out its function, but no longer bore directly on the side-by-side strands, only on the wooden billet, so that regardless of the strain applied the loop could be slipped with ease.

Paul tried the new arrangement until he was satisfied that he had solved the problem, operating the pull-cord first from the rear, and then twice more from the cockpit. Finally, whistling a jaunty catch beneath his breath, he once again tied the half-bow to incorporate the billet of wood, then walking forward, dropped the pull-cord into the cockpit so that all was ready for the off.

There were still the sparking plugs to refit, but even though the rain had stopped Paul wanted to wait until the last moment before drying off the ignition components: he did not want dampness causing a problem in starting the engine. He walked back up the slope and looked south across the fields, startled to see the tip of the spire of Bertincourt church, rising above the trees. The mist was clearing rapidly now.

He turned to the practicalities of the take-off. With the field in the lee of the woods there was no breeze to speak of. Once he had negotiated the slope, however, he would be facing as lengthy a take-off run as any. He looked along the grass verge, measuring its width with his eye. If he *could* swing the machine slightly to the right as he cleared the woods then he would give himself even more space before having to consider lifting over the railway embankment; additionally the grass would offer a firmer surface than the ploughed field itself. True, he would be very close to the trees, and it would have to be carefully done, but it was a course of action to be kept it in mind.

Paul had been conscious for some time of a feeling of discomfort and now the job was nearly complete he could ignore it no longer. He took a careful look around to ensure that all was clear, and then made his way back to the aircraft. Here he scoured the site for every redundant scrap of rope and wire, gathered all those articles he no longer needed, and carried the discard past the root where he had cached the Very pistol and even deeper into the woods. Finding a bank, he pushed them into a crevice, kicking over them what must have been decades of fallen vegetation. Then, retracing his steps a little, he spent some moments gathering an adequate supply of dock leaves, found a bush close by and began to struggle out of his lower garments. Moments later the thought struck him that he felt more vulnerable now than at any time since he had forced-landed. How hateful it would be to be captured like this!

Dusk was still a good two hours away but even as Paul struggled back into his gear he found himself nervously consulting his watch. It would be equally hateful getting caught merely because he had waited a while too long. On the other hand it would be foolhardy to attempt to cross the lines before failing light gave him a reasonable chance of winning clear. So, he would refit the sparking plugs the moment he got back and then make his decision.

To his disgust he discovered that his cache for the Very pistol had pooled with water. Accordingly he discarded the spare cartridge, even though its waxed case would probably have protected it. The cartridge in the pistol had fared better so having wiped it on his coat he replaced it and locked the barrel back into place. He tried to stow the pistol but his coat was fully buttoned and belted while his pockets, though amply sized, were now bulked out with the sparking plugs. The sparking plugs! And with the thought of them his spine chilled, as it had done in that moment of revelation outside the barn. To have risked so much! And the lives of so many people! It was the sort of thing nightmares are made of and he set off at a trot, signal pistol in hand, as if to leave the memory behind him.

After the mist and drizzle the leaf carpet underfoot was soggy and soundless, and it struck home that since Henri had gone a whole army might have sneaked up on him without warning so engrossed had he been in his work. Red Indians, so books would have it, habitually walked through the woods without snapping a single twig. Now he knew how it was done: they waited until everything was soaking wet.

It was the horse Paul saw first, or rather the steam rising in clouds from its sweat-damp hindquarters; a tall leggy chestnut, its ornately plaited mane and brushed tail betokening the esteem in which the animal was held. As it chanced the dismounted rider was unsighted by the bulk of its flank and this gave Paul time to check his stride and step back behind the nearest tree. Heart pounding, he eased himself up so that he could peer between the branches of a fork, thankful for the deadness of the ground which, if it had concealed the arrival of the horseman, had at least done the same for him. Discovery was what he had feared from the first but that it should happen now, when he was so close to the off, made his blood boil.

Just then the rider moved into sight, to stand fondling the horse's muzzle while casting earnest glances into the woods on every side, a tall, smartly turned-out German officer in some form of undress uniform, out riding for the pleasure of it, evidently, before the day was too far gone. He wore a regimental peaked cap with the chinstrap fastened, a long grey-green topcoat unbuttoned from the waist, and black, highly-polished riding boots elegantly set off by silver spurs. His face was perplexed, and he was frowning now as he slowly walked the horse around to give himself a better view, stooping slightly and ducking his head from side to side to see between the trees.

At length the officer led his mount to the edge of the clearing and looped the reins across a low branch in order to give his full attention to the de Havilland. Paul watched as he began a tour of the machine, slowly walking around it, pausing to finger the leader's pennant, now dangling limp and damp from the interplane struts, and stopping, rather longer, to ponder over the tethering rope, obviously puzzling out its purpose. He was clearly ill at ease for he frequently paused to peer into the woods as if sensing that someone was watching, at one time looking directly at the tree where Paul had taken cover, but without seeing him. Paul himself was casting anxious glances up the slope, fearing that other riders would be in company, but as the minutes ticked by and it became clear that the officer was on his own he began to unbrace, and even to see a certain black humour in the situation.

The German had stumbled upon a British aeroplane which was obviously being prepared for flight. He was alone in a secluded part of the woods at the mercy of anybody who wanted to take a potshot at him: at best any confrontation would be man to man and the issue, therefore, open to doubt. The officer had no real alternative but to summon help, but he was in a quandary, for the moment he turned his back he ran the risk of losing both pilot and machine. It was plain that he had no other option but to ride off for assistance; it was simply a question of how long he waited before he went. For Paul it was a matter of patience, and of praying that no other Germans appeared before this one made up his mind. A matter of patience! He smiled thinly, watching the man's fingers beating a nervous tattoo on the drum-tight fabric as he deliberated.

Clearly the German authorities were lagging behind those of the French who, months ago since, had posted notices telling the populace what to do in a situation like this and how to disable an enemy aeroplane so discovered. Paul remembered spelling it out to himself, '*pour empêcher le départ, en brisant soit la queue de l'aeroplane, soit une roué*'. Well, he seemed to be in the clear there. The German had walked past both tail and wheels without doing any damage.

At last, however, the man seemed to make a decision and walked slowly to the rear of the nacelle, throwing back his greatcoat as he did so. He bent over the engine, obliging Paul to crane away from the tree to make out what he intended. Only it came to him on the instant: the ignition wires! The smile vanished from Paul's face. And suddenly he was running from cover, crashing and stumbling through the bushes and shouting at the top of his voice: if the wires were yanked out now he would never get away!

Alarmed, the German whirled to face him, and Paul saw the pistol aimed at the cylinders. So, not the ignition wires but the engine itself! The officer must have already taken first pressure on the trigger for as he spun about so the gun went off, the shot whining away through the trees. But he recovered like a cat and even as he completed his turn, fired again, a hurriedly-aimed snapshot which knocked Paul's right leg from under him and sent him sprawling face down into the leaves.

Paul lay there stunned, spluttering in the dirt, his right arm trapped beneath his body, not yet conscious of pain in his knee. He looked up into narrowed steel-blue eyes, seeing lips thinned with tension in a face white with shock, and the pistol, wavering markedly, but only inches from his face, and he braced himself against the shot. Time seemed to freeze, and the only movement was from the horse, snorting and rearing, and with every lunge threatening to pull free of its tether. It seemed an age before the man's eyes dropped, then it was to take in, not without concern, the blood welling from the side of Paul's knee. A moment later he lowered the pistol and turned back towards the engine, steadying himself to take aim at the cylinders once more.

'*No!*'

Paul screamed out the word, pushing to his feet to hop and flounder forwards, mad with desperation. The German turned, for a scant heartbeat stupefied by this berserker attack, then took an involuntary pace back. '*Nein!*' he yelled piercingly.

But Paul staggered on, seeing only the pistol, hardly three feet from his head. He saw the gun leap, and felt a burn on his cheek, and then the man found his stance and was taking proper aim, two-handed now, the muzzle coming down towards Paul's stomach. Only, as if by reflex Paul's finger tightened and the Very pistol, even now discounted by any conscious thought, went off in his hand and there was a bang, and a flash, and Paul fell sideways as his right knee gave under him. He saw a trail of green fire, smelled pungent smoke, and heard the horse bolt frantically off up the incline.

But the German officer was rolling on the ground, his hands clawing at his neck, and he was screaming and screaming, only soundlessly, for the cartridge had taken away most of his throat, and with it his tongue, and his vocal cords. The ricocheting flare had soared away into a low parabola, and was already tumbling unbalanced about its axis to burn itself out among the furrows. If the glare, and its smoke trail, did not attract someone's attention soon then the riderless horse certainly would.

Gingerly, Paul lifted to his feet, leaving the Very pistol where it lay. He pressed his hand to the side of his knee and steeled himself to look down at the blood oozing past his fingers. Tentatively he bent his leg, and now he began to feel pain, though faint, as yet, like a vestigial memory of his old hurt, for this new wound was still quite numb.

He limped across to the German to see if he could help him, but there was no movement. He checked the wrist for a pulse, only his hand was shaking too much, so to be certain he felt inside the tunic. Still finding none he pulled at the collar to turn the head, shuddering as his fingers touched raw meat. The eyes, so vital only moments before, had dulled and were wide and staring, but strangely the features reflected nothing of the agony in which the officer had died. Paul could see now how young the man had been, and conscious still of the sympathy he had shown when Paul was helpless on the ground, of how he had held his fire, the bile rose in Paul's throat.

He spat the taste from his mouth. Then spat again in self-disgust. This was not war as he had grown to know it in the air. And yet – he took stock. True, it was not war as he knew it. But it was war, just the same. And it was survival, and accordingly he should find no cause for repugnance. He fingered the burn on his cheek: that shot, at least, had been meant to kill, and the next, aimed two-handed, and with deliberation at his stomach, would have killed. Paul hobbled towards the de Havilland, his hand already groping for the plugs. There was no call for regret here. And besides, this was neither the time nor the place for it, even had there been.

But that the regrets would come in time, Paul knew even now, along with so many others, visiting his sleep to haunt his nights, no matter how the years stretched on ahead.

He pulled the branch off the motor and threw it into the bushes. The square of kitchen oilcloth he folded and tossed over the wing into his seat. His gloves, though wet, he would need in the air. But the silk scarf, wetter still now, he wound tightly around his knee in an endeavour to staunch the flow of blood. He unbuckled his coat belt, and transferring it to just above his knee, used Basquin's screwdriver to twist it – windlass-like once again – as a tourniquet. Then he turned his attention to the Gnome.

Initially Paul merely eased the propeller around, eyeing the cylinders as they spun in unison, turning the engine over through a few revolutions, feeling for any stiffness. There was no sign of mechanical damage, nor did the lubricating oil appear to have congealed enough overnight to cause any restriction. So far, so good! With suddenly unsteady fingers he unwound the first few plugs and used the rag to wipe around the sockets. Then he began to fit them, his fingers trembling so badly at times that once he dropped the spanner and saw the blood spurt from the scarf as he knelt to retrieve it. Now he was working feverishly against both time and pain, driven on by the knowledge that more Germans would soon be on their way.

He finished tightening the plugs and began re-securing the ignition wires, despite an increasing light-headedness forcing himself to stop after each operation to double-check his work. Finally, satisfied that all was as it should be, he wiped the area with rag until not a trace of moisture remained.

He was becoming increasingly nervous too, he knew, breathing harshly through his mouth, and glancing up the slope every few moments, aware of the fear churning in his stomach. There was one more job he had planned to do if he had time, although it seemed a waste of effort now. But now was not the time to make new plans, experience telling him that in his present state he was better following plans made in more rational moments.

He took the last two lengths of rope and the two remaining lengths of baling wire and set out to rig the ropes as supplementary fore and aft bracing stays along the damaged booms. He had settled upon his anchor points before leaving for the farm and now he fumbled to connect the first rope, not pulling it tight but leaving himself several inches of slack. Then, using one of the wooden pins Alphonse had fashioned he entwined it through the slack and used it, too, windlass-fashion, until the rope was quivering-tight and would give no more. Only it took an inordinate effort, Paul found, to hold the pin one-handedly while lashing it to the rope with baling wire to stop it spinning free.

The second rope, intended to take some strain from the lower tail-boom, gave him far more trouble than the first, especially the securing of the pin, but finally it was done. How much strength the rope stays would give in case of need was anybody's guess, but that was the way he had planned it and in the absence of a ten-hundredweight cable – a twelve-gauge solid-drawn wire or a five-sixteenths flexible cable – or any other compatible cable, it was the best he could do. He ducked back outside the booms and, reeling and light-headed now, took a final look around to ensure that all was set.

The thought of reprisals had been nagging at him. As had other considerations. But it took an immense effort of will, Paul discovered now, to propel himself over to the body. Would a Very flare be classed the same as Buckingham incendiary ammunition, and having used it against a man – albeit inadvertently – would he be deemed guilty of a war crime against the Hague Convention? There were burns around the chin but no more than powder burns. Indeed the charge, fired at point-blank range, seemed to have torn its way through before igniting so that Paul doubted whether even the doctors would be any the wiser regarding the weapon used. But suppose the Germans decided that locals had been party to the killing? That was something Paul simply could not risk.

He searched his own pockets for paper without success and in the end pulled open the German's tunic and took out a wallet. Inside there were letters, closely written on both sides – so unlike Catherine's sparse missives, he reflected –, but he eventually found a blank space on the back of a photograph. It was a picture of a young woman, a wife, or a sweetheart, only Paul tried not to let the portrait register. His field pencil was blunt and coarse but after a while he printed out: 'THIS OFFICER WOUNDED ME. WAS KILLED DOING DUTY. CAPT COWLEY, RFC.'

He would like to have added his condolences, and something about gallantry, and courteousness, but there was no space, and forced to be content, Paul placed the message on the man's chest, retrieving the pistol – a Luger – and using it as a weight. He was not at all sure that he was doing a wise thing in identifying himself, but better that, than to have civilians blamed.

Straightening up, Paul staggered. He knew that he was losing a serious amount of blood and although he had tightened the tourniquet as much as he dared he was beginning to feel increasingly woozy. That it was time to go was underlined as he reached for the edge of the cockpit, for there was a burst of noise from the south and the unmistakable sound of an aircraft engine, not too far away and growing in intensity. The weather must have cleared sufficiently then and aircraft were taking off from Bertincourt just beyond the wood. The machine passed without coming into sight above the trees, but it sounded fast and powerful as it made off towards the west. It was enough to spur him into life and he was clambering awkwardly onto the footrest before the engine note began to fade.

He took his weight on his left leg and reached over to switch on the petrol. After that he checked and re-checked, setting everything for the start, for with his wound he had to anticipate that there was going to be no second chance if anything went wrong. He stowed the oilcloth and the last rope fragments on the seat, and pushed the tools into his pockets. Then, leaning on his elbow he tied a loop in the pull-rope so that, in case of need, he could slip it over his shoulder. He took a final look around, and then remembered the Very pistol. Carefully he eased himself to the ground and retrieved it from where it lay, half-buried in the leaves. In its absence the chances were that the Germans would assume that the dreadful wound was caused by a ricocheting bullet fired from an ordinary revolver.

The numbness was wearing off now and the pain was beginning to bite. Paul had long learnt to live with a certain amount of pain, and from the self-same part of his body, and he wondered if the nervous system became habituated to pain in any way. First indications now suggested that the answer would be a resounding, 'No!'

He reached up into the cockpit, balancing on his left leg as before, and reloaded the Very pistol from the rack. There were still a few flares left. He had been concerned about prowling children the night before: how then, had he forgotten to remove the flares! Flares! One had flown back into the propeller and nearly killed him in the air, another had saved his life on the ground: best of three then. He snapped the signal pistol shut and pushed it into the stowage.

Now he took the time to make one final check of the engine controls: if he flooded the engine then he could expect trouble, the Gnome detested being allowed to run over-rich. He would start on gravity fuel-feed; everything else he had set using all his experience. And now the time had come to put that experience to the test. He hesitated over the main switch but the rising level of pain decided him, and he flicked it on. Then he let himself down to the ground.

It took, Paul found, a draining application of will to force himself to recheck his tethering rope, but he did so, meticulously, paying special attention to the wooden billet in the slip knot, ensuring that it was still in position. Next he weaved his way inside the booms, staggering slightly, and nearly falling, but gathering himself, to run a finger under the valve of the lowest cylinder, establishing, with satisfaction, that petrol had indeed drained out. Now he took one of the foreshortened propeller blades in his hand. Gingerly he eased the engine over once, and then twice, fully conscious of the fact that the magneto was live, but only too aware also that his strength was giving out. He could make it once more round to the cockpit – he was going to have to – but even that would require a mammoth effort. He steadied himself, putting all his weight on his left leg and dangling his injured knee as far out of harm's way as possible. And suddenly he was staring into the eyes of the corpse. He took a deep breath, '*Hals und beinbruch!*' he called, and swung down with all his might. 'Break your neck and leg!' their fliers told each other before take-off, and that was supposed to bring good luck!

There was a eruption of sound as the engine caught at first swing and clouds of smoking castor-oil billowed around him filling his eyes and his nose and his throat. The cylinders blurred into life with the propeller discing and beating back an instant gale of leaves and dirt into his face. Gasping, but elated, Paul ducked between wires and booms to pull himself along the trailing edge of the lower wing. Maybe the exhortation brought luck after all!

He was determined to keep his hold on the machine no matter what happened as he half-hopped, half-sidled around the tip of the wing. He looked back towards his tethering rope. It was quivering and stretching and he could see the wheels creeping forwards as the fibres were tested to their limit, but the rope was holding the strain, and that was all he asked of it.

He clung to the edge of the cockpit and the pain washed up and sickened him. He pressed his cheek against the lacing of the nacelle while he gathered his diminishing strength and then, balancing on his left leg, pulled himself up to poise on the edge of the cockpit. Not daring to think about what he had to do next he jolted one-footed down to the seat and used both hands to bring his right leg over the edge. It flopped, now agonisingly alive, to the floor, and if his scream was lost in the roar of the Gnome yet he was swallowing vomit as he fought off the pain, dropping into his seat and finding the rudder with his left foot.

The engine was bellowing its protest but running sweet and true and despite the truncated propeller blades there was no trace of abnormal vibration: nor did the revs seem at much variance with the norm. Paul blipped the thumbswitch to slow the engine, swiftly checking around the cockpit before making a minute adjustment to the fine setting. He pulled on his helmet, and his gloves, wet though they were, blipped the engine once more, and then let it run full out. The pull-cord was in his hands, and bracing his left leg, he heaved on the rope. And nothing happened!

The engine roared on, the machine itself held in tightest thrall by the rope. Paul cast a frantic glance over his shoulder. Behind him a myriad leaves whirled in a demented pirouette. The tailplane was shuddering under the strain, but so far the booms seemed to be taking it well. Paul tugged again, but to no avail. And he knew the dry and bitter taste of failure. So after all this, he was to be beaten! In desperation he passed the pull-cord loop across his head, and fighting the weight of his failure, and oblivious to pain, pushed to his feet to throw himself bodily forwards against the rope.

This time there was no restriction, the slip knot gave at once so that he lunged heavily onwards, near-winding himself on the spade grip of the Lewis. His right leg was a mass of agony and as he snaked himself back into his seat and grabbed stick and fuel lever his sight misted over so that he thought he was going to pass out. But the machine had lurched, and the rope was tugging at his shoulder as it pulled clear of the tree and the de Havilland was moving forwards, slowly, if far from surely, up the slope.

It was touch-and-go during the first few feet, for even as his vision cleared so gravity and inertia in concert allied themselves against the endeavour, while the slick, wet earth was mush beneath the carpeting leaves and the shortened propeller, so suddenly suspect once again, seemed to spin away inside a vacuum. Paul hardly dared breathe. They were moving at a snail's pace. Whereas he needed speed. Speed! And airflow over the rudder to supplement the slipstream in case a swing developed.

Only as the machine nosed clear of the woods, and finding the gradient milder, and despite the retarding effect of the sodden plough, began to gather pace, did he exhale, and gulp in another hasty breath. For now the airspeed was registering, and then not only registering, but rising, and Paul forgot the pain and his faint-headedness as he fought to change the course.

He was running on rougher plough now and he tensed his stomach as if to take the pounding for the damaged booms. But the rudder was answering and he jabbed with his right foot, towards the trees as he had planned, not managing to blot out the pain, and biting his lip and tasting blood on his tongue. The nose swung gamely, however, and now he was correcting back to the left and running smoothly down the wide grass verge.

The trees were close, but they were streaming past, the tufted grass beneath his wheels blurring into a river of green. A wheel bounced, and then the other, only for the machine to settle heavily. The railway embankment was inexorably closing with him from the left, and he could see the end of the wood now, and beyond it, for the first time, the roofs of the village of Bertincourt. And then the stick was firm beneath his palm and the rumbling died away. And he cried aloud in pure relief. For the de Havilland was in the air again.

Chapter Twenty-One

The little scout wanted to soar, as if elated at being back in its own medium, but Paul needed to take its measure and held the nose down to gather speed, lifting only enough to clear the trees. And at once he was glad he had restrained its climb for as he passed into the open so he found himself almost on top of Bertincourt aerodrome! Indeed a machine, an Albatros, having just taken off, was heading down the far side of the woods. Paul eyed it worriedly but it continued on its way, banking steeply and climbing off towards the west. But already two more were rolling, heading only just across his line of flight, and after getting airborne and looking around they were bound to see him. Paul was only too well aware that once they were fairly in the air he could neither outfight nor outrun them and he cursed the timing that had led him straight into this hornet's nest. He looked to left and right but could see no way of avoiding the issue.

The rising tide of pain as he banked into a turn, nosing down to stay at treetop level, only added to the sickness in his stomach. And although he was barely over the aerodrome boundary yet already a single line of tracer was coming up at him from the hangars to the left! He kept the turn going, feeling the strain, driving thoughts of fractured tailbooms from the forefront of his mind and pulling even harder, forcing the de Havilland to quarter-in behind the enemy pair. The first of the machines – they were the newest Albatros D-types, Paul registered – was already in the air and gaining speed. Paul levelled his wings. The leader turned his head and seeing another aircraft so close, swerved frantically to avoid a collision, rolling left, his downgoing wings brushing the grass so narrowly that Paul expected him to cartwheel into the ground. Instead the German reversed his turn and used the speed he had left to counter what he now perceived to be an enemy attack.

Like the gunner firing from the ground the enemy leader's reaction spoke well for his reflexes for the de Havilland had appeared out of nowhere to menace him on his own doorstep. But Paul had the advantage of position as well as surprise and the Lewis, ready-cocked – and despite being cold and having sojourned overnight in the open –, loosed off half a drum into the leader's cockpit without a hitch. It was little less than murder and the Albatros, only just above the stall even before the shots went home, simply continued rolling until it hit the ground and crashed below Paul's nose.

The second pilot had even less of a chance, for having had his attention fixed on keeping station behind and below his leader's tail he had no idea that Paul was there. His leader's unaccountable swerve proved fatal, as in skidding left to avoid a crash the follower put himself directly into line with Paul's gunsight. There was no manoeuvring to do, no deflection to consider, Paul's wings were level, he simply steadied out his own skid, and loosed off the remainder of the drum. He must have hit the pilot in the back for the Albatros reared up on its tail and climbed sharply before stalling and nosing heavily, wing down, into the ground. But even as it fell a third machine was pulling away from the lined-up scouts and accelerating across the field.

Paul's mouth went dry. It was too late to run, for even in top-class condition the de Havilland was out-matched and would have been caught long before it reached the lines. With no other option, therefore, he first dipped his starboard wings, then – fighting down the flood of agony in his knee – ruddered right to widen the angle before sweeping left into a teardrop turn, banking near vertically and pulling hard, back to meet the still-accelerating machine.

By now tracer was arcing over him, seemingly from all directions, but Paul shut it from his mind and concentrated on finely positioning himself to meet the other head on. He rolled wings level, holding low, and watching the shark-sharp nose lifting off and coming fast. The expended Lewis drum was reluctant to release, and when it came away the airflow nearly took it from Paul's hand, and he shuddered, remembering the Very cartridge – would he ever forget it! Then he had the drum secure, dropped it at his feet, and banged another into place.

The other pilot was no novice for he was firing even as he left the ground, his twin-tracers curling over Paul's head. But it was a case of wrong time, wrong place, for Paul was below him, his wheels nearly brushing the grass. Which meant that to bring his guns to bear the German would have to drop his nose; except that he had no height to play with. Further, Paul's head-on position denied him space to use his superior speed; he had to collide, fly into the ground, climb, or turn, and whichever he chose Paul had him cold. He chose to climb and Paul simply maintained his attitude and fired into his belly from below, resolved to let the drum run through. But there was no need, and he released the trigger. A grey wisp of smoke issued from the enemy scout's engine and was swept away in the slipstream, the propeller faltered, the machine sank heavily to the ground, and broke up.

'No *élan*!' Paul gritted. Nor was it. As with the horseman back there, this was simply survival.

He dropped, if anything, lower still, pressing on the stick, trusting to the wheels to tell him when he was too low, lifting over the wreckage, and praying that it would not blow up until he was clear, holding his course then and pointing at the line of readied scouts. Seeing that two had starter crews in attendance, Paul swung his nose their way, opening fire as the Lewis came to bear. He marked strikes on the first machine, and kicked up dirt near the second. But the handlers had scattered from both and Paul judged that he could be well clear before they collected themselves enough to get another under away.

The ground defences were chasing him now, in full strength, but lacking co-ordination, and Paul held low, continuing his turn to the left as the tracer began to fall behind. He found himself heading back towards Vélu Wood and he steered close to the edge, seeking what protection he could find. Just short of the logging track, he discovered, a lorry had skidded to a stop and was spilling troops who now froze at his approach: so the horse had been found – and even a five minute delay would have been fatal to his bid for escape! He chose not to open fire on the men but lifted over them to treetop height, using what might be only a momentary respite to slacken off the tourniquet.

The wood unrolled beneath him with not just the central ride but an unexpected complexus of patterned paths, and suddenly he was flashing roof-high across Vélu Chateau, but in a left turn, effectively unsighting himself from the Basquin house. Paul ruddered straight, hooking his left toe under the rudder pedal to help his right leg, and heading west, shaking and breathless and weak with nausea. He spared a glance for the sheds of Vélu aerodrome but all seemed quiet, with no scouts at readiness. His leg was drenched in blood and his head reeled each time he looked at it and he pulled for height, afraid of passing out and piling in before the senses could return to him.

Time fragmented. There were lucid periods when he saw his surroundings with great clarity, and others when he flew on in what seemed to be a dream. He skimmed an infantry bivouac with tents set out in geometric lines and saw men startled from their ease, springing to their feet and staring after him. There were open fields with chalk-white roads and isolated farms, and showers of heavy tracer streaking from a wooded prominence, twinkling fireflies disappearing as he closed his eyes and laughed. A dead and ruined village with its church tower still intact, mourning over its desecrated street; and a man in field-grey, with a dog, sitting on a wall and calmly waving up at him.

It came to him that he was trailing the tethering rope still, and he pulled it in one-handed, pushing down the coils to pad his leg and watching as the fibres too glistened red. He began to look for pinpoints but with no conviction that they would appear, for the landscape had a fatal hue such as he had never seen in waking. The trees took on mesmeric shapes and reached at him to drag him down: mere phantasmagoria, and he fought them off with conscious lassitude, saving his energy for his reawakening.

Yet it intrigued him to pull at the stick, and see the trees shy off below; then to push, and see the grasses blur and furrow as he passed: it was the finest dream of flight that man had ever had. And there was pain and fear and the bull-like throbbing of the Gnome, and moments when he could have sworn his fantasy was all too real.

He sat up abruptly, suddenly alert, his knee a sickening fount of pain. He would land the moment he crossed the lines, choosing any field that promised rapid aid. Not waiting for an advanced landing-field, but putting down anywhere near a road or camp where he could get assistance. No *élan!* A hole appeared in his left upper wing and he smiled as he looked over his shoulder to see fabric peel back to the spar, to cling there, snapping like a pennant in the wind.

Diane's singing voice was soft and low and thrilled him to the core but the fine soaring baritone now bursting from his own throat must be the match of hers on any day. And what grand, wild, wind-lashed songs he knew, and what words came flooding through his mind! Stirring words that carried tuneless, timeless strains and came to him without a single trick of thought ...

He no longer seemed to be heading west, but north-a-bit of west, and for a seeming age he leant his forehead on the coaming to puzzle out this curious phenomenon, his good leg straight to counteract the engine's torque, eventually looking aside to howl with laughter as he swept across the forlorn wreckage of a tank. The once-tiled roofs of Hébuterne came swaying at him from his left and he felt for the map but it was lost beneath the coils of blood and he was unconcerned for he knew his way from here.

He looked to left and right, irritated that the others were not tucked in close. After all the weeks of practice Dick, at least, should have learned to keep station. And Simpson had gone off after that Aviatik. Give him a flight of his own, and soon, to calm him down, or he would kill himself: he would have a word with the major when he got down. He turned over Hébuterne, setting course for the field, checking off the familiar landmarks one by one, holding track, and peering narrowly towards the lowering sun.

One side of his face was stinging and he was not feeling all that well. And his height-keeping seemed erratic so perhaps that explained why the others would no longer fly close station on him. But it was hurtful and smacked of disloyalty. Perhaps they thought they could do better? But he had the leader's pennants fluttering on his interplane struts. He giggled: he had an extra khaki-green one too, infinitely longer, of stripped-off fabric, on his wing! He altered course to the left, glad that it was the easy way, for the aircraft no longer seemed to answer to the right.

He saw the sheds and waved the flight in close. The windsock was pointing the wrong way, he noticed, and that was annoying and he would have a word about that too. And who had left his lapstrap dangling free? He held off, and touched, and blipped the motor as he bounced, and held everything central, and touched again, and stayed down. He developed a swing to the left and instinctively pushed on right rudder to correct but right rudder still refused to answer and he watched the swing develop until eventually it ceased to interest him and he reached over and cut the switch, and as an afterthought, the petrol, and heard the motor die.

And then there was a silence, shattered by a klaxon and a bell, and men were running across towards him and calling and pulling at his shoulders, and he knew that he was being sick and suddenly he wanted to weep because none of them would keep station with him in the air and now they would not let him be alone.

Chapter Twenty-Two

There were loud voices and soft voices, irritating voices and comforting voices, voices that soothed him, and voices that frightened him; all of them unintelligible. There were shapes moving away and shapes looming close, shapes that bulked over him, or moved about him; and noiseless, shadowy presences sensed but never seen. There was bright light, disturbing and threatening; and there was darkness, concealing and protective; warm friendly darkness into which he could snuggle squirrel-like, drawing it around him to shut out all that lay beyond.

And there were faces, floating like candle flames fluttering in a breeze; faces disembodied and far off, and faces pushed close into his own; and smells: of tobacco, of carbolic soap, of tart breath, and faint perfume. And features, brown eyes, severe mouth, the shadow of hair above a female lip. He said once, 'Your nose is too long.' And heard a startled gasp.

There was movement, and stillness. And unseen hands that pushed and probed and lifted and pulled; warm hands, and soft, that cherished and drew darkness around him; and brisk, dry hands that prodded and jabbed and tore away the darkness, exposing him to the light. And then there was the sobbing – and the warm hands again, and the brown eyes, and the darkness.

And then gradually there was subdued light, misty, like gauze, no longer menacing, and the voices were clearer, though still unintelligible. 'Warm Hands' was not beautiful but he loved her soft, caring eyes, and the faint trace of hair along her upper lip, and her breath that smelt of warm milk when she bent to rearrange the pillows.

'Thank you,' he said.

She smiled, and stood back from the bed. 'He's awake, doctor,' she called. And there was darkness again, but now it was irksome and he longed for the light.

There was a booming voice, breaking through the darkness but bringing little light, its tones not altogether cold but unbendingly authoritative. And one earnestly opposing it which lectured and reasoned, harangued and instructed, propounding theories and fine ideas until he could stand it no longer and opened his mouth to tell it to be quiet. And only then knew it for his own.

He was left alone, and later the light came. But it was lamplight, and pooled at the far side of the room, and it was bright and his eyes pricked until he closed them again, and the darkness returned.

The sheets were turned down neatly with practised precision, and they were white and crisp – but well-worn for there was a finely stitched darn where his hand lay. There was a frame over the bed holding the clothes from his leg and it had been concerning him for some time. There was a sister at the bedside but she was looking away, out into the room. She was tall and very slim and her hair was swept back primly under her cap. Paul could not see her profile but he knew that her eyes were soft and warm and that there was comfort in her smile. Her hand rested on the counterpane and he reached out and touched it.

'Have I lost my leg?' he asked.

She turned to him at once, bending close to look into his eyes, and there was milk on her breath and although he had never liked milk, now it was warm and comforting and brought him solace.

'Of course not, goose!' she said with brisk familiarity.

And at that he turned and slept.

There were two of them standing at the foot of his bed, their backs towards him, discussing what was recorded on a clipboard. One was a captain and one a major, both in white coats, with stethoscopes in evidence. Paul thought they might be talking over his case but for fear of interrupting them he waited until he saw the clipboard replaced at the foot of his bed.

'My right knee's been a problem for some time,' he told them then. 'It was a motor bike, you know. Doctor Petter can tell you about it. Mr Petter, I should say, for he's a surgeon.'

Both looked up, surprised.

'Oh, you're back with us already. Jolly good!' said the captain cheerfully, and moved to Paul's side to examine him. The major watched. A man of middle-age, with thick-rimmed glasses and a corpulent stomach, acquired, no doubt, in some comfortable practice, forsaken now, as like as not, for the duration. 'Yes, we spoke to Mr Petter on the telephone two days ago.'

'How is he?' asked Paul.

The major ignored the inanity. 'You're obviously feeling fine,' he observed tartly, 'but I'd like you to have a little more sleep.' He nodded to the captain and Paul felt a touch on his arm. And once again he slept.

Paul was hungry when he awoke, ravenous, and he could remember eating nothing since Angele had passed around the food in Alphonse's wagon. The sister was there, Sister Carmell; and it came as no surprise to him that he knew her name. The major was still there too, or rather, was there again, for it was dark beyond the window and Paul could no longer see the trees or the turreted corner of the chateau where doves had fretted and – so he had fancied – kept him from sleeping for the last two nights.

'Ah, Cowley, you're awake,' said the major. 'Had a good rest?'

'Magnificent, sir,' said Paul truthfully. For he really did feel magnificent. But the frame was still in place above his leg. The sister had hurried over and was readjusting the pillows behind his shoulders, smiling at him conspiratorially, as if there were secrets shared.

'I'd like to get up and walk about a bit,' Paul said. It was a question, posed in the guise of a statement. And there was one reply above all that he was dreading.

'I'd like you to have another good night's sleep first,' said the major, 'Then we'll see.'

Why were they always so bloody evasive?

'Have you taken off my leg?' asked Paul in blunt desperation.

The major walked to the side of the bed and pulled back the covers. 'Well?' he asked brusquely.

Paul tensed himself to look down. And felt his lips twitch. 'It's still there,' he smiled.

'Of course it's still there,' snapped the major. 'Where did you think it was? Good God, man, it was only a simple flesh wound!'

Paul caught Sister Carmell's eye and grinned. The major was examining the dressing.

'Had it been giving you much trouble?'

Alarm bells sounded in Paul's mind and he said, 'Nothing noticeable.' It never paid to be too forthcoming with doctors, they had too much say in things. Like who was fit to fly, and who was not. The major looked up exasperatedly.

'When this insane bloody war is over,' he burst out, ostensibly to the ceiling, 'we'll get hold of some of these people and look into what passes for a brain.' He turned to Paul. 'What was it, afraid they wouldn't send you back to your regiment? Afraid they wouldn't pass you fit enough to come out here and get your bloody head blown off?' He checked himself, remembering. 'Oh yes, you're an aviator, of course. Couldn't bear the thought of not floating about in those contraptions of yours? Of missing out on the Great Game?' He turned to the nurse. 'You know, Sister, I wanted to be an engine driver. Dreamed about it for years. But I grew out of it. Now, I'd like nothing better.' He said to Paul. 'That knee of yours has been bothering you for a long time. Probably since just after you were discharged from Mr Petter's care.'

Paul eyed him.

'But you've never reported it. Not to Mr Petter, not to the military medical authorities, not to anyone. Isn't that so?' He did not wait for Paul to reply but carried on, 'Had you only spoken up it could have been set right in moments but no, you had to slink about like an adolescent convinced he's contracted syphilis from some backstreet –.' He glanced aside at the sister and broke off abruptly. 'D'you know what Mr Petter did to your knee?'

Paul nodded. 'He explained it fairly thoroughly at the time to show me how it would work. I'm an engineer, you see, and he thought I'd be interested. He drew it all out for me, the pins and plates and things.'

'And things!' repeated the doctor in disgust. 'Well, what happened is that one of "the things" came adrift. There was always a chance of it happening if you went at it too strenuously at first – they'll have warned you of that?'

Paul thought again of his treks in the Lakes and the backward descent from Sty Head Tarn after his knee had locked. Undertaken far too soon after the operation, as he had suspected at the time, and had had cause to regret far too often since.

'Ah! strikes home, does it?' The doctor had read his change of expression. 'But you declared yourself fit and well and nobody thought it necessary to doubt your word. After all, we do credit patients with a certain modicum of common sense. Though so often I wonder why.' He pointed to the offending knee, now free of its dressing. 'What was it this time? A gunshot wound, obviously.'

'A Luger, or that's what it looked like.'

The doctor nodded. 'That's what I thought, same calibre anyway. And fired close range – like this.' He ran his finger over the flash burn on Paul's cheek, now a rough and reddened patch of tender skin. 'Well, that won't spoil your beauty. And as for the knee, the bullet did you a bit of good: virtually pushed the 'thing' back into position – left us with very little to do.'

'Then I'll be able to walk again?' burst out Paul, relieved.

'Well of course you'll be able to walk again,' snapped the major, 'What do you think I've been saying? But another full night's rest, at the least, before we think about it. Sister Carmell will see to that, won't you, Sister?'

She smiled in reply and the major bustled off, muttering beneath his breath.

'Some bedside manner,' grinned Paul lightly.

Sister Carmell looked fondly after the departing physician. 'He's tired,' she said. 'They're all tired, and there's so much work to do.'

And Paul looked at the dark shadows beneath her eyes and at the tense lines around her mouth, and nodded, reduced to silence.

'Then if my leg isn't that bad, why the cucumber frame, and why all this bed rest. And why do I feel so completely wrung out?' Paul asked the captain – Captain Armitage, he had discovered – next day.

'Because you really were, as you put it, wrung out,' the captain told him. He looked at Paul steadily for a moment or two and then seemed to come to a decision.

'The wound was a lucky thing for you in a couple of ways,' he said quietly. 'Although it was trivial it was undoubtedly painful and it cost you a lot of blood. But had it not been for the gunshot wound we wouldn't have looked at your leg and the knee would have gone on causing you more and more bother. The cage is to ensure the covers didn't disturb your rest.'

'In a couple of ways?' prompted Paul.

The doctor paused. 'If you hadn't stopped the bullet, we wouldn't have got our hands on you and forced you to take a rest.'

'Forced me?' Paul searched the doctor's face. Then reflected. 'You mean I was shell-shocked?' he asked. 'Headed for the loony bin?'

'In so many words,' the captain replied. 'Call it shell shock, if you wish. There are other words for it, none of them very kind, and none of them bearing much semblance of the truth, as so many poor devils are finding out. In your case, well, we were lucky.'

'I was lucky,' amended Paul feelingly.

'Yes,' said the doctor.

'Right then, it's time you were asleep,' Sister Carmell declared when the doctor had gone about his other duties.

'So you've been sending me to sleep to stop me from going loopy?'

She pursed her lips. 'I shouldn't concern myself too much about that. But you'd lost a lot of blood remember, and you were very weak for the first four days.'

Paul looked down at his hands and noticed how white they were. 'I dare say I'm a bit weak yet.'

'You'll soon be back to normal.'

It was only then that her words struck home. 'The *first* four days? Well, how long have I been here?'

'Today's the twelfth of the month. Eight days.'

Paul laughed disbelievingly. 'Nobody gets eight days' rest in the RFC. Or "Boom" Trenchard himself would be down to look into it.'

'He was,' she told him evenly. 'And you were exceedingly rude to him, Captain. Now do as the doctor said, and get some sleep.'

It was another two days before Major Upton, the senior surgeon, allowed Paul to leave his bed, but after that he was always on his feet, with the aid of a stick for the first day but after that insisting that it was time he walked unaided. The doctors applauded him in this and as the pain and the swelling diminished and he built up strength with exercise and good plain fare he began to concern himself with when they would let him leave.

The chateau where the hospital was located, Paul discovered, was one of several houses belonging to a family of wine producers – largely champagne – whose main business was centred upon Rheims and who had offered the house to the government as a hospital and rest home, first to the French, and then, when they moved to the south of the Somme, to the British who replaced them. Most of the patients were relatively senior officers suffering from minor illnesses or mishaps which did not warrant sending them home to England, but some were badly-wounded cases who needed to build up strength before facing the sea crossing and specialised surgery at home.

Paul, it became clear, was typical of a third category of patient who, although only slightly wounded, had become the subject of enlightened treatment by doctors who had recognised his state of war-nerves for what it was. As he already knew, scores of other men were not so lucky. Some were forced to soldier on, some were 'Returned to Depot' in disgrace, some were court-martialled, and all were made to suffer indignity; some soldiers, as posted orders confirmed, had actually been shot – for cowardice. RFC commanders, it was true, tended to be quite enlightened for the most part, perhaps in view of the nature of the job their men were doing, and if they noticed a pilot getting 'overtired' could quietly get him sent home to a training establishment. Notwithstanding which Paul counted himself among the very fortunate in the way things had turned out for him.

Now that Paul was up and about he had been allocated an attic room of which he was the sole occupant so that for some days past he had experienced no difficulty in getting the undisturbed rest the doctors demanded, needing no drugs, and heeding no sleep-stealing doves. The night before, however, six more beds had been brought in, for despite the onset of the November rains it had become clear that the offensive was not yet to be called off and that the hospitals were readying themselves for the next phase of the slaughter.

From the first day after Paul came off sedation he was allowed visitors and he had been gratified by the number of pilots and aircraftmen from all the flights who found their way to his room, for getting there at all represented a tidy journey.

Among early visitors had been Major Hallam and Roly Clarke, the former, before leaving, tasking Paul to write a formal report on his last patrol and his subsequent return to base. Dick Fisher and Chalky Whitehead, together with Alfie Cox and Simpson had, of course, already written their own combat reports and had been able to supply most details about the fight. Dick, for example, had vouched for the destruction of the Roland Paul had attacked, reporting that it had burst into flames and broken apart before he himself, following it down, could fire a shot. Chalky and Simpson, it transpired, had dived after the other Roland but had lost it in cloud.

Alfie, for his part – as he reiterated when all four of them came to visit –, had seen Paul zoom up into the clouds after the attack on the Roland and had assumed that the Roland's gunner had hit him on the way in. Finding himself alone Alfie had chased after the Aviatik and fired off half a drum before losing it in cloud. He had then returned to base while Dick, having circled for some time, had signalled home the others. Nobody had noticed Paul's abortive attack on the Aviatik but when he told them what had happened with the loose Very cartridge they could not contain themselves, until Sister Carmell bustled in and threatened to send them all packing.

Paul's draft report, written a day or so after he came off sedation, was scanty, for in truth he was only too anxious to have the whole sorry incident forgotten. His ham-handedness had got him into the predicament in the first place, and nothing else seemed that important.

Major Hallam, on his second visit, scanned the draft report, and then frowned. He passed the report to Roly, still eyeing Paul.

'And the machines at Bertincourt?'

Paul was taken aback. He saw the major look interrogatively at Sister Carmell and saw her give the faintest of nods. Paul bit at his lip. He was beginning to suspect that he had done nothing but blab while he was under sedation. And suddenly he thought of the hayloft, and of Angele, and especially of that second time when there had seemed to be no urgency and when they had been less driven by impatience, and he felt hot flushes rising under his collar and could not meet Sister Carmell's eyes ...

'I didn't think the De Hav would stand up to a fight so I had to face them in order to escape.'

Major Hallam took the notebook Roly was holding out to him and read from it: 'You shot the first, and saw it crash. The second sheered off and you saw it roll in, and the third you met head-on and saw him break up. And one you badly damaged on the ground.'

'And missed another one altogether. And smashed my own prop in the first place.'

'Is that why you didn't mention the kills at Bertincourt?'

'There was no corroboration,' Paul said, evading the issue.

Major Hallam flicked a glance at the notebook, and then cast another glance towards Sister Carmell. 'And all with a total absence of *élan* – you were particularly anxious to make that quite clear, it seems.' He stood up. 'Apart from anything else, an agent has corroborated it all. And a few other things.' He waved Paul's draft. 'This report is scrapped, and the one we've written goes in.' He grinned, and his normally careworn face looked suddenly boyish. 'Sister Carmell has already vetted the official report for detail and it's being typed up in the hospital office. We'll have your signature on it before we leave.'

'How's my bus?' Paul asked weakly.

'What's left of it's not too bad,' said Roly. 'One flying wire on the left-hand side, and one or two sparking plugs were well worth salvaging. Apart from that it's been trucked to the depot in bits, the way you brought it in.'

'I'm sorry about that,' Paul told him. 'It really did me rather proud.'

'Corporal Metcalfe looked as if he hardly knew where to begin,' Roly smiled. 'So the major sent him off on his observer's course.'

Paul beamed with delight. 'That's a lad they'll not keep out of the driver's seat for long.'

'Also, Flight Sergeant Moss is intrigued by all the lashings, and the sporty prop,' reported Major Hallam. 'But says he hopes you're not going to start a fashion.'

Paul laughed. 'It's all a bit hazy. I didn't even notice what the prop and the revs were doing but from what I can remember, it seemed to handle pretty well.'

'From all accounts,' Roly grinned, 'it handled spectacularly well. HQ was bombarded with accounts of your progress. The troops swear it was a reincarnation of the Mad Major. You crossed the lines near Flers, and then flew pretty well north-west, slap bang up no-man's-land, went charging back into Hunland, and eventually came out at Hébuterne.'

'You were "frolicking," one artillery report had it,' the major told him. 'Said the Huns were throwing everything they had at you and that you weren't taking a blind bit of notice.'

'I could have sworn I was flying west,' Paul said.

'Flying west?' laughed Roly, 'going west, more likely. Five miles at low-level and not a care in the world. You're lucky you got five yards.'

Two days later there came a diffident tap on Paul's door, barely heard against the wind and rain lashing through the elms outside the window.

'It's open,' Paul called.

The man who entered was tall, fortyish, with pale, almost sallow features, and calm, perceptive eyes. He shambled across the room, threading between the empty beds in a curiously uncoordinated fashion. He wore blue Flying-Corps staff tabs on his collar and the rank of captain, bearing both with an air of faint surprise as if he had awoken one day to find himself in uniform and was still wondering how the transformation had come about. He placed a gentle hand on Paul's shoulder to restrain him from getting to his feet, and sat down beside him, putting his briefcase on the floor and producing a notebook from his tunic pocket.

'Now I know you,' said Paul, smiling just a little warily.

Everyone in the Flying Corps knew, or at least, knew of, 'Take-a-note-Baring'; writer, war-correspondent, poet, diplomat, and much else besides, serving, since the beginning of the war, in the RFC, and now personal slave to the biggest slave-driver of them all. So Sister Carmell had not been making it up about 'Boom's' visit; which suddenly made it all rather difficult.

'Maurice Baring,' acknowledged the other, 'I hope you are feeling better.'

'Aide-de-camp and Notetaker-in-chief to Major General Hugh Trenchard CB, DSO, ADC,' said Paul trippingly, embarrassed, but determined not be caught on the defensive – nor had he displayed any undue act of memory, for Trenchard's style appeared almost daily on one RFC order or another.

Baring gave an understanding smile, and took off his hat, surprising Paul by the extent of his baldness. There was a small scar on his forehead, the legacy of a motor accident, as Paul knew.

'You are formal today,' Baring murmured.

'Today?' Paul probed.

'"Boom, old boy? Boom, my old butcher?"'

As Baring jogged his memory so Paul put his head in his hands and groaned. So it was true then! And that tiresome, tendentious, patronisingly know-it-all voice – his voice – that had babbled on and on! He winced, cringing anew. And as if on cue, Sister Carmell entered the room, inclined momentarily to bridle at finding an unauthorised visitor, but then smiling. Clearly she recognised Baring. Recognised him, and approved.

'The major general not with you, today, Captain?' she asked.

Baring had risen to his feet. 'He's in Paris, on a visit, Sister. I'm joining him later today. Just tying up a few things beforehand.'

'So I see,' said Sister Carmell dryly, seemingly fully cognisant of Paul's discomfiture.

Baring turned back to Paul. 'The general asked me to call in and see you again.'

'Really?' For just a second Paul wished he had full recall of that previous visit. Equally as quickly he was glad it was blanked out.

Baring said mildly, 'Whatever you think of him, Cowley, I can assure you that he feels the losses more deeply than you would believe. Your safe return, therefore, meant a lot to him.'

'Whatever *I* think of him?' queried Paul uncomfortably.

'The other day you were rather outspoken in your criticism of *his* offensive policies – in fact, Joint Allied policy, both British and French – and of the machines he employs. Don't think he enjoyed it, in other circumstances he would have finished you, but you weren't complaining – he would never have forgiven that – and he found it refreshing to hear from someone with no political axe to grind.'

'I wasn't in my right mind,' Paul muttered.

'Just as well.' Baring gave a rare smile, and his eyes crinkled. 'But you made sense, and the Chief will forgive almost anything, even mild criticism, if it's for the good of the Flying Corps.' He paused, and referred to his notebook. 'You had a lot to say about the possibilities of independent, long-range bombing, and the fact that at the moment aircraft and crews are simply being thrown away.'

Paul gathered himself. As well a sheep as a lamb.

'Well,' he said, 'I really believe that the *real* offensive policy must be to bomb the Hun where he lives. As it is, you're not giving the bombing squadrons the right equipment. With the present lumbering old buses it's no wonder casualties are so high. All I ask is why he doesn't slacken off until the new machines arrive. They can't be that far off, and he'd save a lot of valuable lives.'

Baring nodded. 'Yes, that was the burden of your homily the other day. You were a little more graphic then. You weren't pulling your punches.'

'As for trying to sit up and poke the major general in the chest!' said Sister Carmell unhelpfully. And she ran her finger down the side of what Paul suddenly perceived to be a surprisingly long nose. 'Captain Cowley does have a straight way of talking when he is not himself,' she added.

Baring acknowledged that with an appreciative smile, then, fingering the drooping moustache below his own somewhat aquiline feature, said to Paul, 'The general has a favourite saying, "The best is the enemy of the good". He wishes me to commend it to your notice.'

Paul mulled over the saying, infinitely relieved that the general had apparently seen fit to overlook his impertinence. For if the tales were true 'Boom' broke big men daily. After a moment or two he nodded.

'You mean, if he could produce better bombing machines out of a hat, he'd do so; as it is, they're the best there is, and he can't afford to wait.'

'The Germans aren't waiting,' Baring told him. 'And if they switch over fully to offensive operations themselves, instead of holding most of their aircraft in a defensive role, then we are really going to know all about it.'

'But we're losing a lot of men and a lot of machines,' Paul insisted.

'Nearly three hundred machines in the last two months directly due to enemy action,' Baring said sombrely. He had no need, Paul noticed, to refer to his notes. 'An enormous percentage increase the moment the Germans came up with the new fighters.'

'And the *Jastas*.'

'And the *Jasta* attack-squadrons,' Baring agreed. 'The casualties in the last part of September reflected that.' He paused. 'At enormous cost'– he acknowledged Paul with a tilt of his head – 'the Corps has maintained air-superiority, but it's slipping from us, and the Chief will need absolute loyalty – and many more sacrifices – before we win it back.'

Paul nodded. Loyalty, yes, for even the squadrons were aware of the in-fighting going on at the very highest levels as the RFC sought to divorce itself from the army and become an independent Service. Within the Corps, it was true, one frequently heard Trenchard reviled as a butcher, but in the main there could be few in France who did not realise that he regarded the RFC as very nearly his own progeny. A reflection which brought Paul a new stomach-turner: '*What did daddy do in the Great War, Mummy? He called "Boom" Trenchard a butcher to his face, Dear.*' God! Men would sport medals for less!

Perhaps to escape from this latest of emergent mortifications, Paul turned his attention to Baring himself. The man did not appear to be technically-minded and yet since 1914 he had been at the very heart of what was quintessentially a highly technical Air Service.

'Not what one would expect of a poet,' he commented.

Baring was quick to follow the drift of thought. He smiled a little pensively. 'Yet it *is* poetic, seeing the RFC develop; the heroism, and the high endeavour in the clouds – but the nuts and bolts of it as well.' Randomly he flicked back the pages of his notebook, and began to read.

'Taper-pegs; split pins; lorry cushions; bronze obdurator rings, camera plate-cases, brass clips – and every item to be actioned swiftly, or he'll know the reason why.' He closed the notebook. 'And then there's this sort of thing: it's all part of the same whole.' He pulled an envelope from his briefcase and handed Paul the folded paper he extracted from it. 'You might wish to keep it.'

It was a carbon copy of Paul's 'Combat in the Air' report. Not his original. But the version augmented by the squadron. Paul saw the claim at the top, 'Enemy aircraft destroyed 4. One Roland, Three Albatros D-type scouts; Enemy aircraft damaged, 1. One Albatros D-type scout. Casualty report attached.' Scribbled on the margin was Trenchard's own comment: 'Well worth reading.'

Paul felt a glow of gratification, but there was discomfort too.

'And yet what good does it do?' he protested. 'On July the First there we were within feet of all those troops, and we couldn't do a thing to help. And our reports changed virtually nothing, they were still committed.' He could hear the bitterness rising in his voice, but he pushed on. 'As for scouts fighting each other, it may give the troops something to look at but it achieves nothing else.' He shook his head. 'No,' he said decisively, 'We have to hit them where they live. And make it tell. The way things are, the air war – aviation – is nothing but a bloody diversion.'

Baring had been listening intently. Now it was a long moment before he broke the silence.

'If it's any consolation,' he said then, 'I am to advise you that the general has noted your interest in long-range operations and has made it a matter of record once the new machines approach Service readiness. Where more immediate matters are concerned –' he indicated the combat report, 'you will hear what the general has recommended in due course.' He smiled his slow smile. 'The general has another saying: "Get well soon, I hate sick people". – I believe you are to be discharged relatively soon?'

Baring glanced for confirmation towards a suddenly non-committally smiling Sister Carmell.

'Then you are to be sent on home leave – you are due for it anyway.' Baring snapped shut his case. Then opened his notebook once more.

'The question of compensation for civilians aiding Allied personnel is already in hand, but if you would send me specific details of the people you mention I'll ensure that it is properly recorded for future action.' He caught sight of the clock on the wall and lumbered to his feet. 'Dear me,' his smile included Sister Carmell, 'Is that the time? I must get on my way – it will be dark soon and I tend to get lost – I actually lost the general when driving him on our very first outing. I do hope *my* driver knows the way.' He turned to Paul again, and shook hands. Sister Carmell opened the door for him and Paul, looking down at the paper and hearing his murmured thanks, thought he had gone, then found that he had paused in the doorway.

'Military Aviation,' Baring said softly. 'Nothing but a diversion, you say?' His eyes held Paul's. 'Perhaps.– But Cowley, what a *magnificent* diversion!'

'Such an unusual man!' wondered Sister Carmell, as Baring's footsteps faded on the stairs. 'What does he do, exactly?'

An unusual man serving an unusual man. What does he not do? thought Paul.

'He takes notes,' he said.

Chapter Twenty-Three

The day after Baring's visit Paul was once more descended upon by the doctors. There was, it seemed, a certain restriction in his mobility that they were not entirely satisfied with. Suddenly Paul could see his leave receding indefinitely. However, his protest, 'But I've got total mobility!' fell on stony ground.

There then followed a delay of some three days until the swelling around his knee reduced enough to satisfy them and while new X-rays were taken. Summoned to the office on the third evening Paul found the two doctors discussing the plates. Captain Armitage greeted him cheerily but the major barely looked up, leaving Paul to gaze out of the window at the rain. At length they reached agreement: a further – minor – operation was desirable.

'But the knee's almost better,' Paul protested.

'We're well aware that you want to get back to skitting around the sky,' snapped Major Upton, 'but two or three days aren't going to make much difference and you'll benefit from it for the rest of your life.'

'In engineering terms it's just a question of paring away about a thou or so,' Captain Armitage smiled.

'It feels fine,' insisted Paul.

Just the same, he grinned resignedly. Accordingly, the next day, he found himself scheduled for theatre once again. He spent the interim in attempting – and failing – to compose a meaningful letter to Catherine, between times whiling away the hours in watching the rain driving down from the dull, low-hanging clouds and reading and re-reading the little he had received from her over the months.

She wrote rarely, he reflected yet again, and briefly, almost clinically; and always about her various enterprises rather than about what she felt for him. If, indeed, she felt anything beyond friendship. And sifting through her letters now for some positive clue to her feelings – which he had done so often that many were effectively reduced to tatters –, left him suffering from an uncertainty that depressed him even more than the weather and the imminent operation.

Clouding his spirits too, was the letter he had to write to Jacques Delcamp. Sister Carmell had long ago sent off Paul's first brief note, now, in amplifying that one, the omissions alone cost him blood ...

This time Paul was not kept anywhere near so long under sedation after surgery, nevertheless, he suspected that his return to full awareness had been prolonged by at least a day and a night. In fairness to the major Paul had to admit that on this occasion he experienced none of the nightmare-like phantasms he had known before. One visitation, however, stayed with him as he drifted in and out of wakefulness, puzzling him, for he was unable to determine which state it belonged to, that of waking, or that of sleeping.

It took the form of a woman leaning over him and smoothing his hair as he slept. Who he conceived her to be eluded him but as he drifted back towards full awakening he was reluctant to believe that he had merely dreamed her into existence. For a while he played with the notion that it had been Angele, an ethereal Angele conjured up by the culpability of his subconscious, an Angele still breathless from love in the shadows of the barn. He did not look upon himself as a philanderer and his moral sense allowed him to take no conscious pride in what had happened between them; and yet night and day he hugged to himself the memory of their lovemaking, reliving it so vividly in his sentient mind that he feared for his ravings under anaesthetic.

Later, the visitation became Catherine. For there was warmth. But there were kisses on leaving, soft and tender, and achingly familiar; kisses lingering, and unaccountably wistful. Kisses which relegated Catherine to the world of dreams, her only kiss having been the fleeting semblance of a salute in parting, while these struck chords – yet brought no firing thrill, only melancholy echoes of a half-remembered pain.

Then, as the drowsiness died away and Paul recalled the aseptic redolence of starched linen as the visitation bent over him, he became sensible that it could only have been Sister Carmell herself, and he laughed at his fancies. And yet still there came the haunting remembrance of a subtler, more sensuous perfume to hover tantalizingly on the very edge of recall, bringing keen regret that something so real should be nothing but a dream.

It was rain, beating in flurries against a loose casement that brought him from his torpor, awakening him to the fact that he was ravenously hungry. At which he turned upon the pillow, and slept again.

Well-fed and well-rested after breakfast and a good night's sleep, Paul finally waved a reluctant goodbye to his cherished visitant, even venturing to joke about her to Sister Carmell. The good sister's easy response certainly drove away all mystery, and thoughts of guilt. Yet startled him beyond all measure.

'That would have been Nurse Cousins,' she told him lightly, refilling the drinking glass on his bedside table.

'Nurse Cousins?' For a moment Paul regarded her blankly. And it was suddenly inconceivable that he had not thought of Diane from the beginning. Now the visitation swung into perspective, the half-forgotten, so-familiar touch of her lips, the evocative musk of her perfume, the vague regret breaking through to his consciousness despite the comfort of her presence.

'She's a VAD nurse's-aid at the main hospital and her father – he's a general it seems – found out where you were.'

'Is she coming again?'

'It would be difficult just now.'

Paul understood. Since the thirteenth of the month the guns had not ceased their drumming-in of what seemed set to be the last bloody fling of the Somme battle before increasingly severe weather finally put a stop to further lunacy for the year. The other hospitals were filling up and the Chateau had now been ordered to expedite the dispatch of all but their most serious cases in expectation of yet more casualties. Diane would have little time for social visiting, little enough even, for rest.

To Paul's surprise, however, she was ushered into his room just after dark only two days later, a bare ten minutes after he had flung himself on to the bed exhausted but delighted at having walked for three hours non-stop without a stick. What surprised him even more was to see Sister Carmell still hovering, doubtful-eyed, at the door. Then he looked at the girl, and Sister Carmell's misgivings – whatever they might have been – went completely from his head.

In part, of course, it was the nurse's uniform, but it was above all the gauntness of Diane's face, the dark rings around her eyes, and the starch-white skin, pale-drawn across her cheekbones, that made him look for long moments before sure recognition flooded through. It was hardly five months since he had seen her, yet she seemed to have aged by quite as many years. There was tiredness in every line of her body and pain behind her eyes.

'Diane!'

His feelings must have shown in his face for she smiled through sudden tears, and hurried across the room towards him.

'I only have a few minutes, Paul,' she said, physically restraining him from swinging from the bed, 'my transport's waiting. But Sister Carmell says you're off home tomorrow.'

As Baring had done days before so Paul looked for confirmation now, but with a final frown of perturbation the sister turned and left the room.

Diane laid her cheek on his. Her face was cold, and as she stood back, Paul looked at her yet more keenly.

'You look so tired.' So dreadful, he meant!

'It's been a bit hectic,' she said simply. 'And I've just a touch of this flu that's all the rage.'

'Would you like a cup of tea? I'm sure Sister Carmell would be glad to oblige.'

'For a mere nurse's-aid? I'm sure she wouldn't!'

She chuckled, and there was the ghost of the old Diane in her smile. But a pathetic ghost, gazing with such tragic eyes – and his heart went out to her: that there had been some profound change in her, he was certain, but how to establish what it was?

'I'm on duty in half an hour,' she was explaining easily. 'But hearing a run was on, I begged a lift. The driver's collecting medical supplies, we've run so short.'

'It's great to see you.' It was a weak response, he was only too conscious of that. And yet he was beginning to get over the shock. If he could hold her here just a while longer, maybe he could get her to talk about what it was that burdened her so: Catherine, he was certain, would have divined her trouble in just a glance.

'Sister Carmell told me you'd visited a while back, but I was still groggy. I thought I'd dreamt it.' And something else was irking him. He frowned. 'What was up with her just now? She looked upset.'

Diane shook her head. 'She's probably afraid I'll disturb your rest. But I'll only stay a moment.'

'You can't rush off,' he protested, 'there's so much to catch up on. How long have you been over here? And how's Harry? We hear the Rifle Brigade have –.'

She put a finger lightly but firmly on his lips. 'Never mind about me,' she said. 'According to Gramps, you're the celebrity. He tells me everyone at home is complaining that you've told them nothing. Only that you've had your leg put right and that you're due for a spot of leave.'

Paul was mystified. Told them what? For if the truth were known, until Baring's visit he had expected to be admonished, rather than commended, merely for making the best of his own bad job.

'I ruined a perfectly good aeroplane. And put a lot of fine people at terrible risk.' he said uncomfortably. 'So there's nothing much to tell, as such.'

'Certainly nothing worth a Military Cross and a *Croix de Guerre*,' she smiled. She held up a hand to stay his disbelief. 'That's what Gramps says.' She got to her feet and when he tried to protest again, said, 'I told you this was just a fleeting visit.'

She leant down and kissed him on the lips, and with her femininity came the memory of his dream, warm, wistful, and everlastingly endearing. And he smiled fondly into her care-strained face, her dear and valued, yet unaccountably-troubled, face. She smiled back. And then, before he could formulate the words he sought to hold her with, she walked briskly across the room, turning as she got to the door.

'Cheerio, my dear! Give Gramps my best love, won't you? I'm longing to see everyone again. And although you'll see them months before I do I'll still write and tell them all how well you look.'

And she closed the door behind her.

Christ, girl! Paul thought wildly. How can I tell them how *you* look? Washed out, wasted, sick on your feet. And with such torment in your eyes.

Suddenly determined on action he swung off the bed. His knee had stiffened after his protracted exercise and he stumbled at the door, cannoning into Sister Carmell as she was about to re-enter the room, her head turned worriedly over her shoulder.

'Sorry!' he grunted, half-retreating, yet pressing onwards notwithstanding in his desperation to detain the girl.

'She's gone,' Sister Carmell told him. Then, her voice sharpening as he persisted in trying to dodge around her, 'Let her be.'

Paul was taken aback by the unaccustomed acerbity of her tone, and perhaps because of that allowed her to ease him away from the door.

'I'm sure she's not well,' he said.

'I think she has flu,' the nursing sister agreed. 'And she's been overworking. They've been inundated over at main – working practically non-stop for two days now.'

'But she was quite different from the way she's always been. There was something odd about her.'

'Being out here. It's bound to have made a difference.'

He frowned. 'No, that wouldn't be it.'

'It's true that you're going home, anyway,' she said brightly, and he knew it for a deliberate change of subject. 'I daresay you'll hear officially tomorrow.'

Paul thought for a moment. 'Wouldn't it be possible to phone through – maybe they'd rest her?'

'I think we'd better let her take care of things in her own way,' Sister Carmell said firmly, and forestalled any further protestations by pulling together the heavy curtains, plunging the room into darkness. 'Get some sleep. I don't want you tired out before you even start your journey.'

Early next morning, during rounds, Major Upton stiffly pronounced himself satisfied with Paul's progress and discharged him for immediate return to the United Kingdom. Paul thanked him, but found himself waved back to the bed where he perched on the edge, a frisson of unease raising gooseflesh on the backs of his hands.

'You've probably deduced, Cowley, that I've kept you here rather longer than some might consider necessary,' the major opened brusquely. 'You see, I happen to agree with Mr Petter that your main trouble was never the physical injury to your knee but the guilt-feelings you'd built up around it.' He ignored Paul's reflex grunt of rejection and went on, 'When I first examined you I was struck by the high state of tension you exhibited. It worried me far more than did your knee.'

'But everybody gets the wind-up – nerves,' Paul protested. 'It's natural. Nobody in their right mind wants to be in this shambles. There'll always be risks in flying, but not like this out here.'

Major Upton nodded. 'Agreed. But in your case it was just a little different. It concerned me, as it concerned Mr Petter.' He raised a calming hand, as if aware – impossible though that would have been – that Paul was seeing once again the tortured face of Andrew Barton. 'Neither one of us now has any doubt that the problem has been resolved, so take off that worried look.'

The surgeon's own face was expressionless.

'I intend to spell things out in everyday terms. I am sure that you will understand. And act accordingly. To go back only as far as we need to, let's look at your motor-bike accident and the guilt-feelings you built up over that.' If he sensed Paul's scepticism he ignored it, spelling off points against his fingers. 'One! You felt guilty because in a moment of carelessness you had jeopardised your future in flying. Two! Knowing that your carelessness caused concern to so many people – your parents, the cottage folk, the various medical staffs – increased that guilt. Three! You even felt guilt for the machine you were riding, the –'

'The Rudge.'

'No matter,' the major frowned. 'The point is, you even managed to conjure up guilt feelings on behalf of that – an insensate machine!'

Paul remembered only too well that Catherine had called attention to his treating the bike as if it had a personality of its own, nevertheless he made a audible sound of disagreement.

'I am a very busy man,' the major snapped irascibly, 'and in less than half an hour I expect to get very much busier, so please do me the courtesy of not grunting. Whether you accept what I say, is entirely up to you. Whether you act on what we recommend, equally.' He went on, his voice brisk, but now without the irritation, 'You have a highly-developed sense of being responsible. Of being morally accountable. You can push things into the background but you can't shrug them off – better for you if you could. But that's your make-up. And so you came out to France in a state of subconscious tension, already burdened with the guilt you had assumed after the accident. Now add the strain of war flying, and latterly the responsibility for four other flying officers and their machines, and the cumulative effect becomes evident.'

He sat back. 'And on top of this you were suffering a constantly nagging pain that was steadily draining your energy – and further burdening your subconscious by worrying that by not declaring it you had let Mr Petter down.' He pursed his lips. 'I suspected it the moment I began examining your knee. It had so clearly been troubling you since the beginning that it led me to the correlation and eventually to contact Mr Petter.'

Paul remained silent.

'Now,' said Major Upton more gently, 'the knee will settle – although I want you to use that stick for another week or so, regardless of whether you feel it's necessary or not –, and with freedom from pain you may cheerfully discard all your self-adopted cloaks of guilt.'

He paused, and went on, his voice as brisk as ever. 'Take my word for it. Or not. But at least mull it over. What I want you to do is neither difficult nor arcane. Simply – be less hard on yourself.' He displayed outstretched palms. 'That's all there is to it. But it will keep you out of trouble.'

Paul bowed his head. The gooseflesh had gone but he was at a loss for what to say. Be less hard on yourself? The major had been watching him.

'Your combat report, for instance.'

'But it was my fault ...'

The other snorted. 'Nobody is going to fix you up with a little man to stand at your shoulder and whisper, "Cowley, thou art mortal", every time the crowd roars approval. You'll have do that for yourself. But give yourself credit. You might have made an error, yet, as everyone else agrees, you didn't do too badly after that.'

Despite himself, Paul felt the beginnings of a grin.

The major nodded abruptly. 'That's right, don't take yourself so damned seriously. Give yourself a chance, man.' He walked to the door. 'Captain Armitage! Are they ready?' He turned back to Paul. 'If you want to discuss it when you've had time to think, then simply call Mr Petter.'

The captain appeared, and nodded. 'All ready, sir.' he reported.

'We have urgent need for this room, Cowley,' Major Upton said shortly. 'So don't shilly-shally over packing. But first – Lesson One in self-approval!'

Paul dutifully followed them out of the room to the main staircase where Sister Carmell, joining them, ran a swift eye over him before reaching up to remove a scrap of cotton wool from his tunic. At the centre of the entrance hall, perfectly aligned with the ornately-patterned tiles, was a greatcoated detachment of French soldiers, tall, helmeted, of impeccable bearing, and mustachioed to a man like veterans of Napoleon's Imperial Guard. They were formed up in an open-fronted square centred by a short, trim, much-bemedalled colonel with piercing eyes.

Still only half-crediting what was happening, Paul, with Sister Carmell at his shoulder, ready to assist, descended the stairs, brought his heels together before the colonel, and saluted. The last salute he had given, he remembered, had been to Henri, in Vélu Wood. Major Upton called patients and nursing staff to order and the hallway quietened as a small bronze cross was pinned to Paul's breast. Next, to the delight of all the onlookers, the colonel raised himself and bussed Paul on both cheeks. Spurs ringing he then stepped back, saluted smartly and made a short, echoing speech – not a word of which Paul really understood – before stepping forward again to shake Paul's hand.

The brief ceremony over, Major Upton gave the order to carry on, and restrained pandemonium broke out as the assembly began to return to their duties. Like automatons and without an apparent word of command, the French guard of honour about-turned as one man and marched away down the steps, their precision raising a half-serious ripple of appreciation from some newly-arrived infantry-subaltern patients hanging over the balcony. At which point, with his departing guard drawing all the attention, the French officer leaned closer to Paul and in perfect, unaccented English, said quietly, 'Captain Cowley, the Republic awards you the *Croix de Guerre* not only for your victories in the air but also for the concern you have shown for the French citizens who assisted you. I refer both to your recommendations made through your own Service, and to the note you left exonerating the local populace. Our agents report that the local German commander too, has made known his appreciation, declaring that had you not taken such a step he would have been required to carry out reprisals. I salute you, sir, and wish you a speedy recovery.'

'Humph!' said Major Upton, as the French party drove off down the drive. But there was a twinkle in his eye and for just a moment Paul thought he might be about to see him smile. But then ambulances began to arrive, churning into the gravel drive, and the moment was lost. Sisters and orderlies headed towards the huge main doors, and

Paul made his way, step by reflective step, back towards his room to pack.

So, his first lesson in self-approval! He smiled a little wryly, squinting down at the cross on his breast, then looking, very much more searchingly, inside himself, assessing his reaction to the decoration in the light of what Major Upton had said. But all he could see was his ham-fistedness at the controls, and all he could feel was a little niggle of shame. Clearly this self-approval business would take a good deal more than a tiny bit of practice.

The expected influx of patients, it was clear, had finally begun. For days now it had become evident from reports flooding back from ambulancemen and casualties alike that the renewed offensive had taken the form of an attack across the River Ancre, barely yards from where Paul had watched it all begin back in July. Yet again, it seemed, it had been a story of unbroken wire, only this time of stormers overrunning the protecting barrage, instead of the reverse, and falling in droves under their own shells, of machine-gun fire, and of tremendous cannonading by German artillery from Bucquoy: the same batteries whose unsubdued existence had so appalled Paul on Day One. A story this time, of an attack through glutinous mud – and of the depleted attacking forces being beaten back once more to the battered trenches from which they had started.

But some objectives, according to reports received, were not only carried, but held, significantly where the ridge between Serre and Beaumont-Hamel shielded the attackers from the Bucquoy guns. Thiepval, and the Schwaben Redoubt, had fallen at the beginning of October, now, in this final convulsion, Beaumont-Hamel – with all its cellars and subterranean works – fell, as did thorny St Pierre Divion.

In an effort to carry Beaucourt village itself, bitterly fought for by the Royal Naval Division and the Rifle Brigade – Diane's fiancée, Harry Peterson's, unit –, three tanks were employed. One was knocked out before starting, one bogged down – but the survivor created such havoc as to force the final surrender! General Cousins, Paul mused, might get some wry satisfaction from that.

Grandcourt however, bloodily repulsed all attacks, while Serre, deep within the enemy defences, and entered as Paul had reported on that first day, was not so much as approached.

And already the weather was closing in, and the snow would be showering on the stormers and the supports, and on the newly-dead-and-wounded of the day, covering too the bones and khaki rags yet lying on the self-same slope where July's freshly-dawned sun had bathed their fall. No doubt the Ancre, broken-banked, would be placidly flowing from the high ground still – as would, if far less placidly, the torrent of the maimed.

The recently arrived convoy had proved to be but the initial trickle of a flood, the backwash from this latest tide of battle arriving just as Paul was about to board his ambulance. His kit was already loaded but the driver, although with understandable reluctance, agreed to wait while he made a final attempt to locate Sister Carmell. She had proved impossible to contact earlier but he found her now, stationed in the entrance hall, imposing order upon a melee of nurses, orderlies, patients, doctors, stretcher-bearers, and local staff, directing them this way and that like a policeman on point duty; or like a shepherd.

More ambulances were expected at any moment, Paul knew, and not all the last arrivals had yet been dealt with. The hall was littered with unquiet casualties tagged by the forward aid stations and now awaiting verification of their medical status, the habitually-hushed corridors buzzing like hives as yet more beds were trundled into place. Sister Carmell saw him across the crowd and came at once, a frown furrowing her brow. 'Paul.'

He smiled, holding out his hand. It was always difficult to know what to say in parting, especially when as indebted as he was, and more especially at a time like this, amidst all the bustle and confusion of the moment. He knew how much he owed to her care, yet he was lost for words with which to express his gratitude. Only, even as he searched for a way to begin, it struck him that she was uncomfortable too, and he realised with sudden uneasiness that this was the first time she had ever used his given name. An orderly wheeling a trolley full of bedding stopped to ask for instructions and she turned aside to direct him, her voice brisk and controlled. But Paul saw the pinched whiteness about her nostrils and knew that she had unwelcome news to impart.

'Diane?' he asked intuitively as she turned to him again.

She nodded, her face still taut from managing the chaos about her, but with sudden sympathy in her eyes.

'Paul, last night when she came here. She had just found out that her fiancé had been killed up at Beaucourt.' She assessed him sharply, then went on, 'I could see what a state she was in, but she seemed to be a sensible girl. Wouldn't let me give her anything because she was going on duty, and told me quite calmly that she wouldn't upset you. She asked me not to tell you until you were committed to leaving.'

Paul gazed dully before him. Then it had been grief tearing Diane apart! And he *was* committed to leaving – his allotted ambulance had critical cases aboard. And now three more orderlies were clamouring for attention and a noisy argument had broken out between two of the civilian staff who were gesticulating animatedly heedless of the fact that they were blocking the entire corridor. Sister Carmell looked at him helplessly, and he nodded, and backed away, raising a hand in a wan, unseen farewell.

The trip home was tediously long, a far cry from the last crossing Paul had made ferrying the Fokker. Most of the time he spent at the rail, huddled into his greatcoat against the chill of the sea breeze, deliberately choosing an exposed position in order to be alone with his thoughts. Around him were seemingly like-minded figures, each endeavouring to find solitude amid the general throng. A throng who, with peril behind them for a space, laughed and joked, and broke his reverie once in a while with wind-wracked fragments of raucous song.

For weeks now Paul's main consideration had been getting home. Home, had meant Catherine. Times without number he had pictured himself arriving at the Darlington salon with Catherine answering the door. Although beyond that he had never dared dwell. What had nagged him constantly was that he had no way of knowing what he really meant to her. If indeed he meant anything. In the short time they had spent together she had seemed so warm and friendly; it had been as if they had known each other all their lives – yet nothing had been said. Neither then, nor since. Did all the passion rage in him alone, he had constantly asked himself? Her letters permitted no more certain an interpretation. But Home had meant Catherine, nevertheless, although the uncertainty had been becoming more than he could bear.

Home, had meant flying again. Paul was due for ten days' leave but his return to flying duties would certainly be delayed until his knee had fully healed. He had harboured plans however, of cajoling Frank into getting him aloft at the earliest opportunity: Sopwith Pups, he had reasoned, were becoming available in increasing numbers while the de Havilland bomber should also be off the stocks. But scout, bombing-machine, or humble trainer, he had intended to find his way into the air again the moment he could. The moment he had settled things with Catherine.

Now, however, as the destroyer escort zig-zagged back and forth, neither Catherine nor his own return to flying held the forefront of his thoughts, for as seagulls stooped to skim the white-spumed waves he saw only Diane's pain-filled eyes, crying out her need.

It could be, he brooded, that Frank could arrange to get him back to France. A ferry flight, perhaps. Even just a flip. It might not be possible for a day or so, he realised that. But he must get back, no matter how briefly, having failed her so utterly in her hour of need.

The white cliffs swam mistily into view, and he shook his head despondently, turning gratefully to accept a mug of soup proffered by a bearded sailor. Later, as the gangplanks slid ashore, so the rain began to fall.

Frank was there to meet him at Charing Cross, grinning at the sight of his stick. 'Dray horse actually step on you this time?'

Similarly recalling their first meeting, Paul smiled. 'Give me three weeks, then watch me,' he boasted. 'Even now it's just that the docs insist on my not overstressing it while I'm on leave.'

In fact the leg was already much better than he might have hoped for and only at the fullest bend did it give him discomfort, and that only because of the rawness of the operative scars. There was no trace of the deep-seated pain he had learnt to live with for very nearly two years before Vélu.

Frank peered into his face. 'For a sorely-wounded warrior you look remarkably fit.'

Paul nodded soberly. 'I was lucky. They forced a lot of bed rest on me. I was on my way to the asylum, they told me. I'm not sure they were right but I must say I feel a lot better for the rest.'

Frank grunted. 'Fatigue,' he said reflectively. 'No sane mind can put up with things out there too long. As you say, you might well be one of the lucky ones.'

'I felt fine enough before I got hit,' Paul said. 'After that I suppose it was the loss of blood. That and the pain. Otherwise I like to think I'd have kept going indefinitely. At least, until my leave came up. Most of the chaps do, after all.'

'Who's to say,' agreed Frank.

He grinned, poking at the space below Paul's wings. 'Improperly dressed, young man! I saw the approval to the French for your *Croix de Guerre*, and there's an MC in yesterday's orders. You won't have seen 'em yet. Here!' He reached into his pocket and took out two fragments of coloured ribbon, the green with thin-red-vertical-stripes of the *Croix de Guerre* and the white-blue-white of the Military Cross, the latter's glaring newness throwing his own well-worn ribbon into the shade. 'There you are. We'll get Laura to do the job for you: must make a show for the ladies.'

Paul shook his head in weary disbelief. So Diane had been right. The *Croix de Guerre,* and now the Military Cross for what was basically nothing but a crass piece of handling.

'If the truth were told,' he said, 'I should have been court martialled for cack-handedness.'

'Confessions later,' Frank stopped him. 'Laura's preparing a snack. We presume you'll be travelling north? Darlington? Or Derby?'

Paul sobered. 'Derby. You've heard the news about Diane's Harry?'

Frank sobered in turn. 'Yes, from that chap, Tom, at the general's.'

'Tom Lelliot, the general's factor.'

'That's the man. Harry's father rang the general.'

'The thing is, Frank,' Paul was unable to play down the urgency he felt, 'I feel I've simply got to hop back to France to see Diane. I wanted to before leaving but it simply wasn't possible. She doesn't say it – you know Diane – but she's terribly cut up. Although she's being very brave. Frank, could anything be arranged? A two-way ferry, even, straight there, then back a few hours later?'

Frank looked at him closely. 'Before you do anything else?' he asked, after a pause.

Paul shook his head. 'I know it might take a day or two, so I'll go up to Derby tonight. To assure the general that Diane's bearing up.'

'And Darlington?'

Paul looked down at his stick. Where did this strange reluctance stem from. Was it pride? Militating against Catherine seeing him reduced to a stick? Or was it unashamed faintheartedness that was making him so drastically re-arrange his priorities?

'I'll not feel easy until I can get back over,' he said.

There was another pause. Then Frank clapped him on the shoulder. 'Very well,' he said. 'Then I'll do everything I possibly can. Now, let's not keep Laura waiting ...'

It was dark when Paul rang the bell at the Hall and there was no sign of life although the taxi had slowed at the gates to allow a saloon-car out. Jenkins answered the door, his face showing relief at the sight of Paul.

'I'm glad you've come, sir.' His eyes were dull.

'If I could have a word with the general?'

'I've made him take a sleeping draught, sir. The doctor's just left.'

'A sleeping draught?' Paul desisted from chewing his lip. There was something wrong here! The general had hardly known Peterson. – But of course, he would be thinking of Diane.

'If he's not actually asleep, Jenkins,' he pressed brightly, 'Perhaps you'd tell him from me that I saw Diane only last night. She's dreadfully cut up, of course. And she's a bit down with flu. But she's bearing up. Tell him she's a fighter. That she'll pull through. That he shouldn't worry himself over much ...' He stopped short. Realising that the soldier-servant's composure had crumpled utterly.

'But Miss Diane's dead, sir.'

Chapter Twenty-Four

An old friend of the general had phoned from the War Office two hours before. Diane had been found when the nurse sharing her room had come off duty. That Diane had taken something was clear. Paul, still stunned, shook his head.

'Look,' he said slowly, after a while. 'Don't disturb the general now then. But the moment he wakes up, tell him what I said. Diane was tired, she'd been overworking, she had flu, and she'd just heard about Lieutenant Peterson. But nothing in her manner suggested *this*. Tell the general – that something else must have happened, something that shocked her out of her senses.' He nodded, his own mind too dazed to think clearly. 'Tell him that.'

Even as he made to step from the flags to the drive, he turned. 'The moment you think he can stand it, get him to phone the War Office. Medics stick together, as you well know, but he can pull strings. Someone will know what really happened.'

For himself, Paul sought his solace in the distant hills, riding through the night, ignoring lighting restrictions and following his headlamp's beam. At length he parked the Rudge, and totally discounting trespass-signs and keepers, began an abstracted climb of Kinderscout, never hurrying but toiling upwards at a pace in keeping with his thoughts, convinced, no matter how he worried at it, that Diane's only aim on leaving him had been to lose herself in duty, to burrow into work, a gravely injured creature seeking comfort in its den.

Sitting, gazing unseeingly down into night-bound Grindsbrook, he searched his mind to recall exactly what her parting words had been. Something to the effect that she would write home. And something else, implying that she too would be seeing everyone. And he remembered the tenderness of her parting kiss, the tenderness that belied the coldness of her cheek. The girl who had kissed him then – he knew beyond all doubt – had never meant to take her own life, that girl had meant to live.

So, something had happened after she had left him. Something so cataclysmic that it had tipped the balance and sent her over the edge. What it could have been Paul could not conceive; what it had been, might never be known; but in those wind-lashed hours of tryst amongst the hills he did find solace of a kind, solace that offered at least a foothold on the future, knowing now that whatever might emerge in time, he for one would always keep the faith. But what a kind and loving, troubled heart had passed away!

Despite his nightlong vigil Paul was back at the Hall first thing next day. The general was up, and he was taking it hard. He seemed shrunken, more truly his age, and the veins on the backs of his hands were pulsating visibly.

'I loved her, despite her weakness,' he told Paul, staring into the distance. 'She seemed lively and gay, but she needed an anchor. Needed someone to give her stability.' He lapsed into silence. 'From the first, Paul, you lifted her up, spurred her on. I had high hopes for her then.'

Paul thought of the summer house and shifted uncomfortably but as if the old man had followed his thoughts he raised a staying hand.

'You were good for each other,' he said. And again he fell silent. 'In those last few months, you see,' he resumed after a while, 'we grew very close.' He smiled. 'She was always particularly gratified at putting you in touch with that young woman of yours.' He saw Paul's expression and smiled again. 'I've met your Catherine, you know, and so has Diane.' He paused. 'So *had* Diane.– You didn't know?' Paul shook his head.

The general grew introspective, his thoughts once more with Diane. 'I saw Diane twice, on visits to France. She was tired, as they all were, but she was fulfilled at last. Her superiors spoke highly of her sense of duty. Nothing was too much trouble for her, they said. She would spend hours with cases other VADs found too harrowing.'

He grimaced. 'Possibly they were humouring me. People do that to generals, at times.' His voice, uncharacteristically had a lost quality.

'She was run down, sir,' Paul told him. 'And she'd got flu. But I'm convinced that she was determined not to let Harry's death put her under. That she intended to bury her grief in work.'

The silence lengthened until at last the general sighed. He shook his head, wanting desperately to accept comfort, but unable to.

'It all came together, flu, and overwork, and Harry's death.' His shoulders drooped. 'It was in her nature.'

'No, General!' Paul's protest came out more stridently than he would have wished, but he shook his head firmly. '*No*, General!' He put his hand on the old man's shoulder. 'She did need an anchor, perhaps we all do. But she was not weak. We can only guess at her state of mind after she left me, but whatever happened, believe me, Diane is as much a casualty as any soldier destroyed upon the battlefield.'

The old man was gazing into the flames, but after a while he gave a brief nod. Paul, seizing upon this positive response, went on. 'A man giving way after weeks of shelling isn't simply weak, General, you know that. See Diane that way, too.' He stood up. 'In a fortnight, it seems, I'm to attend an investiture at the Palace. *Me!* But it's Diane, and those like her, who should be attending.'

'I may be wrong,' Paul said to Jenkins as he left. 'But I think he'll be up to phoning soon. I'm convinced that something happened to upset the scales. Something General Cousins ought to know about.'

Jenkins nodded. 'Like you seem to say, sir, Miss Diane wasn't a quitter. It's only ...' He paused.

'If we're wrong?' Paul prompted.

'That's right, sir. It won't do the general no good then.'

'The doubt isn't doing him too much good as it is,' Paul pressed fervently. 'Besides, I'd stake my life on there being something more.'

'But it ain't your life you're staking, sir.'

Paul squeezed his shoulder understandingly. For Jenkins to come that close to impertinence to an officer was a measure of the old soldier's concern.

'If 'e don't make the call within the hour, sir,' Jenkins promised grimly, 'I'll put the bleeder through myself.'

At just after one o'clock Tom drew up at the cottage.

'Paul, the general asked if you'd mind coming over. I think it's something about Diane. He's still very low, of course, but he seems to have bucked up a bit. Would you mind?'

The moment he entered the library Paul could see what Tom meant. The general was haggard and weary, but his eyes were alive and there was a set to his shoulders that had been absent earlier.

'I'll never forget how you championed Diane,' the old man began without preamble. 'And now I think I've got the full story. It's not pretty. Just another futile blunder!' He shook his head. 'It seems there was a sharp engagement at dusk, the day before yesterday, a Hun attempt to re-take Beaucourt.'

Paul nodded – later he would tell the general about the tanks. Later.

'Some of the wounded, it seems, had just been classified, when the Regimental Aid Post itself came under sustained shellfire. The medical officers caught the first salvo. The surviving wounded were gathered up – still under heavy fire – and bundled into the nearest transports.' Paul grimaced, closing his eyes against the hellish picture. 'When they arrived at the hospital it seems there was considerable confusion. And four men who had been tagged for immediate surgical attention were warded with twenty others only lightly wounded. So Diane, coming on duty a few minutes later, was briefed that the ward contained only slightly-wounded patients.'

Wearily, the general shook his head. 'They were so short of staff that Diane had been placed in charge of two wards. In the other ward, it seems, there was a shell-shock case. He began screaming and the other VAD, a girl fresh out from home, became hysterical.'

He looked up. 'The girl had to be persuaded back to duty. And the soldier had to be settled for he was disturbing the others who would have been keeling over with fatigue, quite apart from their wounds.'

Paul could well picture their possibly paramount need to rest.

'According to Diane's report, when she returned to the first ward most patients were sleeping so she spent some time with those who were seeking her attention – for bedpans and because their dressings had come loose. That seen to, she started a systematic bed-to-bed inspection.' The general's face mirrored his agony.

'She walked to the first bed, and found that far from sleeping, her patient was dead. Then she went to the next bed, and found that patient dead too, and to the third, and finally to the fourth. Imagine! Yet she told the doctor she had failed to check them earlier.'

Paul shivered, and the full significance of the situation coming home to him, his mind reeled. But had the general, he wondered, made the connection; with an infant Diane, gaily tripping into her parents' bedroom, to come upon the asphyxiated corpses of her mother and her father – the general's son? Hopefully not. Hopefully he never would! Yet without warning, and after all these years, the girl had yet again come face to face with her childhood horror: expecting smiles, to meet once more the gape of Death!

The general fell silent, and it was several minutes before he resumed detailing the tragedy.

'In their initial shock both the doctor and the sister accepted what she said, thereby tacitly accusing her of negligence and of killing her patients. Certainly that's how she seems to have seen it. An hour later the doctor collapsed from exhaustion. He'd had no rest for well over forty-eight hours, the sister for rather longer.'

He sighed. 'Diane finished the shift, handed over to her relief, and wrote up her report. A model report, they say. Except that in it, despite recounting her actions on taking over the ward, she still blamed herself for killing the four men by negligence. It was early next morning before the truth came to light, when they read her report, and had listened to what the other VAD, and the soldiers in both wards had to tell them. But by then it was far too late.'

His voice dwindled away. Moving to console him, Paul met the soldier-servant's eye, paused, and stood away.

There was nothing to be said. No consolation to be offered. Not at present. But the picture was agonisingly clear. Her nerve ends raw, exhausted by months of sapping overwork, to experience a nightmarish déjà-vu that was only too piteously real; caught at the highly depressive stage of influenza, desolated by Harry's death, her self-condemnation apparently reinforced by superiors who had hitherto regarded her highly; and then, in the small hours when the human spirit is at its lowest ebb, finding herself alone – something she had always dreaded, as she had made known to Paul in the summer house –, it was little wonder that despair had engulfed her.

Nine months before, blaming herself for her mis-routed patient's death, she had been able to take it out on Paul. This time, there had been nobody. That it was a misunderstanding, stress bearing upon stress, only made it more tragic, but looking back as he eased the door to Paul was persuaded that possessing now even some facts would allow the old man to begin, at least, to progress through his grief. And that, at present, was as much as anyone could hope for.

Paul spent the rest of the day moodily working in Mrs Cossey's garden. He had tried to contact Catherine but the staff at Darlington's King's Head Hotel, who habitually took messages for her, reported that she was away and not expected back until next day; they did not know her present whereabouts. Paul was aching to see her, quite literally, and yet, he was afraid. For surely her letters – which now he once more fell to studying – positively shrieked that they had been penned by a friend, rather than a lover. And gnawing at him unremittingly was his awareness that the existence of any deeper tie between them might well be but a product of his own uncertain mind. He knew that Mrs Cossey was watching him, aware of his agitation, but not saying a word, merely smiling sadly, and keeping her own counsel.

In the evening he telephoned once more. Ted, the night porter of The King's Head, was unable to tell him anything new, except that Catherine was expecting her own telephone any day now, news which, at the moment, only frustrated Paul more. He tried to book a room for the next day, only to find that none were available, however Ted obligingly booked him in at the hotel next door. After that, although he did his best to rally the others in the cottage, Mary and her mother in particular, both of whom had known Diane all her life, he found the evening even longer than the dragging day.

At times he pondered over the revelation that Catherine had met General Cousins. And even Diane, too! Yet her letters had told him nothing beyond reporting her several weekends at the cottage with Mrs Cossey, Mary, and Tom. Now he pressed for every detail of her visits until even ever-patient Tom could take no more.

'For goodness' sake!' he burst out finally. 'Get yourself off up there. Faint heart, and everything else you told me, remember?'

Next morning Paul was up early, although he felt compelled to delay his departure for Darlington in case the general had need of him. He was unable to fully account for this deep-seated compulsion, although his relationship with the old man had always evolved alongside his relationship with Diane rather than as an offshoot of it. He was certainly aware of a sense of responsibility, and of affection too, indeed a sense of near-kinship. But wherever the compulsion was rooted, being at hand had become much more than a matter of duty.

At just gone twelve Tom drew up at the cottage door. 'It's General Cousins, Paul. He knows you're waiting to go but he'd like a word.'

'Something new about Diane?'

Tom shook his head. 'Not strictly – but best let him tell you. And after you've seen him I'm to drop you at the station.'

That the general was beginning to pick up was clear the moment Paul entered the library. The old man was standing by the fire but there were piles of documents scattered across the table and Paul realised that he had been working through them. From his bearing it was obvious that he had regained a lot of his normal vitality.

'Sit down, Paul.' The general gestured towards a chair. 'I understand that you're finally off to see that young woman of yours. And high time, too.' He smiled faintly, and his eyes were strangely soft. 'I know that, in part, you've delayed for my sake. It's the sort of consideration I've come to expect from you.'

'She isn't due home until later today,' Paul disclaimed, embarrassed.

'She intended travelling up late last night,' the general contradicted. Then stopped. 'Perhaps I should have mentioned it, but with everything ...' His voice tailed off. Then he resumed, 'She'd been in London with my lawyer and her backer – Abercrombie, isn't it?'

Paul furrowed his brow. 'He's a merchant banker.'

'That's him.,' the general nodded. 'Think you'll be marrying the girl?'

Paul opened his palms appealingly. 'We've hardly met, really, sir,' he said, facing the fact himself. 'I honestly don't know how she feels.'

The general snorted, canting his head. 'We had long talks, the two of us, whenever she came a-visiting, did you know that?'

Paul shook his head. 'Until yesterday, sir, I didn't know you'd met.'

'Well, now you do. And she's got her head screwed on. Knows where she's going, I can tell you.' The general gestured around him, embracing not only the room and the house itself but the farms, the meadows and the woods, taking in all that went to make up the demesne. 'She sees, as I do – and as Diane did – that places like this must change. I told her the plans I had, and the decision we'd come to, Diane and I, before the lass went off to France.'

He lapsed into silence for a while but when Jenkins tapped the clock he went on, 'Diane intended moving to Harry's place. She knew I wouldn't want to carry on here for more than another year or two. She suggested proposing that you run the place for me. A home of your own, with Tom as participating factor.'

Paul chewed his lip. He was not sure that he was taking this in.

'Now, with Diane's – death.' The general hesitated but then spoke the word firmly, as if to help expunge a ghost. 'Things have changed significantly. I have no heirs, and unless, when you consider the matter, you have any objections, I intend to deed the whole concern to you, as I would have done to Diane.'

Paul drew in his breath but the general held up his hand. 'What I'm putting to you here is the product of many months of thought. You already knew of my plans for Tom and Mary. There's no time to discuss it now, but just a bit more you might bear in mind. You can mull it over at leisure.'

He pointed out of the window beyond the gates to where the expanse of the Big Meadow lifted, in a barely perceptively slope, to the horizon. 'You showed Catherine an aerodrome.'

'Catterick.'

'Was it? Anyway, she says the aerodrome seemed much smaller than the Big Meadow. She also says you have ideas about developing aerial journeying after the war.' Paul opened his mouth, but the general stayed him with a palm. Pointing through the window he indicated the downhill slope towards the river.

'Finally, the Old Mill. Your Catherine dragged me down there to look over the buildings. They haven't been used for twenty-five years to my knowledge but she maintains that they'd be ideal for setting up some sort of clothes business she has in mind.' He paused. 'Now you begin to see what we've been up to behind your back.'

'And that's why she's down seeing Mr Abercrombie?' Paul murmured. All wonder aside, he was vaguely troubled, although instantly dismissing his misgivings as absurd. He was also assailed by more than just a shred of doubt as to his own ability to become either a businessman or a landowner, let alone both. True, he had his dreams about aviation, but they had always been dreams without form. Now it looked as if Catherine had taken steps to give them substance.

'Has she actually signed to buy the Old Mill?' he asked. He could not credit it of himself, yet he could not deny this feeling of unease. Of dawning resentment, even.

The general shook his head. 'I hope it won't be necessary, it's part of the estate. Besides, she refuses to do anything until she has your full approval. So although the preparatory work's done –' he waved a hand at the paper-strewn table, 'it awaits your yea or nay.'

Paul felt that he ought to say something, even a disturbed, 'Thank you.' But his mind was spinning and he could not yet grasp what had been offered him. Once again the general forestalled any attempt at speech. He stood up, and taking Paul's arm, walked him from the room. 'You go away and think about it. Discuss it with that young woman of yours, and then come back and let me know how you feel.'

Paul stopped by the car door and bent towards the older man. 'As you say, sir, now's not the time to thank you, but believe me ...'

'Nothing more to say at the moment,' said the general brusquely, 'but plenty to do. Now be off with you, before you miss that train.'

Tom glanced aside at Paul as they got under way. 'I wanted to talk about it, Paul, but what with losing Diane, and everything ... I thought it best to wait. But it's quite a notion, isn't it?' The subject broached, they continued to discuss it throughout the journey, although Paul found himself strangely unable to enthuse.

'Catherine's even more of a doer than I'd imagined,' he said dryly.

'And it unsettles you?' Tom braked to a halt beneath the bulging-eyed dragons on the station clock.

'What if it's just the business opportunity she's interested in?'

Tom reached behind him and swung the grip from the back seat. 'Ask her if that's the case,' he said easily. He touched the medal ribbons on Paul's tunic. 'After all, according to these you're pretty brave.'

Paul merely grunted, hitching high his knapsack of doubts as he boarded the carriage. Only how willingly he would have thrown off such a burden! But one gesture of abnegation he could make. He brandished the walking stick, and as the train jolted preparatory to departing, he handed it down to Tom. 'Sling this for me?'

'Nice piece of Jersey cabbage stalk that,' Tom observed, eyeing it appraisingly. 'You sure you won't need it?'

'Never again,' Paul said decidedly.

'Man of Iron Will, eh!' Tom smiled. 'Then just remember it when you meet up with Catherine.'

Chapter Twenty-Five

The train journey seemed interminable. Paul had to change at York and he tried to phone The King's Head from there but could not even raise the exchange. After that he spent the time staring out of the window, his mind so overbusy with his thoughts that he only rarely became conscious of his surroundings. But one thing was clear. He was beginning to come to terms with Diane's death himself now, although still with a lingering stab of conscience. For who could tell what the right word, spoken during her visit, might have meant just hours later, on that baneful night? His mind had been filled with how she looked rather than how she felt. Had he only been more perceptive!

It was a bitter irony that the general had spoken of Diane's weakness, for had she not possessed the core of strength that had seen her through that childhood horror; had she given way at Harry's death; had she been less caring of her patients, and colleagues, or less conscientious; had she even excused herself, just for an hour or so, from her responsibilities, giving way to what she would have regarded as self-indulgence in order to take the briefest rest; then she might never have taken that dread step. But it had never been in her nature to excuse herself, and convinced that she had killed her patients, she would have admitted of no way back to grace. The taking of her life, Paul divined, had not been an act of weakness but rather one of strength, a strength empowered by an indomitable, pitiless, quite unalterable conviction that there could be no atonement, that nothing would suffice but tooth-for-tooth retribution.

Only, life persisted. And as the hours dragged and the miles dawdled by, Paul's mind played more and more upon his coming confrontation with Catherine. For months he had been writhing in the toils, agonizing over the nature of her feelings for him. Now his fears were festering on this new begetting-ground, the fruit of the general's revelations regarding the Old Mill. What had she in mind? Affection, or merely gain? For uncertainty, like jealously, fed vilely.

Paul must have dozed, for he became aware of a clerically-collared gentleman shaking him by the shoulder. The carriage door was open and clouds of steam were billowing past. His grip was on the platform.

'Darlington,' said the cleric, smiling. 'You were having such a good sleep it seemed a shame to wake you, but I read your luggage label.'

Paul thanked him, feeling that he had been asleep for ever.

'You and yours deserve a good sleep after driving off those baby killers,' said the clergyman earnestly. 'I was in Hull in June last year and I saw how indiscriminately bombs from Zeppelins kill.'

Paul nodded. Twenty-four civil dead, he remembered, and mumbling something suitable, and feeling like a sham, bent to retrieve his grip.

Most of the other passengers had already disembarked, the bustle of their passage echoing under the high, glassed vaulting of the Victorian roofing, and Paul followed on, falling further behind as he idled beneath supporting arches pierced with circles and with stars. A clock, equally ornate and quite as gaudily painted as that at Derby, jerked to its next minute in the way of station clocks, and he realised that the salon would probably be closed by now. And then, as he faced the fact that within minutes he would be knocking on Catherine's door, his nervousness returned full force.

He paused for a while across the road from the station's tower, and stood, flanked by public houses, gazing down to the river and the town on the rising ground beyond. The wind was keen but it was heaven-sent after the carriage, where any attempt at ventilation had filled the air with locomotive smoke, and initially, when he walked on, it was with his greatcoat folded across his arm. Then it occurred to him that Catherine might think he was making an ostentatious display of the ribbons newly-sewn beneath his wings so, chagrined, and feeling somewhat cheap, he hurriedly slipped the garment on.

The road fell only gradually, nevertheless his knee protested at the gradient, but good humouredly, with none of the old, sap-draining pain. He came to the gently babbling Skerne, then wandered on, the rattle of a tram drowning out the river's murmur. High Row opened out before him, then Prebend Row, and ahead, Mr Pease – the hatless Mr Pease –, gazing steadfastly into space: no self-doubt for that Victorian paragon!

The Borough Hotel was on the right, just short of the statue. Paul was expected, a smiling receptionist proffering the register.

'Ted, from The King's Head, wasn't sure how long you'd be staying, mind, so I've provisionally marked you in for just one night. Would you care to see your room before you book in?'

Paul hesitated. What to do? Hurry off and face his fate right away? Or wait, freshen up, try to collect himself, and then go round? With seeming inconsequence the memory of his first opportunity to loop an aeroplane came back to him. His first visit to Darlington had been to see a loop performed. It had been somewhat different when the time had come for him to perform the manoeuvre himself: then too putting it off had only made it harder to face.

'If it's all right with you,' he said, 'I'll go out for a while first.'

'Then I'll put your case inside the cloakroom, sir, out of harm's way.'

He passed The King's Head, a passage made so often in imagination, and turned down the side road, his thumping heart drowning out his footsteps on the paving. As he had expected, the salon was closed, the curtains drawn over the window and a slide-sign regretting that the establishment would not re-open until next day. He listened, stilling the pounding of his blood, his hand poised, uncertain. There was not a sound from within, and in a mixture of dismay and hope he realised that Catherine might be at another of her premises. He raised his eyes, seeking solace from the sky, but all he saw was rain-bearing scud. So not even the sky was in his favour! Not even the sky ... He knocked firmly, too firmly, in his determination to have this done.

For a while there was no response at all, and then he heard light footsteps hurrying down the stairs. He stepped back, and the bell jangled as the knob turned. And suddenly she was smiling down at him, her eyes sparkling, her face alight with joy. And on the instant all his fears dissolved, his spirits soaring, climbing, as it were, from clouded shadows into sunlit glory.

'Paul!' Her finger was at the corner of her mouth, her eyes flashing over him, pausing when they came to his knee, then flickering up concernedly to read what they could in his face. The light in their blue-grey depths made his senses reel.

He tapped his knee. 'Better than ever,' he assured her.

She laughed throatily, and leaning forwards, drew him into the shop, letting the door swing to, spinning to face him as the bell jangled.

'I've been expecting you all day,' she told him, running her hand up and down his lapel. She pointed to a telephone. 'It was only installed at one o'clock. I spoke to General Cousins, but you'd just left.'

'Catherine!' He reached out for her, blindly. Suddenly everything else seemed far away and meaningless, the war, the new Sopwiths, the Big House, the Old Mill – even Diane –, everything that mattered was here before him.

'Oh, my dear!' Her voice broke. She was aware of his doubts, he knew. His doubts, his travails, his fears ... And suddenly her hands were pulling, bringing his face down to hers. Her lips were fresh and demanding, and there was fire in every fibre of her body as she moved to press him close.

Minutes later, she broke away, and gazed up at him breathlessly. 'Any doubts now?' she gasped.

He grinned, somewhat inanely, he was sure, experiencing difficulty in regaining his own breath, but reaching out for her once more. She held up a restraining hand. 'How long are you home for?'

'For a month or so, at the very least,' he told her. 'Probably longer.'

'And how long a leave have you got?' she persisted.

'Ten days.'

She gestured at the floor. 'No luggage?'

'I've booked in at The Borough.'

She nodded, and picked up the telephone.

'Borough Hotel, please,' she said and then, after a while. 'Is that you, Betty? You have Captain Cowley's luggage there, I believe. Would it be possible to have the porter drop it round here? – No, he's decided not to.' She listened for a while longer, smiling, and then colouring slightly, but eventually nodding in satisfaction. 'Right away?'

She paused. Then, taking Paul by surprise, looked up into his face. And he saw in her eyes what he had vainly yearned for in her letters. What she read in his he might wonder at later. For without looking at the instrument she shook her head.

'No,' she said decidedly. 'On second thoughts, don't bother the porter. We'll call around for it later.'

Quietly then, she replaced the receiver, and turned to him, her hands coming up to his face. And as he reached out so she came fiercely, and hungrily, and unreservedly, into his arms.

Dedication
Eamonn Mills, of Alicante, whose enthusiasm for Yeates' *Winged Victory* brought this 1988 series out of limbo. Though adding much to the new edition, Eamonn died just before publication, on 4 July 2008.

Acknowledgements

Jenni Bannister of Book Printing UK.

Proof reading:
Clive Teale, Nottingham, aviator; additionally for technical advice.
Frances Meeks, Nancegollan

Critiques:
Margaret Poulson, Nottingham
Eamonn Mills, Alicante
John Scaife, Weston on Trent
Nicholas Armfeldt, Helston, author, world traveller

Technical vetting:
Air fighting: Gerry Franklin AFC RAF, Tactical Air Combat Instructor
Rotary engine handling: Chris Morris, Chief Engineer, Shuttleworth Trust
Military history: Arthur L ('Bunny') Bleby, Lt Cdr RN

Notes: a glossary would be inappropriate for this fictional series, detailing, as it might, the plethora of aircraft types and the biographies of the historical personalities encountered, of Trenchard – 'Father of the RAF' – and Maurice Baring, in particular. It is hoped that any relevant terms are made clear in context. A few notes, however, might prove pertinent.

Morale (p.8). The contemporary usage was 'moral'.
The Very (p.72), sometimes Very's (p16.), signal pistol, often – understandably – rendered 'Verey', is, in fact, named for its 1877 inventor, American naval officer Edward Wilson Very
Albatros (p.10). The combat reports of many First World War fliers read like schoolboy compositions. Accordingly, the German fighter, the Albatros, was variously rendered in the plural as Albatroses, Albatrosses, and Albatri.

Historical note
The background of this series is the air war from 1916 to 1918. Paul Cowley, a pioneer aviator who believes that the war has sent Aviation off track, reflects front-line views. These, however, are tempered by those of staff officer, Frank Taylor. Yet both men, being of their time, share an outlook far removed from that of the jaundiced generation who wrote of the First World War in the depressed late-1920s and whose portrayal is still popularly held, notwithstanding research and (since the 1960s) the re-emergence of more balanced contemporary material.

Selective References

Air Ministry, (1960). *Flying Instructor's Handbook. AP3223D*. London: HMSO
Bacon Gertrude (1915). *All about flying*. London: Methuen
Barber, H, (1916). *The Aeroplane Speaks*. London: McBride.
Baring Maurice (1920). *RFC HQ 1914 – 1918*. London: Bell
Blunden Edmund (1928). *Undertones of War*. London: Cobden-Sanderson
Borlaise Matthews, R., (1917). *The Aviation pocket-Book 1917*. London: Crosswood
Boyle, A, (1962). *Trenchard*. London: Collins
Burls, G.A., (1917). *Aero Engines*. London: Charles Griffin
Chamier, J.A, (1943). *Birth of the Royal Air Force*. London: Pitman
Cole, C, (1969). *Royal Flying Corps Communiqués 1915-1916*. London: Donovan
Conan Doyle, A., (1917). *The British Campaign in France and Flanders, 1916*. London: Hodder
Duchêne, Emile (1912/14). *The Mechanics of the Aeroplane/Flight Without Formulæ*. London: Longmans
Edmonds Charles (Carrington) (1929). *A Subaltern's War* 1964 Preface. London: Icon
Fokker, A, (1931). *Flying Dutchman*. London: Routledge
Graves Robert (1929). *Goodbye To All That*. London: Cassell
Handley Page Ltd, (1949). *Forty Years On*. London: Radlett and Reading
Harvey, W.F.J, (1969). *'Pi' In The Sky. (No. 22. Squadron)*. Leicester: Huston
Holmes Richard (2004). *Tommy*. London: Harper Collins
Jane Fred T, (1918). *All the World's Aircraft*. London: Sampson Low, Marsden & Co Ltd
Johns, W. E, (1932 et seq). Instructor and DH4 bomber pilot. Early *Biggles* are good source
Jones, H.A, (1922-1937). *The War in the Air: (Bombing Operations, Air Fighting)* Oxford Press
Kermode, A.C, (1932/40). *Flight Without Formula/Mechanics of Flight. London: Pitman*
Lanchester, F.W, (1907/8). *Aerodonetics/Aerodynamics*. London: Constable
Lewis, C, (1936). *Sagittarius Rising*. London: Davies
McCudden, James. T.B, (c1918). *Flying Fury: Five Years in the RFC*. London: Bailey Bros
Neon (Mrs Marion W. Acworth), (1927). *Great Delusion*. London: Benn
Ogilvy, D, (1977). *From Bleriot to Spitfire: Shuttleworth*. England: Airlife
Oliver Stewart (1925). *The Strategy and Tactics of Air Fighting*. London: Longmans
Oliver Stewart (c1927). *Aeolus, (Refuting 'Neon', The Great Delusion)*. London: Keegan
Raleigh, W, (1922). *The War in the Air, Vols 1, 2*. London: Oxford University Press
Royse, M.W, (1928). *Aerial Bombardment – International Regulation of Warfare*. Vinal
Sargant, W, (1957). *Battle for the Mind*. London: Heinemann
Sassoon Siegfried (1937). *Complete Memoirs of George Sherston*. London: Faber
Saunders, H, St. George, (1944). *Per Ardua – 1911-1939*. London: Oxford UP.
Slater, G, (1973) *My Warrior Sons – Borton Family*. London: Peter Davies
Solano, E. J (1915). *Drill and Field Training*. London: Murray
Swinton Ernest (c1938). *Twenty Years After. 3 Vols*. London; Newnes
Von Richthofen, Rittmeister Manfred. F, (1918). *The Red Air Fighter*. London:
Woodman, H, (1989). *Early Aircraft Armament, to 1918*. London: Arms and Armour Press
Yeates, V.M, (1934). *Winged Victory*. London: Cape

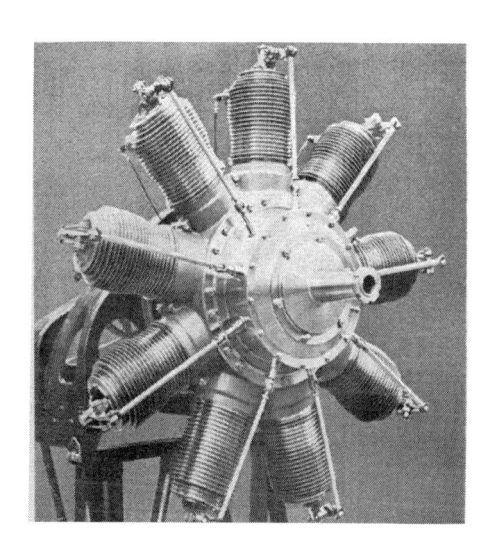

Monosoupape (single-valve) Gnome rotary engine, without propeller, on a test rig. The crankshaft is fixed, the crankcase, cylinders, and the propeller rotate.

(Burls, G.A., [1917]. *Aero Engines*)